FINDING HEKATE

FINDING HEKATE

By

Kellie Doherty

Desert Palm Press

Finding Hekate
Cicatrix Duology – Book 1

by Kellie Doherty

ISBN: 9781942976066
ISBN (epub): 9781942976073
ISBN (pdf): 9781942976080

Desert Palm Press
1961 Main Street, Suite 220
Watsonville, California 95076
www.desertpalmpress.com

Editor: CK King
(https://www.facebook.com/RavensEyeEditing)
Cover Design: Rachel George
http://www.rachelgeorgeillustration.com/portfolio/)

Printed in the United States of America
First Edition April 2016

For my family who always believed in me.

AKNOWLEDGEMENTS

First I'd like to thank Lee and the lovely staff at Desert Palm Press for believing in my story and for putting it out there in the world. Second I'd like to thank my friends: my Writer's Ink crew—Sheila, Brianna, Sy, Melissa, Deric, and Bonnie—for helping me hash out the idea, my Jitters Critters folks—Molly, Louise, Brooke, Tam, Lizzie, and Mike—for helping me polish it, and the many others for cheering me on throughout the process. And finally I'd like to thank my family—Ed, Deb, and Jessie—for always believing in my writing and pushing me to do more.

FINDING HEKATE

Chapter One

MIA FOLEY'S LEFT PALM began to ache. She squeezed it into a fist and willed the pain to leave her. It didn't work. Her eyelids fluttered open, but in the darkness of her cabin she might as well have left them closed. Untangling herself from the sheets, she stood and stretched. A chill seeped into her bare feet from the deck, and she vowed to get a rug at the next stop. Of course she wouldn't. She dressed, wanting to go back to sleep. Of course she wouldn't do that either. She had a job to do.

Mia pulled on her captain's jacket last and stumbled over to the mirror by the hatch. It took only a few steps to cross her small cabin. Her crewmates likened the space to living in a metallic coffin. She hated that image. Tiny, yes. Cozy, too.

"Lights." Her voice, slurred with sleep, stuck in her throat. The ship understood. The orbs above the mirror brightened. She stared at her tired reflection before leaning down to lace her boots. The black pants, camisole, and jacket ensemble always made her feel like a villain right out of the 1800s. Yet it kept her and her crew out of harm's way when trouble struck. Easier to slide into the darkness and hide in the shadows if the trading went awry. Besides, the dark Ariien fabric was soft and strong. A good combination. She patted her breast pocket. The soft crinkle of paper reassured her the list was still there. Paper might've gone out of style generations ago, but the material was easiest to hide. She tucked it deeper inside her pocket and shook the sleep from her arms. The yellow symbol on her jacket's shoulder caught her eye: a tiny spaceship surrounded by three multicolored stars, the Across the Stars trading company logo.

Since Mia had to keep running from the hunters, trading seemed to be the perfect solution. Traders moved around. They kept a lower profile than most. And the units, while not extravagant, would allow her to live a decent life. She'd been captain six months on this ship with no hint of her followers. Until last week, that is. The pain in her hand had only increased. With almost four years since the *Jubilee*, Mia wanted to relax. She couldn't.

Her gaze strayed to the bedside table bolted to the deck. To the cracked and rusted breathing apparatus resting there. She'd spent two and a half of those four years on Baubo, a backwater planet known for its limited inhabitants and terrible air quality. She'd hoped the murky atmosphere would quell the hunters. Or at least slow them down. When they found her, Mia stole away on a high-warp transit ship named *Xi*. Thankfully, that ship wasn't on the list. She got off the ship before the hunters could find her again. She hoped that *Xi* would lead the hunters far away, and maybe it had, for her new ship, the *Eclipse*, certainly wasn't fast or powerful. Still, even after all this time, anxiety blossomed in her chest at the thought of what she should be doing. What she'd been forced to do for all these years. The explosives should be rigged. The timer should be started. She should be far away from this crew by now. But she wasn't.

Sighing, Mia pushed the nerves away and ran her fingers through her thin hair. A few short, red strands fell to the deck. Though the chopped cut wasn't her style, out in space it helped to not have a lot of hair to grab onto. People were dirt poor and fought dirty. Just like her. According to her crew, the hairstyle showed off the atmospheric blue of her eyes. Really, who cared out here? Jeff's idea of a smooth line, probably. She pulled a pair of gloves from her jacket pocket and yanked them on, her nails snagging on the frayed edges where the fingers had been cut off. She still hadn't fixed that. Maybe Will could.

Mia fidgeted. She shouldn't even think about taking her gloves off in front of someone else. Too much pain lingered beneath the fabric. Too many unanswered questions. She thumbed the scar on her left hand through the material. Too many memories. She knew Will could fix the blasted frays. It unnerved her, the things she remembered about this particular crew. She shouldn't be so close to these people, and yet, found she couldn't help herself. Waving her hatch open, she walked out into the corridor and straight into her first mate, Cassidy Gates.

"Galaxies!" Cassidy's brown eyes widened as the armful of bowls and forks she had been carrying tumbled. The metal bounced harmlessly off the deck. Cassidy cringed and picked up the fallen dishes.

"Oh, blast it. Sorry, Cassidy." Mia bent down and helped her friend. She shouldn't even call Cassidy a friend, but she couldn't help it.

"Don't worry. It's a great way to start off the morning though, eh?"

Mia managed a laugh at the old joke, like they could really tell the time of day out here in the black. Her palm spiked. Despite that it felt as if a knife had shoved itself into her old wound, Mia forced herself to breathe. To be easygoing. She had to. No one had seen through her disguise, not a single crewmember on this or any other ship she'd been on. The ache dulled again.

It wasn't as hard with this crew. They made it easy, actually. Mia led the way down the corridor and into the square kitchen cabin. Cassidy went straight for the built-in sink behind the bar on the far side. Mia claimed one of the bolted-down chairs butting up against the bar. She folded her arms, left tucked under her right, but smiled at her crewmate's grumbling. Perhaps she had been on this ship too long.

"It's times like these I wish we had an AutoChef on this boat. At least we could make it wash the dishes," Cassidy said.

Mia knew it was a lie. Cassidy liked to cook. To bake, especially. Cassidy unlatched the metal cabinets. When she turned to put some cloth on the bar, Mia saw it. Her black camisole had acquired an even darker stain. The rehydrated kax berry and gava grains—a favorite breakfast of Cassidy's—splattered nicely on the fabric. The rusted hinges squeaked in protest as she shut the cabinet. She turned to Mia, wincing.

"And some good Skadian oil too," Cassidy said.

The twinge in Mia's hand worsened. She ignored it, unwilling to recognize the sign. The signal for her to run. To leave this crew behind. To do things she couldn't even speak of. "Well, at least now I know another one of your secrets."

Cassidy's eyes narrowed, tilting her head to the side, the question clearly written on her face.

"It's obvious." Mia smiled. "Skadian women never learned how to eat properly, even when the recipe is a staple on their planet."

"Pah! I wasn't the one who spilled tea on myself yesterday!" Cassidy smirked. "Or gava grains last week. You make more messes than I ever could."

Mia arched an eyebrow. "And yet, you're the one with the stain."

"Not for long." Cassidy swiveled back around, pulling her shirt off in a huff. She turned on the water and rubbed the dark cloth. "Don't let Will or Jeff come in, 'kay?"

"Sure." Mia got up to stand by the hatch. Cassidy's low rumbling voice carried above the water's hiss. Snippets of "stupid bowl" made Mia frown as did the continuing sensations in her palm. She shook her hand as if trying to fling the sensations away then stilled. If she ignored it long enough, maybe they wouldn't find her. Maybe she wouldn't have to run. Maybe she wouldn't have to leave this crew. As if on reflex, Mia touched her jacket pocket. The paper inside grew heavier each time. Maybe she could stay. She glanced at her first mate, who scrubbed the cloth in angry, quick motions.

Even the slightest jest grated Cassidy's nerves. A few months back Will had teased Cassidy when she spilled some gravy during dinner. Nothing harsh. Will never was intentionally harsh. Cassidy's eyes darkened all the same. He couldn't see that his humorous comments stung her. A thicker skin might help. Mia could teach her more than a few things about developing one.

But, as Mia's gaze traveled up the small of her crewmate's back, she could hardly think of skin prettier than Cassidy's. A smile spread on Mia's lips once more. The yellow bra Cassidy wore clashed with her pale skin. She never could coordinate well. Out here, no one should care. Mia certainly shouldn't. She should be initiating her plan, one honed over years of use. Her palm began to pulse. She should be leaving by now. Instead, the swaying of Cassidy's violet and brunette locks captivated Mia. She marveled at her crewmate's bravery in keeping it long, and dyed, even out here.

Cassidy spun so fast she sprayed water all across the bar. Mia, quick to react, shielded her face and groaned when her jacket caught some of the spray.

"Seen enough?" Cassidy winked and stuck out her tongue. She pulled her top back on, smoothing the wrinkles out as it fell over her well-toned stomach. The camisole looked great on her. Too great. Cassidy practically flew around the bar and linked her arm with Mia's.

"You were really staring." Cassidy's eyes sparkled. "Didn't you get enough on that last planet we were on? You were gone for quite a while."

"I was doing the job and you know it."

Cassidy pushed her teasing further. "Well, maybe Will or Jeff—"

"Don't even finish that sentence." Mia cut her crewmate off. "Those men aren't worth my time. I'll wait until the next stop and see if there are any good catches there. Will or Jeff. Two crewmembers sleeping together? Imagine the consequences." Mia broke the connection first and stared at the ceiling. The agony in her palm seared. She glanced back at Cassidy.

"Yes." The skin around Cassidy's eyes crinkled. "The consequences."

Mia could not find her voice to respond, so Cassidy led them to bridge. Without warning, a sharp, electric crack echoed in the corridor.

Smoke engulfed them. Debris flew into the air and banged onto the other side of the bulkhead. Flames shot out of the vent like an engine backfiring.

Mia turned away, lifting her arms to protect herself. Her heart pounded, but the explosion didn't scare her, something much more dangerous did. Surely the Acedians couldn't have shot their way into the ship. She would have heard them. Felt them, even. She lowered her arms and searched the smoky corridors. Empty. She strained her ears against the ringing that clouded her hearing. Were there footsteps? Had they been boarded? Silence, a ringing silence. No, of course the *Eclipse* hadn't been boarded. Jeff would've called the alarm. Will would've notified Mia of the proximity alert. Finally, it clicked. Another answer. Mia's heart calmed. Will.

"I'm going to kill the idiot," Cassidy muttered.

Mia agreed. William Dee always fiddled around with wires he shouldn't. His creativity could be used elsewhere, piloting the ship, perhaps. The man decided on building bombs as a pastime. He hid them in empty spots below the walkway. It seemed he had neglected to defuse this particular one. Any other captain would've locked him in the brig for such negligence, but not Mia. Hidden bombs could be useful when the time called for it. Useful to her, especially.

She glanced around once more, assessing the old bulkheads now instead of the walkways. The entire ship was old. With small passageways, and even smaller cabins, an explosion like that could've damaged quite a bit more. Thankfully, only the immediate corridor suffered. The explosion scraped a few sharp edges onto the dark metal. Thankfully? She was too close to this ship. To these people. Mia raced the last few feet to the bridge with Cassidy on her heels.

"Will," Mia shouted as her crewmate came into view. He attempted to run in the other direction, but his retreat wasn't soon enough. Mia smashed her fists into his arm. "What were you thinking, putting an active bomb in the ship's duct like that?"

"I was only trying to store it there! I didn't mean for it to go off. And it was a small bomb anyway." Will groaned, his Paradousian accent elongating the s's into a soft hiss as he tried to explain his reasoning.

Mia stopped hitting him, her eyes widened. "A small bomb anyway? That's your excuse?" She gestured out the bridge's viewport. "Do you know where we are?"

"Of course I know where we are," Will said.

"Obviously not. You decide to put a bomb on my ship? Jeopardizing my crew? Out in the middle of nowhere? I should have you thrown into the brig!" Mia shoved her hands onto her hips. Her palm throbbed. Could the Acedians detect explosions inside ships? She didn't want to know.

Will shrugged. "There are plenty of planets around. Pargon is twenty klicks off our bow. We don't even have a brig to throw me in anyway. And who would even fly this boat if I wasn't around?"

The conversation stalled as Jeff slid in between them, facing Mia. She glared at the two men. Jeff looked so much like his younger brother. Stand them together, and the one distinguishing feature of the burly, green-eyed twins was hairstyle—Will's shaggy locks, Jeff's buzz cut. Their square-cut shirts stretched tight over their dark skin. She cocked her head, questioning his sudden intrusion.

Jeff pointed out the viewport. "We may have some trouble."

Mia huffed a response then looked to where Jeff pointed. Her anger dissipated. They had found her.

"Blast it!" Mia threw herself to the viewport. A ship loomed large, sleek, and ever closer. She could recognize their design anywhere—Acedians. Her left hand seared again. It had to be them. Her heart pumped faster. Her arms started to tremble. No, she had to be strong in front of her crew. She had to be strong for them. And besides, the Acedians wouldn't take her without a fight. Not yet.

"Who are they?" Will asked.

Mia's jaw tightened. Her crew didn't know of her history with this particular race. They didn't know how wanted she truly was by these people, or how difficult it was to get away from them. Or how difficult it was to get away a second time. A third time. They didn't know, because she hadn't told them. She hadn't told anybody.

"No one we want to deal with." Mia had to make her crew leave the ship somehow. They wouldn't understand. Or she had to leave herself. A twinge tightened in her chest at the idea of leaving her crew behind. Of destroying the ship and saving herself once more. She hated the Acedians for making her do this, forcing her to make this choice again and again. But the Acedians would do terrible things if they boarded the ship. To her and her crew. And they could still run. She glanced at Will and Jeff, before her gaze finally slid to Cassidy, who merely titled her head in question. Yes, she had become too close with this crew.

"We have to leave." Mia straightened. "Now."

"Leave?" Will and Jeff had identical looks of shock on their faces, mouth parted and eyes wide.

"It's just a ship. Nothing to worry about," Will said.

"Yeah, we don't even know if it's actually trouble," Jeff said, his accent slipping in now. "I only said that to get you two to stop bickering."

Cassidy merely stared at Mia.

"Look. I'm captain of this boat and you blasted well have to listen to me." Mia took her post, square in the center of the small bridge and closed her hands into fists. She hoped they didn't notice how much they trembled. "I don't care what you think. I don't care what you say. They're trouble. And we have to leave. Now."

As if to emphasize her point, the enemy ship fired a warning shot across their starboard bow. The shot flitted past them, bathing them in a sudden aqua light, only to be replaced by the dull white orbs on the bridge. A static-filled voice filtered over the comm system.

"Mia Foley."

Mia stood as straight as possible while attempting to calm her screaming mind and make a rational decision on whether to shut the comm off by shooting it, or by simply pushing the button.

The voice came again. "Mia Foley. We know you are in there."

The static grew louder over the intercom, but Mia was sure she heard screams filter through as well.

"We have come to collect you, Mia."

Mia's left hand twitched.

"We have come—"

The voice on the comm didn't have a chance to finish that sentence. Mia threw her entire weight onto the control panel and pushed that blasted button.

We have come. Those three words echoed in her thoughts. She grimaced, hoping her crew couldn't see how frightened she was. We have come. She'd heard those words too often. Her hand twitched again. A scorching pain flew from her palm. She pushed her right hand into her left. Maybe she could smother it. Smother the hurt. We have come. Her thoughts reeled. How did they find her so soon? How did they know where she was all the time? Why didn't they just leave her the blasted well alone? It had to be the scar. Her memory leapt back to her first encounter with them. Her vision shadowed and shifted out of focus.

She couldn't see them. Her captors. Mere shadows dancing on the metallic walls of her prison next to her bloodstains and the dried stains of who knew how many others. Strapped to a cold metallic table, face down, she screamed. Her clothes had been ripped to shreds. That was nothing compared to what they did to her body. She suspected that at least two of her ribs were broken. Her long hair had been yanked out in so many places and so hard, droplets of blood leaked onto her forehead.

One of her captors pulled her left arm around her back and forced her palm upward. A loud hissing sound came from the far end of the dark cabin. A bright light suddenly entered into Mia's field of vision. Slowly, her eyes readjusted to the piercing onslaught of a white and red glare—what was it? Her captors must've figured she could make out the symbol for they laughed, and the light drifted away. She connected the dots. Red and white. Hissing. It had to be.

They were going to brand her. Like a common animal. She thrashed, but the bonds held fast. The powerful grip held her steady. Too powerful. Her own hand shook under the pressure of the great brute.

Something pressed into her palm, and the agony started, as if she had stuck her hand in molten lava. Her hand shook. The brute tightened his grip. The suffering pushed past her hand and coursed through her entire left side. Fire rushed through her veins, through her skin, through everything. Nothing would stop it. Nothing could. Her screams reached their peak. The pressure on her skin lifted, the throbbing subsided. Mia fainted.

Mia's right arm shook. She became aware of the pressure on her shoulder, of her jacket pushed down by a heavier weight, of warm breath on her cheek. The bridge snapped back into clarity. Cassidy shook her, saying something that Mia couldn't make out. A flash of aqua washed over Cassidy's form. Another shot streaked outside the viewport. The shot connected with the hull, sending blue sparks skittering. A blinking red light on Jeff's panel warned how the shot also tore an outer layer off the ship. Mia's hearing finally clicked back into place.

"Captain!" Will's shouts filtered through.

Mia turned toward the sound of his voice, grabbing onto Cassidy's hand and squeezing it to reassure her crewmate she was back in the present.

"We're running out of options here, Captain," Will shouted. "They stopped the warning shots and now they're trying to disarm the ship. We're making a run for it."

"Good." Relief flooded her. So her little journey into the past hadn't disrupted the flow of her crew too much. "How are we holding up?"

"Not good." Jeff's hands flew over the screen of his control panel. Mia didn't need Jeff to expand on his statement. The flashing lights confirmed they didn't have enough time to make a different decision.

Another flash of aqua. The screech of hull tearing away. The shot ricocheted off the hull and beyond their line of vision. The ship lurched sideways. The shot had to have connected with one of the aft wings. Hissing came from down the corridors. Small explosions sounded, metal tearing against metal. Orange flashes sparked into life and died again. Chaos. Utter chaos. Mia scowled. Chaos made by only one of their ships. Not ten, not even two, only one ship attacked the *Eclipse*. She pressed her lips together. They wouldn't force her hand again. Not yet. Not while this crew could still get away. The chatter on the bridge hummed: Will updating her on the position of the enemy ship, Jeff trying to contain the hull breaches, and Cassidy manning the guns and shooting back at them with everything this little ship had.

Even with the upgrades to the energy beams, Mia knew this ship had no way of beating the Acedians without proper shields. And, of course, a transport ship wouldn't have shields. Mia grimaced. How could she pick such a weak crew? Usually by this time, she'd be gone. The crew would be, too. Her throat tightened.

"If they keep this up we'll be drifting in no time," Jeff muttered, his body curved over his control panel. "I'll try to reroute some power from the guns to help."

"Will, we need more speed," Mia said. The ship shuddered under another shot, and she had to grip the back of Will's chair to keep steady. "Do a full engine forward, maybe we can get out of sensor range and shake them at Shei. No." Mia faltered. Were there any other planets close enough? She scanned Will's control panel. Shei. Quar. One tiny, yellow dot stood out to her. It had to be Pargon. "Head for Pargon's outer belt. Cassidy, stop firing the moment Will does the forward blast. We don't need to give them help targeting us. Jeff, seal the outer breaches. I don't need to have pieces of my ship flying off. We need all the scraps we've got."

"Aye." The bridge echoed with her crew's reply. They carried out her orders. The silence lengthened, grew heavy. The ship shot forward. Their momentum brought the *Eclipse* far enough out of range of the enemy's guns, and they reached the rock barrier creating Pargon's outer ring. As Will navigated through it, Mia relaxed a little, remembering why she chose such a crew. Not weak. Sneaky. A ship as small as the *Eclipse* could squeeze through floating debris better than the massive hunk of metal following them. The Acedian ship drew back. They'd have to wait for an escort to guide them through. It would give her time, but not much. She could stay with this crew for a little while longer. Her heartbeat slowed. A shiny, silver planet loomed ahead of them while their—no, her—enemy drifted behind.

Chapter Two

PARGON LOOMED EVER CLOSER, the cities glinting as the solar panel roofing both absorbed and reflected the sun. Mia eyed Jeff's tracker. Their ship was a tiny blue blip on the screen, her enemy's a crimson smear, foreboding, but drifting farther and farther away. Pargon's belt had saved them. The enemy had given up for now. That is, until they realized Pargon's belt was just that, a belt, and not a complete sphere protecting the world. It seemed like this particular Acedian ship didn't have the technology to extend their sensors more than a few klicks away. Mia's hands shook, from fear or adrenaline she didn't know. Next time, they might not be so fortunate.

"Will, let's see how close we can get to the surface of the planet." Jeff looked at his brother. "If we get close enough I might be able to communicate with them using the short-range comm system."

Will shook his head. "That won't work." He pulled the controls up a bit and the *Eclipse* slowed her forward momentum. "They would shoot us out of the sky when we got too close for their liking."

"He's right," Cassidy said, rolling her eyes. "Pargon tends to be wary of people they don't know."

"We've been here before." Jeff tapped his foot on the deck. "They should recognize the symbol we have on the hull."

Will slapped Jeff's leg to make the movement stop. "You just want to get off the ship."

"Well, of course I do." Jeff's eyes narrowed. "We need to fix this girl up before we fly again. You think the outer hull would have survived another impact? I barely contained all the breaches. We need to get more supplies from the surface of Pargon."

As if to agree with Jeff's statement, a hissing erupted from the corridor leading away from the bridge. Cassidy glanced down the corridor for a second before meeting Mia's gaze and raising her eyebrows. The brothers still bickered back and forth about the supplies and the challenge of getting onto Pargon—possibly illegally—without being blasted. Mia frowned. No mention of the ship that tried blasting them out of the sky. Will brought up a good point. They'd never get close enough before one of the Pargon gunners decided the *Eclipse* looked better on fire. But no matter how antsy Jeff was to get off the ship, he was right. His screen alone showed six different areas of the *Eclipse* that needed repairs.

"We go in." Mia's sharp tone halted the fight. She folded her arms. "We send a comm-burst like Jeff suggested. Stay far enough away to not pose a threat. We don't need any more hull damage, especially not from their lasers."

Cassidy nodded. Thankfully, the *Eclipse* didn't look like much of a threat anyway in their current condition. The head council of Pargon, a group of elders elected by their people, seemed to think the same, and the *Eclipse* settled down on one of the landing platforms outside the main city. Mia and her crew meandered to the stern hatch leading outside. Crates littered the circular loading bay. They hadn't moved their latest shipment to storage. Hadn't she told the boys to do that yesterday? Mia shoved some of the containers to the side and shot Will a glance.

He shrugged. "Sorry. We meant to get to it today."

Mia winced. Until the Acedians fired at them. Would they bring that up?

Cassidy smiled. "I can't believe Pargon still has lasers. You'd think they would have gotten a magwave turret at least."

Mia shook her head. What kind of crew was this? Weren't they curious about the ship that nearly killed them? She didn't push it. She never would. But she didn't join in either.

"Lasers might be older tech." Jeff twirled his metal wristband around and leaned back on the bulkhead. "They're effective, though. One direct blow from a well-aimed beam would burn a hole into any ship, regardless of what the engineers used to build it."

"Unless they have a shield, of course." Will pushed a tiny, rusted, square explosive, one of his homemade bombs, behind one of the crates.

"Which we don't." Cassidy bundled her long hair up into a ponytail and tied it with a piece of black fabric from her pocket.

"Which we should." Will's green eyes flicked toward Mia.

A frown pulled at her lips. Of course they should have shields. "Enough."

Her crew fell silent. It surprised her that they mentioned nothing of the attack. Surprised, and annoyed her as well. Any crew would've by now. Strange.

The bulkhead opened upward, air whooshing out until the *Eclipse* had pressurized with the new atmosphere. Light from Pargon's two suns washed into the bay, their combined rays as bright as the glare off a metallic shard. Which is exactly what this city was. The temperature peaked at one hundred and twenty. Luckily, today it stayed in the one hundred degree range. Still, a bead of sweat dripped down Mia's back. She took off her captain's jacket, slipping the list into her pants pocket. She always kept the paper close, in remembrance of the lives lost and for her own safety. Couldn't have anyone finding it. Her eyes adjusted to the rays bouncing off the platform and rested on the darker buildings that made up the city.

"Ugh," Cassidy muttered, holding a hand to shade her eyes and yanking her camisole up a bit to reveal her pale stomach. "Why does it always have to be hot in these places?"

"Just deal with it, Cassidy." Will strutted past her, chest high and dimples etched deep in his face.

"Some people aren't tolerant of the heat like us." Jeff threw himself over his brother's shoulders. "That's what you get for being from a frozen world."

"Skadi isn't always cold." Cassidy's ears darkened to a shade of pink.

"Ten out of twenty months it is." Will laughed.

"All right," Mia said. "Time to split up and gather the supplies we need. Cassidy, you go with Will to the Nutriment and get some food powder, but be sure to grab some fresh fruit and vegetables if they have any."

"And spices." Jeff fell off Will and ruffled his hair. "We can make anything taste good with spices."

Mia wiped her brow, her hair already matted. Idiotic heat. "Jeff, you come with me to the Tin Roof and see what sort of metals we can scrounge up."

Her crew paired up. They seemed determined not to mention anything about the ship chasing them or about Mia's odd reaction. Very strange. It would only be a matter of time before they brought it up. Will and Cassidy walked off to the right, heading toward the marketplace. Scuffed, glass-fronted rooms were filled with farmers waiting for shoppers.

Will pushed up the black sleeves of his shirt and brushed his hair back as he walked. Cassidy's shoulders slumped. Her ears had faded back to pale pink. They would work fine together, as long as Will didn't try anything too stupid.

Jeff sidled up to her, hands shoved into his back pockets. Mia looked at the man. Sooner or later, Jeff would be the one to break the silence that had fallen over the issue of the attack. He seemed the type.

"So, where's the Tin Roof again? I can never remember where anything is on this planet." He started walking in the wrong direction. "It's too shiny for its own good."

"Well," Mia replied, typing in the code to close the hatch and pulling him the opposite way. "We need to get to the outskirts of the city. Which means straight to the other side."

A crowd gathered to gawk at the *Eclipse*. Mia strolled through them. Patrols were there, too, ones who would keep the ship from harm. She spoke to a particularly dapper young officer, promising a high transfer of units to his account if he could keep strange folk off the ship. And to buy himself a drink because he looked like he needed it.

The kid, who couldn't be more than eighteen, nodded and tightened his grip on his stunner gun. The stunner wouldn't do much damage—a cheaper design than the magnetic wave guns the military used—but the shockwave it dissipated would hurt enough to stop someone. Despite his age, Mia knew she could count on him. Pargon had always been a clean and safe harbor. The officers kept anyone unwanted off the streets, with an effective kill-all-who-disobey law that kept the evildoers off this particular planet. She'd picked Pargon for that reason. As for the unit transfer, she'd get Cassidy to do it later. Mia didn't have the ID tag for it anymore anyway. Too easily tracked. She thumbed the side of her wrist. Her time on Fissure took care of that. She grabbed Jeff away from a pretty, raven-haired gawker and led him off the landing pad and into the city.

"Did you have fun flirting with that patrol guy?" Jeff's coy smile was like his younger brother's, but his dimples weren't as deep. His smile reached his eyes without even trying. Mia shook her head.

"Come on." He walked next to her, admiring the sights and giving her sidelong glances every once in a while. "He was cute."

"Cute." Mia bumped into a tanned girl wearing a white mesh fabric cleverly covering the necessary areas and a loose-fitting, semitransparent coat that fell to her knees. Pargon fashion stumped Mia sometimes. The girl even had knee-high sandals. Mia hadn't seen footwear like that in years. All of her deals were on less chic planets, more boots and less skin. "Sure, he was cute."

Jeff's smile widened. "Not your type, right?" He put his hands up and flopped them down in a mock imitation of a woman. Mia threw him a glare. He put up his hands. "Not like I care, of course."

She ignored him after that. Buildings towered over them, skyscrapers with glass fronts and houses that bulged into the street. Narrow offices melted into roads made with a mixture of metallic shards and rock, everything paved or plated with different substances specifically designed to absorb the heat. Floating orbs hung over the walkways and roads. At night, those orbs would glow a soft white. Mia stared. She couldn't help herself. How anyone could have enough time to build such structures was beyond her. She barely had enough time to find a ship, much less a crew.

The mass of people on the walkway swelled, as a new wave tumbled out of the sleek office buildings. It must be time for lunch. Mia's stomach growled. Will and Cassidy had better buy a lot of food. Many of the city dwellers passed them by, unnoticed, but a few did double takes. White was the predominate color of this planet, the fabric lightweight. Even the men wore the white mesh. Mia hated the color. Too easy to notice. To be fair, their own dark outfits stood out in this crowd. An easy mark if the Acedians made it through sooner than expected. Her camisole already stuck to her back, and her pants clung to her legs. She picked up her pace, knowing Jeff could keep up. A woman pushed past them, her right iris a different color than her left. Mia tensed. Had it been silver? She looked back over her shoulder, trying to get a glimpse of the woman. No, the eye had been orange. She was sure of it.

Jeff grabbed onto Mia's shoulder. "Did you see her eye, she's wearing a Comp-tact! I hear they actually hardwire them, so the wearer doesn't have to say anything."

Mia nodded to show she heard over the hum on the street. She knew of the advanced tech system, but Jeff rattled on anyway, twenty-five and still acting like an excited child. "All they have to do is think, and suddenly the web is right there. Everything on cyberspace is available, no hassle, no control panels. Just a simple little eye piece."

Yes, she had to admit it was a pretty ingenious piece of technology, though an orange eye was easy to spot. Advanced technology reigned on this planet. A gaggle of women watched in awe as a bubble of gray transformed into a desk, then a table, and then a chair. NIN morphing tech, Mia recalled. Children held education rings, holoimages of history, science, and math displaying in front of their eyes. One child seemed fascinated by a terraforming lesson where a useless planet transformed into a bounty.

Jeff, open mouthed, pulled her to a stop as they passed a group of white Shifting Pads capable of transporting people from one side of the planet to the other. The technology could even shift people planet to planet, as long as the planets were relatively close to one another. As they watched, a young couple stood on one of the oval pads and dematerialized from view. A wide grin on his face, Jeff swiveled to Mia. She shook her head and guided him away. Shifters were military tech, too easily tracked. The moment she stepped on one, the Acedians would find her. She rubbed her left hand. And they already found her fast enough. She eyed every person that passed, waiting for an Acedian to appear.

Beyond Jeff's wistful admirations, Mia overheard a few snippets of conversation, mainly about work and relationships. A few whispers caught and held her attention. Some of the businesswomen were conversing about a rather large and unnamed ship circling the border ring. One squeaked how the ship might be rogue. Another uttered how odd it was for the ship to linger. Clearly, it couldn't pass through the ring, and yet it didn't try to go around. The ship hadn't requested an escort either. Some tension left her body. The Acedians hadn't landed. Odd was the buzzword whispered throughout the streets. *Odd* was the word that resonated in Mia's head.

The Tin Roof's sign flashed over the hustling crowd, and Mia didn't need to look back at her companion to know disappointment crossed his face. The sigh he exhaled was more than enough. He waved the door open, shaking his head. Mia followed him inside. A cool blast of air hit her. So, the owner had finally decided to install the ColdAir coils the Vespa government had issued for the hotter planets in their system. The air brushed her skin, leaving goosebumps in its wake. Spotting a water jelly station beneath the coils, she grabbed a handful and popped a few of the squishy, translucent beads into her mouth. The jelly flooded her tongue with fresh, semisweet water. Cool air and cool water jelly all at once. The place to be on a hot day like this. She squeezed behind two elderly women gazing at an automatic cleaning robot that dated back to the 2300s, and weaved straight for the gun and dagger display in the far corner.

"I'll look in the back," Jeff said as he passed her to get to the sheet metal room.

"Be sure to get the layered hybrid if they have it," Mia replied. "We need as many sheets as we can get to fix the hull, not to mention the tears inside."

"I know," Jeff shouted, heading deeper into the shop. Metals of all different shapes and sizes were piled high within the front room, and the bulkier sheets were kept in the back. "You'd think I hadn't been working on ships for over five years with the way you baby me."

Mia smiled at his retreating back. He had a fair point. But it was her ship. Sort of, anyway. She'd hate to have them find out she'd stolen the blasted thing. She turned to the guns and daggers, many of them older designs, yet still high quality for used gear. She picked up a dagger, admiring the hilt. Flames etched into the metal no doubt honored the Vespa government, but within the flames another design shimmered through. Snow? Mia squinted. Yes, rough-hewn, like kids' paper cut outs.

"Pretty, isn't it?"

Mia jumped. The voice had come out of nowhere, it seemed. A man, in a white blazer, slid around the pile of metal next to her and into her line of sight. Mia recognized the pointed eyebrows of the shop owner. His dark eyes found hers.

"Yes," Mia agreed. "It's quite unique."

The owner disappeared again, making a bit of a ruckus as he left, leaving her shaken and feeling dumb about it. The owner shouldn't have been able to sneak up on her like that. He probably wasn't even trying, but she'd been too distracted to hear the noise. Surely, she couldn't be that off? Goosebumps traveled over her skin. Mia rubbed her arms to chase the feeling away. Tensing when an eye color seemed off, jumping when the owner had only meant to sell a dagger? She was tense from the attack. Too tense. Even this crew would notice.

The scar on her hand burned. She clenched it within her fist, closing her fingers around the pain. She frowned, looking inward. She hated the guilt she carried around from her past. She tried to wear it like a shield, keeping others at bay. The ache was always there, a dull reminder if she needed one, but when a ship of theirs was around the feeling doubled. Her sign to get moving. To do horrible deeds because the Acedians forced her to. Because she needed to, to save herself.

They had to track her using the scar. Mia never knew how. It was just another wound from her travels. Her crew knew nothing about it.

And would, hopefully, never know. She couldn't let anyone in anymore. She couldn't let what happened on the *Scarlet* happen again. She knew she shouldn't. Still, this particular crew amazed her.

Even when they were away from the danger, not one of them brought up the attack. Even though she had acted oddly. Even though the *Eclipse* was damaged. Even though she gave no explanation for her actions. Mia knew she would have to talk about it sometime, and perhaps this crew would be able to handle it. Perhaps this would be the crew she could tell. She could confess her deeds to. Perhaps not.

"El Cap-ee-tan!" Jeff's voice floated over from the back. He soon joined her, a cart hovering before him regardless of the heaping pile of metal stacked upon it. Another cart lagged behind.

"Something the matter, Mia, other than the obvious?" Jeff raised his eyebrow at her rigid position. Mia shook her head and turned away. They meandered to the front of the shop to pay, but Mia noticed Jeff continued to stare at her. Now was not the time to speak her fears.

"That will be three hundred for the sheet metal and thirty for that dagger." A screen appeared on the counter, brightening the owner's features from below. He inputted the information and holoimages flashed up, showing the metal they bought. Jeff tapped *Eclipse*'s coordinates into the screen, as well as the extra supplies needed. A timestamp appeared at the bottom, flashing yellow. "The materials will be at your ship early tomorrow morning, around five."

Mia nodded and nudged Jeff. He waved his arm over the screen, and the ID tag embedded in his skin glowed. It would show his name, homeworld, and account information. The info appeared on the holoimage, scrolling upward, but Mia paused it at the extra thirty for the dagger. Dagger? She looked at Jeff whose green eyes traveled down to her waist. The short knife she had been gripping a few moments ago rested in her belt.

"It's a nice piece," Jeff commented.

"Yes, it is." She gave the dagger a once over. It seemed she hadn't forgotten everything. Her body remembered skills she tried to push away.

When they arrived back at the *Eclipse*, Pargon's two suns were falling fast and the crowds thinned in order to make it home for dinner. Will and Cassidy had already reached the ship and stored their supplies. They'd had a good run for food, and both Will and Cassidy were enjoying handfuls of fresh kax berries while lingering outside the *Eclipse*. Mia's mouth watered, as she punched Cassidy on the shoulder and slapped the back of Will's head. Cassidy grinned. She was used to Mia's way of showing enthusiasm. Will was not so accommodating.

"Hey!" He rubbed the back of his head. "What the heck was that for?"

"These, you dolt." Mia plucked one of the round, green berries out of Will's heaping handful. The kax berry was as large as her thumb, and he had plenty.

Will tucked the fruit closer to his chest. "I don't go bashing my friends whenever I want a piece of fruit."

"Well, I do." Mia leaned on a carton of food still outside and marveled at the mention of them being friends. Her chest tightened. Friends. She looked upward at the darkening sky. Way too close. But when Cassidy meandered over to stand next to her, Mia could not contain her grin. She bit into the ripe fruit, savoring its sweetness as it flooded her tongue.

Cassidy laughed. "It's a good thing we don't get fresh fruit everyday or he'd have brain damage."

"It's a miracle he doesn't have it already," Jeff said.

Will sputtered, pale-green juice spurting from his lips, and grimaced at his brother. "Like you're one to talk! I got a higher MES score than you. And you've probably lost millions of cells from working with gases all the time."

"Hey now, respect your elders. I am five minutes older than you." Jeff wiped juice off his brother's chin and started to unload the carts, making a ruckus as he did. He walked to the hull, leaned down under the *Eclipse*'s belly, and went to work. The fuse-gun sparked, injecting preprogrammed microbots into the hull and welding the metal plates into place, but Jeff still cursed up a storm at the work the *Eclipse* needed.

Mia winced. If any Acedians were on this planet, it wouldn't take them long to find her crew. But since the Acedians seemed less than accommodating to the Pargonian rules, maybe they had more time than she assumed.

Cassidy rummaged around in the crate next to her for a moment and pulled out a rumpled package. She presented it to Mia with a smile.

"Here," she said, her voice light. "I got this at the market for you. The wrapping is horrible, I know."

"What is it?"

"Just open it, you'll see."

Mia ripped open the flimsy package, feeling the weight of such a gift in her hands long before seeing what was actually inside. Once the wrapping fell away, the gift became even heavier.

"Gloves," Mia whispered, turning the soft fabric around in her hands. Stitched with white, the black cloth seemed soft, durable. It gave somewhat between the fingers and stretched, only to regain its original shape.

"I figured you might need another pair, since the ones you have are falling apart," Cassidy murmured.

Mia glanced up at Cassidy. Her brown eyes crinkled at the corners. For a moment, Mia's voice caught. She cleared her throat. "Yes, but...why did you feel like you had to get me a gift?"

"It's for being a good captain these past six months, as a thank you." Cassidy shrugged. "Aren't you going to put them on?"

"Later, I will. Thanks," Mia murmured, unsure of what else to say.

Cassidy nodded, touched Mia's arm, and walked away, grabbing another piece of fruit from Will's pile and munching on it as she left.

Mia shook her head at Cassidy's odd behavior. It was shaping up to be a nice night, and Mia found she was glad to have one. Peace and quiet stayed here. Real quiet, broken only by laughs of kids and the random yip of a nearby pet. No shadows lingered here, no suspicious people jumping out at her as she ate fruit with her crew. Her actions in the Tin Roof were novice. Idiotic. Her scar, once so painful, had dulled into a simple ache. The Acedians were far away.

She grabbed a box of yellow carotas and wandered inside her ship, stopping by her cabin to drop off the gift and heading to the kitchen. She washed and cut the carotas, then dumped them into their disintegrator. By morning the carotas would be reduced to a fine powder, easily made into soups and stews, yet still retaining all their nutritional properties. Eggs worked best at the rehydrating process, as they reformed their original scrambled shape. Other foods tended to turn into mush. Still, it was better than nothing, and her crew would thank her for it later. Cassidy appeared by her side, grabbed her arm, and yanked her back outside. Cassidy shepherded Will as well, and soon they were all gathered around Jeff as he hunched under the *Eclipse*'s belly.

"We need to find some work," Cassidy began, looking at each one in turn. Mia was not the only one who sighed in their little group.

"Work? We just got here. Can't we enjoy ourselves first?" Will's face fell, as he leaned back onto the *Eclipse*. His arms dangled at his sides and shoulders slumped. Mia could swear he looked twelve.

"No." As tired as Mia was, Cassidy was right. "We should look for a deal tonight. Maybe see if we can settle it in the morning."

"Perfect!" Cassidy smiled, walking toward the city while Will and Mia followed. Jeff stayed behind to work on the ship, although it was highly unlikely he would finish the repairs tonight.

"At least we look professional." Cassidy straightened her camisole and doubled back to straighten Mia's as well. Cassidy's fingers brushed against Mia's stomach as she did so, and heat rushed up her skin even at that slight touch. Mia ignored it. Or tried to, anyway. She knew the tricks of the trade.

The only impression they made on these people was the first. Cassidy took that idea to heart. Traveling as much as they did, it was hard to have repeat customers, and they relied heavily on techno-chip to techno-chip to stay in the business. Mia pushed her new dagger farther into her belt and held onto the hilt as she walked. Perhaps not the right message to send to people, but the back of her neck still tingled. Rather be alive and prepared than professional and bleeding.

"You stay in the back when she does her pitch," Mia muttered to Will.

Will nodded and fell in line as they approached the first store and strolled inside. Cassidy's confidence was breathtaking to watch. Her passion knew no bounds.

"Good evening! We are Across the Stars trading company." Cassidy was in full businesswoman swing, shaking hands with an elderly woman and flashing her best smile, before Mia even reached the counter. "We have many different items from other worlds that could be helpful to your business, if you're interested."

Sheryl, they later learned, was quite interested. Chopped gray hair fell over her blue eyes. She nodded along each time Cassidy stopped to take a breath, and leaned forward, placing her hands on the counter that separated the two women. Both were promising body signals.

A shadow fell on the floor, but Mia didn't turn fast enough to see who passed. Acedian? No. Of course not. If they found her they would attack. Rolling her shoulders and trying to relax, Mia glanced around the store to see what sort of things they might be able to trade for. Sheryl had a good eye for quality trinkets: miniature ships controlled by headset and voice commands, technopets with fur so realistic even Mia wanted to touch them, and even personal disintegrators, all set up in displays around the edges of her store.

A technocat awoke from the robotic pet display and pawed its way over to Will. He scratched the machine's furry ears, and the technocat purred. In spite of herself, Mia grinned. It reminded her of the technodog her parents once bought her. Even the brown and white markings were the same. They had years together, their family of three becoming four. Her smile faded. Before they were killed by the Acedians. She never did know what happened to her dog. She turned away.

A faint scent of muskiness lingered in the air, even though the open door tried to hide it. Mia closed her eyes and rubbed her temple. An elderly person, with miniature flying ships and technopets. She suppressed the sarcastic remarks bubbling within her. It was always beneficial to get a good reputation, on any planet, with any client.

Settling her hand on her hip, Mia could feel her pulse in her palm. The steady rhythm calmed the constant suffering more than her mind could. She opened her eyes. A shadow drifted outside the door, and her fear spiked again, hand closing fast over her dagger. Her eyes narrowed, and the room grew silent. The shadow illuminated. Once again, not Acedian, just a man walking past. She softened her grip and shook her head. Idiot. After a time, her heart slowed back to normal, and the conversation between Cassidy and Sheryl gradually began to register in her ears once more. Their voices grew louder and clearer with every breath she took. The tapping of Will's foot became more distinct.

Sooner than expected, Mia shook hands with Sheryl, and Cassidy gave her a techno-chip to hang on to with the promise to come back in the morning. Sheryl, in turn, gave them a bundle of cookies tied with an orange and yellow ribbon. "They were made entirely by my AutoChef. I call him Harley."

An AutoChef...here? Hekate had one, too. Sheryl motioned to a silver, human-like machine curled up in the corner. At the mention of its name, the machine activated and stood, waving them out the door. Mia swallowed the lump forming in her throat. Too many things were reminding her of the home she lost so many years ago. Soon, she found herself standing in the hazy light of the three moons.

Cassidy skipped ahead. She loosened her hair from its high ponytail. Her locks fell gracefully down to her shoulders. Mia shook her head before any distracting thoughts could form. Why did her first mate have to be so pretty? And why did she have to care? Caring would make it harder to leave. She risked a smile though and called out, "Done for the night?"

"Of course!" Cassidy glanced back over her shoulder, and Mia's heart missed a beat. "I can't possibly make Will stay out anymore, just look at him."

Will lagged behind. He stuffed his hands deep into his pockets and walked slow. His eyes trained on the moon and his thoughts clearly up in the stars rather than on making deals.

Cassidy walked backward, lacing her hands behind her back and tilting her head. "Why must you always look at the moon? Every planet we go to, you look at the moon."

"I like moons," Will muttered. "What's it to you anyway?"

"Well, it's a romantic, starlit night, everyone else is asleep, and you have two gorgeous women walking with you. I find it offensive."

Mia shook her head at Cassidy's attempt at a barb. She always made herself an easier target when dealing with him.

Will glared at her. "Well, maybe it's because you're not—"

Mia shoved a hand over his mouth. "If you can't talk nice," Mia interjected, using an adage her mother once used, "don't talk at all."

Either Cassidy had not heard the anger in Will's voice or simply ignored it, because she continued her barrage of questions. "Don't you like being planet-side?"

Will heaved a sigh in Mia's direction. She shrugged. Her crew meshed so well together. A sudden pang pierced her heart. She grimaced. Too well. She matched her pace with their awkward loping, but kept her eyes on the shadows. Her palm still tingled, after all.

"No, I don't like being planet-side. Why do you think I became a pilot? I like stars. I like space." He gestured at the sky, catching Mia's attention. "I'd rather be up there than down here."

"Don't you care about the deals we make?" Mia asked.

Will frowned. "No, I don't care about the deals. Especially when it's with an old woman with worthless trinkets."

Cassidy waved the retort away. "Oh hush, you know as well as I do that stuff would sell well on family shuttles. And maybe we can go visit Paradous. They always have families landing there." She poked him in the side. "We could visit your family."

"Like my folks would want trinkets." Will rolled his eyes, but a hint of a smile flashed on his face.

Mia grinned. Cassidy always knew what to say. "Maybe one of your sisters would want a technopet," she suggested.

"Elizabeth is thirteen years old." Will tried to sound exasperated. Failed. His eyes crinkled at the sides like his brother's. "And Sarah would just laugh at me if I gave it to her."

"You never know." Cassidy glanced at Mia. "Elizabeth could really like it."

Will reached the ship first and led the way inside, a definite change in his attitude as he sauntered down the corridors to the ship's living room. Once he was far enough away, Cassidy turned to Mia and shook her head.

"Men." Her low voice seemed to ring in the silence. "How do people live with them?"

Mia laughed. "I haven't the faintest idea."

She pushed the button to close the hatch for the night, and both women walked in as the bulkhead closed. Cassidy had successfully teased Will out of his funk for the moment and, with a little luck, they would all simply say their good nights, drift off into their own cabins, and go to sleep. The Acedians wouldn't attack tonight. They couldn't. And maybe Mia finally could get a good night's rest. A small sliver of hope rose in her. Perhaps, she wouldn't have to discuss anything at all tonight. When Mia stepped into the living area, it was clear she had never been more wrong.

Chapter Three

MIA SIGHED AS SHE meandered around the living area, gathering the necessary elements of a good cup of xarianflower tea. Its three other occupants lounged about, watching. Tea cubes, liquid milk, and even sugar, it seemed Will and Cassidy had done an excellent job at restocking their supplies. They even bought five cartons of water jellies. Must've been Will's doing. He liked the sweet taste. The convec buzzed. Mia placed a cup with the cube into the machine, letting the steaming liquid pour down. The cube dissolved, and the water turned deep violet. She reached into their tiny fridge for milk. A whoosh of cold air ran over her hand and arm as she grabbed the pale carton. The liquid milk would only last a week or two and they'd be back to substitute, a gritty sour substance. Mia mixed the liquid milk in, watching the violet swirl into a lighter tint. Silence seemed to dominate the cabin. Someone coughed behind her.

"Mia." Jeff's voice floated over to her. Her grip on the cup tightened. So, his patience had snapped first. Seemed about right. Yet Will had the history of recklessly foraging into sensitive subjects, not his older brother. She turned toward them.

Jeff opened the cookies. The bright ribbon fluttered to the deck. He motioned for Mia to sit next to him. With Cassidy on one side and Will on the other, there was no more space for her on the couch. She unlocked one of the metallic chairs by the counter with her free hand and scooted it closer to the group, locking it back into the grooves on the deck. Jeff munched on a cookie, passing the bundle around.

Cassidy made a face but took one anyway. "I'll never understand why people have bots make their food for them. Baking is easy!"

Will stuffed two cookies into his mouth. When he spoke, crumbs followed his words. "Only because you can actually bake."

Mia tensed. If he made fun of Cassidy's baking skills she might have to hit him. Cassidy loved to bake, and she did it well. Quaint, perhaps, since an AutoChef could do it faster, but Mia liked that Cassidy embraced the older traditions. The traditions of old Earth. Because of people like her, those practices would never die.

Cassidy just laughed and passed the bundle to Mia. Taking one of the dark cookies, Mia swirled it in her tea before popping it into her mouth. Sweet. Too sweet for her liking. Cassidy's breads were better.

Reaching over, Will snatched Mia's cup out of her hands. Some of the tea spilled onto the walkway, and he wiped it clean with his sock. Mia arched an eyebrow and eyed the ribbon still on the deck. The brothers always made such a mess.

"How many times do I have to tell you idiots to clean up?" Mia picked up the ribbon and held it up for the brothers to see. They shrugged.

Cassidy stared at the piece of fabric. "That has such beautiful colors."

"Really?" Mia asked. Cassidy nodded. The colors were a bit much, the vibrant orange and yellow on the ends melted together in the center of the ribbon. Too cheery for Mia's liking, but when Cassidy looked away, Mia pocketed the silky fabric. She closed her eyes against the brightness of the cabin. If only they would all just go to bed.

"So," Will said.

A prickling sensation ran down the back of Mia's neck. She opened her eyes. Will tapped his hand on the side of the couch. If she'd been watching, she would've recognized the signs of his growing agitation.

He glared at her. "Why were we attacked earlier?"

Mia sat up a bit straighter, folding her arms so her left hand was hidden from view.

"Oh, nice segue," Jeff whispered. "Really nonchalant."

"What? I don't care." Will kept his eyes trained on Mia. "We need to know."

Let the reckless foraging begin.

"We should know who attacked us. And why we were even attacked. And why they wanted you in the first place."

Mia looked at the brothers, banded together. Her eyes narrowed. What to tell them, the truth? Perhaps. Her hand shook under her elbow. She clenched it into a fist. They might be able to handle it. But not now, not planet-side. They might not be able to handle it as well as she would like.

"They're pirates." She cleared her throat. "Rogue men and women who follow ships and steal whatever they can." Partially true.

"Pirates?" Jeff's eyes narrowed. Blast. Did he know pirate strategies? Recognize the difference in shooting patterns?

"Yes, pirates, outlaws, criminals, whatever you feel comfortable calling them. For me, they're pirates." Mia's heart pounded. It seemed like the cabin lights dimmed, and the bulkhead next to her loomed larger. It happened every time. That feeling.

"How cool." Will pumped a fist into the air, his gleeful attitude slowly creeping back. "We were chased by pirates."

Jeff spoke over him, "Why were they chasing us?"

"We're a trading ship," Mia replied. "The hull bears our symbol. A symbol of traders." A pang thudded close to her heart. She ignored it. Kept going. "The pirates must have seen it and decided we were perfect targets. Jeff said so before, we do hold some pretty valuable items on the *Eclipse*."

"Yeah." Will nodded. She had won him over. He must have only read about pirates, never encountered them before. "It makes sense that they would come after us."

"It makes sense that they would attack us," Cassidy spoke up from her corner of the couch. Her round eyes reflected the light so much they shimmered. Mia nodded, keeping her expression in what she knew was a neutral and inquisitive manner as Cassidy continued, "That doesn't explain how they knew you."

Mia was silent for a moment. She blinked. Her fingers clenched so tight they hurt.

"They knew me from my past dealings with them," she began. Good, that was the truth. She did have a past with the Acedians. The list in her pocket seemed to burn.

"Past dealings?" Cassidy leaned forward. Both brothers had gone silent, watching and listening to her reasoning. Mia knew they would be the ones trying to find a crack in her statements. It was a technique they used in the trading business.

Mia chose her words carefully. "Yes, I had an encounter with those pirates before joining your business. They tried to raid a transport shuttle I was on. I was able to evade them, but not before seriously damaging their ship." Memories of explosions flashed into her mind, of needles cutting flesh, of screaming children, before she could push the images down.

Cassidy frowned. "How did you get away?"

"I was able to get to one of the escape ships." Bright white lights, annoyingly blue seats, cold metal belts secured her and an escaping family. The *Oasis*. Her first ship. "I got away, but not before they saw my face. Not before they got my name."

"How did you know it was the same ship? The same pirates?" Cassidy seemed to want to know everything. Mia couldn't give her that. Not yet.

"I never forget the markings on a ship." Mia grimaced. She always knew. "Especially one that tried to attack me, one I tried to destroy."

Cassidy blanched. "How did you try to destroy it?"

"I grabbed the charges from one of the fallen officers and threw them into the pirate's hatch." That part she had altered slightly. She knew if she added a bomb Will would be on her side. Sure enough, when she stole a quick glance at him, he smiled. Even Jeff looked impressed.

"That's all well and good," Cassidy said, staring at her. "How did they know you were on this ship?"

"They must have seen me get on the ship. Or when we made deals on other planets. Or heard my voice on the comm. I haven't a clue." Mia threw up her hands in mock exasperation. She lowered her voice. "They're pirates. They have technology that we don't. Who knows what sort of equipment they stole from other planets. We barely got away the last time."

Cassidy fell silent, resting her elbows on her knees. Mia couldn't read Cassidy's face, and she prayed to every god listening, Cassidy couldn't read her own. She was already in too deep with these people.

"They were pretty close to blowing us up. And you said they go planet-side?" Will shook his head. "Man, I've never seen one face-to-face. From the looks of their ship, I think they'd be scary as a super nova."

"The people of Pargon seemed to be frightened of them." Jeff nibbled on another cookie. "I overheard one of the officers telling another that Pargon had put up their defenses, lasers and rail guns."

"The people of Pargon are scared of everyone." Mia rolled her eyes. Jeff seemed to need a push before he'd believe her. Lucky for her, she had the perfect argument ready. "But they have a right to be scared. These particular pirates loot worlds, too. They have some powerful guns on their side, both in space and on foot. We're lucky we got away. Think about what that power could do to planet-side."

Silence fell over the group. Jeff glanced at his brother, who nodded. They seemed to telekinetically agree her argument was sound, because Jeff mirrored his twin's movements. Perhaps not completely sound, but manageable as a good story. Even Cassidy seemed willing to let the matter drop. She leaned back into the couch, grabbing a pillow from behind her and holding it on her lap. Her fingers twisted the strings straying from the pillow's fabric. Mia let the story lull in the air.

"We were lucky to get away," Jeff broke the tension, echoing Mia's words. His voice quieter than it had been before. "Our ship was in a pretty bad condition."

"How much of it did you get fixed today?" Glad to get off the topic of the attack, Mia latched onto the repairs. It probably wouldn't be the last time they'd discuss the "pirates." Though perhaps she would be the one to bring them up next time. And perhaps then, she could use their real name. Acedian.

"Not much, honestly," Jeff admitted. "Mostly patches. I have to wait for the other supplies to do the serious work. If all goes well, I should have it completed by the morning after next, maybe even late tomorrow evening if I can have some help."

Mia nodded. "We'll see what we can do. Will can lend a hand, and maybe we can hire some extra help."

"Oh great, I get William." Jeff raised his hands in celebration.

"Like fixing the ship is something I really want to do." Will slapped his brother. "That's your charge."

Jeff yawned and stretched. He got up, shook his boots off his feet, and grabbed the last cookie. "I'm going to bed. I'll see you crazy people in the morning."

Will yawned as his brother retreated into the corridor connecting the living area to the personal quarters. The shadows in that particular corridor of the ship did look mighty inviting.

"Blast it," he muttered, yawning again. He got up and followed his brother. "See you in the morning."

Mia grabbed her cup, placed it in the sink, and glanced toward the couch. With only one occupant, the seat looked huge. Cassidy watched. She didn't speak. Didn't move. Didn't even reply goodnight when Mia whispered it into the stillness.

Happy to be engulfed in the shadows, Mia made her way to her cabin. She reached the hatch to her quarters. The boys had already gone into their respective cabins, and silence filled the space. Here, she could at least show her true face, let her eyes look to the deck, her mouth turn downward into a scowl, and her hand shake unimpeded by anything. Let her shoulders slump the tiniest bit. Here, she could be herself, and no one could stop her. Here, she could truly be afraid of the choice she must make.

Behind her, something moved. Mia tensed as a warm hand rested on her arm, her ears sharpened to the noise of another person breathing, and her eyes fixated on the circular pattern of her door hatch.

"We had discussed it earlier, you know." Cassidy breathed into the darkness. "The conversation, I mean."

"Will blurting it out wasn't really part of the master plan, huh?" Mia could feel Cassidy behind her. Her crewmate couldn't possibly see her face, so Mia kept the scowl in place, kept her head tilted downward, and her eyes on the hatch.

"No," Cassidy replied.

"Did it go as planned?"

"No." Cassidy shifted as if to get between Mia and the hatch, but only succeeded in sidling next to her.

Mia turned her face away. Who knew how far Cassidy could see. "No?"

"The conversation went better than planned actually, for you anyway. Both boys believed you." Cassidy's hand felt too warm on Mia's arm. "I didn't."

"Oh?" Mia shoved the word out, afraid if she said anymore her voice would give her away. No one had ever seen through her lies.

Cassidy squeezed her shoulder. "No. There's something you're not telling us."

"I told the truth," Mia said.

"Maybe. Not the whole truth."

Mia remained silent. If Cassidy did suspect anything, Mia would only make it worse, and more obvious, trying to deny it. Why did Cassidy have to be suspicious anyway?

"It's okay," Cassidy's voice was quiet, so quiet Mia had to strain to hear it. "It's okay if you didn't tell us everything. It's okay if you have secrets."

No, it wasn't okay. They could be killed for her secrets. Horribly and senselessly murdered because of her. Or worse. Her eyes burned, tears threatening to fall. She had to make her decision soon.

"But please," Cassidy's voice cut through Mia's thoughts. "Please. When you do feel strong enough..." Cassidy's hand entwined in Mia's. With Cassidy's help, the warmth and confidence in her grip, the shaking slowly stopped. How did she know? Did she know? "When you feel ready, please tell us."

Cassidy squeezed her hand once more and left. Her boots clicked down the hallway. The shadows licked her figure until she was completely engulfed by their darkness and could be seen no more. A sliding noise echoed in the corridor. She had entered her own cabin.

Mia stayed in the corridor a moment longer. Or perhaps an hour longer, she couldn't tell. She waved open the hatch, took off her boots, and fell into bed. Even with the comfort of Cassidy, memories came unbidden in Mia's consciousness. The ones she tried hard to ignore. The faces she tried so hard to forget. She pulled the list from her pocket and stared at it. Four ship names had been penned on the paper, penned by her. *Oasis*. Her first ship after *Hekate*, the family shuttle she'd been born on. After her parents died. After she'd been branded. She was so young. So afraid. *Scarlet*. Whenever she remembered that ship, her thoughts immediately went to Freya. To her first love. *Luminaria*. The ship where she didn't care anymore. And finally the *Jubilee*. The ship where she didn't have any time. Where she couldn't warn anyone. Tears again sprang up in her eyes.

Her anger spiked, and she crumpled the paper in her hand, tearing off her left glove in one smooth motion. She dropped both on her bed, staring at her scar. At the puckered triangle and spiked lines. At her veins running beneath it. She hated the Acedians, but most of all, she hated herself. Hated what the Acedians made her do in order to stay safe. In order to protect herself. In order to run. She destroyed ships for blasted sake. Mia's shoulders shook. She killed people. The tears finally ran down her cheeks.

The Acedians had forced her. Forced her! She never wanted it to go that far, never wanted to take lives, but the things the Acedians did to their captors...it was worse than a quick death. The cabin seemed to tighten around her. She hugged her knees. Mia always tried to make it quick, always placed the bombs in the areas most likely to do the most damage, always activated the alarms. She always activated the alarms. She always tried to save people. Always tried.

A while later, Mia rubbed her face, drying the tears. She smoothed out the list and tucked it into her pocket once more. The gloves Cassidy gave her caught Mia's eye and held her gaze. Sighing, she raised her own hands up once more, eyeing the glove covering her right hand. The ripped and frayed gloves had taken a beating, more than their fair share. She yanked that one off, too. The new pair pulled on easily, slipping over her fingers as if made for her, snug but not overly so. Comfortable. The white stitching shone bright in the dim light by her bed. Had Cassidy given Will or Jeff such gifts? She certainly hadn't seen her do so. Mia allowed herself a small smile.

She took out the ribbon. So bright and cheery. So Cassidy. Mia ran her fingers through the silky fabric. Cassidy had given her so many gifts in the past six months. Food, clothes, little trinkets here and there, but gloves? Gloves were personal, a gift shared by friends. Maybe more than friends.

A crazy, idiotic idea captivated Mia. What if she gave Cassidy a gift in return? She had never given anything to any of her crew before, never had the chance, or if she was honest with herself, the motivation to do so. In her weaker moments, she had allowed herself to grow attached to this crew, these strangers she now called friends. Maybe, just maybe, she could ease some of the guilt by doing so.

Images blossomed in her imagination. Mia grabbed some spare wires from the hidden compartment beside her bed and began twisting them into shape. She stayed up late that night, creating Cassidy's gift. When Mia finally closed her heavy eyelids, the sense of fear boiling in her stomach since the attack subsided just a bit. Not much, but enough to let her fall into a restful and dreamless sleep.

Chapter Four

A SHARP PAIN WOKE Mia. She rubbed her hand while getting dressed, kicking her used clothes to one side and pulling on new ones. Black camisole, pants, and boots. She glanced at the mirror before shaking her head, remembering where they were. Pargon, the planet that might as well be inside the sun. She frowned, tore off the black camisole and found a white one, stripping out of her black pants for a lighter gray. Waving open the hatch, Mia walked out of her cabin.

She passed by the place where Cassidy had stopped her with only a slight hesitation. A lingering smile pulled at her lips. Mia wandered down the corridors, and the most delicious smell hit her even before she reached the kitchens. Wash meat? Like on Fissure. The idea flitted through her head before she realized she'd registered the salty smell. Mia's stomach growled. She was almost there when something struck her on the shoulder. The person sped around the corner into the kitchen, but not before Mia saw a flash of black hair.

"Will!" Mia shouted, reaching the kitchen a few moments behind. She rubbed the new twinge that blossomed from the impact.

Will stood by the sizzling pans Cassidy had set up, snatching a crispy strip. "Don't blame me, it's the meat."

Jeff appeared at Mia's side and sidled past her, his eyes apologizing on his brother's behalf. He smacked Will on the head. Fast. Jeff was fast. Surprisingly so. Mia leaned on the hatch.

"Meat," Jeff said. "It's the only thing that will get Will up faster than a naked woman."

"Jeffery." Will landed with a thump on one of the stools. "Not in front of the ladies."

She locked her gaze on Will. "You had better watch where you're going or next time—"

"Yes, yes," Cassidy interrupted from the corner. She dumped white floria powder into a pan, splashed some water in it, and shoved the pan onto the burner. The powder boiled. "Or next time Jeff won't be there to apologize for your actions and protect you from her fiery wrath."

Will frowned. "You didn't even let her get to the good part!"

"I don't care," Cassidy snapped, shoving the pan over to them. It was now filled with scrambled egg whites. Portioning the food, she handed three plates out, sliding two extra pieces of meat to Mia and keeping one plate for herself. "If you two start that up, the food will get cold. Again."

Mia took her plate and smiled, grabbing a fork and stabbing some eggs. Cassidy never liked the morning quarrels. When they first became a crew and Will found out Mia was not a morning person, he had made it his personal mission to annoy her at least once every morning. Thus, they always dissolved into a barrage of colorful insults cascading across the cabin. Cassidy never quite learned to appreciate their friendly banter. Mia watched Cassidy rustle around, making and serving tea for everyone before eating anything herself. Or perhaps, she'd simply never found a way to participate.

"She's right you know." Will scraped his plate clean before anyone else. "The food was slightly off temperature."

Cassidy glared at him, sitting down and finally starting to eat her breakfast. "That's only because I let yours cool off a bit."

"What's wrong?" Jeff stared at Cassidy.

His question lingered in the air for a few moments, and Mia finally took a closer look at Cassidy. She had picked a similar outfit as Mia, with the exception of white pants instead of the gray. She scowled, her eyes bloodshot, and she slumped in her seat.

"I didn't get any sleep last night," she sighed.

Mia should have blushed when Jeff's eyes first flitted toward her. Men. Only one thing on their minds. "Why?"

A moment passed before Cassidy answered the question. "I just thought I heard someone outside my cabin."

The brothers straightened in their chairs, and Will asked, "What?"

Mia tensed, trying to remember if there was ever a time when the Acedians used her own crew against her. There hadn't been. And she would've sensed them long before they entered her ship.

"Did you see someone?" Mia leaned toward Cassidy, wanting to protect her, to hold her hand at least. Maybe her fears of being watched the day before were vindicated after all.

"No." Cassidy shifted her eyes from Will to Mia, then dropped her gaze and continued. "When I went out to see who it was, there was no one."

"Why didn't you wake anyone else up?" Jeff got up off his seat and started to pace. He threw his plate into the sink. The clanging rang throughout the corridors, reverberating until the noise died away. His agitation seemed understandable. Troubling, though. He was usually the calm brother.

"I didn't want anyone else to worry." Cassidy's voice rang sharp, as she shifted her body slightly away from them. Obviously, she regretted even bringing the subject up. She ran a hand through her hair and continued in a lighter tone. "Being on a new planet always does strange things to me. Like I said, there was no one there. Remember that time we were on Gyre and every time I walked into the ship I swear I heard someone whispering 'twinkle, twinkle the great star above'? Maybe it's like that."

They grew quiet, digesting the information. Pushing her tea away, Mia watched Cassidy, reading her movements. Mia sighed. The story was convincing enough, but Cassidy's body language betrayed more than her words. She was lying to them. Shoving eggs into her mouth, ignoring Will as he poked her in the side, not looking at any of them. Agitated. Embarrassed. Mia tore her eyes from the two. Everybody has secrets, but it was far easier when she was the only one hiding something.

Mia motioned to Will. "Go check around her cabin. See if there are any markers of an intruder. If so, tell me. If not, go outside and help Jeff repair the ship. The new supplies should be here."

Both men sighed and left, turning into the corridor and heading aft. Cassidy and Mia were alone. The scent of breakfast still hovered in the air. Cassidy sat by the bar, her plate long since empty, her cup two-thirds full. Wanting to do something for her, anything, Mia walked around to the other end of the bar and reached for the sugar and milk. She poured some into Cassidy's cup, sliding the tea back to her. Cassidy looked at the drink, then at the one who had given it to her. Mia realized then that behind Cassidy's brown eyes lived many secrets. As if reading her mind, Cassidy smiled. She drank the tea in one gulp.

"Come on," Cassidy said. "We've got work to do, too." She led the way out of the kitchen and turned down the corridor, the same way the brothers had gone.

Mia ran a hand over the metal bulkheads, her fingertips catching on the uneven plating. She breathed deep the manufactured air. Of course, everyone was allowed to keep secrets. Blast, she had plenty of her own. But Cassidy? That just didn't sit right. Cassidy came back, grabbed Mia's hand, and pulled her outside the ship, yanking her out of her thoughts.

"You're always so slow." She let go of Mia's hand when they reached the sunlight. She threw her arms out so suddenly Mia bumped into one, but the fact that Cassidy had just slapped her captain in the chest barely registered. Cassidy twirled on the spot. Her hair flew out around her like a multicolored aura. "It's a gorgeous day!"

Mia could only gawk at Cassidy's change of emotion, like the earlier events had never happened.

"Oh," Will shouted as he grabbed the supplies off a hover cart. "You don't like the sun."

Cassidy turned toward him and pointed at the sky, matching his pitch with her own. "There are clouds today."

Jeff grinned at their argument and slipped under the *Eclipse*'s belly again, a bright orange light flaring to life and searing to white, as he repaired sections of the ship.

Mia and Cassidy grabbed their packs, hooked comm pieces in their ears, and left the brothers behind, walking into the city and discussing where to hit first. Mia looked up, watching the clouds burn off as the sun rose higher in the sky. The rays broke through.

"How many techno-chips do you have?" Mia asked.

Cassidy fingered her pouch for a moment. "I gave one to Sheryl, and we have to go back. I've only got three more."

Sheryl. Mia sighed. That old woman would probably trade new tech for a musty shawl. Not good enough. However the morning dawned successful. They traded three jars of bosyn jam to a particularly homesick, elderly man for a piece of tech he didn't know how to use. Cassidy was more than happy to trade, recognizing the detection cube. It was an older device used to warn against radiation. They could use the wiring. Cassidy used all of her charms to glean an opae necklace for just a few trinkets from Cigarian. Opae was the local gemstone that both women knew would fare well with women on other planets. Plus, Mia's scar hadn't hurt since she woke up. She took that as a good sign.

"We should go visit Sheryl now." Cassidy nodded in the direction of the old woman's shop.

"You just can't get her out of your head, huh?" Mia replied.

"Don't you know it. Old women are so appealing," Cassidy said, smiling. She eyed Mia. "Although I have my sights set on someone a bit younger."

Mia ignored the comment, walking slightly behind Cassidy so the brunette would not see the heat creeping up Mia's neck. She shook her head. Way too blasted close. They meandered into the marketplace, intending on cutting through it to get to Sheryl's. Pargonians crowded the area. Mia automatically tensed when a stranger approached them, but the woman threw her arms around Cassidy's neck.

"Cassidy!"

Cassidy pulled back, eyes wide and mouth slack. She didn't return the hug. "Katarina." Cassidy glanced at Mia, who stood back to give the two some room. The woman turned to Mia, her green eyes and obviously fake orange hair catching the light. Her tanned skin looked slightly off hue, almost to the point of matching her hair.

"You must be Captain Mia," Katarina said in a high-pitched voice. Squeaky almost. "I've heard so much about you!"

"I'm sorry that I can't extend the same courtesy," Mia replied. "It's nice to meet you." She held out her hand, and Katarina shook it. The woman's hand felt too light for Mia's liking. She let go. Cassidy shifted her weight, glancing at Mia and Katarina. Was that a blush rising on her ears?

Cassidy pulled Katarina's arm. "Can I talk to you over here?"

Katarina nodded, and Cassidy guided the woman away, speaking in hushed whispers and glancing back every so often. Still, their voices floated over, angry. Mia tried to move away, tried to give them some privacy. Strangers pushed her closer instead. Finally, Mia glanced at the pair.

Katarina's high voice burst through the hum. "That's not what you said last—"

"I know." Cassidy placed her hand on the woman's shoulder. "Look, I'm sorry. I never should have contacted you. We never should have—"

"But we did!" Katarina backed up, shoving Cassidy's hand off.

"I know. It was a mistake," Cassidy said.

"All because—"

"Yes." The surety of Cassidy's response threw even Mia.

Katarina pushed her way through the crowd, holding her hands to her face. Cassidy followed after. Her manner seemed determined, her walk hard, shoulders squared. Mia turned away, even though she knew Cassidy wouldn't stray from Katarina's receding form.

Mia found herself looking in the window of one of the shops when a reflection caught her eye. A man glanced her way, and, through their reflections, their eyes met. The back of her neck tingled. The man looked simple enough in a light blue shirt and matching pants. Simple. But his face was too serious for someone looking for something to buy. His boots, too scuffed to match his pristine outfit. His hazel eyes, too piercing. A searing pain jolted from her hand. She closed her fist, too distracted by Cassidy's recent conversation to do anything different. The man's eyes narrowed as they flicked downward and back up again. His reflection in the window shimmered in the heat and vanished as he turned a corner. He was one of them—an Acedian.

Her heart beat furiously against her chest, a bird struggling free of its cage, pushing her to run away from the threat. She couldn't move. The Acedians were here on the planet. That meant they could've been on the *Eclipse* somehow. Could've been outside Cassidy's cabin. Who knows how many they could have planet-side right now. They could've landed somewhere without her knowing it. But how could she not know? There had been signs. She had been feeling off ever since the *Eclipse* landed. Her palm pained her last night and this morning. Mia cursed and jerked herself to move, doing exactly what her body told her not to do and followed the man around the corner.

Chapter Five

MIA'S MOVEMENTS WERE FORCED at first, weaving around the shoppers at a brisk pace. It seemed unreal that these people were just going about their daily lives, while an Acedian lurked in their midst. It frightened her how well he seemed to blend in, how normal he appeared.

Sweat ran down her spine. She cursed the blasted sunlight. Choosing lighter clothes must have allowed her to blend in with the crowd. The man noticed her only after she had made the fist, her natural reaction to the agony that pulsed through her palm. He might not have noticed otherwise. She cursed. Idiot. Alerting the enemy to her own whereabouts. Even if she didn't know the Acedians had landed on this planet, it was still a rookie mistake.

She pushed past the shoppers, her movements fluid and fast. She wanted to get closer to the man, wanted to finally get answers. Most of all, she wanted him taken out. His blond hair kept bobbing in and out of her sight. They were in a less populated area now, on the outskirts of the city.

Mia immediately understood why the man had led her here. It was a stagnant place. The perfect place for a trap. The man stopped in an open area and looked around. Mia was almost close enough to touch his shoulder, her heart pounding so fast she was sure he could hear it, when he turned toward her. It wasn't the Acedian from the reflection. She couldn't believe it. Her jaw slackened. He uttered a surprised "Oh!" at discovering her an arm's length away, then shuffled down a joining alley, leaving her alone.

Mia tensed. She had been sure to keep her eyes on the man from the reflection. Where did he go? She searched down the alleyways surrounding her, but saw nothing. Music jingled and voices hummed softly from the direction she had come. Her ears picked up nothing else close by. Where was the man?

A sudden, painful weight crashed onto her back. Before she could react, a strong arm linked around her neck, while another snaked around her stomach, and she was yanked to the ground. Her head hit the gravel. Her eyes lit up with stars.

The attacker let her go and stood. “Looking for me?”

Gravel embedded itself into her cheek, cutting slivers in her flesh. A boot came into her line of vision, but she didn’t move quickly enough and grunted as it connected with her shoulder. Agony spiked up her arm. The force of the kick was enough to make her roll away from the next one. She struggled to her feet.

The man laughed. “You’re not as tough as my boss led me to believe.”

Mia circled around and mirrored his movements, fingering her belt. What did she have? Her gun lay safely tucked away in her cabin. The knife! She moved her hand toward her back, until she felt the cold steel of the handle.

The man lunged, his huge hands balled into fists. She sidestepped the attack, raising her weapon. He twisted, grabbed her hand, and wrenched it sideways. The knife grazed his ribs. His shirt ripped, a distinct and unfortunate sound. The knife had missed his flesh. The overpowering stench of his warm sweat surrounded her.

“A dagger, really?” The man’s voice grated against the silence that shrouded the alley. Mia wrenched her hand out of his grasp, and they fell apart, circling each other. Her breath came in gasps. She forced herself to breath, slowly. To not be afraid.

He nodded to her weapon. “Isn’t that a bit old fashioned?”

Mia hated conversationalists. He was trying to make her talk to him. Why? To give up information on the rest of her crew? *Perhaps it was for the best,* another voice whispered. Her eyes narrowed. She shook her head. For the best? Never.

He lunged again. When she tried to sidestep, a sharp twinge spiked up her leg. She balked and moved in the opposite direction. Too predictable. Her fear was getting the better of her. The man smiled as his fist sunk deep into her stomach. His putrid breath filled her nose. Mia grunted and slashed the dagger at his neck. He yelled. Her weapon sliced a red line across his jugular but didn’t go deep enough.

His fist came at her, and she threw her arm up. Luckily, it was a glancing blow. Mia threw her body back, smashing against a hard surface. She cursed. She had backed right into the blasted wall. The man smiled again, that idiot smile they all give when they think some poor defenseless doehorn is theirs for the taking. She brought the dagger up in front of her chest.

His hands moved quickly, diving into his belt and pulling out needles, throwing one after the other at her. One grazed her side, making her gasp at the sting of the wound. The others bounced off the wall as she moved to evade them. Mia plunged her dagger into his shoulder and ripped it back again. He cried out, backing away from her blade.

Mia slashed again. He was too far out of her reach and the blade sliced only fabric. A swath of tan cloth hung down, revealing a triangle of marred flesh underneath. Dark lines swirled across his skin. Scars. She forced her gaze back to her attacker's sneer. A voice not her own echoed in her mind. *Pretty, aren't they?*

The voice jarred her. Scared her. Shock coursed through Mia as realization hit. A telepath? Was that even possible? She backed up a pace, and that slight movement, that slight repositioning of her body, caused heat to knife up her leg. The place above her ribs pulsed. Each breath brought a new wave of agony. She was losing this fight. And he seemed to know it.

The man winked. *You've seen mine. I should get to see yours. I've heard it's his best work yet.*

His gaze flitted to her hand. Her palm seared, and she clenched her hand into a fist. His hazel eyes met hers once more. She couldn't help herself, having an Acedian so close, she had to ask. "Whose best work?"

As if in reply, the man moved. Fast. Far too fast for her eyes to follow, the man stood a few feet away from her and then was next to her. Half a blink would be too long a time. His fingers curled around her wrist and slammed her hand back into the wall behind her. The knife clattered to the ground. His other hand pushed into her chest, shoving her body back into the wall. Strong, overly strong, even. He smacked her fist away, almost before she swung with her free hand. And too fast. He punched her face. Stars burst into her vision. A stream of blood poured from her nose, tickling her lips and chin.

"You'll find out soon enough," the man said.

He shoved his weight into her right side; an elbow to her neck pinned her to the wall. She grasped at the last tendrils of breath fleeing her lungs. He removed something from his eyes, and now silver eyes held hers. Contacts. He grabbed her hand and bit the fabric that covered it, sliding the glove off. Cold air rushed around her clammy skin.

The man's eyes widened as he looked at the triangle that puckered and blackened her skin. Jagged lines splayed out of the triangle itself. A thin line pierced the shape, winding like a snake, in and out of the scar.

"He was right. It is beautiful," the man muttered.

Mia narrowed her eyes, unable to fight back, unable to even move, gasping for air, as his weight pressed into her. Beautiful? Never.

His eyes locked onto hers once more. His voice took on a mocking tone. "I bet Jeffery would look simply dashing with one of these burned into his flesh. And I bet his would be even more stunning. Practice is key with the cicatrix ritual, you know."

At the mention of her crewmate, Mia struggled and thrashed against the weight that held her. The action did nothing to push the man off of her and managed to expel the last of her energy. Her attacker raised an eyebrow, bashing his forehead against hers. Stinging radiated from the impact.

You think your crew is safe from us?

Her vision blurred around the edges.

Do you think their families are safe?

A punch to her shoulder knocked her to the ground. For the second time, Mia's head hit the gravel. She gulped in air. She watched as the man smiled down at her, rustling around in his pocket for a moment before pulling out a tiny device. A distinct click echoed in the still air. A tingling sensation ran down her arm like water dripping down a limb on a cold, wet night. Her vision blurred in the center. Something slammed into the side of her head, followed by dizziness and a blinding white light. A single thought filtered through.

Soon, you will join us. Soon, we will see what you're really made of.

Unconsciousness pulled Mia into the black.

The black receded, swarmed, melted into blurry shapes above her. The stench of blood and burnt flesh filled her senses.

Paintings?

No, the shapes solidified as her eyes refocused onto what resembled branding irons from old Earth. Prongs to burn the cattle of old. Different, bulkier. Triangles, circles, squares, each distinct with lines cutting through them, spirals winding around them, or other patterns disfiguring the perfect symmetry of the form itself, as if molded by an artist. The prongs hung from the bulkhead above her, dangling over her as she lay strapped to the table, waiting for the Acedians to return. One in particular caught her eye, a simple circle with a line cutting across it. Next to it, hung a triangle. Mia blinked.

She woke. The alleyway flooded with music as Mia regained consciousness. The tingling sensation lingered in her arm. She tried to shake away the pins and needles traveling down to her elbow. She pulled on her glove, grabbed her dagger, now dripping blood, and stood, struggling past the pounding in her head and the aches of her body. A throbbing in her leg still hindered her.

After a moment to breathe and gather her courage, Mia looked down. A dark red stain blossomed from where a needle pierced her thigh. She grimaced. Needles. Thin and silver, their weapon of choice, with spokes that splayed outward, embedding the device within the victim's skin. Deadly if hit in the neck or chest, but a thigh wound wasn't so bad. These hunters would resort to anything to capture someone. She was thankful that her crew couldn't see her now. They would ask too many questions.

Looking around, it was impossible to tell which direction her attacker had gone. His last thoughts echoed in her ears. Join them? Never. The nasty little voice clawed back into her mind. *Why not? Life would be so much easier with us.* She ripped the needle out of her leg and pushed those foreign thoughts away, shoving her hand on the wound.

Mia glanced at the sky. The suns had moved, but not much. Good, she hadn't been out long. Maybe her crew hadn't noticed. The crunch of footsteps snapped her attention toward an empty alleyway. Was it empty a few moments before? There was no way to know, no visible way to detect any more of their kind. Her scar seared. She refused to close it into a fist. No need to alert any others who might be lingering. Mia followed the music.

Every step was punctuated with a throb, as if the needle were still lodged in her thigh. She removed her belt and wrapped it around her leg as a makeshift tourniquet over the hand-sized bloodstain. There was no way Cassidy or the others would miss it. She'd have to make something up. A fight? Wouldn't be a lie, but it would be suspicious. An accident? Perhaps. The lie would endanger her crew. But they were already in trouble.

Throwing her pack over her shoulder, Mia touched her earpiece. Clicking it three times signaled the brothers. Will's voice filtered through the device. "Yes, oh great captain?"

Mia could have slapped him. She spoke as calmly as she could while running, which wasn't that calm at all. "Ready the ship. We leave in fifteen minutes."

"You're in luck," Will said. "We just finished the repa—"

She flicked the device off before he could finish. Hopefully, her crew would be ready. Hopefully, the *Eclipse* would be ready.

Thoughts racing ahead, she burst into the marketplace. People milled about, each one no more familiar to her than the next. There could be more of their kind on the planet's surface. There had been no outward markers on her attacker. He didn't look any different than anyone else here. A suspicious glare, maybe, but that was only after he'd given himself away. The Acedians she'd seen before always had marks, scars on their faces or necks, distinctive outfits. And they were always attacking someone, attacking everyone, not leisurely walking around on a planet. Not casually stalking someone under the guise of buying vegetables. Not using contacts to hide their true eyes. Fear flooded her system. Her breathing grew rapid. Hairs stood up at the base of her neck, and a chill shivered down her spine.

A woman bumped into her and did a double take at her appearance. Mia winced. Blood ran down her check, bruises mottled her skin, and her life seeped out of her thigh. They could be anywhere, anywhere. That woman could be one of them! Anyone could be one of them.

Her heart skipped when words not her own cascaded through her. *Do you think your friends are safe from us?* Her crew. They would have no idea what hit them. The throbbing from her wound dissipated. Pounding footsteps that were not her own made her stomach clench in fear. They were here. Close to her.

She barged into Sheryl's store and waved the door shut, slamming a fist into the control panel and effectively locking the door. One quick look and her heart sank. Cassidy was not there. Sheryl's surprised gasp drew Mia's attention. The elderly woman leaned over the counter, a hand fluttering over her chest. Mia rushed to the counter. Better be having a heart attack, woman. Anger and apathy washed over her, uncontrolled and unexpected.

Mia placed a hand on Sheryl's shoulder. "When was Cassidy Gates here last?"

It seemed as if Sheryl regained her composure but didn't answer the question. Sheryl blinked. The world could have spun around three times before she finally answered.

"Cassidy, that wonderful young woman who sold me a cleaner-bot?" Mia nodded, her heart pounding in her throat matched the thumping on the door. The woman spoke so unbearably slow. "Yes, she was here, just a few minutes ago, with a woman who wanted some help outside. She left before I could give her this. It's my son's old Compact."

A crash reverberated behind Mia. She barely had time to grab the little box Sheryl handed her, before a needle lodged in the elderly woman's forehead. Sheryl slumped to the ground. Mia ducked and rolled, hearing another needle ping off the countertop. She crashed into the shelves. One of Sheryl's old clocks hit the floor beside her—its hands still moving around the face. A sharp pain in the back of her head blurred her vision for five terrifying seconds.

Tick

Mia was young again, just a teenager, running away from the shadows that chased her. The shadows with scars on their faces.

Tick

She shoved people out of her way. Tendrils of fear grabbed her heart and squeezed the reason right out of her. The pounding of the man's feet grew closer.

Tick

She looked behind her. A giant brute of a man, a scar running across his neck, was almost on top of her. She ducked under the needles he threw. A woman called out, "Forget the girl!"

Tick

The man didn't listen. She ran. Her foot caught on cracked plating, the rusted metal sheering her brown socks. Her hands flew out to catch herself, and pain shot from her palms to her shoulders. She spun around, scooting backward. Her eyes watered too much to see.

Tick.

Mia's vision finally cleared. The attackers spun around, distracted by another crash. She dashed toward the door and behind a display of old blankets. Officials barged their way in, a herd of white and blue. It seemed the patrols of Pargon finally got the notion that these Acedians could be dangerous. After they chased after her through the streets. After they killed Sheryl.

"It was a woman. She came in and went insane." A deep voice spoke.

Mia peeked around the blankets and saw two patrol officers crowding beside her attackers, two men and a woman. Deep-voice pushed a needle into a holder on his wrist behind his back. "She fled before any of us could stop her."

One officer hesitated, but the other said, "We'll send out an alert for her. Can you describe her?"

Idiots! Mia took this as her cue to leave. There would be many more Pargonians in the shop soon, investigating the death. She stayed close to the floor and snuck out, putting as much distance between the shop and herself as possible. Blast it. She had to find Cassidy before they reached the *Eclipse*.

Mia got to the edge of the marketplace, and she saw Cassidy standing beside Katarina, squeezing her arm and smiling as if nothing was wrong. As if their earlier argument had never happened. Just a simple day on the job. She walked straight to Cassidy's side and put a hand on her shoulder. The conversation between the two women died. Katarina tensed as she brushed Cassidy's hand off her arm and looked away from Mia.

"I just got us a time-sensitive gig on Paradous. We need to leave now," Mia said, as casually as possible.

Cassidy took one look at her, eyes widening as she took in Mia's haggard appearance. "Who the quasar did this to you?"

"I'll tell you later, okay?"

Concern dominated Cassidy's features, furrowed eyebrows and tilted head, entirely focused on Mia. She moved closer and put her hand on Mia's shoulder. Her touch seemed gentle, not playful or teasing, but soft. Had something changed? Her brown eyes filled with worry. If only later would never come. Cassidy glanced around, squeezed Mia's shoulder, and nodded. Cassidy seemed eager to leave the company of Katarina and said her goodbyes and followed Mia back to the ship.

The two women made it onboard moments later; the sirens started blaring from the speakers of the marketplace before the hatch clicked shut. The screech rang through the corridors, bouncing off the bulkheads. Cassidy cocked her head at the noise, shrugged, and walked to the bridge. Mia exhaled a sigh of relief. They would break atmosphere and be on their way to Paradous long before the patrols could contact all the ships.

The brothers were already on the bridge, going through the checks needed to start the *Eclipse*. Cassidy sat and smiled at them. She seemed too thankful. Too ready to leave. Mia filed this away in her mind and looked out the viewport.

"Guess what, crew," she said. "We're going to Paradous." The brothers whooped. Paradous was their home.

But Mia saw them—Acedians. They were standing around the ship, watching as the *Eclipse* rose into the air. Their eyes seemed to penetrate the ship's hull, the viewports, and the air between them. The *Eclipse* hovered close enough for Mia to see a flash of their eyes, their dull gray eyes, like a reflection on a piece of metal. She heard a thought clearly not her own. *Time to go to Paradous.* It dissipated as the *Eclipse* flew farther and farther away from Pargon. Mia clenched her jaw, as the ship broke through the atmosphere and blasted their way into the dark horizon. The Acedians were gone for now, but she breathed no easier.

"Who were those people, Mia?" Cassidy's quiet voice filled the cabin.

"No one we want to meet again."

"Hey." Will interrupted them. "What happened to your leg?

Chapter Six

MIA SAT ON THE TABLE in the *Eclipse*'s infirmary, a cabin with too many instruments in too small a place. Cramped, just like everything else on this ship. Cabinets, bolted to the bulkheads, held simple tools: an old helotube, antiseptic foam, blood-clotting pills, and pain medication. Pillows and blankets lay scattered on the deck. No need to get blood on the off-white fabric if she could help it. Her hands shook, as picked up the helotube. The precursor to the helofoam now used, the helotube seemed awkward in her hands. She hadn't used this technology much. The rounded end seemed fine. The needle-shaped point on the other end worried her. And she didn't have a clue how to work the tiny screen on the side. It flashed with purple and gold lights.

As she slowly unraveled the cloth covering her wound, Mia made a mental note to get an assuage kit on the next planet. Even the *Scarlet* had that sort of tech. Spraying some foam on this wound would have been much easier than whatever this tube would do to her. The cloth fell away. Blood pulsed out, dripping down her thigh and pooling behind her knee on the table. Mia shuddered and popped one of the many pills. The blood-clotting pill in her mouth melted, flooding her tongue with a coppery, gritty taste. The pill worked sooner than expected and her blood thickened. Her hand hovered over the wound, eyes trained on the tube, wondering what could be inside that would help her cut. She thumbed the screen on the side.

"You think you can do everything by yourself, don't you?"

Will's voice made her jump, and she pressed harder on the tiny screen. A soft hiss escaped the helotube, and something poked her skin. She didn't bother to look up, staring at the tiny gold pin in her leg. She pulled it out and inspected it. The needle portion splayed outward, much like the Acedian version.

"And you shouldn't sneak up on people when they're performing surgery." She flicked the pin away and covered the wound on her thigh with a bandage, trying to staunch the flow of blood. The pill worked to calm her immediate worry.

"That's not surgery." Will moved toward her, leaving the hatch open. "And that's not how you hold a helotube."

"Well, if you're such a wonderful doctor, why don't you do it?" Mia's voice lowered, too aware of the hatch and how easily a voice floated down the corridors.

"Fine, it may take a while." Will put a hand on the bandage, lifting it up for a moment to examine the cut. Mia fidgeted, her gaze still flitting toward the open hatch.

"Did you want me to close it here, or shall we go somewhere more private?" Will asked.

Mia gave him a startled look. His steady eyes held hers, not accusing, just watching, as if he knew this was something meant to be secret. When Mia nodded, Will retied the bandage, grabbed the supplies nearby, and offered his shoulder to Mia. She leaned on him as she got off the table, even more so as they hobbled toward the hatch.

Once outside, Mia grimaced, stood up straight, and walked without Will's help. He cast a questioning look her way, but didn't verbalize his thoughts. They stopped outside his cabin.

"Does your place have an infirmary I don't know about?" Mia raised an eyebrow in Will's direction.

"My cabin has plenty you don't know about, Captain." He winked.

Mia chuckled. "Do I want to go in there?"

"Too late to change your mind." Will waved his hand over the controls, and the hatch slid open. He went in, tilted the mattress up, and helped her sit down. He waved the hatch closed. She wiggled out of her pants, sliding the Ariien fabric carefully over her wound. The surface brought chills to Mia's thighs as she waited, arms and legs crossed. Being half naked didn't bother her. She chewed on the pills Will gave her. More grit, more metallic taste. Mia wondered if they ever made oral medicine that tasted good. She doubted it.

It was the first time she'd been in Will's cabin, and the clutter of fallen clothes and magweights thrown about made the space feel tiny. Mia had knocked over a rather large pile of archivists when she walked inside. Will moved with the grace of a man who knew his surroundings, stepping over or around the fallen tech.

The acrid smell of burnt metal hung on his clothes. A hole in his shirt was a small reminder of the help he'd given his older brother in fixing the ship. There were multiple holes in his pants as well. Will, clearly, was out of his element maintaining the *Eclipse*. Mia smiled. The things family members did for one another. Her smile melted as she remembered her own family. And of her surrogates, Clin and Sheyla on the planet Fissure. The ones who took out her ID tag and kept her safe for a little while. She ran a hand through her hair, scratching the back of her neck, and pushed the thoughts down. Mia noted that Will attempted to look anywhere but at her bare legs, as he gathered his tools.

"Sorry about the metal," Will said. He looked at the gauze pad on her leg, slowly turning red with blood. Mia's bandage wasn't doing its job. "I didn't want you to get blood on my bed."

"Don't worry about it," she said. "I'm used to the cold."

"Well, in that hole you call a cabin I'd expect nothing less." Will finally sat down in front of her, placing the helotube beside him. The needle-like end pointed toward her, and Mia's arms quivered. She leaned back on her hands to make them stop. Her camisole scooted up a bit on her stomach, revealing a tiny patch of skin above the blue band of her underclothes. She pushed her shirt down and looked at the tube.

"I wasn't aware of your skills with medicine."

Will glanced up at her, the orange specks within his hazel eyes reflecting the light. He waited a moment before answering, taking the time to push up the sleeves of his jacket and running a hand through his hair, smoothing back the black strands that occasionally fell over his eyes. His skin was even darker than usual, the suns of Pargon taking a toll on his complexion. "Well, Jeff fixes ships. I fix people—sometimes. I took some classes back at the Academy, trying to find something easier than piloting."

Mia snorted. "So you chose medicine?"

Will picked up the helotub. "I took one class. It was an important class. I learned a lot." He dropped his gaze guiltily. "Okay, I learned how to do one thing, use a helotube correctly. It was back before helofoam was even created. And it took me all semester to learn it. And I eventually failed the class. But at least I learned one thing, right?"

"One thing?" Mia started, then quickly settled again, trusting him to do his best. *In order for them to trust you until the end*, another voice whispered. She ignored the strange voice in her head. "Yes, one thing's okay."

Will scoffed. "My parents didn't think so. Supposed their units went out the airlock with that class." He finally looked down at her bare leg. "What about you, any classes you failed?"

"Surely, learning one thing deserves credit." Mia made a lame attempt to push the conversation back to Will. It would be only too easy to guess she had not attended the Vespa Academy.

Will considered her words. "I figured as much. Until I got my score, of course."

Mia saw his eyes lingering on the wound on her thigh, but his hands were still hovering over her skin. She could practically see the bubble of nerves causing him to stay there. She put her own hand over his and pushed it down. Will winced as his hand touched her leg.

"Get going, this cut can't heal itself," Mia said.

Will's smile faded as he bent to work on the task at hand. A wrinkle formed on his forehead. The silence stretched, but Mia couldn't work up the nerve to talk anymore, half expecting Will to ask about how the cut was made. Here they were in his cabin, together, and he didn't ask about her wound. Nor why they had to leave Pargon so suddenly. Mia watched, unable to look away, as Will pushed the screen six times, puncturing her skin with six pins. The tiny needles dug into her flesh. Ironic that one needle gave her this wound while others would help heal it. She winced.

"Not a robot, eh?" Will paused in his work, rummaging around under his bed.

She cocked an eyebrow.

He grinned. "You took most of it so well I was beginning to wonder. You didn't even limp when we walked over here. A grown man would be hobbling."

The tiny golden pins glinted, framing the wound. Stupid Acedian tech. The needle had opened within her flesh, and the splayed barbs made a four-inch long gash when yanked out of her skin. A rookie mistake.

Will pulled a bottle of Paradousian beer, the strongest this side of the Zan Nebula, from beneath his bed. He handed it to her and continued his work. "I was beginning to think this was just a tiny paper cut to you, like you had been through much worse."

Mia held her breath, faking her sudden stiffness as a reaction to the pins in her leg. She downed a gulp of beer. It was stale and overly bitter.

He fiddled with the helotube and the device glowed purple. "You winced. So, I know you're normal."

"Well," she said between sips. "I'm glad you've decided I'm not a robot."

Will pointed the glowing tube at her wound. A purple bubble grew out from the helotube's tip. The bubble met her skin, and, as soon as it touched the pins, popped, transforming into a gleaming liquid. Her skin tightened, the liquid pulling the pins closer together as it closed her cut. Soon, a line of gold pins and purple liquid was all that remained of her wound. He leaned back to admire his work.

"Hopefully, it'll heal quickly," he said. "Remember to take your vitamins and call me in the morning."

Mia rolled her eyes. "How about I bang on your hatch instead?"

"Sounds like a plan. We can get someone to look at it on Paradous. There's a nice med section at their Academy." Will got up and moved away, giving her some semblance of privacy in the process. Mia unfolded her black pants and pulled them on. The gray ones would never be usable again. It surprised her that Will didn't turn around to look while she dressed. He surprised her daily, these days.

Will turned around and cocked his head, his black hair falling toward his shoulder. "If you'd like to stay that would be great. Otherwise I'm done here. Either way, you're going to have to move."

Will cleaned the cabin, moving his bed back into place. Mia was shocked again by Will's silent acceptance of her injury. No word of the cut, or of their speedy escape, or even of the Acedians watching. The silence between them suddenly seemed heavy, so she asked the only question that she could think of to fill the space.

"So, do you consider anyone else a machine? Or is that lovely term reserved for just me?"

Will ignored the question and fixed brown sheets around his mattress. He took a deep breath. "Just you."

Mia blinked. Just her? Sure, she wasn't too terribly loving to the crew, but she was being much warmer than normal. Usually, by this time, she would be off the ship. Usually, by this time, they wouldn't be around anymore. A sharpness formed in her chest, a knife to her lungs, twisting at the memory of the crews before this one. The pocket of her pants burned, the list safely inside. Had she ever before worried about these people suffering what should be their undeniable fate? She was in too deep.

"Thanks," she muttered. Of course, the first crew she decided to be nice to would decide otherwise. It only now occurred to her that such a thing mattered.

"I didn't mean it like that," Will said, a bit too loud for such a small cabin. He put a hand on her shoulder, misinterpreting her conflicted emotions for hurt. "It's just, when we first met, you were...well, cold. Calculating. We were a brand new crew, barely glued together by Cassidy's crazy idea. You didn't eat with us or talk to us. We were becoming something, and it seemed like you didn't want to be a part of it. I mean, you're the captain, and you didn't want to get to know us at all."

She wasn't supposed to get to know him. She wasn't supposed to get to know any of the crew! Her own foolishness at actually getting familiar with the blasted crew, getting to like them even, finally swam into focus. What if the Acedians came again? What would she do? She closed her eyes, wishing Will would just leave her alone.

"Captain," Will said. She didn't open her eyes at the plea. "Mia, you've gotten warmer. You laugh with me and Jeff. I mean, it's pretty clear that you and Cassidy are—" He faltered. Mia had opened her eyes and silenced him with a glare. He started over. "It just took a little bit to get to know you, that's all."

Mia nodded. A lump was forming in her throat. Will squeezed her shoulder once more as if to make his point then let go. She smiled and left, too concerned over her sudden clash of emotions to speak. She waved the hatch closed on Will's concerned expression. Her hand ran along the sides of the corridor as she walked, fingers catching on scratches here and there on the rusting metal. Idiot. She was in way too deep.

Time to go to Paradous.

"What?" She pushed a finger next to her ear and waited for the reply. She switched her earpiece on in the process, but that meant the earpiece had been off. No one had spoken to her through it. The voice didn't belong to either Cassidy or Jeff, and Will was probably too worried to contact her now.

Time to go to Paradous.

There it was again. The voice sounded deep, definitely a woman's. She listened hard. Silence. Too much silence, maybe? She waited for the lights to flicker on and off, or the floor to fall out from under her, anything that would suggest she had finally snapped. Nothing happened. The lights stayed on, if a bit too dim for her liking, and the deck was solid under her boots. She tapped her foot just to make sure.

Wait until they're asleep.

Blast it. The voice was inside her head. Again! How was that possible? She had a sinking suspicion as to who it might be. But how did one of them get on the ship and inside her head? The telepath man from Pargon. The nagging thoughts not her own. Were all of the Acedians telepaths? Her heartbeat quickened, and her breath grew ragged. She stalked down the corridor. There was only one place where one of them could hide on her ship. Only one spot the brothers might not have looked.

Get them in their sleep.

"Shut up," she mumbled.

"What?" Cassidy's hurt expression was suddenly before her. She had walked right up to Cassidy without even realizing it.

"I wasn't even saying anything." Cassidy's expression changed into a bewildered stare. She hooked her arm in Mia's and led her in the opposite direction. The gesture made their bodies swing close together, and Mia felt the warmth of Cassidy's shoulder next to her own. Yet Cassidy was much too somber. Her glare pierced through Mia. Looking straight ahead, Mia made her talk first.

"You're way too uptight. We apparently got another gig on Paradous, and apparently it's urgent. We should be celebrating. Apparently."

"You're saying apparently way too much," Mia muttered, deliberately walking slower than Cassidy and hoping she'd get the point. She didn't.

"Well, you didn't come to Sheryl's, and you made a deal. Which apparently was urgent, because you practically dragged me away from Katarina."

"Whom you wanted to be dragged away from," Mia inserted.

"True," Cassidy said, her voice higher than it usually was, which Mia interpreted to be a bad sign. Her and Katarina did have a fight after all. Must be a touchy subject. Cassidy continued, "That's beside the point. Apparently we don't get to know anything about this said deal you got us. We don't know whom you made it with. Or what they want from us. Or what they want us to trade."

"I haven't gotten around to telling you about it," Mia snapped, her anger flaring. This wasn't the right time. There was an Acedian on the ship. On her ship.

Kill her before the others can. Slowly.

Couldn't Cassidy hear the voice? No. Cassidy was still walking, still fuming, still ranting. Nothing showed that she had heard a mysterious voice inside her head. Mia was almost glad.

"Well, get around to it. Because, I think you're lying." Cassidy's blunt manner shocked Mia. Cassidy had never confronted her like this.

She unhooked her arm from Mia's, stopping their forward momentum. Her friend's lips contorted in a frown and her face tensed, but hurt glimmered in her eyes.

"Do you now?" Mia shifted her weight back. There never was enough time for this.

"Yeah." Cassidy put her hand on Mia's arm. Her eyes met Mia's, searching for answers. When she spoke again, her voice was calmer, quieter. "Galaxies, I'm not stupid. I saw how you looked when you came to get me. Wild, scared, not at all the controlled woman I've come to know. I saw the blood on your leg. Who was the quasar that tore up your thigh? Something happened. And you needed to get away. Off of Pargon."

Mia tensed. There was no way Cassidy could have known. She tilted her head sideways, putting what she hoped was a bewildered expression on her face. Cassidy rubbed her hand over Mia's arm and up her shoulder. The warmth from that single action sent shivers through Mia's body. Cassidy stepped closer, closing the distance between them.

When she spoke it was as quiet as it had been the night before. "I don't like that you felt you had to lie to me. Please, tell me the truth. I want to help you."

Mia's heart sank. Cassidy's eyes were all but pleading now. Those eyes almost made the truth fall from her lips. It took all Mia had not to tell her. There was no way Cassidy could handle it. No way they would have enough time to discuss it now. Not here. Not now. Mia breathed out.

"Cassidy," she said, her voice matching Cassidy's quiet tones. "There is something I need to tell you. Later. In private."

"You promise." It wasn't a question. Cassidy's quiet voice betrayed the hurt underneath. Mia had broken some line, crossed some boundary. No time to dwell now. Cassidy cocked an eyebrow at Mia's silence. The ventilator clicked on. The breeze took a few strands of Cassidy's hair and waved them in front of her face, the purple and brown dark against her scorched skin. The suns of Pargon had burnt her pale cheeks into an angry pink. Mia pushed the strands back behind Cassidy's ear with shaking fingers. Her fingers grazed the side of Cassidy's neck, before she dropped her hand. Even now, even with the Acedian threat, Mia couldn't believe how pretty Cassidy looked. She remembered the gift, how she so desperately wanted to give it to Cassidy one day, and how she desperately knew she shouldn't.

"I promise," Mia said. It surprised her that she meant it. Definitely way too deep.

Cassidy nodded and let her hand fall off Mia's shoulder. Mia missed the weight of it. Her first mate turned and walked toward the bridge, the space she had filled now empty. The sudden draft of air carried the warm aroma of sinna. Cassidy's favorite spice lingered after she left. Mia breathed deep before walking in the opposite direction.

Kill them all.

No kidding. She ran toward the storage cabin to confront the monster hiding in its depths. Here she was, protecting the people she was supposed to be distancing herself from. Now was the time to plant explosives—in the aft compartments of the engine to make the explosion bigger. To gather supplies—guns, food, water, clothes. To rig the escape shuttles, this boat had four. But instead she was racing toward the very thing she'd planned to pin their deaths on. To protect them! How did this happen? How did she let this happen? She liked Cassidy, and the brothers were insane, but friendly. She learned more about them every day, chatting with them, sealing herself to them. She'd gotten too close. It was bad, and she knew it. It was just so blasted lonely being a runner out here in the black.

A thought fluttered through the confusion. Maybe it's okay to be connected. Maybe it's okay to be part of a group. A twinge from an old battle wound from the *Luminaria* reminded her that leaving these people was the best thing to do. Not killing. Just...leaving. The idea made her ache even more. She couldn't leave. Not now. It shocked her how close she was to these people after spending only six months with them.

"Mia Foley." The monster stood right before her. She didn't recognize the woman who knew her name. She was just another one of them.

The woman stood six feet tall, her white, mesh outfit stark against the storage containers. Her body seemed lithe among all the bulky crates that surrounded her. Gray eyes captured Mia's own. Brown hair flowed in long, wavy locks past her shoulders. Mouth turned downward. Her scars stood out prominently, one on her forehead, another down the side of her neck, and still another running over her collarbone. Mia stepped through the hatch and waved it shut. Shivers ran down her body, her instincts and fear kicking in, as she circled the woman. This is what she would look like if she ever became one of them. Apathetic. Wild. Acedian.

The woman's eyes tracked Mia as she moved around her. The woman stayed perfectly in the center, holding a single stunner trained on Mia's heart. One she probably stole from Pargon.

"How did you get onto the ship?" Mia's question echoed in the silence.

"That is no matter."

"I beg to differ." Mia stopped circling the woman. Her arms flexed, balling her hands into fists for the second time that day. Too many times for her liking. She eyed the weapon in the woman's hands. She could not get around that gun. The scar burned.

"What does matter," the woman said quietly, "is how you located me."

None of her business.

Oh, yes it is.

Mia's eyes narrowed.

The woman smiled, a lackluster smile. Her eyebrows raised, crinkling the scar that decorated her forehead. "Didn't know we could do that, did you? If you can hear my thoughts without me forcing them on you, your bots must have been activated during that scuffle on the planet."

Letting silence fall between them, Mia searched for a way to get the upper hand. Bots? Activated? She didn't understand. Didn't need to. Not right now. The cabin was spacious enough to hold thirteen crates, all packed and labeled, ready to trade off for something else. But for a fight? It was way too small for her liking.

"It is a bit tiny, huh?" The woman's grin widened.

Mia hated that the woman could read her thoughts. She tried to stop thinking. It didn't work. The air breathed heavy and sour. Mia's nerves stretched tight, almost to the breaking point. The woman stood there. Waiting. Watching. Infuriating.

"Mia, it's time for dinner!" Jeff's voice came over the earpiece so loud and so suddenly, Mia nearly jumped.

The woman's hand twitched, her finger inching toward the trigger. Mia lunged forward and was at the woman's side faster than she should have been. She didn't process the information, didn't care how she did it. Instead she knocked the gun out of the woman's hand, punched the woman in the stomach, and knocked her legs out from under her in one liquid motion. The woman smashed down onto the floor, a crumpled mess of white and limbs.

It's already begun. Your transformation.

Mia scowled. She snapped the woman's neck. The crack bounced through the cabin, reverberating back to Mia more times than it should have.

It was only after she stood up again that Mia realized what she had done. The entire fight lasted only a few moments, and she had barely broken a sweat. Her breathing came easily to her. She raised her hands in front of her face. Her body quivered as shock came, crashing in waves against her. Another death. Sorrow shook her from the depths of her body, swimming up inside of her until she could bear it no longer. Another death. Another life. No. Not another life. An Acedian. Mia stood there for a long time.

"Come on, it's getting cold." A voice chattered in her ear.

That voice brought Mia back to the surface. She buried the sorrow with mound over mound of reasons why this death was okay, why this death was acceptable, and hoped the emotion couldn't filter through again. Her hands stilled. Mia pushed the storage crates aside and eventually found the biggest. She clicked open the top. It held a few technopets. These were things that could be easily hidden in the corner of the cabin, farthest from the hatch, and she did just that.

Lifting the woman into the container proved to be difficult. Her limbs were awkward. The clothes ripped on the sides of the container so loudly, Mia found herself shushing them quiet. As if that would do anything. She listened. No other voices invaded her thoughts. No whispers except her own. The silence unnerved her. She clicked the crate top closed and pushed it over to the disposal hatch at the far end of the cabin. Garbage piled high on the other side of the hatch. She waved the hatch open, shoved the crate in, and closed the hatch again. The combination to jettison the crates appeared heavy to her fingers. The numbers slowly appeared on the screen. Silently, the crates were sucked out into the blackness of space.

Mia clicked her earpiece. "Be down in a few seconds. What are we having?"

As Jeff rattled on about dinner, she walked toward the hatch that led to the corridor and looked back. She ran a hand through her hair. Nothing too out of place. Good. Her hands straightened her jacket and fixed her gloves. She looked down at herself. Nothing too out of place. She sighed. Good. Waving the hatch shut, she slowly began the long walk to the kitchen.

Chapter Seven

MIA REMAINED QUIET THROUGH dinner. She had detoured to the bridge to see if the nav system had picked anything up, but no suspicious ships tailed them, and the space off the bow was clear. The woman must have snuck on before the ship even took off. Not good. She'd have to check every cabin each time they left a planet. And Mia could not shake the horrible feeling lingering over her since her fight on Pargon. She remembered the man's words, "Do you think their families are safe from us?" No, they weren't safe. None of them were. She had never stayed with a crew after the Acedians found her. She didn't know what they'd do. The trip to Paradous would show if their threats were real.

Around the table, the rest of the crew chatted and laughed through dinner. If her crew found out about the Acedians, their questions would uncover the truth about why Mia was on this ship in the first place. Why she'd randomly appeared that day, six months ago, claiming to be a captain of her own ship. Claiming to have built the *Eclipse* from the ground up. Claiming everything and promising nothing to the small business desperate for a way to reach the stars. Gray goop sat untouched in front of her. Jeff called it soup. Its sour scent mingling with a deep earthy aroma killed her appetite. Probably a mixture of old food powder they were trying to use up. She swirled her spoon in the dark liquid, the color sparking a memory deep within. Her thoughts drifted back to the first day she met Cassidy, that cloudy day on Paradous when she chose her next victims.

"Hi, my name's Cassidy Gates." A young woman clothed in a shocking hue of orange extended her hand. She couldn't be more than twenty-three or twenty-four years old. A brisk wind swirled the skirt of her dress around her legs. Clouds gathered overhead, darkening the sky. "You must be Maria."

"Mia," she corrected, grasping Cassidy's hand in her own. "Mia Foley."

The woman blushed a deep pink. "Oh, Mia, sorry about that."

"No problem." Mia let go of the woman's hand first, turning slightly so the woman could see her ship. She watched the woman's eyes widen as she surveyed the Eclipse. Rounded shape, rail guns, and a decent engine, Mia knew it wasn't much to look at compared to the military boats on this planet. The woman—Cassidy—captured Mia's attention, though. An orange dress with yellow boots? And purple highlights in her hair? Must be an artistic type. She wanted to make a quip about it. Instead she said, "She's a good ship. Easy to fly with the right pilot."

"Speaking of which." Cassidy gestured to the two men standing behind her. One stood at attention, hands behind his back, eyes staring straight at her. The other had a more relaxed pose, shoulders slumped as he gazed at the ship. Both wore white shirts and thick brown pants, nothing elaborate. Nothing like their apparent leader. Mia looked back to Cassidy.

She pointed to the slumped man and the other one in turn. "This is the pilot I told you about, William Dee, and the engineer, Jeffery. They're brothers. They've both been to the Academy."

Mia raised an eyebrow. Brothers who've been to school. Like they've actually seen anything. She was supposed to be with these people for a while, this time around, so it was nice to know William could at least fly. An engineer would not go amiss either. She stuck out her hand, shaking both in turn.

"I'll give you a quick tour." Mia led the way into the ship and down the corridor. The tour was short, just the kitchen, bridge, engine room, and crew cabins. They could learn everything else later on, if they wanted to. If her plan worked.

"The first few months will be fully funded," Cassidy was saying, as they walked the corridors. "Just to get our hooks in with the planets, generate some business."

"Funded by who?" Mia glanced at her, surprised that such a tiny business would get that much support so fast. Cassidy didn't answer, and Mia didn't ask again. They crowded into the bridge, and here, Mia spoke to the pilot. "She's got a MagPrint Drive. Are you familiar with it?"

"Yes," William said. "It's a navigation device that searches for, and locates specific magnetic fields around habitable planets then gets pulled toward that planet."

Said like he'd been chewing on a flight manual for a while. Correct, though. His brother, Jeffery, spoke up, "He'll do the driving. I'll navigate. I know the system just as well as he does."

"It's easy enough to understand," Mia said. Pilot, engineer, and navigator. Good. She flitted her eyes to the woman. What would this woman do on her ship? The brothers looked toward Cassidy. She searched the bridge, seeming to analyze every detail. There was a signal exchanged between the three—Mia couldn't catch what it was—and the brothers exited the bridge, giving her a smile or nod as they left. Cassidy turned around to face Mia.

"I realize you have to be captain of this ship, and I think we'll work well together," she said, a sharp note punctuating each syllable. She took a breath and let it out, as if dreading the next words. "I also expect to be second in command here. This is my business."

Mia tilted her head in acknowledgement of her condition. A smile played on her lips, realizing in the same instant that she had captured her prey. "You know about the MagPrint Drive, too, right? It's a new feature."

"The MPD should get us to Paradous in a few hours," Jeff said, both echoing her memory and pulling her out of it at the same time. He yawned and motioned to Will. "Just put her on autodrive and let her go. Long enough to take a nap, I'd say."

Mia put her spoon down, leaving her dinner untouched, and hoping they wouldn't notice her silence. Cassidy noticed. Her eyes found Mia's. She cocked her head sideways, clearly waiting to ask a question and unable to with others around. If her thoughts had a voice, Mia knew the words would be tumbling out.

"A nap." Will snorted. "More like an inquiry with our dear captain here."

Mia leaned back as all heads turned toward her. An inquiry? Surely, Cassidy wouldn't have told them. She glanced at her. Cassidy was angry, but it was the calm sort, leaning back in her chair, one arm thrown over the back, while the other rested on her crossed legs. Faking her easy manner. She smiled, but the corners of her eyes didn't crinkle. No, if Cassidy ever came to know the whole truth about Mia, she would be fearful. Not angry. Terrified. She wanted answers. They all did. The silence was broken by the steady hum of the engines.

"Well?" Mia folded her hands in her lap.

"Well." Jeff leaned across the small table. "For starters, what's the job on Paradous? We can't rely on Cassidy forever."

"On Cassidy?" The shock in her voice was the same it had been months ago. Mia never did learn who actually funded this little jaunt into the business world.

"Of course." Will pushed his bowl away. It scraped across the table. "She only has another month set aside."

"It's not like the business is going to Helix!" Cassidy's voice took on a defensive edge.

"No, it's not," Will said. "I just meant we need to solidify our asking price for trade. We can't go trading bots for blankets, you know? We'll need fuel for the *Eclipse*. And spare parts in case something breaks. And enough to pay for food, of course."

"It's a simple job, an exchange." Mia jumped off of Will's idea, making it up as she went. "They wanted the extra Comp-tact Sheryl gave us in exchange for five hundred units."

The brothers seemed leery at the prospect of such an easy job. Will sat up in his chair and cleared his throat, and Jeff scuffed his boots on the deck. A straight exchange for units was rare. Mia didn't even need to look at Cassidy to recognize her displeasure. She could feel Cassidy's anger seeping toward her.

"I know." Mia looked at each one in turn; lingering on Cassidy's crossed arms and increasingly irked expression. "It seems shady. That's why we need to check it out. It could be a great deal or it could be a wash. They got our name from somewhere, and we need to be sure it's a reputable source."

"Besides," Cassidy's voice cut into Mia's. "If it doesn't work out, we can always stop by to visit your family."

Mia was sure to keep her face as straight as possible. She couldn't believe what had happened. Cassidy covered for her. She glanced at her out of the corner of her eye. Cassidy was all smiles, yet Mia could not help but notice that her grin never did reach her eyes. She sat too still in her chair, too rigid. She had spoken too nonchalantly.

"And speaking of that nap," Mia knew her segue was idiotic. She couldn't help it. She had to get away, to think, to be alone. "I have to get some sleep. Doctors orders, you know." She looked toward Will, who smiled and took the bait.

"Ah, yes," he said, "rest and relaxation for that leg."

Looking anywhere but at Cassidy, Mia got up from the table. She didn't look at Cassidy when she picked up her bowl of soup and dropped it in the sink, nor did she glance at her when she spoke to the brothers.

“Will, get back on the bridge. You can sleep when we get planet-side. Right now, I need you there.” She turned her gaze toward Jeff, thankful that Cassidy wasn’t sitting between them. “Jeff, I checked the nav system. Be sure to keep checking for pirates. We don’t want to be surprised by them again.”

They nodded, no questions asked. Pirates were worrisome enough to make her crew cautious, not cause for major alarm. Mia knew she couldn’t get too crazy about the apparent pirates who dominated space. But the Acedians always lurked around the major Vespa solar systems. The military couldn’t pick them off fast enough, didn’t understand why there were always more of these attacks, and couldn’t break through their disguise. She also knew she couldn’t be too lazy about them.

Hooking her fingers in her belt, she walked out of the cabin. Not once did she lay her eyes on Cassidy. No contact, not yet. The tightness in her chest was easier to ignore than the glares Cassidy gave her. She waved her cabin’s hatch open and closed, pulled off her boots, and flopped onto the bed. Cassidy was angry, she knew, but the time still wasn’t right. It wasn’t private enough. Cassidy couldn’t know. Not yet.

The list in Mia’s pocket grew heavy again. Heavier than it had in a while. She pulled out the parchment and set it close on the shelf next to her bed. The list landed next to Cassidy’s finished gift, a wristband Mia created for her though never had the courage to give. Perhaps it was for the best. She turned away. In the dim light, far away from her fellow crewmates, she allowed herself to tremble. Curling up on the cot, pulling her arms around her knees, Mia couldn’t help but wonder what a normal life would be like. A simpler life. Her thoughts drifted back to *Hekate*. What a home would feel like. Her loneliness settled over her once more, at first a comfort, now only seemed a weight, pushing down upon her. For now, Mia would fret enough for all of them. Her dreams, much like her life, troubled her that night.

It must have been hell inside the great ship as it tore itself apart. The noise must have been horrendous. Metal screeching upon metal is one of the worst sounds to hear. The fire itself must have smoldered, bursting forth in every direction, eating up the oxygen. There would have been the screams, the silent notes of those sucked out the darkness and the frightened shouts of those destined to be next. The ship slowly burst apart.

Out here, in the calmness of space, not a sound could be heard. Nestled in the infinite backdrop of stars, the breaking apart of the

Luminaria looked almost beautiful, despite the hundreds of people dying onboard. The fires bubbled out of the ship, forming blue and yellow globes until their oxygen source depleted. Out here, there were no screams. No screeching of metal against metal. No fires. Only silence.

She, at least, was safe, waiting for someone to hear the distress call and pick her up. Her stolen spacesuit pumped warm air over her skin. Blood dripped down her hip, oozing from the gash on her side. Now she could only watch. A sharp pain spiking up her left arm, radiating from her hand, drew her out of her reverie and reminded her to have sorrow for these people. These people did not deserve this death. And neither did her parents.

She narrowed her eyes. There was almost no way anything could reach her once she jettisoned. Something had. A man. No, only a body floated the distance. She saw the skin shriveling in on itself, masses of dark frozen shards trailing behind. A red and black tail on a human comet. Hands contorted, legs broken and bending where they should not, the body floated toward her and slowly turned its frozen face. There, in the dark of space, she saw it. She heard it—the silence screamed.

Mia twisted away from the bulkhead, jerked the sheets off her, and searched her cabin for help. She scowled as her gaze found Cassidy's white-stitched gloves resting on her bedside table. How in the universe was she supposed to escape from the Acedians if she let herself fall for one of her victims? It wouldn't do. Cassidy's face surfaced in her memory. Was Cassidy a victim? Were any of them?

The smell of freshly baked bread drew Mia into the corridors, two hours later. Cassidy's vexation had sparked her urge to bake. Mia smiled at her transparency, always with the baking. Warm hazii fruit lingered in the air and made her mouth water as she wandered closer to the kitchen. Mia hadn't eaten the fruit in nearly a year. Cassidy must've gotten it on Pargon. It was only after Mia stumbled in the corridor that she realized her feet were cold. No familiar click echoed her steps, just the muffled padding of her socks. The chill from the floor traveled up into her ankles and calves. The dual fights had tired her more than she realized. She had not even been coherent enough to grab her jacket, nor the list. At least she had been sane enough to grab her gloves. The warm scents of Pargon-made butter and sinna pulled her farther away from her cabin.

Mia wavered in the corridor for a moment, between the frantic urge to put on an attire more proper for a captain and the overwhelming scent of Cassidy's freshly made bread. Her stomach made the decision. Surely, everyone could hear the rumbling. The smell was so overwhelming, Mia could almost taste it. She had just reached the kitchen when their conversation reached her ears.

"My family is amazing," Jeff said. A burst of anger flared within her. He was supposed to be on the bridge. A light flickered along the bulkhead. Unlike the solid glow their electric fixtures emitted, this light seemed to quiver a bit. Softer. Candlelight? Mia pushed her back against the cold hatch that led to the kitchen. She could listen here in the shadows.

"I can't wait to see them. It's been forever," Jeff said.

Cassidy's voice floated out into the corridor. "Really? I would like to meet them."

"You didn't seem too thrilled about it earlier. The look on your face. Did you and Mia have an argument or something?"

"It doesn't matter. What are their names again?"

"Elizabeth and Sarah. Sarah is the older. I'm older than both by a few years. I'm even older than Will by a few minutes." There was a rustling noise, and when Jeff spoke again, his voice was muffled. "Liz is the smartest of the bunch, way smarter than Sarah or Will, but don't tell them I said that."

"I won't," Cassidy replied, her voice softer than it usually was.

A jolt of jealousy replaced the anger she'd felt before. They were sitting alone together, in candlelight, ignoring their duties. Talking.

"Will misses them too, of course." A thunk came from inside the cabin, followed by a yelp.

"Of course I miss them, you idiot!" At the sound of Will's voice, Mia's anger flared again. Her emotions seemed to boil close to the surface since she was attacked. Now both brothers were ignoring her commands? Idiots. The Acedians could be right in front of them and here they were, sitting around, chatting, and stuffing their faces with bread. As she moved to go into the kitchen, Will's next question stopped her.

"What about your family, Cassidy?" There was a clacking of chairs, and the sound of scuffed footsteps. Will had apparently scooted closer to Cassidy and Jeff.

"Mine?"

Curious, Mia stopped just short of the hatch and leaned in to hear Cassidy's reply. She had never heard of Cassidy's family before. Never figured to ask. But now, in the darkness, a burning need to know more about Cassidy filled her. She wished she wasn't hiding, lurking in the darkness like some stalker. She wished it was just her and Cassidy talking.

"Yeah," Jeff said. "We've talked about our siblings. Spill."

"My parents are dead."

The jolt had nothing to do with hunger, or jealousy, or any other emotion. It started in her midsection and jerked its way up her spine. Her head bumped into the hatch. Stars twinkled briefly in front of her eyes, as her memories took hold of her.

She was thirteen again, hearing the screams of families on the shuttle, the families being torn apart. Literally. Blood poured out in rivers onto the deck, and a strong hand pulled her away. Her father picked her up and swung her around, her feet scraping against the metal bulkheads, as he ran down the corridor to her mother, a fiery redhead with tears in her blue eyes.

"Don't worry, sweetheart," she said, kissing her forehead. "We'll be safe."

One of the Acedians stabbed a needle into her mother's neck. Blood splashed onto Mia's face. Her father dropped her, bellowing in rage. He was brought down, arms snapped at odd angles, and his neck broken, blue eyes sliding closed as his brunette hair fell across them. She saw the man who killed her family shift his gaze to her, a brown scar clearly cut across his neck. She ran.

Mia blinked, and the kitchen snapped into focus. It took her a moment to realize she was in full view of her crewmates. The shocked look on their faces mirrored the look on her own. She quickly yawned and stretched, rubbing the back of her head with one hand while reaching out to the counter with the other. The ruse worked, and after a quiet "Hey, Captain," from Will, the two brothers looked at Cassidy once more.

Will leaned forward. "Dead?"

"My parents had the boline radiation from old Earth. The one accidentally created by the scientists when they developed the magnetic wave technology?" When the others nodded, Cassidy looked down at the table. "I guess they had it in their genes or something, because my grandparents had it and so did their parents, my great-grandparents. When my folks found out, they got me checked right away, but I don't have any in my body."

Jeff cocked his head to one side. "I didn't think the radiation could be transmitted through the bloodline like that. Especially after a hundred years. It should've burnt out long ago."

Mia moved around the kitchen, making herself a cup of tea and trying to hear their conversation over the rustle. Jeff was right. The radiation should have been contained on Earth. Nothing got past the Vespa government's defense protocol.

"I don't know, honestly." Mia turned to see Cassidy shrug. "It was strange. I guess new technology, new dangers. They had all of the symptoms, nausea, vomiting, fever, headaches, ulcers, super-sensitive skin." Cassidy's voice caught. "They hid it from me for a long time. They were both really weak. It probably didn't help that our home planet was so cold all the time."

"So they died from it?" Will settled deeper into the chair, leaning back as far as the thing would allow.

"Not from the radiation, no." Cassidy's eyes darkened. "When the government found out, they decided that in order to contain the radiation, they ordered the military to come and 'properly dispose' of the new victims."

Will took a quick look at Jeff, who mouthed "they killed them." Will's eyes widened. Mia's did the same. She sat down on a stool next to Cassidy's, only now realizing she'd been wrong about the candlelight. A commemoration pyramid flickered instead. Family members of the deceased used the device. It could call up an image of their dead loved one held in cyberspace. Sure enough, a couple floated between them, and, with brown eyes, brown hair, and beaming smiles, they had to be Cassidy's parents. Mia's throat tightened. Her friend stared at the image for a moment then looked down and picked at the threads of her shirt.

"I was nineteen at the time." Cassidy's words lingered in the air, smothering all other conversations. A weight pushed them to the deck and held them down. Even Will shut up. Mia wanted to hug Cassidy, to hold her in her arms and whisper that everything would be all right, that she would never have to feel that suffering again, that she would never be alone again. But she didn't. Mia stayed on her chair just like the others. Waiting. Cassidy seemed to rouse herself from whatever dark place she had gone to. "It was sad, of course. I was young."

Will snorted, a black laugh. Jeff punched him on the arm. Mia did the same. Their two whacks were enough to shut him up again, but not without Will casting a meaningful look at his brother, who only shook his head.

"It was...it was okay, after a time," Cassidy muttered. "They gave me a lovely childhood and a great foundation to build from. For the short time I was with them, they made me stronger. I was able to go to the Academy on Skadi, get a business certificate, and start my own trading company, all by myself." Cassidy's voice brightened. Her smile was genuine. "I was able to meet you three, form friendships, and have more experiences than I ever would've back home. There was nothing to leave behind when I started Across the Stars."

"You don't have any brothers or sisters?" Mia asked, astounded by her friend's abilities to see the good in everything.

"No, I'm an only child." Cassidy took the cup from Mia's hands, blowing off the steam. She took a sip, eyes sparkling. "No worries, everything I got was brand new. No hand-me-downs."

The brothers chorused, "Lucky," and looked at each other, grimacing.

The sullen cloud that formed when Cassidy mentioned her parent's death had dissipated. The brothers relaxed. But, Mia could tell from the silence and the brothers' downturned eyes that their thoughts were not in this cabin, possibly not even in this moment in time.

Mia's own thoughts drifted as well. How did she not know about Cassidy's parents? How had any of them not asked? Cassidy always seemed so cheerful. It was almost unbelievable that something so horrible had happened to her, so young. She truly was amazing. Mia could almost love a woman like that. Mia felt herself falling into something so powerful, her entire body tingled. She had to get away.

The hum of the engine room filled the silence as did Cassidy's quiet sips of tea. Mia shook her head and pushed her back harder into the chair. There was no way she could be feeling these things for Cassidy. No way she should even be allowed to have any feelings for her whatsoever. She was dangerous. Not what Cassidy needed.

Every time Mia glanced at Cassidy, the tingling would continue, as if all her senses were tuned to Cassidy's being, to how close she was, the way she moved, looked, smelled. Mia rubbed her arms, goosebumps suddenly prickling her bare skin. She had to get out. Jeff cleared his throat a few times, breaking the silence with coughing noises, which only served to grate on Mia's nerves. Why weren't those blasted brothers on the bridge like she had ordered? As if on cue, Will shifted his body slightly, accidentally knocking into the table.

"William. Jeffery." Her sharp voice echoed in the small kitchen, completely shattering the silence. She rose. "Didn't I order you onto the bridge?"

The attempts to talk their way out of her admonition only infuriated her more. She barely listened to a word they said in their defense, speaking over their mingled voices.

"The fact is, I did." Her anger must have shown because both brothers quieted. "And since you can't seem to follow a simple order, I'll have to do it for you."

Mia stalked off, too angry at herself, too annoyed at the brothers, too close to Cassidy to stay. First she let herself get attached to this crew, and now she was developing even deeper feelings for Cassidy. So stupid. She had to get out. At her cabin, moments later, she waved open the hatch. Even without stepping inside, claustrophobia hit. Too closed off, too cluttered, too small.

Her gaze landed on the newly finished wristband, tightly wrapped wires and ribbon hiding the miniscule knife inside. The gift irked her, the time she'd spent idly creating it could have been spent formulating a new plan. The fact that she had made it specifically for Cassidy annoyed Mia more. She took two strides into her cabin, yanked her boots on, and grabbed the list from the table. She snatched the wristband from her desk and strode out again, waving the hatch closed behind her. She walked, blindly, her thoughts consuming her too much for her to really care where she went.

Mia found herself on the bridge, slumping in the pilot's seat. The cushion seemed hard under her. Uncomfortable even. How did Will even sit in it? She should not care. She fingered the wristband. Were there no trash compartments in this cabin? No, there never had been. Mia shook her head and threw the wristband onto the control panel. She rummaged under the seat, her fingers finally contacting the smooth astroprojector he stashed under there for long treks in the deep. Setting the projector on the panel, she flicked it on. The cabin filled with images of star systems, moons, and planets close by. The starchart took up the entire cabin, its brightness dimming the MPD's warping effect on the actual stars outside the viewport. Mia reached out and touched one of the holoimages, a brilliant blue sun. The sphere shattered, swirled, and, once Mia pulled her hand back, reformed itself.

She picked up the wristband again, this time cradling it in her hands. Her craftsmanship had been tedious, the twisted wires created intricate patterns through the orange and yellow ribbon. The knife remained hidden, but usable, the sturdier wires holding it in place. Cassidy would only need to slip her fingers into the circles by her wrist, and the knife would slip free. Mia tried it a few times, just to be sure. It worked fine. A tiny weapon, yes. Still, effective in close combat if the need arose.

"You look cold." Cassidy's tone was light.

Mia stuffed the wristband next to her, hoping her body would conceal it from its true owner. She took a breath to calm her now quickly beating heart and turned to Cassidy. The woman had an armful of blankets from the couch and a plate perched precariously on top, holding a slice of bread. She maneuvered her way into the cabin, flopped down in Jeff's chair, and set the plate on his control panel.

"I brought blankets," she said.

"So I see." Mia eyed the blue sheets.

Cassidy gave her one and spread another over her legs. Even though her body was nothing but warm, Mia spread hers over her legs as well.

"I brought you some bread, too." Cassidy handed over the plate, and their fingers touched for a moment. Heat ran through Mia's fingers, hand, and arm from that slight contact. Tingled. Had Cassidy felt it too? Mia's first mate smiled. Maybe she had.

"Thanks," Mia replied. She took a bite, the soft hazii bread giving easily and tasting of warmth and spice. Hazii fruit always tasted sour to Mia. The way Cassidy melded the flavors brought out a subtle sweetness. Why did Cassidy have to be so amazing? She knew Mia was keeping secrets from her.

"I know how much you like my bread."

True, but did she realize how much Mia liked her as well? For now, Mia couldn't tell, Cassidy's movements were too much like friendly gestures and nothing more.

"Did you know that star is called Polaris?" Cassidy pointed to the bright white orb burning between them.

"No. My folks called it Hekate." Mia crossed her legs before realizing that such an action might call attention to the gift hidden beside her. The wristband seemed too obvious now. Cassidy glanced down. Mia quickly asked, "Why do you call it Polaris?"

Cassidy looked up again, a smile pulling at the corner of her mouth. "Well, my understanding is that Polaris was the guiding star of old Earth. From the way Jeff speaks, it was this beacon of light for the sailors to follow when they got lost out at sea. Why did your parents call it Hekate?"

Mia shifted her gaze to the holoimage, old memories of her family shuttle coming back to her. Of the *Hekate*. Because that was what their ship was called. What their home was called. It only now dawned on Mia that perhaps her parents knew the star was called Polaris. That perhaps they knew the lore surrounding it, but chose to rename it after the ship they were on in hopes both of them would lead them home. Mia gripped her plate tighter. Or maybe, somehow, they knew the ship wouldn't last long. Knew Mia would need something else to guide her. To remind her of home. She couldn't bring herself to say that. Not now. Not yet. She coughed to cover her silence and shifted in her seat, but could not move far enough over to cover the gift. "That's what Jeff said, huh?"

"Yeah, take it or leave it." Cassidy stared at Mia's thigh.

Heat crept up Mia's neck. The orange ribbon contrasted starkly with the black cushion.

"What's that?" Cassidy nodded.

The heat intensified, and she put the plate on Will's control panel. Why was she blushing, blast it all? She wrapped her hand around the wristband and shoved it over to Cassidy.

"I made this for you," Mia muttered, not looking at Cassidy, rather at the gift instead. It looked feeble, unworthy of her first real showing of affection. Blast it all. Mia should have used golden wires instead of the silver plated, should have wrapped the ribbons tighter so it wouldn't bulge at the base, should have used another color because Cassidy's cheery attitude would diminish the sunset hues.

Cassidy gasped as she took the wristband. Mia glanced up. A bubble of hope rose within her.

"It's so pretty," Cassidy finally said. Her eyes never left the wristband, her fingers running over the designs woven within. "Why did you make it for me?"

Mia wanted to say, 'For being an amazing, brave, gorgeous woman I happen to be falling for. I know this is a meager attempt at affection. It's all I can manage,' but she couldn't bring herself to utter the truth. "For being a good...a good first mate." Because even that sounded like a hollow reason, Mia held out her hand. "Here, let me show you how it works."

Cassidy obliged. It shocked Mia how easily she gave up her hand, wrist, arm to her. Mia placed Cassidy's hand on her leg so she could use both hands to fashion the wristband. Cassidy's hand, soft and warm, distracted her, and she fumbled with the latches on the top, the circles not wanting to clip securely closed. She cursed herself for guiding Cassidy's hand to her leg. There was an armrest right next to them, why didn't she put Cassidy's hand there? Idiot. The heat reached her ears, warming them just like Cassidy's gentle hand warmed her thigh. Finally, the clasps closed.

"It's a—" She stopped, cleared her throat, tried again, "It's a wristband, see?" She took a breath to calm her racing heart. This wouldn't do. Mia made a point to not look at Cassidy, focusing instead on the pale forearm in front of her, now decorated with the gift she had created. She lifted Cassidy's hand off her leg, turning it over. Her gaze flitted once, and only once, to Cassidy's palm, clean of any markings or blemishes. Even her palm was beautiful. Mia blinked and focused again on Cassidy's wrist.

"It doubles as a weapon," she murmured, gaze still firmly focused on the wristband.

Mia slowly pulled the knife from its hiding spot beneath the folds of ribbon and wires and, in the process, her own wrist and hand grazed Cassidy's fingers. For a moment, a split second at best, feather light touches tickled her skin as she drew the knife out. Had Cassidy intentionally done so, or was it a reflex? Mia swallowed the lump that rose in her throat. She showed her the tiny weapon, finally gathering the courage to look at Cassidy's face. A small smile tugged at the corners of Cassidy's lips.

"That's so...practical." Cassidy withdrew her hand to study the wristband.

Practical? Mia's face fell. She looked away, focusing on the starchart. On *Hekate*. A weight pressed on her arm. Cassidy's hand. Cassidy's smile widened, reaching and crinkling the sides of her eyes. The brown of her irises caught the light and glimmered. Cassidy leaned forward, gently took the knife from Mia's hand, and slipped it back into its spot between the ribbons and wires.

"Thank you, Mia. I love it. And the colors are gorgeous," she whispered.

"I figured you might like them."

"Oh?"

"You wore an orange dress and yellow boots the first time I met you," Mia said. When she had sized the woman in the orange dress up as a victim. When she assumed she got the best of Cassidy. When Mia wanted to use her. She pushed those thoughts away, acutely aware of Cassidy's hand still on her arm.

Cassidy's hand tightened. "You remember?"

"I have a good memory for details," Mia replied, heart thudding in her chest. There was a pause, a comfortable silence. She wanted to tell Cassidy how she felt. Wanted to confess her feelings.

"I covered for you, you know," Cassidy whispered, leaning forward.

They were close now, so close. Cassidy's breath tickled Mia's nose.

"I know." Mia's breath hitched. The truth almost fell from her lips.

A knock broke the moment. The hatch slid open to reveal Will and Jeff. Will smiled at the two and gave them the thumbs up. Cassidy quickly stood, but Mia stayed in Will's chair.

An ugly look transformed Jeff's face for a moment, and only a moment, before it flashed away. He cleared his throat. "Sorry for interrupting. We're going to be arriving at Paradous in a few minutes here, and we both wanted to be on the bridge."

Will walked over to his chair, flourishing a bow and extending a hand to Mia. "If you will, my captain, I simply must take over." His smile broadened into a cheesy grin.

Mia rolled her eyes and slapped his hand away, fully aware of how close she had come to telling the entire ship about her feelings instead of just Cassidy. She stood and allowed Will his throne, backing up into the center of the bridge while Cassidy took her post on the guns, and Jeff crept to his navigation chair.

"We should be exiting MPD in three," Jeff's voice had an aggravated clip to it, his eyes remained focused ahead. "Two." Will's hands flew over the panel, preparing the *Eclipse* for the deactivation of the drive. "One."

The MPD deactivated, and the *Eclipse* shuddered as her pull through space ended. The stars separated themselves once more. The dark void of space could be seen clearly again, with only speckles of light on its surface.

Will and Jeff ran through the usual checks to see if all had faired well during the pull, then the crew glanced at Mia. Will gathered the plates and set them on the deck. "Are we a go to enter the atmosphere?"

"Yes," Mia replied. "Take her down easy, Will. Jeff, be sure to ask nicely where to land."

"Aye, Captain."

The planet loomed in front of them, and they cruised down to break atmosphere. Jeff called to the surface with the fixed transmitter, and Cassidy leaned back in her chair. Finally the excitement of being back home overwhelmed the sense of order within the bridge.

Will whooped. "Paradous!" He punched the air. "Home sweet home, we should be touching down planet-side just in time for lunch. Mom should make snapper stew! It should be right in front..." His voice petered off as he saw the planet's surface. His hand dropped back onto the control panel with a crash.

"What the..." Jeff stood.

"What happened?" Cassidy leaned forward in her chair, straining to get a clearer view. What should have been a lively city, bursting with people, was now a charred wreck, a few stragglers littering the streets. The *Eclipse* flew slowly over the city and veered around the ever-increasing blanket of black air, slowly expanding outward. Mia's shoulders slumped. Blast it all. It seemed the Acedians had kept their promise.

Chapter Eight

THE DAMAGE HORRIFIED THEM into silence. The city looked nothing like its previous glory. Smaller structures were only masses of glowing, molten metal. Flames licked around the towering skyscrapers, reduced to blackened skeletons of framework.

"This is the *Eclipse*, *ES5*, requesting permission to land." Will's voice constricted, hands tense above his control panel.

"*Eclipse, ES5*." The voice that filtered through the comm was firm, authoritative. Military. "What is your purpose on Paradous?"

"We're here on business, a trading company called Across the Stars." Will stopped for a moment. He took a deep breath. "And to check up on family. The navigator and I have folks down there."

A long pause greeted them on the other end. Will and Jeff exchanged tense glances, as did Cassidy and Mia. Long minutes passed with no acknowledgement. Finally, the authoritative voice rang out into the bridge. "*Eclipse*, permission granted. Land on the west pad. It's the least damaged. You will be escorted to a safer location."

Jeff keyed in the necessary coordinates and nodded to Will, who edged the *Eclipse* closer to the tiny moon's surface. They were close enough to see the hordes of frightened people massed together in the square. The buildings burned around them. Trapped.

Five massive ships, bearing the green Paradousian seal, flew overhead. Mia could only watch, open mouthed, as the beauties passed by. Sleek and narrow, these ships claimed their sky, swarming around the square, and dropping curtains of gray machines over the flames. Picobots programmed with only a single objective. The tiny robots linked together to climb up and over the flames. They were a subset of NIN's morphing tech. In moments, latticework bubbles surrounded the buildings. The masses within the square were safe. But the amount of people seemed smaller than she remembered. A horrible thought crossed Mia's mind. Where did the rest go? The *Eclipse* touched down on the landing pad, just outside the gray bubbles.

"We stay together." Mia knew the brothers would not take kindly to this order. Staying together would make it easier to leave. She had to be firm.

Cassidy muttered a quiet "Aye, aye." The brothers said nothing.

"Do I make myself clear?" Mia pushed Will and Jeff's chairs around to face her.

"Why?" Will's question hung in the air a moment too long.

Jeff broke the silence. "Because you ran away from Pargon and now you can't stay on Paradous as long as you originally planned, right?" He stood with a huff, face-to-face with Mia. Would he finally snap? "What are you running away from, Mia?"

His question stung more than that blasted Acedian needle. She had to clench her jaw to keep Captain from spitting out. Now was not the time for this argument. There was no good time for this argument. She folded her arms, both to keep herself together and to keep him out.

"I don't feel like getting shot again. Someone took out half this moon. Like it or not, you're on my ship and you follow my orders, or I'll hurl you out into space."

It was a stupid threat. A stupid lie. She knew it as soon as the words flew out of her mouth. Her anger got the best of her. She glared at Jeff, but knew she had gone too far. She'd never threatened this particular crew before. Will sat quietly in the corner, watching his brother fume before he exploded again.

"Do you honestly think your threats mean anything to me?" Jeff threw up his hands and let them fall. He jabbed Mia's chest. "For all I know you could be lying. I know you've done it before."

Mia took a step back, slapping the hand away. He knew she'd lied? Why stay on the ship? How much did he know? She focused on Jeff's furious gaze. Her muscles tightened. Not a word nor breath escaped her lips.

Jeff stepped closer, inches away. "You come back onboard with this pathetic excuse of a job to get us off Pargon, way ahead of schedule, without explanation. You were completely beat up, leg bleeding like it was cut off. Did you say anything to us about it? No. Will even had the decency to patch you up, and you didn't even tell him."

She should have. Will would have been satisfied with anything, and she should have given him something. A fight maybe, a suggestion of a struggle at least. She had been too shaken up to think straight. Too surprised he hadn't asked. Why hadn't he asked? She kept her face blank.

"What happened?" Jeff shifted slightly away from her. "Why did you get beat up? Why did we leave Pargon so quickly?"

The cogs in Mia's mind worked furiously. Nothing clicked together. Caught. They caught her. A boom echoed down the corridor. She turned toward the noise. Her heart pounded. What could she say? That she brought this terror upon them? That she had a scar connecting the Acedians to her? That she had murdered others, just so she could survive? Another boom echoed. Her secrets, her lies, her past. Mia drew a deep breath. A third boom shook through the bridge. The comm system flared to life, a solid orange light in the corner of her vision. A hand moved away from the panel, Cassidy's hand.

A voice burst through the intercom. "Attention." Mia's gaze shifted from Jeff to the speakers. The voice spoke again, accentuating each word. "Exit the ship immediately. You must undergo clearance and are about to be boarded."

Mia turned back to Jeff. His mouth formed a thin line, his jaw twitched.

"We have to get off the ship." Mia said the words slowly, calmly.

"Yes," Jeff said, arms folded tight over his chest. "We do."

"Exit the ship immediately," the voice over the comm said.

"Let's go." Mia led them down the walkway, the bulkheads looming closer than usual.

Jeff followed close behind, stopping her with a hand on her shoulder. "We're not done."

"No, we're not," Mia replied, shaking his hand off. She looked back and caught his eyes with her own. "While you're on my ship, Navigator, you listen to my orders. Got it? And we stick together."

Jeff tilted his head at his title, but as he looked away Mia heard a quiet, "Aye aye."

The outer hatch opened slowly. The acrid smoke singed Mia's nostrils and eyes as she looked at the destruction. In her periphery, a gray bubble encompassed the glowing buildings that used to be homes. Jeff turned toward the housing district. Will lingered close behind, ignoring the people who waited just off the walkway.

Clad in gray and orange, three Vespa soldiers aimed MWGs at their chests. One blast of the magnetic waves could incapacitate a human in seconds. Could kill in less if the pulse was high enough. The high-intensity magnetic field wave would disrupt the electricity of the body. It would be useful against the Acedians. Mia had never successfully gotten her hands on one. The military guarded their tech too closely.

Three more soldiers sported shieldbands; glowing, opalescent, head-to-toe shields that sparked and flickered every few seconds as the bands charged the protective force. Those would be useful, too. Cassidy had disappeared from Mia's side, and she felt distinctly nettled by Cassidy's absence. A deep breath in and out calmed her. Mia hesitated for only a second then stepped out to face the soldiers.

Another cloud of smoke floated over her, burning her lungs. The picobot latticework contained most of the damage, but buildings on the far edge of the city still smoldered. Towers of gray bubbles rose in the distance. A hand touched her shoulder, a few steps before she reached the soldiers.

"Your jacket, Captain." Cassidy cocked an eyebrow at the uniformed personnel. Mia returned the gesture. It was odd that Vespa would station the military on such a small moon. Mia's nerves were still strung out, but they relaxed slightly in Cassidy's presence. That woman could calm a meteor shower.

Mia walked down the ramp. She glanced down, seeing the massive crack spidering from the left side of the pad, shoving sections of metal up. The least damaged indeed. A few short steps took her into the circle the soldiers formed, blocking their path. She glanced back. Cassidy gently touched Jeff's shoulder, pulling him around. Will stood rigid, still searching the fires.

"Will." Jeff's voice seemed to snap Will into life. He shook his head and stumbled down the ramp. Jeff's eyes gleamed in a way Mia had never seen before. He grabbed hold of Will's arm and started walking.

The soldiers stepped in their way. "We need to hold you for questioning."

"Breach questioning to Davy Jones! Scan our ID tags. This planet's our home." Jeff pushed the sleeve of his shirt up, thrusting his forearm toward the officer. The officers exchanged looks. The shieldband soldiers stepped back, still forming a wall, but the soldier in front of Jeff, a burly man, stepped forward. The jumpsuit he wore caught the light, shimmered. He took out a small scanner and waved it over Jeff's arm. A green light blinked to life and a holoimage flashed into view, showing Jeff, as well as a list of specs known about him. "See? You'll find the same with Will."

Will had already pushed up his sleeve and another soldier, a wiry young fellow, was waving a scanner over his arm. Upon seeing the data, the three soldiers powered down their shields.

Jeff looked at them. "See? Jeffery and William Dee, homeworld Paradous. These are my crewmates—Mia Foley and Cassidy Gates—we'll vouch for them. I don't have time for blasted questions." Jeff's voice strained against the chaos around him. A crazed look crossed his face. He pushed past the armed soldiers, dragging Will with him. Mia took three wide strides and planted herself in front of Jeff, Cassidy a step behind her.

"Follow the order, Navigator." Mia's voice lowered. There was no way she would stay on this planet if the Acedians had hit. Too risky and stupid. More of them could be hanging about. They had to stay together in order to leave together.

"You never give orders, Mia. Why should I follow this one?" He shifted his weight. She mimicked his movements.

"It's Captain." She raised an eyebrow, tilting her head ever so slightly.

"No, it's Mia." Jeff wasn't going to back down. "In the six months I've known you, I've never called you Captain seriously and don't you deny it."

"Fine," Mia spit out the word with venom. Her plan spiraled out of control. "You have to follow orders, Jeff."

"No. I'm going home and quasar anyone, military or otherwise, who gets in my way!"

Pushing past the soldiers, he dragged Will along. Will muttered a quiet, "Sorry, Captain," as they rushed past. Panic that engulfed the city swallowed the brothers. Mia worked, unsuccessfully, to calm herself. A shadow fell over her. At least Cassidy stayed behind.

"I assume they were the pilot and navigator who had folks on this rock?" The voice came from behind Mia, and she turned. The admiral's rank was easy to identify by the multicolored bands on his shoulder. Boreas stood out, stitched in black on sleek fabric hugging his chest. The jumpsuit fabric glinted just like his soldiers', and Mia knew that metal fibers were woven into it, protecting the wearer from harm. His stance was at ease, hands smartly behind his wide back. His mouth turned downward into a deep frown. A swarm of soldiers flocked him, standing just beyond hearing but close enough to rush to his aid, if need be. A lieutenant stood at his right hand.

"I have to apologize for my pilot and navigator, Admiral Boreas," Mia said. He looked impressed by her quick assessment of him. "They do have family here. We can track their location with our earpieces." Mia pushed back her hair and revealed the small earpiece they each wore. Static filled her ear. Cassidy had clicked hers on and, in turn, had activated the rest as well.

Will's quiet voice filtered through the static. "We shouldn't have left so quickly."

"I don't care," Jeff replied.

Mia smiled at Cassidy's quick thinking. They would be able to keep tabs on the brothers, even at a distance, and have an idea of where they were heading. She nodded toward the soldiers, two of whom boarded the *Eclipse* unasked. Their orange and gray uniforms hunched deeper into the corridors, almost out of sight.

"My name is Mia Foley, by the way, and this is my first mate and gunner, Cassidy Gates." She motioned beside her, bringing Cassidy into the admiral's view. He nodded. Mia tilted her head at the retreating backs of the soldiers within her ship. "I didn't give them permission to board my ship."

The admiral frowned. "I cannot apologize for the intrusion on your ship, but I can give you the reason behind it. Follow me."

Mia nodded and allowed herself to be escorted away from the *Eclipse*. Tightly clenched in her hand, her jacket swung beside her knee. Mia didn't need to hear the screams, feel the heat on her skin, or see the destruction, to know who did this. To know why.

She scrutinized the admiral instead. He was tall, taller than most, muscular like all military soldiers tended to be, and heavy handed with his weaponry. An MWG hung on one side of his belt, and a picobot blaster, not likely programmed to create gray bubbles, made for the counterweight. A knife was clipped onto one of his black boots, and a few sonic grenades on the other. A man after her own heart, a comrade in a different situation perhaps. Hard brown eyes and a graying buzz cut completed his dominating appearance.

This was the man she would be going up against. A battle of wills to see how well her ruse would work before their probes crushed her ever-thinning hull of a disguise. It wouldn't take long for them to become suspicious. Even Cassidy had qualms with her story. She'd have to leave this blasted moon faster than expected.

"What do you think we'll find?" Will's voice wavered in the earpieces.

"I don't know." So did Jeff's.

A quick glance behind, and Mia saw Cassidy trekked closer than usual. Cassidy watched her surroundings. However, she seemed more intent on listening to the brothers' conversation, putting a hand over her ear in order to hear better. Four soldiers marched behind them. Vespa military made the eccentric combination of orange and dark gray intimidating.

They walked into a warehouse, and the door slammed shut behind them. The screaming and pounding of feet stilled to a quiet rumble outside. People filled this warehouse. She could easily see the difference between the Paradousian scientists, officers, and the military. Paradousians clad in their colorful wraparound or draped garments, officers clad in black and white, and military soldiers standing in formation. A frumpy man, balding to a shiny scalp, his brown eyes dull, was dressed only in green, wraparound nightshirt. His dark legs bare, his feet, slippered. Head Governor Jamees Arieg stood in front of a screen and assessed the incoming reports. The white light washed over him, contrasting greatly with his dark skin and throwing his wrinkles into sharp relief. More displays flickered as people added new information. The large room hummed with orderly life, a stark comparison to the chaos outside. Boreas led them toward the middle of the control center and stopped just before a translucent monitor, hovering inches above the floor and towering up toward the ceiling. Mia's earpiece crackled.

"Will, look at our house! It's wrecked. I can't even see the steps."
"Where are Mom and Dad? Can you see them?"

Admiral Boreas motioned to the screen. "On this screen you'll see the last two hours of security feed from the spacecams. There will be no sound. This is why we have to search your ship, Captain."

He pushed a button on the monitor. The display melted to a mottled white, reforming into a clear likeness of Paradous. Images flashed on the screen: the tiny moon, serene in its place on the fabric of space; ships came and went. The spacecam switched to its ground unit. A bulky transport shuttle landed on the east pad. Five or six people disembarked and milled around for a while. Mia tightened her hold on her jacket. Her hands grew clammy. The Acedians who had followed her on Pargon. Something called all the citizens into the city square, and they moved like ants on the screen. It seemed like all of Paradous had gathered before it happened.

Flashes of light obliterated the sensors for a moment's time. Within that moment, utter pandemonium broke loose. The sensors cleared. The screen filled with explosions. Fires and shots ripped through buildings. One shot shattered the glass cooling system and a surge of water broke loose. Another blasted through the sensor lens and the scene flicked to a different camera. The Acedians marched down the winding streets. Cassidy's hand pressed on her arm. One by one, the buildings caught fire, marking the paths the Acedians chose in orange and red.

Mia's stomach tightened. She had to keep watching. The skyscrapers around the square caught fire, but the people in the square remained unharmed. Each time a flame licked too close, or a building collapsed, a blue light would shimmer in the air, protecting the Paradousians from harm. The officers tried to quell the onslaught. Their defenses fell, their counterattacks failed. The Acedians could not be stopped. A bubble shield protected the Acedians. The ones on the ground and the ones in the ships cascading through the sky. Each barrage of weapons fire hit the shield as they marched through the city or flew overhead. Each barrage was answered by another weapon, so fierce no one knew the extent of the damage until the ship had passed. Aqua light spiraled across the screen until, one by one, all the sensors were destroyed.

"Mom? Dad?"

Jeff's voice, in her ear, made Mia jump. Cassidy started beside her.

"Mom, Dad!" Joy infused Will's voice. It deepened. "Where are Liz and Sarah?"

The monitor winked off. Mia attempted to unclench her jaw. Blast it. Seeing the horror was worse in silence. Her imagination filled in the sounds. The screams. The weight lifted from her arm and Cassidy moved slightly away. Admiral Boreas stood by the screen, hand lowering from the images he shut down.

Cassidy's whisper broke the heavy silence. "What made everyone gather in the center like that?"

"A city-wide announcement. A grand opening for a local restaurant." Jamees Arieg moved closer as he spoke, drawing his nightshirt close to his body. "We have them from time to time. They bring the people together for grand openings of shops, weddings, anything to celebrate. The announcement was lucky. My people survived because of it."

"Your people survived, because the attackers let them live." Admiral Boreas folded his arms. "Make no mistake about that, Arieg."

"Still, that force field kept them safe," he replied.

"Or kept them contained," Cassidy muttered. Mia stole a curious glance in her direction. Cassidy was right, contained citizens were easier to pick from than a hoard rushing from place to place. Mia turned to the admiral.

"Any casualties?" She could barely get the words past her lips.

"They shot to wound, not kill. Only one citizen died," Admiral Boreas answered. "A hundred or so were captured, however. We'll get a more accurate tally once the headcount is complete."

Mia turned away. Such an offhand way of saying lives were torn apart. Her list grew heavy again. Too heavy.

"Lucky," Cassidy said, slumping her shoulders in seemed relief. "Only one death, there could have been thousands."

"Not so lucky for the ones gone missing," Jamees Arieg replied.

"Not so lucky for the family dealing with the death of their own." Mia's statement hung in the air, a cloud over their already stormy conversation. Only one citizen died. That wasn't an accident. It was a target hit. She winced. A target hit because of her. She knew immediately which family would be targeted. The Dees.

The head governor of Paradous nodded, eyes lowered to the ground, and moved away.

"Who were they?" Cassidy asked.

"No one," Admiral Boreas said in a grave voice. "Just a shuttle transporting families to Skadi, the snowy planet on the outskirts of this solar system. The sensors picked up nothing out of the ordinary. The Paradousian offensive couldn't get past their shields when they left. Some new technology they've not encountered before. Harrison!"

Footsteps raced toward them as the officer answered Boreas' call. He stopped just short of Boreas, leaning forward, as if trying to get as close as possible. An overachiever probably. Mia shook her head. Great, he'd ask questions, too. A mop of curly, black hair adorned the kid's face, his brown eyes shone. The cut on his neck glinted against his dark skin. He hastened to smooth his crinkled uniform with shaking hands. Jer Mi Harrison was stitched in black on his collar.

"See this man?" Boreas gestured toward the young man, who straightened a bit. Boreas could only be asking to prove a point. Mia nodded. "He is one of Paradousian's officers, a fine young gentleman, doing his duty to protect this moon from any threat." Harrison's chin lifted a bit. A smile played on his lips.

Mia's earpiece crackled again.

"Liz!" Will sounded panicky.

"Where's Sarah?"

"Mom and Dad won't say."

She tried to ignore it, focusing on the admiral.

"This is the same officer who was unable to protect his home from criminals. Paradous is not the only inhabited planet targeted. We've had a string of these attacks, on multiple planets." The admiral tapped a finger on the control screen next to him. Five solar systems appeared, all tinted with the orange and gray of the Vespa government. In each system, at least one of the planets flashed a deep red. "Unexplained manslaughter, using these weapons." He tapped again and an Acedian needle appeared, long and silver. Deadly. "A case was just made on Pargon concerning Sheryl Stargazer." The monitor blinked off. "There's city-wide destruction and missing inhabitants, just like here. Thousands went missing from their homes, their streets, and the safety of their planets. No deaths were ever recorded during these abduction cases. Until now."

Sheryl. Her again. Mia kept her expression calm as the familiar name washed over them. Surely that would not go unnoticed. Her heart pounded in her ears. The air leaked quickly out of her ruse. Blast. The *Eclipse* would be making a hasty departure.

"Dead? No, that can't be right," Will protested in her ear.

Mia stole a sideways glance at Cassidy. Her eyes grew wide as she processed the news and tears welled in the corners. Mia shifted sideways until her shoulder touched her friend's. Cassidy moved away.

"Sarah," Cassidy whispered. A tear traversed the smooth skin of her cheek and slipped off her chin, but she quickly wiped it away.

The news did not come as a shock to Mia, the death of her crewmates' sister. She had known since Boreas mentioned the planet only suffered one death, a single death in what should have been hundreds. Of course, the Acedians had targeted one of Mia's crewmembers. Of course they had. Though, the people gone missing would suffer a fate worse than death. The Acedians would be processing them now, would be far away from this planet to access their new victims. She tightened her hold on her jacket.

Boreas continued, "The local officers cannot seem to handle this type of surprise attack, so the Vespa government sent us in. The ships associated with the attacks are unremarkable, seemingly innocent vessels. They can come in a range of styles—family transports, trading shuttles, carrier ships, even a few warships have been used. Anything and everything can, and will, be culpable." He narrowed his eyes, as if attempting to detect any signs of evil by sight alone. His scrutiny lingered on Mia and Cassidy. Harrison fidgeted. She was almost sorry for the boy. He had gone from being a proud officer of the Paradousian law to a slouching youngster in a few breaths of Boreas' assessment. She turned her gaze back to Boreas, hooking her left hand on her belt. At least the scar remained hidden, but they had to get off this planet before anyone connected her.

Locking eyes with the admiral, she allowed the words to roll off her tongue. "So, that's why you searched my ship."

He nodded.

"Have you found anything that would convict us?"

Boreas brought his arm up and pushed a code into his white wristband. A screen flickered to life. His eyes traced back and forth through the information for a few moments, before he lowered his arm again. With his mouth set in a line and eyes narrowed at Cassidy, his voice came out slow and calm.

"No." He brought his gaze back around to Mia "My men found nothing unusual on the ship." Mia tensed, dreading the next words. "We have to take you in for questioning, all the same. If you would be so kind to cooperate?"

It would be suspicious if they didn't cooperate, so Mia nodded. Harrison led them to a quieter place in the corner of the control center, where four chairs faced a blank wall. Harrison took two away. Cassidy sat down in one, her eyes tracing the floor panels. She said nothing, clearly in shock. Harrison stood before them, an archivist lighting his face from below, and flicked the screen. Mia leaned back in the spindly chair, waiting.

Sobbing filtered through her earpiece.

Cassidy's lips tightened. Someone's strongly spiced cologne made breathing harder than it should be.

Harrison took a deep, easy breath and asked the first question. "Your names are Mia Foley and Cassidy Gates?"

Cassidy didn't answer, so Mia replied for both of them. "Yes."

"You work for a company called Across the Stars."

Mia nodded. "Yes."

Harrison tapped the screen. "You were recently on the planet Pargon? On business?"

Mia figured Cassidy would answer the work-related questions, since she was technically the owner. When nothing came from her, Mia replied, "Yes."

"Did you meet an elderly woman by the name of Sheryl Stargazer?" He glanced up.

"Yes." Mia kept her voice calm. "We conducted a business transaction with her."

"Did you know of her death before today?" Mia felt, rather than saw, Cassidy's eyes on her, but she answered the question. "No." It wasn't like confessing was an option here. She had to lie. Could Cassidy tell? A quick glance affirmed her worry. Cassidy's eyes had narrowed. Blast. Of all times to come out of a state of shock.

Harrison tapped the screen again. "You were seen leaving Pargon quickly. Did anything happen?" Mia knew if she answered any other questions, her carefully constructed seal would be broken, air would rush out, and her disguise would crumple into a tiny ball from the sheer force of space. Her ruse might already be shattered by Cassidy's sharp mind.

Mia saw her friend's leg jerk. Cassidy leapt up. She kept on shaking her head, her hair swinging wildly against her back. Wisps of it brushed against Mia's face until she leaned away.

"I mean no disrespect." Cassidy's back was toward Mia, but she could imagine the look of sarcasm that confronted Harrison. Mia smiled. "I'm not going to just sit here anymore while our friends needs us. We're leaving."

Without waiting for a reply, Cassidy turned, gave Mia a scathing look, and walked out. Wrinkles formed across Harrison's forehead. Slowly, Mia rose from her seat. Harrison took a step back, misconstruing her rise as a threat. Rookie. Admiral Boreas marched over to her, as she, too, prepared to leave. The sea of officers, scientists, and soldiers parted for him.

"I have to go with my crew," she said simply, and walked away, knowing all too well it would not be the last she would see of the admiral.

Chapter Nine

MIA TOOK THREE STEPS out of the warehouse before Harrison grabbed her arm and circled in front of her. His eyes caught hers. What was the boy going to do now? A lecture was common, an order expected, but the silence Harrison maintained was not. He looked at her, through her perhaps. For a few moments, he did nothing else. Screams punctured the silence as frightened people bumped into them, holding out screens that flashed their loved one's faces in the air, looking for their family gone missing. Flashes of brightly dyed but singed clothing passed by her, along with the scents of smoke and burnt hair. Over Harrison's shoulder, Cassidy's black camisole and pale skin disappeared into the rest of the hurried crowd. Finally, Harrison took a deep breath.

"I cannot allow you to go, Miss Foley." When she didn't reply he continued, "There are still some questions that need to be answered." A hint of pain registered in his eyes. "And you should let go of me."

Mia blinked. Let go of him? Her eyes flitted down, and a jolt rushed through her. Her hand gripped his forearm, his black and white jacket sleeve crinkling under the pressure of her hold. She loosened her grip. Harrison gasped and rubbed his arm.

"Sorry," she muttered. "I didn't mean to hurt you."

She hadn't. She hadn't meant to grab him in the first place, but apparently her body did that of its own accord. Just a reflex, probably. The boy kept rubbing his arm like it actually hurt, badly. What a quasar.

"I can let your first mate go. However, we still have some questions for you."

He extended his palm toward the warehouse, but his eyes lingered on the remains of a nearby building. White screens hovered overhead, displaying the faces and names of the missing. Mia tilted her head. Harrison's eyes betrayed him, and her first impression of him changed. Under that eager exterior was just a boy, a boy trying to impress his new boss, but a boy just as afraid as anyone else. A boy who wanted to get back to his family, as quickly as possible. To see if any had been stolen away. She wilted a bit, shoulders slumping, head down.

"Look, I should be with my crew," she said softly. "Our other two crewmembers lost a sibling in the attack."

Harrison's eyes widened. Mia pushed on, hoping her new assessment of this officer was on point. "Tell the admiral that I'm sorry about her actions. It wasn't the right way to handle things. We had just heard, over our earpieces, and she just broke, I guess." She kept her voice steady, loud enough to be heard over the clamor around them, but quiet enough to appear sincere. "You should concentrate your efforts on helping the citizens and officers. We all should."

Harrison looked to the screens draped above them. A woman in a crimson coat replaced a man with green eyes. Harrison looked away. Mia followed his gaze. The stream of people parted from a new scene of horror. A black-haired woman hugged an officer. She cried out again, sinking lower to the ground. Her blue dress tore, the elegant, draping design so common in this part of space ripping at the seams. She didn't seem to care. The corner of Mia's lips turned upward at the sight. The scene could not have been more perfect. An example of the citizens needing help, needing guidance in this troubling time when their homes burned.

"Look, you can send another officer over later, to ask any questions you might still have." Mia broke into Harrison's thoughts as he watched the woman. He turned toward her. "Sound reasonable?"

"Expect an officer to arrive tomorrow." Harrison held her gaze for a heartbeat longer before turning away. Just before opening the warehouse door, he turned back, a curly lock of hair falling over his eye. "My condolences to the two who lost their sibling. We've all lost something in this attack."

He slipped back into the warehouse. Mia spun on her heel, facing in the direction Cassidy had disappeared. Her eyes slid past the people rushing around her and landed on the young woman still kneeling on the cracked cement. Her tears splashed onto the man, marking the white fabric of his shirt. A needle was embedded deep into the man's shoulder. Medics now surrounded them. The man would live.

"Where's your smile now?" Mia jumped at Cassidy's voice beside her, lips tightened, hands pushed into her hips. Cassidy's dark clothing stood out from the brightness swirling past them. She had become a shadow Mia hadn't even known was there. When Mia had nothing to say in response, Cassidy's voice grew low and dangerous. "Where's your smile?"

A sob echoed in Mia's ear.

Cassidy's eyes flitted to the side as she listened to the brothers mourning. She grimaced. Without meeting Mia's eyes, she spun around and walked away. People swarmed around her, all trying to get to the safety of someplace else. The clothing—yellows, blues, greens, pinks—seemed to engulf Cassidy with their cheeriness, but no one was happy here. Cassidy fished a tracking device from her back pocket and clicked it open. The tracker glimmered for a second and winked off. She altered course, crunching over shards of glass and ruined metal. Mia followed.

Blast. Cassidy strode ahead, her anger a buffer of cold air constantly between them. Had she smiled? It shocked Mia to recall that she had. She wasn't that heartless. But she had killed others. Agony speared deep each time she remembered someone dying by her hand. At each memory, darkness spread into her essence. But not to the extent of her smiling at another's suffering. Another's loss.

Cassidy bumped her, breaking the buffer. The nudge brought Mia out of herself and back into the chaos on Paradous. Only a two-story skeleton and a few steps that led to an empty doorway remained of the Dees' residence. Pungent wafts of burnt metal drifted toward them.

"The picobots didn't reach this sector of the city fast enough to save anything," Cassidy mumbled, looking around at the road. The buildings lay in ruins, their residents sitting helplessly on sections that had fallen, or stumbling toward a nearby warehouse. "Their house was beautiful. I saw pictures once. All these homes were."

"They're nothing, now," Mia replied, ignoring the shocked look Cassidy gave her. Mia looked past the wreckage and settled on the warehouse the survivors seemed to be drifting toward. "I'll bet that's where they are."

"Probably."

Cassidy started walking toward the warehouse. Her boots tread the ground slowly, gingerly, as she stepped over the broken remains of the homes Paradousians had deserted. As she moved, Cassidy's fingers were constantly flicking against the middle finger of her other hand. Mia trained her eyes on the ring, unnoticed before now. Even as the gentle light of the rising sun washed the wreckage, the ring glinted. Mia made a mental note to ask about it later. Quietly, Cassidy moved away from Mia.

Another sob ripped through Mia's eardrum.

She winced at the sound. A few hurried steps took her to Cassidy's side. Mia gently removed the earpiece from Cassidy's ear, startling Cassidy in the process, and did the same to her own. She placed them both into her belt pouch, not meeting Cassidy's questioning gaze.

"There's no need to listen to that." Mia nodded to the warehouse that loomed ahead of them. "We'll see soon enough."

Cassidy nodded. She walked a few more steps alone, then looked back. Their eyes met. It seemed Cassidy's anger had melted...or had been shelved for later. Mia couldn't tell. A breeze swirled around them. Cassidy shivered. A few steps brought Mia closer as she held the jacket out for Cassidy.

"You shouldn't be cold," she muttered, not looking into those brown eyes.

Cassidy nodded her thanks and slid the dark jacket on. Now, Cassidy really looked like a shadow. She led the way to the warehouse and opened the door. Maybe being a shadow would be better in here.

The crowded chaos within the warehouse contrasted with the organized base that lay just a few streets over. Tear-stained cheeks watched them wherever they turned. Families and friends huddled together on the floor in heavy blankets. Joyful reunions of families burst forth into the steady hum of conversation, laughter bouncing loud across the wide walls. Sobs echoed far longer than the laughter. At least they were safe, for now. The Acedians wouldn't hang around once they got what they came for. She frowned. Once they eliminated their target.

Cassidy's shoulders slumped at the sight, her hands shoved roughly into her pockets as she walked past strangers. Mia looked at the chaos and had to force down a perverse bubble of joy—was that joy?—rising in her chest. Better them than her. The thought flickered through her like a firefly on a darkened night, and at first Mia tensed, thinking it was an Acedian trick. When she heard no others, realization slowly dawned on her. It came from her. The scar on her hand stung briefly.

"Maybe I am that heartless," she muttered. Cassidy glanced back. Mia only shook her head. "Did you find them?"

Cassidy didn't need to answer. In the far corner of the warehouse, the Dee family huddled around a heap of belongings piled between them, clothes and archivists mostly. Mia's gaze slid over the family members. Will crouched in the corner, farthest from her and Cassidy. Mia could see the top of his black head peeking out from under his hands. Jeff sat next to him, staring off into space, green eyes glazed over.

Next to the brothers, a dark-skinned man, with inky black hair and dark green eyes, who could only be their father, grasped the woman sitting beside him. The woman, their mother, tan-skinned and slender, with curly brown hair falling over her face, clutched a holocard. Her blue eyes rested on the youngest female sibling—Elizabeth, just thirteen if Mia remembered correctly—who lay curled up on a blanket on the other side of the circle. The mother and father were dressed haphazardly, their brown overcoats settled over wrinkled, white nightwear, their boots, untied. Elizabeth wore a green nightgown and matching slippers. The girl pulled the nightgown's ties, tightening it as if the fabric could protect her. Mia's stomach lurched to see there were bloodstains on the bottom of the gown.

Mia cleared her throat. The noise jarred Will to his feet. He walked around his family to reach them and nodded to Mia with a soft, "Captain." There was a sudden movement beside her, and Cassidy flew toward Will, grabbing him into a hug before either he or Mia could do anything about it.

"I'm so sorry," Cassidy said, "I'm sorry about Sarah."

Will broke the hold. "How'd you know?" His voice broke at the end, eyes sweeping past Cassidy to his family. They watched with the curiosity of cornered prey waiting for that last blow to fall.

"I clicked on the comm so we could track you here." Cassidy tapped her ear, but Will understood. He took out his own. "We heard."

The rest of the family seemed to rouse with the sudden presence of newcomers. The husband and wife tightened their hold on each other, and Elizabeth sat up.

Will brought the two women forward into the circle. "Mom, Dad, Liz, this is Captain Mia Foley and our first mate and gunner Cassidy Gates. They're the rest of the crew we talked about."

Mia nodded—what else was there to do?—but Cassidy went straight to their mother and hugged her tightly, murmuring comforts and condolences, and plopped herself right next to Elizabeth. The girl shied away at first, looking at Cassidy with wide eyes. Cassidy gave her a warm smile. Mia could not bring herself to follow Cassidy's lead, straightening her back just a bit and notching up her chin instead. The husband stood up, extending a callused hand that trembled slightly. Mia shook his hand, nodded at his wife, and sat down next to Cassidy. Jeff flicked his gaze to Cassidy, once, and returned to his stupor, eyes downcast.

"My name is Robert," their father said, Paradousian accent much more pronounced than his sons'. He motioned to his wife. "And this is Arai, my wife, and my daughter, Elizabeth. It's nice to finally meet the captain and first mate of the *Eclipse*."

"Yes," Arai said, her voice strained. "I've heard so much about you. If only these were better circumstances." She broke off and clutched the holocard tighter. Robert placed a hand over Arai's.

"It's good to meet you, too," Cassidy said quietly.

Mia smiled and nodded, but inside she fidgeted. The floor suddenly grew uncomfortable beneath her. Great. Now there are more strings to worry about on this planet. Her stomach twisted. She willed it down again. She knew she should talk to these people, say something at least. No words formed, least of all conversations. Only plans of escape shot out before her. Each idea a ship taking course, but none that could be discussed here. The only semblance of conversations they could have would be about the wreckage of their home, which seemed too sad to bring up; the sibling's death, too personal; or the attack, too sudden. Nothing else came to her. She pinched the bridge of her nose and noticed Cassidy glancing toward her. She gave a slight shake of her head. Unable to stand the silence either, Cassidy seemed to shiver, words blurting out in a rush.

"What is that you're holding, Arai?" She pointed to the holocard.

"It's a recording of—" she broke off, staring at the technology. Suddenly, as if burnt, she threw it away. The holocard clattered to the ground. Slowly, Robert bent over and picked it up.

"It's a recording of our daughter's death," he said in a monotone voice, eyes only on the tiny item clutched in his palm. "They gave it to us so we could see what happened, as if we want to watch the scene over again."

Mia winced. Of all the things Cassidy could have pointed out, that was what she chose? Their eyes met. Cassidy seemed to shrink away, eyes misty and lower lip trembling. Was everyone supposed to cry here? Mia quickly looked away. That holocard could be useful. As much as she hated to think of watching it, Sarah's death could provide some clues to the Acedian's attack. Perhaps to the hunter that attacked Mia as well. There was no doubt in her mind that this family would watch it again, and in that moment, Mia would be watching also.

"Did everything go well with the officers?" Will had settled down beside his mother.

Mia looked at him, glad to grasp onto something that was not death or destruction. Or plans of leaving. He seemed to have aged years since he'd found out about his sister's death. His eyes looked darker, muscles tenser, the lines around his mouth etched deeper. Cassidy opened her mouth to speak. Mia got there first.

"Yes," she replied, narrowing her eyes at Cassidy's look. Cassidy's glance skittered away. "They'll probably send someone over later, but, for now, everything's taken care of."

"Good," Will whispered.

A cold emptiness settled over them. Other people came over, offering their condolences for the loss of a sibling, a daughter, a member of society. How Sarah will be missed. How the citizens would band together and find who did this. Find the ones who took their people and destroyed their city. How they would rebuild and start anew. Whispers of sadness broke over the group. The sympathizers came and went, until finally, they were left alone once more. Moments later, a fellow brought a tray of hot beverages.

"I have tea." The man held the tray out so they could reach. Most of them took a steaming cup, the father took two. Arai seemed too preoccupied to take her eyes off the slight piece of technology she again held in her hands. "Be careful now, it's hot. And Paradousian."

A weak ripple of laughter came from the Dee family. Jeff didn't join in. His eyes could have burned a hole through the warehouse floor. His lip twitched. Will kept glancing at his brother with a worried look in his eyes, tensing every time Jeff moved.

"Was that a joke?" Mia asked.

"Ah, you've not visited our humble shores before, have you, Captain?" Robert asked.

"No, I've heard stories about the alcohol. Never about the tea." Mia gave a sidelong glance at Will, whose lips turned ever so slightly upward.

Arai took the cup Robert handed her. "Like the alcohol, the tea is quite strong." She gulped some of the liquid down. Her lips trembled. "It's brewed from only the best minerals, heated until it's boiling, then a large splash of the best spirits is added in."

Mia nodded. She took a sip of the tea and coughed as the spirits scorched a path down her throat. "Blast it!"

Will laughed, actually laughed. He drank a long gulp from his own cup and grinned. "It's great, right? Elizabeth even gets some."

The girl sat up a bit straighter, and then seemed to curl around her cup. She took a sip and attempted to hide the coughing fit. Her face turned a brilliant shade of red. Mia cast a sideways glance at Cassidy, expecting the same reaction. Cassidy sipped her steaming tea gracefully. Not even a sputter passed her lips.

"Tea?" Jeff's voice snapped from the corner. All heads turned toward him. He smashed his cup of tea down on the floor. The liquid splashed onto Mia's boots. "Tea?" He stood, shaking, towering over everyone in his rage. "My sister died today—was senselessly murdered today, and we don't even know who killed her—and we're talking about tea?"

Jeff kicked the heap of belongings in the center of the circle. A pot flew past Mia's arm.

"Come on," he said, walking around them. "Sarah is dead! Do you understand? Dead!"

His foot thumped close to Elizabeth. She shied away from him, scooting toward her parents. Her eyes widened. Tears stained her nightgown. Will stood, putting himself between Jeff and the rest of his family. Jeff didn't seem to notice the movement. He was too busy stomping on a blanket that had fallen in front of him.

"Jeff," Will said. "Please calm down. It's horrible, I know—"

"Horrible?" Jeff burst out, cutting Will off. Jeff glared at his brother. "Just horrible? It's disgusting. She's dead!"

Jeff brushed by Mia's shoulder without seeing her and disappeared into the chaos. Will sighed and closed his eyes for a moment. He opened them and followed his brother. Mia and Cassidy stood. While Cassidy looked at Jeff's receding back, Mia watched Robert. The older man shook his head slowly, mouth withering into a frown, as he watched both sons disappear. Robert put his arm around Arai, who grasped onto Elizabeth's shoulders. A family trying to hold together, as two of their own strayed in the storm.

Cassidy's elbow jabbed in Mia's side. A slight head nod indicated Cassidy was going after the brothers, and a raised brow beckoned Mia to follow. Mia nodded.

Cassidy looked back at the Dee family. "We're going after them. You can stay here where it's safe. Drink some more tea, okay?"

Arai's lower lip trembled, the wrinkles around her eyes lengthening as she struggled not to cry. Mia assumed she was the type to cry alone, late at night, away from her children. Elizabeth's tears flowed freely down her cheeks. She turned around and burrowed her head in her mother's arms. Mia should say something, but Cassidy had already moved off in the direction of the exits.

"We'll try to get back soon," she said. Stupid, yes. It was all she could think of at the moment.

Mia matched Cassidy's long strides. They pushed past strangers, the earlier void broken as they bumped into each other on the way. Mia shoved the warehouse door open and followed Will's receding back around the building. She heard Cassidy's footfalls right behind her as Will led them farther away from the haven and into a different part of the residential area.

A crashing sound led them to Jeff. He stood in the center of a miniature landing site, a blue flier upturned in the far corner. Will stood a fair distance away from his brother, hands outstretched and pushing the air down, as if that motion would calm Jeff. It didn't. Jeff still shook, hands balled into fists at his sides, jaw clenched. Mia and Cassidy moved closer, now just a few yards away from the brothers.

"Breaking things doesn't help," Will said.

"So sayeth the unbeliever." Jeff stalked over to a bunch of metallic barrels and started kicking them. They crashed to the ground. "See?" He motioned to the rolling barrels. "That made me feel better. Therefore, it's helpful."

"That's ridiculous." Will moved closer to his brother.

"You know what's ridiculous?" Jeff began walking again, this time toward the edge of the pad. He picked up a stray stunner on the ground and shot it. A yellow burst of light blew from the stunner, expanding outward and slamming into the flier. The metal crumpled inward. He gestured with the stunner. "It's ridiculous that my sister is dead. It's ridiculous that Sarah was only a teenager and that she was the only one to die."

Jeff smashed his foot into the side of the flier. Mia's eyes widened as the flier lurched into the air and fell back down with a crash. He was stronger than he looked. Much stronger. Jeff turned around and started toward them. Her muscles coiled. She had the insane urge to jump in front of Cassidy, but Jeff stopped inches away. Mia eased herself back onto her heels.

"You know what's also ridiculous?" He stepped closer, until Mia's boot touched his own. His lips twisted into a sneer. "Your stupid secrecy. I'm sick of it. Six months. Six months! We lived under your captainship for six months, and we get little, if anything, out of you." He narrowed his eyes. The stunner, forgotten in the moment of anger, pushed into her side. Jeff's fist shook around it. "A few superficial accounts might satisfy Will or Cassidy. Not me. You were attacked on Pargon, and we don't know why. For all we know, you might have initiated it. I wouldn't put it past you."

"Jeff." Mia tucked her hands into her back pockets so she wouldn't punch him. "You need to calm down."

Instantly, she knew the words were wrong. Jeff's sneer turned into a scowl, hazel eyes darkening with his fury. He dropped the stunner and grabbed her left wrist in the same motion, pulling her hand from her pocket. Mia's heart pounded. The glove still covered her palm.

"Calm down?" His grip tightened. Mia's free hand curled around the dagger on her belt. "You're keeping things from us, most likely endangering us, and I'm supposed to calm down?"

"Let go of me," Mia's voice lowered. Cassidy moved closer and a hand closed around Mia's hand grasping the dagger. Cassidy twisted her fingers between Mia's hand and the hilt, so Mia couldn't grab the weapon properly. It seemed her threat didn't go unnoticed this time.

"No. I'm not going to let go until I get some answers." Movement behind Jeff's shoulder distracted her. Will headed their way.

"Jeff." Cassidy put her other hand on Jeff's shoulder. He shook it off, glaring at Mia. His body hovered over hers. "I get you're upset, I understand. Who wouldn't be? This isn't the right time, though."

Why would Cassidy stand up for her at a time like this, with Jeff so raw? The woman wanted answers, didn't she? But when Mia glanced at Cassidy, Mia knew it wasn't her defense that Cassidy was thinking of. Her eyes portrayed sadness. Cassidy's gaze never left Jeff's face, yet the man never wavered in his own intense scrutiny.

"Don't make me start with you." He pushed her away. She took a step back, keeping her hand on Mia's, even as Mia's own grip tightened.

Jeff's hold tightened, too, making Mia wince. "Six months. You initiated the attack, didn't you?"

The air stilled around them.

"Why?"

Mia's breathing slowed.

"Tell me why." He shouted the last word, yanking her hand down before letting her go. There was a rip. She teetered forward, off balance, and stumbled. Jeff jammed his shoulder into her chest. Cassidy pulled her back from the brunt of his sudden attack. A weight thumped into both of them before Jeff could do more.

"Stop it." Will wrapped an arm around Jeff's neck and pulled his brother away from Mia and Cassidy.

"Tell me why." Jeff kept shouting over and over again, getting louder with each breath. Will let go of Jeff's neck and circled around him, putting himself between his brother and the two women.

"Stop it. This isn't helping." Will stood before his brother. Hands outstretched, palms down, just like when Mia first saw them.

"Isn't helping?" Jeff's voice shook.

"No, it isn't." Will's back was turned toward them, Mia couldn't see his face, but his shoulders shook. Jeff's face scrunched up. Mia was suddenly glad she couldn't see Will's.

"This won't bring her back." Will's quiet voice seemed to calm Jeff's anger. Not by much. Jeff shifted from one foot to the other, rubbing his hands together. His jaw clenched so tightly, a muscle by his chin twitched.

"Nothing can bring her back," Will said, his voice breaking.

"Stop it," Jeff said, his eyes on the ground.

"Kicking things, storming around, getting angry, it can't bring her back." Will's arms dropped to his sides.

"Just stop it!" Jeff finally broke. He shoved his brother, who landed hard on the concrete.

Will's hands and arms broke the brunt of his fall. He sat up. Jeff stared, eyes watering, as the scratches running down Will's palms, wrists, and forearms reddened with blood. Anger and fear crossed Jeff's face for a moment, sorrow trumping both. Jeff turned away from her, from Cassidy, and from his brother. He walked away. Will's shoulders, if possible, slumped further down. The younger brother seemed to crumble into himself. Perhaps his body attempted to protect his heart from any more damage. Or maybe the weight of Sarah's death crushed him. Either way, Mia couldn't imagine a man more beaten down. He sighed once, picked himself up, and followed his brother back toward the warehouse.

Mia and Cassidy stood alone. Cassidy seemed to be lost in her own world, looking up at the sky. The sun had fully risen. Sometime during the fight her fingers had untwined from Mia's.

Cassidy shifted away. "We need to talk."

Chapter Ten

MIA SAT, LISTENING TO the beating of her heart and wondering how it had ever come to this. How her years of running, hiding, and killing all led to this moment. A connection couldn't be made. Yet, here she was, sitting in front of a crewmember that should have been killed a week ago, a month ago, probably. Cassidy crossed her legs and leaned back on her hands. The wristband Mia had given her glinted. Her hair fell over one shoulder, purple streaks catching the light in-between folds of dark brown. She might have looked gorgeous to Mia once, but not this day. Cassidy's unwavering gaze irked her.

The concrete beneath her numbed her legs after only a few moments. Cross-legged, hands clasped on her lap, she waited. The scent of sinna drifted toward Mia. She breathed deeply, hoping Cassidy would make the first move.

Cassidy cocked her eyebrow and exhaled in a huff. "I defended your stupid lie. I shared my history. Now it's your turn. We're alone enough."

"I didn't ask you to do that." Mia kept her gaze steady on Cassidy.

Cassidy tilted her head. "Well, I'm asking. You promised."

"What, are we in school now or something? I don't have to hold to every promise." Mia shifted, uncomfortable. Now was not the time. It wasn't private enough. There wasn't enough time.

Jerking her head to the side, Cassidy said, "You wouldn't know, seeing how you didn't even go to the Academy."

"How do you know that?" Mia could feel the tension start to swell. She forced herself to be calm. To not lose her temper.

"Did you really think I wouldn't check up on you? Blasted, Mia, I'm starting a business here. Of course, I looked you up." She shifted her weight, as if itching to move. Mia knew the feeling. Cassidy's voice hitched itself up a tone. "Cyberspace knows everything but there's not much to say about you. No records of being in school, no records of having a homeplanet, no bio at all. Who the quasar are you?"

"You looked me up?" Mia echoed, her calm starting to waver. No other member of her crews had done such a thing. "When?"

"On Pargon. One of the little things I apparently had time to do while you disappeared." Cassidy's eyes narrowed, her eyebrows furrowing over them. There was a soft line between them Mia had not noticed before. Still, her anger had spiked dangerously high at Cassidy's last words. "I turned up empty. So now I'm going directly to the source. Who are you?"

"None of your blasted business." Mia instantly regretted those words. It took a few moments for Cassidy to respond after that blow and when she did, there was pain in her eyes. The look twisted a knife in Mia's heart. Too deep. Her anger slowly ebbed away.

"It is my business, because this is my business." Cassidy leaned forward, shifting her hands into her lap. "I know you were hurt on the planet. And scared. Why?"

"Nothing you need to know about." Mia couldn't tell Cassidy. She just couldn't. But she wanted desperately to connect, just this once.

"I want to know." Cassidy's quiet voice filled the stillness.

A flash of Cassidy, dead, a needle to her neck, blood pooling around her in a scarlet stain, filled Mia's vision. She blinked, and the real Cassidy swam into view. Mia's lip trembled. She breathed deep, not caring that the smoke still burned her lungs. Just this once. Maybe it's time to let someone in for a change. "I wouldn't be able to keep you safe if you knew."

"I need to know the truth," Cassidy said.

Mia bit her lip. "About what?"

"About everything."

"That's a lot of things." Mia looked past Cassidy. The buildings of the city towered ominously over this area, marring the horizon with their wrecked state. The sun threw shadows across the concrete pad beneath them, making the overturned flier gleam.

"Apparently." Cassidy's sharp tone snapped Mia's eyes back to her. "What happened on Pargon?"

"I got into a fight." Mia stopped as battle raged within her. Tell her. Don't. What's there to lose? Everything she's worked for would be destroyed. Everything's already falling apart. A flash of the *Eclipse* ripping itself apart darted across Mia's thoughts. A flash of Cassidy floating in the blackness of space. Mia's stomach tightened.

"I gathered that, yes." Cassidy rolled up the jacket's sleeves. "With who and over what?"

"I can't…I don't know." Mia looked helplessly at Cassidy. Her chest tightened. The buildings seemed to loom higher, making her feel tiny. Insignificant. There was just so much to go over, so many painful memories to drag up before it would make sense. Even so, the Acedians were far away. Maybe there was enough time. "I don't know where to begin."

"Try starting at the beginning." Cassidy rubbed a hand over her arm and made Mia's jacket ripple and fall back into place.

"I was born on a shuttle craft," Mia said, slowly, softly.

Cassidy barked a laugh. "Not that close to the beginning. I meant—"

No," Mia cut her off. She might as well go all in and see what happens. "It's important for you to understand where I came from, to understand why this is happening."

Cassidy pursed her lips. "Okay, go on."

"I was born on the *Hekate*, a craft with ten other families," Mia repeated. A flicker passed over Cassidy's eyes at the ship's name. Mia pushed on, "The only child of two newlyweds. My mom and dad, Thressa and Lial, carved out a life together as engineers, became successful, had a growing baby, and friends to support them. They had it all on that ship. I grew up there. It was my home, and they were good parents." Mia's throat tightened, causing her to stop. She had never told anyone about her parents before.

The memories rushed back to her. Her mom instructing the AutoChef on what to make, green mash and fish usually. How the food always seemed to taste the same even though both parents raved about it. Her dad carrying her through the ship's corridors, pointing out the viewports at stars and chatting with the other passengers onboard. Playing keep-away with the other kids in the cargo hold. Living a quiet life. Later on, she found out the food was all the same, a protein and carb mixture cut or mashed into different shapes. She remembered her parents laughing when she told them she knew, their eyes twinkling as their secret fell away. Mia glanced at Cassidy and saw a smile tug at the corner of her lips. She knew that expression wouldn't last long.

"I was thirteen." Mia looked away, attempting to push the memory of her parents down. "The ship was attacked. These strange people boarded, slaughtered families, destroyed everything that moved. Including my parents."

Mia's throat closed up again. Memories filled her, blue eyes pleading for her to help, arms twisted at odd angles, blood seeping onto the deck. She felt a warm pressure. Cassidy had placed her hand, gently, on Mia's trembling arm.

Mia blinked the memories away and coughed. "I ran. They caught me and brought me back to their ship and into this awful cabin." Corridors, deck darkened with blood, the table they strapped her onto, screams filtering through the bulkheads. "They tortured me." Cassidy gasped. Mia kept her gaze trained on the concrete slab beneath them. A blackened smudge on its gray surface caught her eye. Mia's left hand closed out of instinct, her other covering it from Cassidy's view. "Not for very long. I blacked out. The next thing I knew they had branded me and let me go."

"Branded you?" Cassidy sputtered.

Mia glanced up. Cassidy's eyes were wide with fright. Sometime during Mia's tale Cassidy had curled herself into a ball, one arm wrapped around her folded legs tucked under her chin. The other hand still rested on Mia's arm. Cassidy unraveled herself, holding Mia's stare. She placed her hand over Mia's and, without even looking down, pulled the fist into her lap. And even though every fiber in her being screamed for Cassidy to stop, Mia let her. Just this once.

Cassidy waited a moment, looking at Mia's shaking fist. At the dark glove that hid her scar. Prying Mia's fingers open, she studied the fabric. It had been ripped on one side and a corner of the puckered mark could be seen beneath the torn material. Mia's pulse quickened. No one had ever seen the scar before. No one but her and the man who had made it. And, if she remembered correctly, that Acedian on Pargon. Cassidy gently pulled on the glove, the cloth slipping over Mia's fingers. Mia held her breath as her hand fell open on Cassidy's lap.

Not a word passed Cassidy's lips as she studied the scar. She gently traced the triangle that marred Mia's hand. The soft touch tickled. Cassidy moved her finger to the line that snaked in one point of the triangle and out another. Each time her finger rubbed over a different texture Cassidy would pause, as if the new feeling surprised her in some way. The rough callused skin tingled, the scar burned with her touch.

Finally she said, "What does the brand mean?"

Mia started at the question, of all the things she would have asked were the situation reversed, meaning wouldn't be of the select first.

"The scar? I wouldn't know." Her reply seemed unfinished, so she continued, remembering the odd word the Acedian used on Pargon. "They call it a cicatrix ritual. I've always figured it was a mark of their group." She paused again. She had never spoke of their name aloud. "Of the Acedians."

"Acedians," Cassidy repeated, eyes still on Mia's blackened flesh. "Are all the marks similar?"

"No, I just know this is one of his. The man with a scar across his neck."

"Maybe it's just a brand of the one who did it, a way to keep an eye on his flock, so to speak," Cassidy said, her voice low. She stopped, her thumb resting in the center of the scar. "Does it still hurt?"

"Every once in a while," Mia replied, shifting a little. She hoped Cassidy would never let go of her hand. "Why do you ask?"

"You use your right hand for almost everything, even holding weapons." Cassidy faltered, took a breath, as if readying herself for something. "And when you're tense or angry or worried, you always close this hand first."

Mia tilted her head. All this time she had been watching this crew, assessing their habits, their lives, their faults, it seemed they had been watching her, too. Or at least Cassidy watched.

She shrugged awkwardly. "It's out of reflex."

"It's horrible, what these Acedians did to you." Cassidy's eyes were still on the scar, fingers still tracing it. It seemed she couldn't look away. Or did not want to look away. "Who are they?"

"I don't know where they're from. They just attack people, attack civilizations. Anybody." Mia stopped, her gaze transfixed on the woman who hadn't shied away from her. The whole truth wasn't out. Not yet. "They're human, but they aren't. They have scars, dozens sometimes, all over their bodies. Most of the time in places that can be easily hidden so they can look normal if they need to."

Cassidy's forehead wrinkled, and she squinted at the mark. "What do all the scars mean?"

"They symbolize a capture or kill." Mia imagined how many marks she would have to etch into her skin had she followed that tradition. Cassidy seemed to be thinking the same.

Finally, she met Mia's gaze. "Do you have any?"

Mia waited a moment, guilt twisting her stomach, as she formed her reply. A breeze chilled her. Or was it the truth that made her so cold? In the end, all she could manage was, "I don't have physical scars."

Cassidy didn't seem to notice Mia's rigid posture. She gasped. "Do you think that's who attacked here?"

"It's why they weren't stopped originally." Mia frowned. "The officers just assumed they were another transport ship docking at Paradous. Not the scourge that would wipe out half the planet."

"And the fight you had on Pargon," Cassidy said slowly. "It was them?"

Yes," Mia replied. "One of them followed and attacked me."

Cassidy's gaze never left Mia's face. Mia fidgeted under her scrutiny. The hum of the Paradousian ships above floated around them, but the screams had died away.

"You lost." It was a statement, not a question that fell from Cassidy's lips.

Mia nodded.

"And Sheryl? She wasn't one of them."

The combination of Cassidy's unwavering gaze and her hand still pressing down on Mia's hand broke her. Shame burned her neck as words tumbled from her. "No, she wasn't. She was murdered by them. For no reason other than she knew me, that I was with her when they attacked me. For no other reason than she was simply there helping me find you, they killed her. I couldn't." Mia stopped, words stuck, bile in her throat. She ripped her gaze off Cassidy's face and searched her hands instead. They shook violently, one hand grasping hold of her arm, the other, in Cassidy's lap. "If I got there sooner maybe I could have stopped them. I could have warned her. I should have done something more. I should've stopped them."

Cassidy closed her hand around Mia's, holding on until the trembling stopped. When Mia finally gathered enough courage to look up, tears formed in the corner of Cassidy's eyes. She glanced down and traced the scar on Mia's hand once more. Again, Mia hoped she would never stop. Never let go.

"And the ship that attacked the *Eclipse*?"

"Also one of theirs." They reached troublesome ground. Mia had hoped the scrutiny would stop at the knowledge of the Acedians. She was wrong.

"Not pirates." Cassidy stopped tracing Mia's scar and lifted her head, catching Mia's eyes with her own. "They said they had come to collect you. Was it the first time they tried?"

Mia's stomach sank and her breath hitched. What to tell her? To say yes would be lying, but to say no? A whole different universe surrounded the question and the ones that would surely come after. Mia could get shipped off to one of the prison planets where she belonged. Still, maybe Cassidy would understand. She had to try. Had to risk it. Just this once.

"No, there were other times when the ship I was on became a target for the Acedians," Mia said quietly, drawing her hand away from Cassidy's reach.

Cassidy rubbed her cheek, eyeing Mia. Fear had already started to build in her eyes. "How did you get away before?"

"I did the only thing I could think of," Mia said. When Cassidy remained silent, Mia pushed on, "I destroyed their targets."

"You...destroyed their targets." Cassidy glanced down then up again as she realized what Mia meant. "The ships?"

"Yes," Mia said.

"Were there people on the ships?" The slow way Cassidy asked that question burned.

Mia flitted her gaze down, unable to trust her voice any longer.

"You killed people?"

Truth, especially a painful truth, often sounds worse when passing through someone else's lips. Mia winced, as if the words had physically hit her. It took all that Mia had to jerk her head down once in reply. Cassidy stilled for a moment as full realization settled upon her. When Mia finally looked up, the fear in Cassidy's eyes was fresh, real. Her brown eyes shimmered with it. As if by reflex, she threw herself backward and stumbled to her feet.

"You killed people?" She trembled. "But you just told me you don't have scars."

"I don't," Mia replied. "I don't kill people for the sport of it, like they do. I don't hunt strangers down and murder them."

The sight of her crewmate—blast it—her friend, so afraid of her made Mia sick. Cassidy kept shaking her head, eyes wide, lips quivering, and stepped back, as if waiting for the punch line on some gruesome joke. When none came, she turned and fled.

Once alone, for even a few seconds, the beat of her heart crashed against Mia, as if with each thud the Acedian cage drew ever closer, locking onto their prey. Tears, unbidden, fell down her cheeks. What had she done? The weight of her decision pressed in on her. The ground seemed to lurch. Cassidy ran away from her. What had she done? She rose to her feet and took off after her, boots catching the uneven surfaces of the cracked stone.

Cassidy hadn't gotten far. It took less than a minute to catch up with her, but during those few moments thoughts jumbled within Mia.

How Cassidy needed to understand, how she needed Cassidy to understand, how she needed someone to hear her out and maybe, just maybe, see why she did those things. Mia needed that much.

Reaching out, Mia grabbed Cassidy's elbow. Cassidy's hand came out of nowhere and connected with Mia's cheek. Hard. Mia recoiled from the slap, stepping backward and stumbling over loose concrete. She grabbed her stinging cheek, still wet from tears.

"Get away from me!" Cassidy's shout rang through the empty street. She cried, too. Mia knew Cassidy's tears were not for the lives lost. The way Cassidy looked at her now, with such fear, such confusion, said it all. Those tears were for something lost between them. Trust. Loyalty. Friendship. Mia couldn't bring herself to even consider more.

"I didn't think there was anything else I could do. I was so young." Mia reached out. Cassidy slapped the hand away, stepping backward. Mia desperately pushed on. She had to make sure Cassidy understood why such horrible deeds were done. "I couldn't live through another attack, and I didn't want to see anyone captured."

Mia flashed through the memories, all the faces she had known for mere months at a time, until the Acedians found her again. All the people she had desperately tried to ignore so, in the last few moments before the bombs exploded, she would not turn back, would not try to save them, would not care. Cassidy's form dominated Mia's blurred vision as reality snapped back. Cassidy had stopped moving away from her, poised to flee and yet motionless, listening.

Mia's breath quickened as she spoke. "There was screaming on the Acedian ship, so much screaming. I didn't want anyone to go through it, to know who they were and to be friends with them even, and have them be captured. The Acedians do horrible things to those they capture. I couldn't handle it." The words tumbled out before Mia could stop them. It had been too long and already she was in too deep with this particular crew. With this particular woman. "So I destroyed the ships. I pulled the emergency alarm before the bombs exploded, some of them got out okay, but most of them didn't." She stopped, her memories grasping her voice, holding it captive. She spit the next words out. "I ended their lives before the Acedians could get to them. Before the Acedians could ruin their lives like the hunters ruined mine. I had to."

The air stilled between them. Seconds, minutes, hours, it seemed, passed before Cassidy spoke again. "You did this when you were younger." The implication was hard to miss, even without the questioning tone. Fear played on Cassidy's face, knitting her eyebrows together. It danced in her body, moving her away, tensing her shoulders.

"I did it four times, four ships, the last of them three and a half years ago." Mia rustled around in her pocket for the list. She handed the list to Cassidy. Cassidy's eyes swept over the crumpled paper, reading the names out loud.

"*Oasis*. *Scarlet*. *Luminaria*. *Jubilee*." Cassidy's eyes met hers. Mia saw Cassidy's chest rise and fall rapidly, her nostrils flared, lips tightened. "Where's the *Eclipse*?"

Mia shook her head. "The *Eclipse* was never on there."

Cassidy kept her eyes trained on Mia's. "Why not?"

"I haven't destroyed it." Mia frowned.

"Do you plan to?" Mia had to make Cassidy believe her. She stilled. "No."

Cassidy's shoulders loosened as that simple word reached her ears. "Why should I believe you?"

"Because if I had wanted to destroy the *Eclipse*, I would have done it when the Acedians attacked the first time," Mia replied evenly. "I wouldn't have ordered us to run."

The answer settled between them.

"Why even keep the names of the ships?" Cassidy asked, shoving the paper to Mia.

"I keep them to remember," Mia began, taking the slip of paper back and looking at the names scribbled on it. "So when this is over, when I finally break free of these people, I can write letters to those who lost someone on one of those ships. To apologize for what I've done."

The answer seemed to pacify Cassidy's inclination to run. With a calmness that surprised Mia, she moved forward, one step closer. It seemed fear had left her, for now.

Cassidy shoved her hands into her pockets only to remove them again. "Do you even feel sorrow for those you've killed?"

The question shocked Mia. Tendrils of guilt and sadness pushed into her soul once more. She slipped the paper back into her pocket, cutting through the emotions within her. "Every day."

"You grinned when you saw that woman in the street today." Cassidy motioned in the direction of the control center.

"I don't know why I smiled. It just happened." Mia shrugged helplessly. "I felt guilty afterward, if that helps."

"It doesn't." Cassidy looked away, her mouth set in a thin line. The wind caressed her face, gently tugging at strands of her hair. They stood in silence for a while, so close to each other Mia could sense when Cassidy breathed and they were still galaxies apart.

"Are you going to run away from me again?" Mia asked, yearning to know the answer. Dreading it.

"You know, in a way, I asked for it," Cassidy said quietly. "I wanted you to tell me, even when I knew it was hard for you. And you told me the truth."

Mia ran her hand through her hair. "You didn't answer the question."

Cassidy stared beyond her. "No, I'm not going to run away. Though I'm horrified by what you did in the past and terrified of what you might do in the future."

Heart twisting with every word, Mia nodded. She wanted to ask another question, just one more, but her soul couldn't bear to hear the answer. For once, reason won, and she blurted out, "Why aren't you more afraid of me?"

Cassidy looked back at her. "I've seen you when you don't think anyone is watching. You try to hide it. It messes with you just the same. Those lives haunt you. As they should and I'm glad they do. It's when you stop caring, stop being crushed by them, it's then I'll be scared of you."

Mia shook her head, knowing all too well that she was afraid of herself, of the person she had become. "Any rational person would be frightened of me now."

"You should be happy I'm not being rational." Cassidy smiled slightly, and shifted her stance, leaning back on one foot, hooking her fingers through her belt. She turned and started walking in the direction of the warehouse. "We should go check on the boys."

Sunlight streamed down, darkening rays washing over Cassidy's back, as her long strides took her farther from Mia. Silence settled over them once more. Mia let herself smile, not a huge one, not overly enthusiastic, but a smile all the same. Mia slipped her glove back on and made her way after Cassidy.

Chapter Eleven

THEY WALKED BACK TO the warehouse in silence. The emotions surging through Mia could not be contained, and a hum escaped her lips. Cassidy looked back at her, eyes questioning the shift in Mia's mood. Let her wonder for a while, sift through her own feelings. At least she's not screaming and running away. Mia's heartbeat matched the speed of her hurried footfalls.

She tried to calm herself, but by the time they reached the safe haven, not even the wails of the injured within could burst the warm bubble growing in her soul. Finally, someone knew about her past. Finally, a person knew about the scar hidden under her glove. And to have that same someone accept her, however tenuously? Amazing.

Inside the haven, the atmosphere had shifted. The Dee parents sat together on the floor, closer to their pile of belongings. Elizabeth was nowhere to be seen, nor were the two brothers. Arai reached through the pile, clutching a snapper, before kissing its forehead and putting the cat-like toy next to her. Her eyes were tinged with red, though she seemed past the point of crying. Robert nodded as Mia and Cassidy joined them on the floor. A young nurse crouched over him and tended to wounds Mia had not noticed during their first meeting. Now, with Robert's overcoat pulled away, it was easy to see the blood on his nightshirt. There was a gash in the fabric and in his side.

Cassidy cried out as she saw the cut. "Are you going to be okay?"

The woman glanced over at Cassidy, a look of annoyance marring her otherwise unblemished face. Narrow gray eyes widened as the woman looked Cassidy up and down before turning back to her patient. Mia almost stumbled back. Gray eyes? Was the nurse Acedian? No. Couldn't be. Mia's scar didn't hurt at all. And why would an Acedian be helping a Paradousian? The nurse's eyes glinted a darker gray than the Acedians anyway. A lock of thick, black hair fell over the woman's shoulder, a dark contrast to her white attire. She hurriedly pushed it back, continuing her work. Mia noticed, with a twinge, that a smile played on the nurse's lips. The nurse used helofoam on Robert's cut.

The orange foam spread, covering the wound, and Robert sighed. Apparently, it was an analgesic, too.

The woman took a quick glance in Cassidy's direction. "It's just a small laceration. Stop worrying. He'll heal." She turned back to Robert. "As long as you don't move too quickly for at least another day."

Robert grunted and put an arm around his wife. The woman in white took off her gloves and put them in a black bag slung over her shoulder. She seemed young to Mia, too young to be an official healer. Nineteen or twenty. Maybe the military had called in more help. With the moans of others calling her, the woman turned and started walking away. Within a few steps, she stopped and glanced back at them over her shoulder. It seemed her gaze gravitated more toward Cassidy than to her patient. "I'll be back in an hour, to see how the bandage is taking. See you soon."

Cassidy nodded her thanks. The warm bubble in Mia fluctuated. Perhaps the overabundance of kindness in Cassidy was not such a good quality. Mia folded her legs underneath her and glanced around the warehouse, careful to not meet Cassidy's gaze. The lights, so bright before, had been dimmed to reflect the darkness growing outside as dusk approached. The air warmed. People spoke in hushed tones, gathered around the clothes and keepsakes collected from the ruins.

"Where are Jeff and Will?" Mia asked, when no conversation breached the silence.

"My sons stalked off to a more secluded area," Robert said.

"The officers moved healthy citizens to a different area," Arai added. "A safe place, of course, so this area wouldn't be so crowded. Elizabeth went with them."

"Are you two all right?" Robert asked, glancing at both her and Cassidy. By the way he examined them, he seemed to know some quarrel had taken place.

"We're fine." Mia was hesitant to say any more.

Cassidy leaned forward. "He was just a bit mad. It was nothing, honest. I'm sure Will can take care of it."

"That boy always had a terrible temper," Robert said gruffly, eyes trained at the wall next to him. His gaze flicked to Mia, who nodded, understanding the hidden warning. He and Arai exchanged a long look. Her lip trembled.

"If you want," Cassidy blurted out. Mia grimaced, knowing Cassidy would do something rash and volunteer to search for them. To help them. It was in her nature to do so. "I can go find them, again, see how they're doing?"

"That might be best," Arai whispered, not to anyone in particular. "Robert, can you please go with her? I doubt they'd want to see me right now."

Robert nodded, got to his feet, and wandered off. Cassidy rose, took a quick look at Mia, and followed the man. Cassidy's receding form weighed heavy on her. How was she to take care of Arai herself?

As if on cue, a stifled sob came from the woman as she pulled a ball from the heap. It seemed to be a useless thing, tiny, with decorative grooves embossed into the metal and a small button on the base. The metal ball looked like nothing to Mia, but Arai held the object close to her. With a shaking finger, Arai pushed the button. An image flashed to life in front of them. Fuzzy around the edges, the image was clearly Jeff, a younger, longhaired version. Similar to the commemoration pyramid, the ball had to be a memorea, a storage device that saved and displayed family images. Mia's mother had one as well that was much smaller, the size of a kax berry, if that.

"All boys have a temper." Mia leaned back on one hand, the floor cool under her gloves.

"Not our William," Arai said, after a time. She pushed the button again and a young Will flashed into view. "William was the troublemaker, playing with things he shouldn't, touching live wires and such."

"He hasn't changed much." Mia smiled slightly.

"He was never an angry boy," Arai continued. "Jeffery's the one who needs calming." She never once looked up from the images that flashed, every push of the button bringing up more holoimages of the brothers. It seemed better to let her ramble. An image hung in the air between them, the brothers, dressed in the finest blue and black Zephyr suits the Academy could manage. Arai took a breath. "Did you know William was the one that dreamt of the Academy?"

Taken aback at the sudden question, Mia struggled to answer. It was only after she made a soft, noncommittal noise, and Arai rambled on, that Mia realized the mother wasn't really asking.

"Jeffery never wanted to go. He only went so he could watch William. He's so protective. Jeffery became an engineer so he could enlist with William as his second. No one would say no to a duo." Mia nodded, even though Arai didn't seem to notice. She certainly hadn't rejected their deal. "They graduated in record time, two years where most took four, excellent grades." Here Arai glanced up from the image, her reddened eyes meeting Mia's. "We were so proud when they joined your crew, helping a young woman start her own business and another with a ship of her own. So proud. It's lovely to meet you, by the way."

"I wish it were under better circumstances, Mrs. Dee." Formality sprinkled into Mia's speech, both as a sign of respect and from nerves under Arai's unhappy gaze. "It's good to meet you, too."

Mia ran a hand through her hair, rubbing her neck as she stared at the woman. Arai pushed the button again and up flashed an image of a young girl Mia had never seen before. Her shoulder-length, golden-brown hair, and green eyes stood out against her dark skin and the even darker background.

"Sarah." Arai uttered the single word then dissolved into tears. Her breaths came in ragged gasps, shoulders heaving against the seemingly crushing sensation of losing a child.

Mia watched for a moment before looking away, focusing on the pile of belongings instead. A mirror caught her attention, her own blue eyes reflecting back at her. The warm bubble of happiness threatened to burst. Thoughts of losing Cassidy drifted through Mia, of brown eyes closing forever, just like everyone else's. The sadness inched deeper. Mia clenched her jaw and breathed.

It was easier this time to push the emotions down. She was able to calm herself in seconds, where usually it would have taken minutes, or longer. Her scar throbbed, as if she had grabbed a chunk of ice with her bare hand. A shuddering gasp from Arai distracted Mia. She focused on the noise, cocking her head to look in Arai's direction.

The mother sat, bawling. And even though it was not her place, even though she felt awkward doing so, Mia moved closer to Arai. The mother's sobs heaved her body this way and that, tears splashing onto her nightshirt, calling attention to the clumsy way the fabric draped around her figure. Even her clothes seemed weak. Pathetic really. The thought skittered in and out of Mia's mind before she could do anything about it. She pursed her lips, wondering what the blast she was going to say to the mother who lost her child. Because of her. Mia shook her head. She tried to think of what Cassidy would do in this situation, how Cassidy would react. It came to her. The mother didn't move when Mia gingerly placed an arm around her shoulders or pull away when Mia wrapped the arm around her in a sideways hug.

Arai buried her face into Mia's shoulder, wrapped her long arms around Mia's midsection, and cried. Teardrops carved a cold path down

Mia's neck as she put her arms around Arai and squeezed in what she hoped was a reassuring way.

Her attempts at consoling seemed wrong, the way she rubbed Arai's back, her quiet murmurs. Regardless of how she tried, her muscles would not relax, would not give in to this woman sobbing on her. Not at all like Cassidy. How could she relate to this woman? An image surfaced in her, of a teenage girl with chopped, red hair desperately clinging to a girl not much older, a blonde with auburn eyes. How Freya had comforted her those long days and nights alone. Mia squeezed Arai harder, remembering how the warm pressure of Freya's body became a reassurance. A rock through her tormented waves.

Wisps of Arai's hair stuck to Mia's chin, nose, and neck. The woman smelled clean, freshly washed almost, no coppery scent about her, no blood staining her clothes. A mumbling noise came from Mia's shoulder.

"It was so frightening," Arai managed. "I had heard the announcement over the speakers, of the restaurant's opening, and I took a bath to clean up. I took a bath instead of spending time with my daughter." She eased herself off of Mia and pushed a hand over mouth, as if trying to stop the sobs. Her face contorted, lines crisscrossing her forehead and around her eyes. She lowered her hand. "When I came downstairs the men had already come through the door. Sarah was just standing there. If anything, the shot should have been aimed at me. Not Sarah, not my baby."

Arai buried herself in Mia's arms again. An image flashed of Mia's mother slumping to the deck. She gritted her teeth against the memories that welled up inside. The happy bubble burst. Tears prickled in her eyes. She wanted Arai to stop recounting her daughter's death, to stop the memories from overwhelming both of them.

After a time, the tears finally ceased, and Arai breathed in what seemed to be a normal rhythm. Mia, too, finally found the strength to speak. "There's never enough time with the ones we love."

Arai drew back, her cheeks blazing a deep red and eyes watering. She searched Mia's face. Her voice trembled. "Spoken like one who's lost someone."

Mia had to swallow the tears bubbling from within, holding herself tense to keep from flying into this mother's arms. "I've lost quite a few, Mrs. Dee." The formality flowed back as she moved away, giving Arai, and herself, space.

"I'm sorry," Arai whispered. "No one your age should hold such sorrow."

She placed a hand on Mia's shoulder, warm, heavy, too much like Freya's, and like Cassidy's, for Mia's liking. Mia turned away, tearing herself from Arai's unwavering gaze. When did this turn into a commiseration for her instead of for a mother who lost her child? Anger flared deep within Mia, replacing the grief with fury, burning away the sorrow leeching into her body. She didn't need this mother's pity.

"Nor should a mother mourn for her own child's death," she said. A horrible truth, but Mia couldn't help it. She had to distance herself.

"True," came the murmured reply.

In spite of herself, Mia glanced up.

When Arai spoke next, her voice was the calmest Mia had heard since they met. "I have people surrounding me to help hold such a burden. Do you have such a thing, Captain?"

The starkness of her words, coming from one who had just bared her soul, hit Mia with such a force she leaned back, as if trying to get away from the truth that rang within them. Of the pain hidden deep in their meaning.

"That's none of your concern, Mrs. Dee," Mia muttered, rising to her feet. "My condolences for your loss. If my crew and I can do anything to help you, or your family, please say so. For now, I must be on my way." As if the last few moments had never happened, she turned on her heel and walked away.

Chapter Twelve

MIA DIDN'T GET FAR. Only a few feet away from Arai, a hand on her shoulder stopped her, and she looked up. Cassidy stood in front of her. The weight of her hand grew heavy, as if she needed support. Mia straightened.

"You should come with us," Cassidy muttered.

At Mia's questioning glance, Cassidy tilted her head. Robert, and the woman in white who had patched him up, lingered behind. The nurse seemed antsy, shifting her weight back and forth, grasping a small, flat device in her hand. Cassidy merely squeezed Mia's shoulder and they wandered back.

Arai looked up as Mia sat down across from her. Mia did not return the mother's lingering scrutiny. Robert crouched next to his wife, and the black-haired nurse hovered around them. Cassidy sat close to Mia, their shoulders touched.

"Nurse Jones has some more information for us," Robert said.

"The military found another undamaged camera." The woman didn't say it was from Sarah's death. Perhaps she couldn't. "They analyzed it already and determined you should be the ones to have it. Here."

She shoved the tiny device in Arai's direction. When Arai did not respond, Robert took the chip. The woman sat down beside Cassidy, stretching her legs out in front of her. It seemed she intended to stay and watch. Mia scowled. How did a nurse get assigned the job of being a messenger? The woman's white trench coat flipped open, revealing a white shirt that draped open at the neck, skintight black pants, and gray shoes. She looked all too comfortable in such a sad atmosphere.

Robert fumbled with fitting the chip into the holocard. With the way he handled it, too rough, too rushed, it seemed he didn't actually want to. Mia understood. What father would? Still, if that chip held information about the Acedians, it could prove useful.

"Breach it! Here," the woman in white scoffed. She leaned over, grabbing both the chip and the holocard. She slid the chip into a tiny slot in the side and pointed to a square screen on the bottom. "If you touch this, it'll start playing for you." Without waiting for approval, she activated the chip.

An image flashed up, fuzzy around the edges. The Dee household appeared. No, just outside the Dee home, this recorder had been pointed into one of their little windows. Through that window, the inner workings of the Dee's residence could be seen, the pale blue walls, the mismatched furniture, the circular rug on the floor. Arai was just walking down the stairs. Elizabeth sat on one of the chairs, facing the window, reading. Sarah stood next to her father. The recorder did not catch their words.

The Dee's door cracked, weaknesses in the wood splintering, shattering forward. Shards scattered on the rug at Sarah and Robert's feet. Elizabeth started, her archivist falling from her hands. Robert and Sarah moved back a pace. Two men, both dressed in loose, brown clothing, barreled in and looked around. Their black vests and dark boots stood out in the lighter surroundings. For a few moments they stood there—the two strangers on one side, the Dee family on the other—as if frozen from fear, from shock, from indecision perhaps.

A movement startled Mia, and she glanced away from the images. Arai huddled against Robert and buried her face in his chest. He stared at his wife. Mia's hairs rose on her arms. Someone was watching her. Mia stole a quick look about. Cassidy? No, she was transfixed on the image before them. The nurse. The woman's gaze fixed on Mia, analyzing her, angry at her even. The device in her hand shook, a vein in her neck pulsed. Why? The nurse smirked, tight lipped, and turned to the holoimage once more. Mia did the same.

One man, the taller of the two, moved his hand fast, too fast for Mia to see, too fast to be humanly possible. One moment it hung by his side, the next it threw a needle at Sarah. She slumped to the floor. The reaction was instantaneous. Elizabeth's scream pierced through the device. Robert bellowed, moving toward the men. The tall one turned and left. His partner threw another needle, slicing Robert's side and dropping him to his knee. The man followed his partner out. Flames started to consume the Dee home. Robert shoved his wife and daughter out. Coming back for Sarah's body.

The recorder picked up something else, something closer. The two men walked into view of the lens. One had his back to the recorder, and the other stood facing it. Their conversation came through clearer. Mia's hand flared, and, for a moment, she tensed. It took her a few seconds to realize Cassidy had jerked beside her, squeezing her hand a bit too tightly. Distracted by that feeling, she missed a small part of the conversation between the two men.

"—kidding, Donavin," the man was saying. "We have to finish this. It's taking too long." A scar traveled above this man's right eye, shadowed a little by the large-brimmed hat he wore. Acedian. Mia didn't recognize him. Another voice answered, lower, deeper, the man facing away from them. A man with blond hair.

"We don't need to worry about that. Don't bring it up again."

"What about the girl?"

"Don't bring it up again! Or are you too much of an imbecile to understand that, Bern?"

"Fine. Is it time to get moving, Charles?" the first man said, sneering at the last word.

The man named Charles Donavin nodded and turned. Mia's breath caught. He looked straight into the lens, as if he knew it was there, as if he knew Mia was there, watching. He tilted his head upward. Smiled. Mia's breath caught. Cold spread from her head down, an icy wave crashing over her frame, freezing both her mind and body. The holoimage paused, stopped with Donavin looking at her, tilting his head up so she could clearly see the long, brown scar running deep across his neck.

Chapter Thirteen

CASSIDY TURNED TOWARD MIA, her lips moved, the words never reaching Mia's ears. Mia found him, the one who had scarred her, the one who had destroyed everything she knew. Everything she loved. After twelve years of searching every blasted region of the galaxy she could reach, after being hunted by them and running from them, she had finally found him.

Mia's vision hazed, blurring all that surrounded her. She compiled everything she knew of this man. At age thirteen she'd first encountered him, a giant menacing figure. A scar across his neck. As the years passed, other things had filtered into her memory: blond hair, brown eyes, and small, crooked lips. The image on the nurse's holocard only solidified Mia's memory of him. Did this woman know more about him? About the Acedians?

A sudden gasp brought Mia back to the warehouse. Familiar black hair and broad shoulders towered over the woman in white, a few paces beyond their seats.

"What else do you know?" Jeff grasped the woman's arm. Will moved next to his brother, and Mia stood. She didn't like the nurse, but she had no doubt Jeff could do some serious damage if he wanted to. People in the warehouse stood up, trying to see, forming a small circle around them. Cassidy's sidelong glance confirmed her agreement about Jeff's temper. Even the brothers' parents rose from their seats.

"She doesn't. She's just the messenger." Will gently pried Jeff's death grip from the nurse's shoulders. The woman stood motionless, unwavering in spite of the man's anger. "You realize that."

Jeff pointed at the device in her hand. "You must know more! Why else would they send a nurse to do an officer's job?"

The man had a point. He shook Will off and moved closer still. Amazingly, the woman smiled up at him.

"Breach it! Do you Paradousians always come on this strong?" She slid a hand along the sleeve of her coat to smooth out the wrinkles. Jeff's ears darkened. He backed off a step, giving the woman space. Her smoldering eyes looked Jeff up and down, much like they had observed Cassidy earlier. "What else do I know? Plenty. But I'm going to tell the admiral, not you. So, excuse me, feisty, I need to pay a visit to the headquarters thwarting their little terrorist attack and give our people some crucial information."

She pushed past Jeff, walking quickly toward the exit.

"Their who?" Jeff shouted. The nurse looked back. Her gaze fell on each member of the *Eclipse*'s crew, Jeff first—arms at his side, jaw clenched in fury—then Will—hovering around his older brother—Cassidy—who lingered next to her. The woman's eyes found Mia's.

"The Acedians," the nurse said, a small grimace passing over her face like the words themselves tasted sour. The raven-haired woman winked at Jeff and sashayed away, her black satchel swinging against her hip with each step she took.

Flabbergasted, Mia could only watch. Her shoulders tightened just from hearing their name. She tried to keep her expression as neutral as possible. She hoped Cassidy did the same. A quick glance showed that she had.

Jeff turned toward his brother. "Acedians? Who is that?"

Will shrugged and put his arm around his brother's shoulders. Slowly, he led Jeff back over to their parents. Mia hoped, vainly, that Will would not see or speak to her that maybe Will would be so involved with his older brother he would not ask of her what he so clearly should. As he passed by Mia he turned to her, eyes dark with sorrow, and whispered, "Captain, find out something, will you, for his sake?"

Mia nodded, and Will walked on. She sighed, watching the brothers slowly make their way back into their circle. Robert and Arai drew Jeff into their arms. Mia looked away, watching as the nurses stopped by each group, whispering something and handing out large bags of supplies. The survivors seemed to rally themselves into motion, children ripping open the parcels to find sleeping squares, emergency rations, and nightwear inside, and adults shoving belongings out of the way to make way for the beds.

Mia's conscience weighed heavily upon her shoulders. Were it not for her dragging Will and Jeff into this, these people would be sitting in their homes, going about their peaceful lives, not jammed inside a warehouse. Did she want to hurt Cassidy's friends as well, Cassidy's homeplanet? Should she break her promise to Cassidy and start planting bombs on the *Eclipse*? She shifted, uncomfortable. Mia silently thanked the controller of the lights for they dimmed even further, blocking her own sorrow from view.

Movement in the corner caused Mia to turn. A nurse stopped by the Dee family and gave them a bag of supplies. Arai nodded her thanks and opened the bag. Cassidy wandered over to them, her dark clothes making her nearly invisible in the dimming light. She knelt down to help Arai with the sleeping squares—setting the boxes on the floor, inputting a code, watching while the boxes expanded into fully furnished cots—while Robert and Will pushed their piles of belongings farther into the corner.

Standing off to one side, Jeff watched. Only when the clothes were laid out did Jeff move again and pull on his nightwear, a long yellow shirt that ended by wrapping around his legs. Kissing his mother goodnight, he slipped into the cot farthest from the others and yanked the sheets over his head. Arai handed out garments and rations to Cassidy and Will, speaking to them each in turn, and walked over to Mia. She tensed uncomfortably, their last conversation replaying in her mind.

"Goodnight, Captain Mia," Arai said. "I hope only happiness follows you into that realm. I'll see you when the sun rises."

With that, she handed the last pair of nightwear to Mia, slipped an emergency ration into her palm, and left, melting into the darkness. Where was she going? The answer penetrated Mia like a needle. Arai was going to sleep in the safehouse next to Elizabeth, next to her only daughter. The garments seemed to get heavier to Mia, the yellow fabric too bright for her mood. She stared at the emergency ration split perfectly down the middle. The top portion was compressed food—usually bread or vegetables of some sort—and the bottom portion consisted of a small square of picobots programmed to heat the food. Far from hunger, guilt wrenched her stomach. She had brought this destruction to these people, and they still gave her food, drinks, and shelter. She stuffed the square into her pocket and dropped the clothes onto a cot.

Will sidled up next to her. Already in the standard nightclothes given to them and looking slightly ridiculous, he raised his arms. The clothes were made for a teenager, not a man. His arms stuck out from the sleeves a bit, the yellow cloth with black piping draped awkwardly around his figure, and the fabric didn't even reach his ankles. Will smiled, a small grin that never reached his hazel eyes.

"Fancy, huh?" He motioned to his haphazard appearance. "They really go all out when a disaster strikes." The jest vanished in the silence between them. Mia didn't know whether to smile or slap him for even attempting the joke. When she did neither, Will continued, "You can settle down with us, if you want. They gave us extra sleeping squares."

She shook her head. "No, I need to keep an eye on the *Eclipse*."

"Why?" Will asked, shoulders slumping a bit.

"The military searched her, and I want to be sure she's all right," Mia replied.

"I'd want you to be close in case." Will faltered. Shifted. "No separating, remember?"

"We can just take a quick walk to the old girl, see how she's doing and come back, does that sound okay?" Cassidy's voice, next to her, startled Mia. She turned, and sure enough, her shadow had returned. How long had she been standing there this time? Will glanced at the two women for a long time before nodding.

"Yes, that does sound better." He puffed out his chest. "After all, we all need to follow the captain's orders." He nudged Mia, who smiled softly in return. Even that simple gesture was a lie. Will put a hand on Cassidy's arm for a moment before wandering back to his family.

Mia and Cassidy walked toward the exit, gingerly stepping over sleeping figures. Cassidy opened the warehouse door, and they slipped through. A cold burst of air hit them. The famous night wind of Paradous howled. They walked into the wind. Cassidy moved closer to Mia. Even with the jacket on she shivered. She rubbed her nose with the back of her hand and sniffed. Mia's ears grew numb as they linked arms.

Cassidy looked downright chilled to the bone, lips quivering slightly, and nose wrinkling. Mia unhooked their arms. Cassidy shifted from the sudden wind at her side, but when Mia wrapped an arm around Cassidy's shoulders, she relaxed again. They walked like that for a while. Cassidy wrapped her arm around Mia's waist in return, sharing warmth. The contact sent sparks through Mia's body. She ignored it. Had to. But when she glanced at Cassidy, Mia noted her first mate had a soft smile on her lips. Mia's stomach did a little flip before she could control herself once more. The wind died down for a moment.

"What do you think they did to the *Eclipse*?"

"I bet they landlocked her." Mia looked at the darkened sky. Clouds and smoke blocked the starlight.

"They didn't do that on Pargon," Cassidy said, her voice almost getting carried away by a short breeze.

"They didn't deal with a full-scale attack when we were there." Mia's thoughts lingered in the darkness for the moment, wondering if the ones taken from this planet were being branded. Just like her. She frowned. The woman Cassidy had been talking to on Pargon flashed to Mia's thoughts. "I'm sorry for pulling you away from that woman, by the way."

Cassidy glanced at her. "Katarina? Don't worry about it. We were done with our conversation anyway." She might have said one thing, but her body hinted at another. She moved away, not much, just enough for chill to seep up Mia's side.

"Who was she?" Mia asked, a little too innocently.

"Just a friend."

A pang of jealousy flowed through Mia. Ridiculous. "Did you hear any more noises on the *Eclipse*?"

"No," Cassidy replied sharply. Mia glanced at her. A faint blush had spread across her ears. Or was that because of the cold?

They arrived at the ship. Mia opened the hatch, and they stepped through. Once inside, Cassidy removed her arm from Mia's waist and led the way down the corridors to the kitchen. Mia followed, watching Cassidy as she sat down on the couch. Nothing seemed removed, but everything seemed off, chairs locked down in the wrong places, cupboards left unlatched, and pillows strewn on the table. The military had been in here for sure.

Mia quickly made some tea and gave one cup to Cassidy, keeping one for herself. Cassidy nodded her thanks. The attitude shifted slightly. It was more...comfortable on the ship. Jealousy still ebbed through Mia's heart over Katarina. Why she should be jealous was a whole other reason she didn't want to deal with. She couldn't be jealous. Shouldn't.

"Charles Donavin killed your parents," Cassidy said, her voice calm and quiet in the ship.

"Yes," Mia said, too startled to say anything else. Cassidy had gotten right to the point, just not the point Mia was preparing for. "How did you know?"

"Your attitude changed the moment you saw that man's face. And with the scar on his neck, I knew he had to be the one." Cassidy scratched her leg, tucking it under her, not meeting Mia's eyes.

"You're quite observant," Mia whispered.

"Well you're quite obvious," Cassidy replied with a small grin.

A rush of desire threw Mia off balance. Mia adored that smile, the way Cassidy's lips turned up ever so slightly as if knowing a secret. A lover's smile almost. The expression faded as quickly as it had appeared, drifting into the darkness like a lost soul.

"What are you going to do about it?"

"Hunt him down," Mia said.

Cassidy sipped some of her tea. "And what will you do to him when you finally capture him?"

It came as a shock to Mia that she had never asked it of herself. She had fantasized about how she would catch him during the long dark nights aboard strange ships and even stranger planets, about how she would hunt the man down and tower over him. Somehow she would make him feel the fear she had hidden deep within her and make him endure the pain. But the dreams never went into what she would do to him. How would she handle herself when face-to-face with this Charles Donavin?

"What should I do?" Mia asked. She searched Cassidy's face, gauging her reaction, as a small frown created lines in Cassidy's cheeks.

"You should do what your heart tells you." Cassidy's eyes caught the limited light and Mia's at the same time, glimmering. That Mia took those words immediately into her soul was a mark of how deep their friendship had blossomed. Cassidy shrugged and pulled her legs up to her chin.

Mia looked at her. That simple remark sparked something. In the midst of all of this horror and destruction, something deep inside her stirred, an emotion she'd tried to conceal for so long gently seeped through the cracks. The woman before her seemed to change, to grow even more beautiful, more radiant. Curled up, sipping tea, and gazing at something unknown to Mia, Cassidy was simply amazing. Mia's mouth went slack, a tingling sensation drifted through her body as realization hit. She was in love with Cassidy. She loved this kind, happy woman who went through Helix and back again, who didn't let her past tarnish her gentle soul. The woman questioned and pushed Mia to no end. The opposite of Mia in all ways, and Mia loved her for it. But did she feel the same way? Too soon to tell.

"What would you do?" Mia's thoughts finally ended in a confusing spiral, much too close to her heart.

"We should tell the others about the Acedians," Cassidy said, shifting her knees out from under her, stretching her legs, and leaning back on the armrest. A sneaky shift in topic.

Mia took the bait anyway. "No."

"Mia, come on." Cassidy tilted her head. "You know more about them than anyone here."

"What about that other woman? The nurse with the holocard?"

"Who, Skyler Jones?"

Mia tilted an eyebrow up at Cassidy's instant knowledge of the woman's name.

As if reading her mind, Cassidy continued, "She told us her name when we first met, remember?" Mia didn't. "She certainly knows what they're called. Maybe she was attacked by them like you." Cassidy sat up straighter, putting a hand on Mia's knee. Warmth spread from Cassidy's touch, but Mia tried to push that sensation away, tried to focus on what Cassidy was saying. "Maybe she got away before anything happened. You're right. She might have some information that you don't. Some information you could use. You should talk to her."

The idea of Cassidy getting overly attentive with the black-haired nurse, who was obviously attracted to Cassidy, riled Mia more than she let on. Plus, she couldn't actually help anyone anyway. She hurt people. Not helped. A simple shake of her head was her only reply. Cassidy slumped slightly forward and removed her hand from Mia's knee. The warmth lingered for a moment then disappeared.

Cassidy frowned again. "Don't be an idiot. These people could really use the information you have. You were attacked by them, scarred by them. You know them."

"Not well enough." Mia hands clenched by her knees, fingers pushing into her gloves. Cassidy opened her mouth to speak but Mia pushed on, "Not well enough to help anyone. Don't you see? If I told anyone the things I know about the Acedians, don't you think they'd wonder how I'd come by such information? There would be questions, accusations, the fact that I destroyed four ships might even come up, and I'd land on one of the prison planets." Maybe that's what Cassidy actually wanted, for her to be shipped off to prison. It was the natural reaction when finding a killer. "Do you want me to go to a prison planet?"

Cassidy looked at her with wide eyes. Did that comment wound her in some way? Her voice got louder. Great, she was angry now, too. "If that's your fear, why did you even tell me about what happened?"

"Because you and your blasted crew would've figured it out eventually." Mia lied through her teeth, praying that Cassidy didn't notice. The truth seemed too personal to reveal right now, even to Cassidy, even to the woman who might return a truth of her own. Even to the woman she loved. "Anyway, I doubt the fact that I got attacked and scarred when I was younger would help the investigation now."

"You never know." Cassidy leaned back. When she looked at Mia again, her eyes were narrow, cold. "It's your decision, Captain. Sleep on it and see what you decide tomorrow."

"I already know my decision, and you can't speak of it either. To anyone."

"Is that an order?" Cassidy seethed at the last word.

Mia sighed. "It is."

"Fine," Cassidy snapped back. "We should go back."

The walk back passed quickly, silently. Mia blamed the howling wind for their lack of conversation. A fight. Already. Mia had already pushed Cassidy away. So much for having her feelings returned. Once at the warehouse, Cassidy went straight for her sleeping cot and curled up.

Mia separated the emergency ration, letting the gray picobots form a plate and watching as the center glowed white hot. She gingerly placed the food square on it. The square grew slowly into a bread loaf, sprinkled with green and brown. The glowing ceased, and Mia chewed on the crunchy bread. A gooey flood of spicy carotas burned her mouth. Mia winced but finished the bread anyway. Finally settling into her nightwear, Mia slipped inside her sleeping cot. The soft cloth slid wonderfully against her tired body. Her eyes closed of their own accord. Before the tendrils of sleep pulled her under, she heard Cassidy's voice, loud amidst the silence.

"I hope Skyler is more accommodating."

Chapter Fourteen

"WHAT ELSE DO YOU know?"

Mia's heavy lids opened to the sound of voices. Her vision blurry, she could not distinguish between the bodies that conversed above her. The ceiling slowly came into focus. Even though only one night had passed since she'd arrived on this planet, her body buzzed with the want of motion. She needed to move, to leave, to run. She forced herself to stay still, silent, listening.

"We know only what Jones told us." The low voice had to belong to Harrison, the admiral's lackey.

"That's not enough to go on," said Will.

"It's enough for now," Harrison replied. "The admiral wants every able-bodied person to search the grounds. He believes some of the missing may still be here. And the murderers might be hiding, too."

On the planet? That's what these people assume? The Acedians wouldn't stay after a raid. It wasn't in their nature. Moving slowly, she pushed herself into a sitting position, letting the sheets fall away. Goosebumps prickled her arms and neck. She shook the sleepy fog from her mind.

"Nice to see you're finally awake, Captain." Cassidy's voice drifted from somewhere to Mia's left. Mia waved in reply, glumly aware of the sharp tone in Cassidy's voice. Of course Cassidy would still be angry. Being forced into secrecy about something that might help others would be hard for her.

"Yes, Captain Foley, the admiral has a job for you and your crew," Harrison said.

He paused while Mia slid out of her bag and forced herself to stand. Her thigh throbbed. She ignored it, well aware of how many eyes were on her. It seemed both her crew and the Dee family had woken well before she had, even Arai and Elizabeth had returned. Thankful the others looked as disheveled as she, Mia glanced at Harrison. In a smart officer ensemble with his curly hair slicked back, he was clearly the best dressed of the group. "Your crew will be the fifth group out, accompanied by another survivor."

"Solid plan." Mia looked at her crew sitting around her. There were dark rings under Will's eyes, a muscle in Jeff's jaw twitched, and Cassidy, Mia noticed with a pang, didn't even meet her gaze. Having another pair of eyes to help search wouldn't be a horrible idea.

"Here's the survivor," Harrison said. "She requested specifically to be with you."

Skyler walked up beside him, clad in gray pants, a white wraparound shirt stretched too tightly over her ample bosom, and a sultry smile no one should be able to get away with. Mia rolled her eyes, as the raven-haired woman sat next to Will, and tensed when Skyler's gaze landed squarely on Cassidy. Cassidy smiled. Mia straightened, tilted her chin up an inch, and stared levelly at Harrison.

"Your team has been assigned the western part of the city. I've uploaded the coordinates in this archivist." He handed over the square slab, heavy in Mia's hand. She gave the device to Cassidy to hold. "Be sure to double check everything. We start immediately."

After a quick change into more suitable attire and a breakfast consisting of white porridge with slivers of agora fruit, the rest of the crew, including Skyler, joined the other search parties gathered at the warehouse door.

Mia, however, drifted off to the sidewall, pulling a nurse along with her. It seemed the cold winds from the night before had aggravated her thigh injury. She had forgotten it until just this morning. Gritting her teeth, she yanked the cream-colored pants up to reveal the patch job Will had done earlier.

The pretty nurse narrowed her green eyes. "When did you get this wound?"

"A few days back. Doesn't matter. Can you fix it?"

The nurse pulled the golden pins out, tore away the shiny purple film, and applied orange helofoam directly onto Mia's wound. The nurse didn't need to answer her question. Mia's throbbing disappeared, instantly. The nurse wrapped a white bandage around her leg and let Mia's pant leg fall to the ground.

"Be sure to change the bandage in a few days and don't overtax your leg too much. You'll be fine."

Mia thanked her and hurried through the crowd toward her crew. She sidled up next to Cassidy and was handed an archivist that flashed to life, depicting their search coordinates as a holoimage. Other holoimages blossomed around them as the rest of the search parties watched their own coordinates appear.

The doors swung open, sunlight streamed in, and the search parties filed out. Mia grimaced at the hopeless cause. None of the missing would be found here, and no Acedian would stay behind after a success like this. Cassidy walked ahead of her, eager to find clues to help the Paradousians. Mia sighed. Perhaps falling in love was not the best option. She brought destruction regardless of where she went, even to people she had never met. She longed to hold Cassidy's hand, to be close to her, to speak to her even. But Cassidy was too concerned with the search. And seemed to be too angry. Perhaps it was for the best.

On the third day a meeting with the admiral and his lackey landed her in a hard chair in headquarters. Time to be questioned again.

"William and Jeffery Dee were cleared a few days ago. They have identification chips implanted in their wrists—a common practice for Paradousian's—as well as family and friends claiming their citizenship." Harrison paced around her tiny chair. He tapped on the screen of the archivist he carried. The screen went dark, then brightened again. A turn of the page, perhaps. With his eyes glued to the screen, he continued to speak. "Cassidy Gates was also cleared. We were able to contact her homeworld, Skadi, and speak to the professors at the Academy there, double-checking the chip implanted within her shoulder."

Mia settled back in her chair, wanting to look calm, although tense with anxiety. The stiff chair crushed her captain's jacket, hard, against her back.

"You, Captain Foley, are slightly more difficult to clear." He looked up from the screen to scrutinize her. A warm sensation spread over the back of her neck. Nerves. "Your identification chip was difficult to place."

Mia instinctively slid her hand over her right wrist, as if she could still feel the microscopic chip embedded in her skin there. "I had an accident. The chip had to be removed."

Harrison tapped his screen again. "And you didn't think to get another one?"

Of course not. Why would she get something that would make it easier for the Acedians to track her? "It wasn't high on my list of priorities."

Harrison made a note. "Indeed. Did you know people are missing from Pargon?"

"I heard about that when we first landed. I hope our searches give us some clues to their whereabouts." She tried not to fidget.

Harrison was quiet for a moment, watching her. "I hope so as well. We might have to take more drastic measures soon."

He bade her good day and allowed her to leave. As she left headquarters, whispers followed her. Pargon had been hit, too. Because of her. Her heart tightened. Fissure. She could only hope the Acedians had not looked there.

A sense of unease filled Mia over the next few days. Unable to decide what to do about her crew, unwilling to think about the consequences of being with them for too long and the actions she must take in order to keep them safe, and unable to talk to Cassidy, Mia felt stuck—trapped. Her temper was on such a short fuse already, it came as no surprise that when Skyler started flirting with Cassidy—a suggestive glance here, a hand lingering too long there—Mia took the actions badly.

Even her crew noticed how Mia tensed around the woman in white. Or, at the very least, Will did. He kept staring at Mia. On the evening of the fourth day, the crew separated. For now, Mia saw no reason to stick together.

Mia sat in the kitchen of the *Eclipse*, fiddling with wires connected to one of Will's bombs. She had found the makeshift device, a crudely created, square explosive, shoved under a deck panel a few months ago. It was a decent place to hide the thing, actually. She only found it by looking for a place to store the bombs she planned to make herself.

Struggling with the tiny wires that connected the autotimer to the ignition spark, she frowned. The tiny labyrinth in her hands could destroy a ship as big as the *Eclipse*. If she placed it properly. The idea clawed at her. She conjured up an image of the *Eclipse* exploding, of Cassidy, Will, even Jeff dying by her hand. Could she live with herself after? Guilt caused her breath to catch. Her finger slipped on one of the metal threads, puncturing her skin. She yanked her hand back and muttered a curse. A red stain blossomed on the tip of her glove. Could she live if they were taken captive? Mia pushed her fingers back into the mass of miniscule wires.

"What are you doing?"

Mia jerked. Her fingers snapped one of the wires out of place. Blast. She fixed the connection and turned toward Will as he spoke again, "Why are you tinkering with my stuff?"

"Technically, it's my stuff, as it's fabricated from components of my ship," Mia replied, pointing to the metallic box. "Where did you even find the extra wire case?"

"In the storage cabin." Will shrugged. He slid onto the stool next to her and grabbed the bunch of wires she had been working on. After a moment's consideration, he looked at her and pointed to the inner workings of the bomb. "You need to connect this wire to the timer and twist these two together. That'll ready the explosive."

The two black wires in Will's hand looked similar, so similar in fact Mia never would have guessed those were the lynchpins in the mechanism. He twisted the two between his fingers and put them back into place, hidden among the other multicolored strands. The wires slid back into the container and the timer secured over it. The bomb looked harmless. A thin layer of rust even corroded the outside.

"Why are you working on this, Captain?" He picked the device up and rubbed a finger over the rust.

"I needed something to do to clear my thoughts." Truth. Though working on the bomb had only muddled her thoughts even more. "I don't like sitting about doing nothing."

"You think searching for survivors is doing nothing?" Will placed the explosive back on the countertop. His steady gaze, slightly altered by his bloodshot eyes, met hers. "Or, you know looking for survivors is pointless, because the attackers took the ones that went missing?"

Smart one. "The latter."

Wrinkles crisscrossed Will's face as he winced, as if the lines could hold back the emotions frothing within him. "I figured as much. Where else would they go?"

Mia chose to consider that a rhetorical question. She shifted on her stool, crossing one leg over the other.

The action drew Will's attention. "How's your thigh? It's been a few days, and you never did come to see me."

She put a hand on her leg. The bandage had puckered slightly from walking, the lumps creating small rolls and divots for her fingers to traverse.

"It's fine." She made a mental note to check on it later, but appeased the frown on Will's face. "I had one of the nurses check it out. She said you did a good patch job."

Will smiled. "Nurse Skyler, maybe?"

"A different nurse." She scowled and looked away. This wasn't where she wanted the conversation to go. The paneling on the far end of the cabin seemed rusted as well. Just like the bomb.

"I see the way you look at her."

"I get the wrong vibe from her. Skyler's been assigned to your family, so I can't avoid her."

"You shouldn't avoid her." The tone in Will's voice caused Mia to glance at him. The smile on his face had diminished slightly, his jovial attitude subdued. Now he just seemed...sad? "You shouldn't avoid her at all."

"She's taking care of your family, not me."

"She takes care of everybody. Me, Dad, Jeff, Elizabeth, Mom, even you." Will's eyes bore into Mia. "You should really tell her, you know."

Who were they discussing? The man could jump subjects faster than a MagPrint Drive jumping planets. Will's quiet attitude made Mia uncomfortable. The shape of his eyes so resembled his mother's. Mia shifted in her seat. She couldn't handle another emotionally distraught Dee member.

"She's a nurse. She's supposed to take care of everybody." Mia rolled her eyes. "That's her job."

Will reached out and grabbed Mia's hand resting on the table.

She leaned back. The sudden movement, the sudden touch, startled her. "Wha—"

"You should tell her, you know." The gruff intensity of his voice betrayed his emotions.

"I'm pretty sure Skyler knows how I feel about her."

Will shook his head. "Not Skyler. Cassidy."

Mia tried to move back, off her seat, but Will's hand kept her in place. How did the conversation shift to this? Mia did not want to talk about her romantic inclinations or relations with Will. They were not his for the taking. Especially not now with the bomb sitting on the counter next to them.

"I don't think that would—" She started slowly.

He interrupted her again. "It would be best, Captain, if you told her the way you feel about her. Before it's too late. Now, before something happens. Before you're never able to tell her." His voice shook. "You don't want to be left with bottled feelings."

Mia stopped trying to get away, her body stilled. Bottled feelings. Blast it, all her feelings came bottled. Walled. Hidden away. She clenched her jaw to keep the words from seeping out.

"She might love you back." Will leaned forward. His elbow nudged the explosive, and it scraped against the countertop, catching Mia's gaze. She stared at the tiny bomb. The truth slipped out.

"I don't want her to get hurt," she whispered.

"There's always that risk," he replied. "It should never outweigh the chance for something good to happen."

Mia looked back at Will. His gaze was focused. He squeezed her hand again, the weight of it too heavy on hers and much too warm. She fidgeted in her seat, removing her hand from under his. Desire trickled through the cracks in her defenses. For a new life. For a new home. For Cassidy. She slammed down the walls again. She would not survive if Cassidy, or any of her crew, were taken. The Acedians would transform them into unrecognizable, scarred, angry murderers. The bomb loomed in her periphery. The list of her kills weighed her down, hunched her shoulders forward. To write *Eclipse* as the fifth ship would be hard, but she had to do it.

"It would be a certainty, not a risk, with me," she replied.

Will shook his head, contorted his face so the wrinkles returned, and got up. He seemed to harden in place for a moment—was he angry?—then relaxed.

"At least take the time to say goodbye before leaving," he murmured. "That's all I wanted for Sarah."

He turned and left, walking slowly out of the kitchen and disappearing as the hatch slid shut. Mia exhaled. She reached into her pocket, drew out the list and a rusted pen. She smoothed the parchment onto the countertop, next to the bomb. With shaking fingers, she placed the tip of the pen under *Jubilee*. Heavy. The pen itself was heavy. Just like every other time she had scrawled a designation onto this crumpled piece of parchment.

Maybe this time could be different, maybe she could push the emergency beacon sooner so her crew could get away, eject from the ship before it exploded. As long as they weren't captured, as long as the Acedians assumed they all had perished. Slowly, so slowly, she penned *Eclipse* onto the paper, watching the ink and her destiny consume that empty space.

***

After Will's conversation Mia vowed to not have anything to do with the nurse, but on the sixth day, the woman's advances became too unbearable for Mia to ignore. Mia and her crew had been directed toward the eastern side of the city. The picobot latticework around this section had crumbled away, leaving behind a burnt shadow of the original structures, yet the weaponry had not completely destroyed the area. They filed into the nearest building. Mia stopped just inside, tired of searching for something clearly not to be found.

Someone came up behind her. The weight of Cassidy's hand on Mia's shoulder didn't come as a shock. The shivers of warmth radiating down her spine did. Calm down, Mia ordered herself, remembering Cassidy's anger. Unwillingly, her body listened. She turned toward Cassidy, waiting for the dam to break and the accusations to surge over her. Seconds passed in silence.

Mia stared at the woman before her. It was almost unfair how good the red, long-sleeved shirt and charcoal-colored pants fit Cassidy. Did she know that scarlet was an attractive color on her? Or how that collar, so close to her jawline, brought out the freckles on her chin? Hair fell over her eyes, a strand of purple drifting alongside her face, and her lips turned slightly downward. Her hand stayed in place. The wristband glinted. Perhaps Cassidy was not as angry as she let on. Before Mia could question the gesture another weight shoved them apart.

"Oh, sorry." Skyler landed hard on Cassidy, smiling as she righted herself. Mia leaned against the wall, glaring. Skyler fixed one of the straps on her camisole—again with the white, did the woman have no other color?—and gave Cassidy a wink. Skyler laid her small, thin hand on Cassidy's arm. "Did I hurt you?"

"No." Cassidy shrugged off Skyler's movements. "I'm fine."

"I know you are." Skyler laughed. She leaned closer, closing the gap between her and Cassidy for a moment, before stepping away

A sharp sensation flared in Mia's hand, just as she noticed a crunching noise beside her. A quick glance down made her gasp. She'd squeezed the archivist into an unrecognizable shape. Feeling Cassidy's gaze on her, Mia tried to shrug it off.

"It's a crummy piece of tech," Mia muttered, feeling heat creep up the back of her neck. Blast it all, why was she blushing? She pocketed the ruined device.

Cassidy smiled and strolled, quite leisurely, down the hallway. Skyler scowled at Mia. Her eyes narrowed then widened. A smirk blossomed on her lips. Sashaying the distance between them, Skyler hooked a finger around Mia's belt and leaned close. The woman smelled too much like Cassidy, all spice and no perfume.

"Don't be like that, Captain," she said. "You're simply much too obvious."

Mia yanked herself out of Skyler's reach, debating how to gut her "accidentally." Skyler nodded slowly and walked off. Steaming, Mia wiped her pants, wanting to burn the fingerprints of the dark-haired woman off them. Her reaction gnawed at Mia. Gutting a person, over a woman? Scratching she could see, maybe, but gutting? Had her thoughts always been this vicious? No, not always.

She was changing. When they'd found officers hurt in the streets, Mia caught herself smiling. Not because they found the officers, but because those men and women had been suffering for days before being found. Was she really that heartless? No, Mia knew herself well enough to know she was not that cold. Guilt plagued her each night. Her victims' faces haunted her. She was truly sorry for what she had done, for the stupid decisions she'd made in her youth. Would a person without a heart have such weight on their shoulders? She ran a hand through her hair, rubbing the back of her neck as tension settled there. But she couldn't deny that ever since Pargon she felt differently. Her thoughts, her attitude, seemed altered in some way.

Mia shivered and leaned on the wall. Since Pargon, it seemed as if ice flowed through her veins. She was faster, stronger, too. How else could she have crushed the archivist? A noise came from the other side of the wall. She looked inside the nearest door just in time to see Jeff throw a chair a bit too close. Mia yanked her head back and the chair landed in a heap at the base of the door.

"What the blasted quasar was that about, Jeff?" Mia shouted through the wall.

"You should have said you were standing there," Jeff replied, just as loud.

Mia picked her way over the debris and saw Jeff tear down the wallpaper as if expecting to find doors hidden behind the rectangular patterns. Mia had hoped the search would quell his rage. Obviously not. She'd never seen him quite so determined or so angry. He darted back and forth into the rooms so quickly, she would have been amazed if he spotted anyone at all.

"There's no one here." She looked at the empty hallway.

He didn't answer, pushing past her and into a connecting hallway. She wanted to say they would find no one because the Acedians would leave no one behind. That she heard no one. Felt no one. She remained silent. Her guilt burned a hole in her gut each time Jeff yanked a fellow

Paradousian toward the admiral to be questioned. He had clearly let his emotions reign.

Will bumped into her, muttering "Sorry, Captain." The younger brother trailed after his sibling, righting the chairs, folding the torn paper, patting the walls as if to apologize for his brother's fury. Will poked his head into the offices Jeff charged past, moving slower but no less determined in the search. Every now and then, he would cast a glance over at her, his tired eyes would lock on to hers and he'd shake his head as if to say, "What's become of him?" No words were spoken on the subject.

The admiral decided to initiate a mandatory rest day after the eleventh, consecutive, twenty-four hour search came up with nothing. Harrison apparently picked the short straw and delivered the news to the survivors gathered around him inside the warehouse.

"A rest day?" Jeff exclaimed when the archivist would not turn on. Other survivors agreed, waving their blank archivist's in the air. An angry hum filled the space.

Harrison raised his hands. "Rest today, please, and tomorrow we will find who did this."

Jeff threw the archivist onto the ground and stomped away. No one stopped him, not even Will. His brother did pick up the cracked device.

"Captain Foley," Harrison's voice rang once more through the high ceilings. "The admiral wants to see you for a moment."

Blasted military. She made her way into the office for her third time. In the early morning light, the admiral's shadow stretched far over the ground and onto the outer walls of the room. She stepped up beside the admiral, glancing over at him. Linking her hands behind her back, she stared out over the city.

The admiral spoke in a quiet voice, "If this doesn't work we're going to search the skies."

Mia looked up at the cloudless morning. "That wouldn't take too long."

Admiral Boreas barked a laugh. "If only. These attacks have been going on for too long, and on too many planets, for us to handle. Therefore, in an effort to stop this horror and appease the families of the thousands gone missing, the military is recruiting volunteers to deal with this threat. We want your ship to be part of the hunting party."

Hunting party. Mia's heart pounded in her ears. That's what she wanted to do, right? Hunt Donavin down? Working with the military was like going into a punctured airlock without a suit, no way out but one. They would find out about her past somehow. And it would make her plan of blowing the *Eclipse* that much harder.

She kept her eyes on the sky. "I'll think about it."

Admiral Boreas nodded.

Mia walked away. She spent the rest of the day not thinking about it, preoccupied by her newfound abilities. Her body had changed. She had more energy now. Mia tested herself—picking up thick metal slabs from the streets and bending them easily, whipping out her dagger and embedding it into the ground faster than normal, lugging around pieces of scrap, much too heavy for her, with ease. Mia knew. The Acedians had done something to her. She looked at her hand, seeing the scar even through her glove. Done more to her.

Mia couldn't get her crew out of her mind. The bomb hiding in plain sight irked her. Mia walked faster, away from memories of Freya, and of Cassidy suffering the same fate. She pushed herself to try one more experiment.

Her gaze latched onto a squat building, much smaller than the ones that claimed the sky around it, tucked away from prying eyes. One of the taller buildings had fallen on top of its white, painted stones. They were perfect for her final test of the day. Jumping.

She readied herself at the base of the buildings. Her vision focused on the first crack, just eight feet up. How could she let herself fall in love? She jumped for it, grabbed for the sliver of empty space. Her fingers found that space easily, pulling her upward. How could Cassidy ever return those feelings? A cold sweat broke out over her body, dripping over her arms and down her back. Another crack, another jump, and she was sixteen feet up. She could move the bomb. Someplace not so obvious.

She gasped, slipped. Recovered. Beads of sweat formed on her abdomen and legs. Tiny rocks fell into her eyes. They watered. Maybe the wiring was wrong inside the bomb. A third fracture, another ten feet up. An image of the *Eclipse* exploding, tearing itself apart as Mia floated safely away. Maybe there was another way. Colder than she had ever been, she shoved her feet against the building and launched herself upward. Maybe she could save them? Save Cassidy. Her fingers pushed against stone, not emptiness. Missed. She saw the building, a flash of afternoon sky, and then darkness.

Chapter Fifteen

MIA JERKED, HER EYES snapped open. Her boots rested on—nothing. There was nothing beneath her, nothing above her, nothing at all. Floating in a void of white and weightlessness, she slowly drifted. Gradually coming to a halt in a somewhat upright pose—she listed slightly to the side—Mia took in her surroundings. Where was she? Surrounded by white, there was no way to place herself, no markers of any kind to determine where she was.

She looked up—the direction she figured was up—and found no darkness piercing the colorless void. Silence. Goosebumps prickled her skin even though the air—was this even air?—seemed warm. She rubbed her shoulders and found herself rubbing soft fabric instead of her skin. A quick glance down. She was now clad in a long-sleeved, white dress that flowed past her knees. White boots covered her feet.

An explosion rocked her, jostling her about. Darkness invaded the white space. Cold air, followed by a hot wave, rushed past her skin. Sharp particles darted into her eyes, making them water. A bright, orange light washed over her. The Oasis. She was sure it was the Oasis. There was no other ship like her. Mia only caught a glimpse before the massive ship exploded.

The ship reappeared, whole and new, as if freshly constructed and out on a maiden voyage. A jolt ran through her. This was how the ship looked to her when she first joined the Oasis crew. She blinked, and her boots hit the hard, metallic walkway within the ship's belly. Recognizing people seconds after they rushed past, Mia blinked again, out of shock.

Glimpses of herself as a passenger flashed by—reading on an archivist, chatting with strangers she would later call friends, eating in the communal dining cabin. She had been merely a traveler in between ports of call on this great ship named after something she desperately sought. This was the ship she hailed with directly after losing her parents, after being taken by the Acedians, after being set free. No one cared that she was alone. No one noticed.

She saw a young version of herself leaning onto the viewport, as close as she could get to the stars winking in and out just beyond the glass. Childish hands pressed against the glass, only fourteen years of age, nothing protected her skin from the chilled surface. Before she started wearing gloves, before she realized the scar was dangerous, her hands breathed free. Mia stood so close to her younger self, she could count the buttons on the girl's blue jacket, the black stitches traveling down the side of her white pants. Could the girl see her? No, a teenager would immediately question a strange woman standing around, staring. Especially a teenage Mia. A shout came from down the walkway, and the child ran toward its source, long, red hair dancing behind her.

Mia blinked.

Surrounded by the scraping of forks, the belching of happy souls, and the scent of warm plumseed pudding, it didn't take long for Mia to place herself. The dining hall, a favorite of hers on the Oasis. Her lithe, young body reclined on a seat, arm draped over the back, and hand rubbing her stomach. An empty bowl of Mrs. Hama's pudding sat on the table before her. Mrs. Hama herself was laughing as she sat down next to the child Mia once had been.

"You don't hold back, do you, child?"

"Well, if it tastes like engine grease, someone should woman up and tell him."

"And you will be that woman?" Laughter sparked in Mrs. Hama's eyes.

The girl grinned. "No. At least now you know why I prefer your pudding over his."

"Ah, so mine tastes better than grease, you say?"

"Marginally."

Mrs. Hama—Em—scuffed the top of the child's head and yanked her into a massive hug, one the girl returned just as hard. An ache tore through Mia as she pulled her gaze away and searched the cabin. Familiar faces saw through her. She may not be real to them, but they were certainly real to her. Mia could see every hair on Chac's balding, gray head. Part of the engineering crew, he'd shown her how to wire things properly, bombs and control panels in particular. They had spent hours together, learning. The cook, Dari, yelled out for her to come get the rest of her meal. His was the gruel pudding she so loathed. He had always been kind, handing out extra to the new girl on board. The background drone of voices remained steady. Dari's shout traversed the distance so easily, Mia had to smile. He had always been loud. Her younger self merely stuck out a defiant tongue. The other crewmates grabbed her from her seat and pushed her toward the evening meal. Everyone had been kind to her on the Oasis.

Mia shook her head, pulling herself from that happy place and into her current dilemma. Her head pounded. Was this the day? Dari dropped a bowl of pudding, and Mia's younger self scowled at the wasted food. Mia's heart began to thud. Surely there were many days Dari's clumsiness caused that to happen, surely it could not be the day that—

A crash echoed down the walkway, just outside the dining hall. The screams began. The captain's voice filtered through the intercom: they had been attacked and boarded. Orders barked out to stay calm, to not worry, and that they had everything under—his voice cut out. Her younger self crouched under a table as feet pounded around her. Mrs. Hama crouched alongside, clutching her. How cold Mia had felt in that moment, as a rapid heartbeat under one ear and confused shouts filled the other.

Mia blinked.

The child was running now, dashing down the walkway, dragging Mrs. Hama along with her, shouting for Dari and Chac to follow. They never would. In mere moments the attack had changed from a forced boarding to an all-out raid. Mia followed the pair, running hard but barely breathing, passing through solid bodies and doors as if they were air. The opening to the pods dominated her view now, white, gleaming, safe. Mrs. Hama cried out in relief.

The gnawing deepened in the pit of Mia's stomach. She knew what would happen next. She stopped running, and the folds of her dress swirled around her legs. She didn't want to remember Mrs. Hama, or Dari, or Chac, or anyone on this ship. Her skin prickled as a chill passed through her neck and the back of her skull, pooling around her forehead and cheeks. Even though she willed them to, her eyes would not close.

The child jumped into the pod and sat down on the blue seat, tugging a silver bar down over her stomach. Mia remembered the metal almost burning her hands with its cold surface. Mrs. Hama stepped into the pod, into safety.

The Acedians had followed them. One of them grabbed Mrs. Hama. She fell into the waiting arms of the others. The pod hatch began to slide shut. A small hand threw a makeshift bomb into the space, following the path of Mrs. Hama. Mia watched as the child's face appeared in the hole, watching the bomb land at Mrs. Hama's thrashing feet.

She watched as the terrified, crying girl mouthed sorry and turned away, disappearing from sight as the hatch sealed shut. The pod's closed hatch reflected her current image, an adult woman, wearing only white, standing amidst the Acedian raid as they dragged a screaming Mrs. Hama away. With a faint pop, the escape pod jettisoned. A few moments later, an echoing explosion blew past Mia. Her bomb had saved Mrs. Hama's life. Mia had always wondered. The blast rustled her skirt, but the explosion did not harm her. It did light up the area, and, on the hatch in front of her, Mia's reflection stared back. A wide, terrifying smile lingered on her lips.

She blinked awake.

Agony tore through her side. Confused, she struggled, couldn't move her arms or legs. The real world blurred, her mind making no sense of the sudden onslaught of bright lights and hazy shapes in front of her face. Blast it! She tried to speak, tried to ask what had happened, why she was restrained. Her voice would not listen. What was happening?

A warm hand pressed itself against Mia's neck. Cassidy? No. Black hair fell in curtains over Mia's field of vision, obscuring the lights from view. Her pulse raced against the hand that lay softly on her neck. Into her blurred vision dipped the face of Skyler.

Her lips moved, but only a few words filtered through Mia. "Lay still."

A sudden pinch at the base of her neck made her wince. A sharp object pierced her skin, and warmth spread throughout her body. What? Her vision darkened to black as she fell once more into a heavy, medicated sleep.

Mia blinked.

The crimson-tinged walkway reminded her of something. Of someone. Judging by the red-trimmed, gray uniforms of the crewmen walking past her, she had to be on the Scarlet. Another ship, only a year after the Oasis had been destroyed. Scarlet wasn't glamorous by any means. The crew were jammed four in a cabin, walkways were narrow and connected in too many places, and meals consisted of cold gruel. It got her off the shuttle she had been stowing away on. It gave her a job.

A woman dove through her, shocking Mia. A flash of blond hair waving against a sanguine coat dashed through the corridor. Freya. Mia moved to the side, as her fifteen-year-old self rushed after the woman.

Mia had been an insignificant part of the electrical engineering crew, merely an assistant to one of the engineers. Freya Glessal took her under her wing when Mia showed interest in wiring. During the weeks they spent together over sparks and copper, a bond formed. Freya's laughter brightened the dark days, and her auburn eyes contained the mysteries of entire galaxies Mia could never quite touch. She had been lost. Alone. And she had the sense Freya had been, as well. They took comfort in one another.

Mia found them laughing, smiling, happy to be around each other. Now the sight made her sick. She forced herself to look away. She could not acknowledge that particular memory in waking hours. Here she was, witnessing herself fall in love for the first time.

It had to be a dream. Surely she could wake herself and not need to see any more of Freya. Mia closed her eyes, willing herself to wake and be gone from this place. Willing herself to leave. To go away. The ache in her side did not return, and the whispers of Skyler did not tell her to lay still. She had not woken up.

Opening her eyes once more, she saw them. Herself still so young, kissing Freya, exploring the older woman's body, pressing the woman against the bulkhead in her haste. Mia blinked. Another scene appeared before Mia, the pair walking down the corridor with linked hands, pushing and shoving the other, pulling back for a kiss. Freya, taller of the two, gathered the fifteen-year-old into her arms, and smiled.

Mia blinked.

They were at the starboard viewport now, looking at the stars. Still fascinated by them. Arm in arm, they found Hekate, Mia's North Star. Freya laughed as the young woman pushed her hands against the glass in wonder. Dark gloves now protected them from the chill.

Mia blinked.

An alarm sounded deep in the engineer's section. An enemy ship was bearing down on them. Couldn't they get more power to the engines? Weren't they trying hard enough? The captain warned of a shot off their starboard bow. Moments later, it connected, knocking equipment and crewmembers to the ground. The girl yanked her lover off the floor and into a safer compartment. Mia moved to follow the two, but her mind screamed no. Why did she follow them? Did she have to see? Yes.

Mia blinked.

The two cowered in an empty shaft. She towered over them now. It unnerved Mia to look into her own youthful, terrified eyes. A hand reached down to grab Freya and hauled her forward, away from the girl's desperate grip.

Mia realized, too late, that it was her own hand grasping Freya so tightly. No longer merely a witness to this scene, a ghost in their world, she'd become the villain. Her other hand held the knife. Shivering permeated her upper body, and her hand moved to slit Freya's throat. Blood seeped down the wound.

A bubble of laughter traveled inside of her. A moment later, Freya's body dropped to the ground, and Mia found herself wrestling with her teenage counterpart. They fell to the deck, and Mia laughed. Not her laughter, not her voice. A deeper chuckle burst forth from her. She did not feel the hand that connected to her face, nor the dagger forced deep into her chest. She did not feel herself fall to the side. The young girl rose. A metal pin the girl wore caught Mia's gaze, but the face reflected there frightened her. Her own face split into a laughing, maniacal grin as her past cried above her.

Mia blinked awake. Her head fell to the side. She gasped for breath. Blast it all the Helix. The sharp ache in her side had subsided into a dull stinging. Someone squeezed Mia's hand, and, as her vision cleared, a deep sense of relief seeped through her. Cassidy's face now swam in and out of her vision. Mia tried to speak. Only a soft moan escaped her lips.

"How many times have you been injured these past few weeks? Three? Four? I've lost count, surely it's been one too many." Cassidy's voice permeated the deep ache in Mia's heart.

She wanted to ask Cassidy what was happening to her. Why these memories, long caged in a dark corner of her mind, suddenly broke free. And how? She could only moan.

Cassidy stirred beside her. Voices raised, both male and female, around Mia's bed, but she had already started losing consciousness. Waves of sleep pulled at her. The warm pressure from Cassidy's hand lingered and left, as Mia drifted back into darkness. Mia blinked.

Her hand rested on a control panel in the corridor. An insignia decorated the metal just above her fingers. Luminaria. With her lover gone and the last few ships ruined behind her, she hardly cared about this vessel. Mia glanced around and, sure enough, there her younger self was, walking straight-backed down the corridor that led to the engine room. Mia followed the girl clad in bulky, yellow overalls, passing by people, recognizable, yet not. She had begun to distance herself here. At nineteen, sullen resentment was expected from a brooding child who was only around to fix the engines. She had reached head engineer status in a few mere weeks and made a few enemies in the process.

No one met the teenager's gaze, nor attempted a greeting of any kind. Walking ahead, Mia stopped to watch her own loathsome expression drilling into the deck. She had played that part very well. Following the girl, she ducked into the engineering room, a grimace playing on Mia's lips as she realized what she was here to do. The cabin was empty, perfect for her plan. Sure enough, slight, young fingers wormed their way into the core of the engine, hiding an explosive deep within the wires and far from prying eyes.

Mia blinked.

Her younger self sat on her bed, crying now, and crossing off the areas where she had planted bombs. Her charges were all over the ship, specific areas destined to save the hundreds of crewmembers from the terror the Acedians brought with them. Her hand shook from the pain in her scar. It was only a matter of time. Mia tried to look away as sobs wracked the young girl sitting in front of her, but she couldn't move. Couldn't turn. Mia remained frozen in this memory. In this nightmare.

In a flash of light, the girl and her cabin disappeared, replaced only by a mirror. Mia sorted through her memories, trying to figure out what this mirror was. Her reflection was twenty-one years old, clad in rough, green pants, tight shirt, and a first mate star pinned to her collar.

Jubilee. The last of the four ships, before becoming captain of the Eclipse.

A high-pitched screech tore through the cabin. The captain had just called all-hands-on-deck. They came too quickly. There had been no time to plant charges. There was nothing she could do to help these people. She would already have left her cabin, already left the ship, not stood, like a helpless child, waiting to die. Ice surged through her veins, from head to toe, she trembled. This time was different, altered. Someone else was in control. The thumping of feet echoed down the corridor, just outside her cabin, as crewmembers rushed to follow the captain's orders.

Her scar chilled. Her hand shook. Her reflection changed, clothes shifted from green to white, pants melted into a skirt, and her shirt into a long-sleeved bodice, forming the dress once more. Her mouth was a twisted line, curling up in one corner to form a smile. Her eyes narrowed—evil.

The idea entered her mind only to scurry away again. She pulled it back, examining its true meaning. The Acedians were the bane of her existence, the scourge of this universe. They had killed hundreds of lives, captured thousands, and ruined many more. Of course they were wicked. No, not them. Her reflection cracked, fractured outward like her thoughts, until even the tips of her fingers splintered. Frost covered her entirely in white and melted away, dragging the splintered remnants of her past down, pooling at her feet. Millions of tiny machines formed her body now, interconnected, woven throughout her skin until they too had crawled away, finally uncovering her true self. Captain Mia Foley stood in the mirror, clad in black, fiery, red hair cut short, a dagger decorating her hip. After years of running from those she deemed wicked, destroying innocent souls in her haste to get away, realization finally punctured her heart and embedded itself in her very soul. She was the evil one.

Mia blinked awake once more.

Chapter Sixteen

BLACK SPOTS BLURRED MIA'S vision. Hull panels, overhead, swam in and out of her sight, dark in some places, light in others. Confusing at best. With every breath, the cabin swelled outward only to crash inward again. Her wrists and ankles ached where something bound them to the surface beneath her. The bed in the infirmary that much she knew from the uncomfortable cushions under her. She was on the *Eclipse*. What held her down? And why?

Struggling slightly and finding she could not move much—not that her body wanted to—folds of cloth grew rough under her palms. Folds of cloth? No gloves? A spark of panic forked through her, and the place under her left ribs twinged with each hurried breath. Counting to ten slowly calmed her breathing. Only a few wisps of dreamland remained, and only one word lingered in her thoughts—evil.

"You get injured too often."

Her head fell to the side. Splashes of color invaded her vision: burnt-orange, long-sleeved shirt; dark, scarlet pants; and yellow fabric holding back amethyst-streaked, brunette hair. Like the sun had settled itself onto Cassidy's form. Mia winced as she met Cassidy's eyes.

"You said that before," Mia's voice came out harsh, garbled, like her vocal cords had forgotten how to work. She coughed, swallowed, and tried again, "You mentioned that before."

"I'm surprised you remember. You were pretty out of it." Mia watched as Cassidy shifted on the countertop, her long legs dipping toward the deck. The rest of the *Eclipse*'s infirmary stretched out around Cassidy—bulkheads formed a convex bubble, shiny equipment, narrow lights in blurred parallel lines overhead—as if Mia just now pieced it together.

A cold cloth pressed against Mia's forehead, drops of water creating a narrow path to her earlobe. She shuddered, yanking her head away only to have the cloth remain, regardless how much she moved. Mia glanced sideways. A pale wrist and arm. A skinny wrist.

"Breach it, Mia, you were an idiot to walk on that leg." Skyler moved her arm away. Mia could now see the condescending look. "Lucky it healed up before you got hurt again, or I'd have two things to fix."

"You fixed me?"

"Don't look so surprised, Captain. I'm a nice person, you know." Skyler winked, a smile lingering on her lips. "Besides, no one else could have stopped the bleed from a wound like you had. As it is, you were still out for a week."

"A week?" Questions tumbled over one another in their attempt to get out first. "How bad was it? What's happened? Why are we back on the *Eclipse*?" She attempted to sit up but the restraints bit into her skin. Wincing, she raised her head and glanced down to her body. She wore all black now. At least the color suited her better. The metal shackles gleamed brightly and held her in place. "Why am I restrained? Did we leave Paradous without my permission?"

A laugh cracked through the air, and a sudden movement in the corner of Mia's vision startled her. She turned her head just in time to see Cassidy slide off the countertop and raise her hand toward someone, just out of sight.

"Will, don't!" Cassidy yelled. The hatch merely hissed closed.

"Will? Where is he going?" Mia glanced back and forth between Cassidy and Skyler.

Neither answered. The air in the cabin shifted. Altered. The silence lingered, uncomfortable, as Skyler checked Mia's side. The wound flared with every touch, but Mia held her tongue. Her gaze caught Cassidy's, who looked away, the deck apparently more interesting than her captain.

"What's wrong?" Mia asked.

"I'm sorry." Cassidy's eyes slid to hers for just a moment then flitted back to the deck.

"Sorry for..."

Those two words were barely uttered. Jeff barreled over, knocking Skyler out of the way. She crashed against the equipment table. The parallel lights above Mia disappeared, as Jeff's wide shoulders blocked them from sight, one hand on either side of her arms. Lines creased his forehead, spidering down his cheeks, past his flared nostrils and his downturned mouth. His eyes frightened her. Barely any hazel could be seen in his irises. Crazed. He was crazed or angry. Or both.

"How could you lie to me? How could you lie to us?" His questions smashed across Mia's face, leaving spittle behind. "How could you do such horrendous things?"

"What are you talking about?" Mia kept her voice even, though her heart thudded. Skyler and Cassidy lingered on one side of her vision. Will appeared at her feet. He must have followed his brother inside. Mia even caught a glimpse of Harrison. Apparently the admiral's lackey found a way on her ship, too. Jeff shifted, demanding her focus.

"Don't act like an imbecile, Foley. I know. We all do," Jeff said.

"Know what?"

Mia chanced a quick look around, scared eyes met hers, even Cassidy's. Jeff leaned in closer, a pungent scent wafting with him.

"What you did to the other ships," he said, his voice getting louder with each word.

Mia stilled. Did he know about the bomb in the kitchen, too? About her plan to set it off as soon as they were in space? About her? She couldn't decide which one was worse.

Inches away from her nose he continued, "What you did to your other crews. Why you're running away from the..." He stopped, as if searching for the right word.

"Acedians," Cassidy mumbled.

"Yes, the Acedians. Why you're scampering away. What you are!"

Mia's breath caught. Her heart pounded. The shackles seemed to tighten around her wrists and ankles. Somehow, deep down, Mia had known Jeff would be the one to catch her, to finally realize who she was. How, though? She'd been careful. She only told one person in her whole life. Not even Freya knew the truth. A weight fell onto Mia's thigh, and she jerked away from it. The weight stayed in place. Mia looked down at Cassidy's hand resting there. Mia stared at her. Cassidy looked miserable, shoulders hunched, eyes averted. Only Cassidy's hand on Mia's thigh connected the two.

After a moment's pause, Mia found her voice. "And what am I?"

She looked back at Jeff. Dreading the answer, dreading the truth, Mia could only hold those dark eyes with her own. The word surfaced again. Evil.

"You're a slaughterer."

Or that could work too. She winced at the archaic word.

"You've slaughtered families. You've destroyed homes, entire crews, ships even, all in the name of fear and some sick sense of kindness. All because you could." Jeff yanked himself upward and stalked around her table.

The others moved out of his way. Cassidy removed her hand from Mia's thigh. Empty chill took its place. The crew seemed more afraid of Jeff than of her. Even Harrison shifted slightly away from the Dee brother. Of course, she happened to be tied down, and Jeff wasn't. Jeff seemed to be working himself up to something, his footsteps echoing in the silent cabin. He stopped pacing by her left hand. Mia could see his chest rise and fall under the orange and gray jumpsuit he wore. Reaching down, he placed a hand over hers, curling his fingers underneath to feel the marred skin of her palm. Under different circumstances, it could have been mistaken for a lover's hold. Here, now, the touch was far from affection.

A rush of shivers seeped from her hand in response to his exploration. A chill permeated her body. Her muscles relaxed. Her breathing leveled out. It seemed something else controlled her. She tried to resist it. Couldn't. She became quiet, a serenity void of emotions.

"Where are the rest of your scars?" His mouth twisted into a deep-set scowl. "The rest of your triumphs?"

The rough calluses on the tips of his fingers scratched her scar, pressed upon it, his grip tightening. Soon his hold pained Mia, but she did not give him the satisfaction of crying out. A slight movement behind Jeff caught Mia's attention. Cassidy shifted forward, inching closer to Jeff. The muscles in her left arm—the only side Mia could clearly see—flexed as she reached forward, eyes only for Jeff's hand.

"Because of you, my family was split apart." His eyes narrowed. "Because of you." His voice cracked. He tried again, growing louder and louder still. "Because of you, my sister is gone! Never coming back." His hand crushed hers, and she couldn't keep from wincing. "Because of you, Foley."

Cassidy leapt forward, grabbing Jeff's arm and pulling him away.

"Do you understand that?" He screamed the words now, pushing against Cassidy, reaching for Mia's trapped form. Skyler rushed in to help Cassidy. With both women working against him, Jeff could not move. Still, his words flew out, slapping Mia with more force than a fist ever could. "Because of you! When were we going to be your next victims? When were we going to get blown up like the other ships?"

With a grunt, Jeff broke free of the two women. Jeff grabbed Mia's pant leg, only to rip the fabric as Harrison jerked him away. Expression tight with effort, Harrison managed to stop Jeff from completely throwing himself at Mia. Already off balance from the lunge, Harrison's extra weight caused Jeff to slip and crash to the deck. Throughout the entire scuffle Mia remained calm, not the usual calm expected from a ship's captain. The calm brought on by something else, something she could not explain. She didn't want to explain it.

"Stop, Jeff. This isn't how we operate," Harrison said, dragging Jeff to his feet. Jeff either couldn't hear him or chose not to. He glared at Mia. His furious gaze could peel panels away from the hull of a ship. That's exactly how Mia felt, her guise peeling away from her inner secrets, leaking the horrible deeds she had committed out into space. Her calm wavered.

"You're evil," Jeff yelled.

A vision blew into her head, her skin shattering, leaving only a million tiny machines roaming her body. The serenity broke, leaving only panic and confusion dripping off her shocked soul.

Harrison yanked Jeff toward the hatch. Equipment smashed to the deck as Jeff struggled to get free. Waving a hand to open the hatch, Harrison nearly gave Jeff the momentum he needed to break the hold, but Harrison countered and pulled him out into the corridor. The hatch clicked shut.

"What are you going to do with me?" Mia asked no one in particular.

Her vision fell on Will. Now that Jeff had left, Mia could clearly see his younger brother tucked away in the back of the cabin. Will's gaze strayed after his brother, and, after only a moment, he started for the exit. He waved the hatch open, paused, and looked back at her.

His eyes never met hers as he said, "Harrison will deal with you." He left. The hatch clicked closed, sealing in the heavy silence inside the infirmary.

"Not really the interrogation he planned," Skyler muttered. Mia watched as Skyler righted equipment and picked up the tools. Cassidy came forward and stopped next to Mia's bedside. Her eyes lingered on the tear in the dark fabric of Mia's pants, exposing a swath of her skin.

"I'm sorry." She reached out to move the fabric back into place. With that movement, she also slipped a piece of paper into Mia's pocket. Mia's list. Realization aimed a hot ball of anger toward herself. How could she have let herself trust Cassidy? Despite herself, Mia's leg tingled when Cassidy's fingers brushed against it.

"Why did you tell them?"

Cassidy winced.

"She didn't have a choice because—" Cassidy put a hand on Skyler's arm and halted her speech. The nurse looked at Cassidy. "Breach it all, you tell her." The nurse started to walk away, paused, and glanced back over her shoulder, a gleam in her eye Mia didn't quite like. "She was intensely attractive at that moment, by the way." Skyler winked.

Mia lunged, heard a binding snap but not break. Skyler smiled, sashaying out. The hatch hissed shut, again. Cassidy walked over to the hatch and punched in the locking code. No one could get into the infirmary now. Not until she unlocked it. She did not turn back around.

"You told them?" Mia whispered, glaring at Cassidy's back. She unclenched her shaking fists.

Cassidy lingered by the bulkhead, farthest away from Mia, her shoulders hunched, head down. Mia could barely hear the word that passed from her lips. "Yes."

"How much?"

"Everything."

"Why?" Mia's eyes narrowed.

Cassidy shrugged, shaking her head as she glanced at Mia, only to look away again. She twiddled with the ribbon on her wristband. "They wanted to kill you, and I couldn't—"

"Kill me?" Mia tensed.

Cassidy backed up a step and rubbed a hand over her elbow. "Because of your scar."

Exhaling, Mia looked away. "How did they find it?"

Cassidy rushed over to the table. She placed her hands on the surface next to Mia's arm. The fingers that touched Mia's skin shook. Mia moved away, scooting as far away as her bonds would allow.

"You were hurt, Mia, bad," Cassidy said. "The wound on your side—I was so shocked to see you like that, bleeding, unconscious. The cut was huge. And I'm no doctor, I didn't know what to do."

"So you removed my gloves?" Mia huffed. The idiot.

"I didn't know what else to do!" Cassidy's voice trembled. She placed a hand on Mia's arm, as if needing the connection, needing her to understand. Mia shook it off.

She didn't want to see the expression on Cassidy's face, or watch the tears welling up in her eyes, so she looked away. The tools next to her seemed more interesting, easier to focus on. She glared at the helotube and bit the side of her tongue. Her breaths came shallow. She had to force herself to be calm, to listen.

Cassidy rambled on. "Your wound, it looked horrible. There was so much blood. I had already contacted Skyler, and I couldn't just sit there, waiting, watching you die. You had walked off alone, disappeared for the entire afternoon. I had no idea where you went, and I wanted to let you know you weren't alone anymore."

Mia looked back at her, tilting her head at that last statement. Cassidy's whole body trembled now. She had moved closer still, leaning down over the table, over Mia, as if closing the space between them would make Mia understand. She fidgeted with her wristband, slipping her thumb under the ribbon, sliding her fingers across the designs. Her eyes searched Mia's face, trembling lips pursed together, a blush crept up her cheeks. Suddenly, she straightened and turned away.

"Your breathing was shallow. The blood kept pouring out, but I had to make sure you—I had to do something. I just wanted to feel your pulse. Your blasted gloves got in the way, so I tore them off. I didn't think anything of it." Cassidy moved further away from Mia, shoulders hunched, breaths coming in ragged gasps, fingers twirling the ring.

Mia's own breathing calmed, muscles relaxed. Cassidy cared enough to stay with her as she bled. She cared enough to sit beside her as Mia slept. She cared enough to be with her now. Not idiotic. Worried. Something inside Mia broke. Her anger disappeared.

Before she could say anything, Cassidy moved. Her eyes burned with an intensity Mia had never encountered before. Cassidy stalked toward her, jabbing a finger at her. She shouted now. "Do you know how I felt seeing you in this infirmary for a week, a whole blasted week? Slipping in and out of consciousness? Thrashing? Terrified, that's how. You're always getting hurt!" Tears shimmered in her eyes. "Curse it all, Mia, I was scared you'd never fully wake up."

"I'm...I'm..." Mia stuttered, stopped. Cassidy's words rang in her ears. She was terrified for her? Did that mean? Could Cassidy have feelings for her? An impossible hope. "I'm sorry."

Cassidy shook her head. She ran her hands through her hair, breathed in, then out. Her hands fell to her sides. She turned and leaned on the table, her back to Mia.

"Well, you should be." A sigh escaped her lips.

"How...how did Jeff take it when you told him?" Mia asked, changing the subject, trying to get Cassidy to calm down.

"Less than pleasantly," Cassidy replied, rubbing her elbow again.

The second time she'd done that. Mia flitted her gaze down to Cassidy's elbow. "What happened to your arm?"

She furrowed her eyebrows and a crease appeared in Cassidy's forehead. "Jeff did it."

Mia's jaw went slack. She tried to move closer but failed when the bonds halted her. "Jeff? What did he do?"

Cassidy kept her gaze on the equipment cabinets. "He wanted to kill you, Mia. The idiot figured you were an Acedian and when I told him you weren't, when I told him you're different from them, he...well, you know how livid he can get sometimes."

"What did he do?" Mia asked again, slower this time. She struggled to get up, at least partially, onto one side, raising her head and shoulders off the table and leaning on her arm. The wound on her side throbbed.

"He pushed me against the bulkhead." Cassidy winced, as if reliving the moment. Mia narrowed her eyes. He hurt her? "He ended up slamming my arm against the hatch. I knew he was angry. I had to stop him. I couldn't let him hurt..." Cassidy stopped, darting her eyes to Mia's face and looking away again.

Mia shook her head, disbelief coiling inside. This woman had fought for her, too? Protected her? Cassidy truly was astounding. After some time had passed, she asked, "Where are we headed?"

"You're going to prison, to the Ghost Nebula."

Mia's throat tightened. A prison planet? She only knew of one. Fissure. Memories flowed back to her. Dust, bleating animals, real food. The family who took her in for a little while. The Peri family. Clin, Sheyla, and their daughter, Viv. A fresh wave of guilt crashed over Mia. The ones she'd lied to. Would the Acedians follow her there, too?

Cassidy grimaced. "To Helix specifically. It's where you'll spend the rest of your life." She did not meet Mia's gaze, rather stared at the bulkhead instead. As if the metal had all the answers.

Mia sagged. "Helix?"

Cassidy nodded. "It's where only the worst criminals go."

At least it wasn't Fissure. Her stomach clenched at the idea of being dropped off at that barren world. But maybe it was better barren. The Acedians couldn't hurt many people there. "It's fitting I end up there."

Cassidy moved to face Mia. She seemed to be steeling herself for something, taking a deep breath and letting it out. Finally, she said in a clear calm voice, "No. It's not."

Mia looked at her. "I'm a murderer, Cassidy, I—"

"You're more than that," Cassidy interrupted. Mia looked away, the cabinets now catching her gaze. A hand pressed down on her shoulder. This time she didn't shake it off. She didn't want to. The pressure comforted her. Calmed her.

"Look at me," Cassidy whispered.

Tears prickled Mia's eyes. "No, you look at me. I'm strapped down to a table and being shipped off to prison! Is that what you want?"

"No," Cassidy said firmly. Mia tore her gaze away from the cabinets and glanced at Cassidy's blush a deeper red, squeezing Mia's shoulder tighter. "Can't you see? I like you, you idiot."

Like? Mia got stuck on that word. But Cassidy seemed to have more to say and Mia desperately wanted to listen.

Cassidy leaned closer, her words, gentle. "What you did, it's in the past. There's light inside you, not darkness. I know, deep down, you're a good person."

"Cassidy." Her voice deeper than usual. No one had ever said that to Mia before. Heat crept up the back of her neck. Wanting to protect her, to thank her, to touch her, Mia stretched her hand toward Cassidy. Her hand stopped, midair, the shackle biting against her wrist and halting her movement. She stared at it for a moment and closed her eyes, sighed. Warmth suddenly encompassed her hand, fingers intertwined with her own.

She opened her eyes and Cassidy sat next to her, holding her hand. A small smile tugged at her lips. Then, as if the *Eclipse* was not heading toward Helix, as if Mia was not a killer, as if everything had changed, Cassidy brushed a stray hair out of Mia's eyes and tucked it behind her ear, letting her fingers linger on Mia's cheek. Mia turned into the touch, chin pushing into Cassidy's palm. Heat radiated from that simple touch. They were inches apart.

"See? Not all bad," Cassidy whispered.

Mia moved her hand to clasp Cassidy's tighter when Cassidy winced and pulled her hand away, holding it up to her face.

"What's wrong?" Mia asked, leaning back to give Cassidy some space.

Cassidy silently held her wrist up for Mia to see. A small sliver of red now decorated her pale skin. The snapped shackle must have caught her. Mia glanced down and sure enough, a piece of metal jutted out from the fabric where it broke. The shackle her crew had put on her. She was going to prison, most likely would die there, and now was the moment she decided to show her feelings for Cassidy? What about her plans to destroy the *Eclipse*? How could she do that now? Cassidy's eyes were trained on the slight cut, examining it, not Mia, even though it was Mia who deserved more scrutiny. No. Despite that she desperately wanted this connection, she couldn't do it. Wouldn't. She didn't want to bring this beauty into her beastly world. Never. The warmth that radiated from Cassidy's touch dissipated. Cassidy shook her head and raised her eyes to Mia.

"You don't think this is a sign, do you?" She cocked an eyebrow, a grin still lingered on her face.

"I can't." Mia muttered, shifting away and tearing her eyes from Cassidy's.

"What?" Cassidy's smile disappeared. She got up off the table, moving away from her.

"I can't. I can't do this."

"But—"

"For galaxies sake, Cassidy, do you see these?" She raised her hands as far as they could go, bringing the shackles up.

"Of course I see them! Didn't you hear me?" Cassidy's voice grew more desperate with each word.

"So you know I'm not good enough for you. I'm dangerous," Mia shouted, ignoring Cassidy's question and trying hard not to look as Cassidy backed away. Mia seethed with thoughts she could not control. Who did she think she was, conversing with a normal human, when she herself was so twisted? So horrible. Deadly.

She had to plant the bombs, had to set them off, had to end this. Mia could see no other way. Her emotions fluctuated, confused calm, calm confusion, until finally she gave into the control, the void. The serenity. For now, at least. The cold seeped again in to her body. This time, instead of fearing it, she welcomed the chilled state. Tears slipped down Mia's cheek, and she hoped Cassidy didn't notice. She trained her eyes on the panels above her, forcing herself to not look at Cassidy. A glimpse of her shocked face, the parted lips, the wide eyes, would surely break the cold.

"Please," Mia whispered. "I don't want to hurt you."

Cassidy turned to leave, the serenity snapped apart. A desperate urge to grab onto Cassidy, to call out to her, to touch her hand at least once more, filled Mia. But only for a moment. The calm flowed over her again, washing those urges away as quietly as a ripple seeps into the ocean.

Chapter Seventeen

TIME PASSED SLOWLY. STRAPPED down and monitored, Mia was only allowed to get up to eat the meals provided to her and relieve her bodily functions. She looked at the wound and found cloth blocking her view. Skyler had done a good job covering her up. Torn by the emotions raging within her, Mia barely wanted to move anyway. The shackles aided her shocked state. Cassidy confessed her feelings. And Mia pushed her away in return. Cruel. But it had to be done. A headache started, a pounding on the left side of her temple. Her eyelids closed on their own, blocking out the light. During the first night, Mia wondered if she would freeze to death here in her own ship. A blanket settled down over her. She opened her eyes.

Cassidy tucked the blanket in, gently pushing her hands under Mia's calves, thighs, the small of her back and arms. "Better?"

"Much," Mia replied.

"Good. You shouldn't be cold," Cassidy murmured, only briefly meeting Mia's gaze. She lingered a moment before closing the hatch. The sadness within Mia leeched out again, moving slowly through the blockades within her mind and soul, warmth penetrating the cold.

Mia's body was sore, her back ached, and her limbs prickled with underuse. Her head grew heavy resting on the pillow, her vision never wavering from the hull of her ship. Her *Eclipse*. Evil. The idea never strayed far from her. Evil and alone. Mia wondered if the two could be synonymous.

But she was never truly left alone. It was the unrelenting tapping of Will's foot that finally caused Mia to glance at him. His hazel eyes seemed to swell and shimmer as she watched. Was he about to cry?

"Why did you do it, Captain?" He blinked away the tears.

"I didn't want to," Mia whispered, narrowing her eyes as if she could decipher part of his soul.

"Did you know they were following you?" Will shifted in his seat. His actions reminded Mia of a child in school, worried that the teacher might call on him.

"Yes," Mia said.

Will tilted away, arms and legs crossed. Clearly, he didn't want to be in this space with her. It seemed to hurt him too much.

"Did you know they'd attack her? That she'd be killed?" Will's voice was a hollow version of its usual self.

"Not for sure," Mia replied, sliding her gaze to the walkway. "But I supposed a family member of yours might be."

"Why?" The question came out low, forcing Mia to look at him. Will leaned forward, the gray and orange fabric of his uniform bunching at the elbow, his eyes flashing in the bright lights.

"They're attacking me so they attack my crew."

A look of what might be sorrow flashed in Will's eyes. He looked away. Jeff stalked in, Cassidy following close behind. Mia expected Jeff and Will to be in military garb, but seeing Cassidy also in gray and orange shocked her. The jumpsuit looked incredible on Cassidy. Still, a pang of loneliness sliced Mia. Did Cassidy switch sides too? Jeff stopped by her feet, hands shoved deep in his pockets, shoulders hunched. He stayed an arm's length away. His fury, with narrowed eyes and a locked jaw, closed the gap all the same.

"You are going to tell me everything," Jeff said, "I want to hear it from you, first hand."

Mia nodded, and, not under torture or duress but in the infirmary of her own ship, she told her many secrets. She related all that had happened to her throughout her lifetime, her entire past out for all to hear. Harrison had slid in after Jeff and was now simply waiting in the corner of the cabin, listening. He had changed outfits, too, from the black and white officer outfit to the military uniform. This didn't surprise her. The admiral's lackey kept gasping like he had never heard such atrocities before. Mia suspected it was a ploy of some sort, perhaps to make her feel worse about her actions. The constant interruptions only succeeded in making Jeff angry.

"Harrison, I swear, if you make another noise I'll throw you off this ship."

"You have no authority to do such a thing, Dee," Harrison said, giving a sideways glance at Jeff while doing so. "Don't try to pull rank with me."

This time no fear passed through Mia, and no concern filtered down through her thoughts. It was as if she was empty. A vessel emptied of any emotion troublesome to the human mind. True serenity must feel like this. After such a long time feeling nothing but anger and fear, she welcomed the emptiness.

The confession ended, and Jeff, apparently satisfied by Mia's direct approach, now rounded on Cassidy. She hunched her shoulders, shrinking away from him and kept glancing at Mia, eyes shimmering.

"You should've told me sooner," Jeff muttered.

"I told you as soon as I figured it was necessary," Cassidy replied.

Jeff moved toward her. A twisting sensation in Mia's core jarred her calm state. Cassidy might be in danger. As every second passed, Mia hated that she could do nothing about it. The shackles were flimsy compared to her new strength, but she didn't want to break free. Not now. Not yet. It would jeopardize the plan she had formed during the night. But if Jeff hurt Cassidy, nothing in the galaxy could stop her. She'd rip him, limb from limb.

Skyler stepped in front of Cassidy, blocking her from Jeff. He folded his arms. The twisting in Mia now turned into jealousy. Her leg twitched. She should be the one protecting Cassidy, not Skyler. Who did this woman think she was?

"Back off." Skyler narrowed her eyes at Jeff.

Jeff's arms jerked, partly untangling themselves. Would he slap her? He pulled his arms tighter over his chest, as if willing them to stay still. His jaw clenched. A muscle in his cheek contracted.

"I need to avenge my sister," he said.

"And do you think Cassidy helped to kill her?" Skyler crossed her arms, mirroring Jeff's movements.

"She might," Jeff replied. "She was helping a criminal."

"I was helping my captain." Cassidy moved around Skyler and faced Jeff alone.

"You were helping a murderer." With that, Jeff exited the infirmary, grumbling under his breath.

Throughout Mia's reveal, Will remained silent, head down, hair falling slightly over his eyes. He got up from his chair and did not look at anyone, as he walked slowly around Mia's bed. His uniform rustled when he moved. Finally, Will glanced up from the walkway and met Mia's steady gaze.

"That must be hard," he said.

By the time Mia figured out Will was continuing their previous conversation about how the Acedians would target her crew, he had already left the cabin. It seemed as if those few words were an apology. On behalf of himself or his brother? Mia didn't know.

Cassidy made a move, at first toward Mia only to switch directions. She sealed the hatch before Mia could say anything. A cold sweat broke over Mia's body and even with the blanket covering her, she shivered.

Over the next few days, she waited, and watched, searing the activity of her crew into her consciousness. Soon, she could predict each of their coming and goings. Skyler visited her often, tending to Mia's wounds. Mia tried to ignore the nurse, but Skyler often spoke of Cassidy, and Mia listened. Apparently, Cassidy wasn't doing well, fighting with Jeff and Harrison, keeping to her cabin, eating very little. It sounded like she was in mourning. Mia knew all too well what crashed against Cassidy and kept her gaze locked on the panels overhead. Skyler would move onto brazenly describing Cassidy's beauty, and Mia grew angry. She did not rise to the challenge. Never did. The frozen sensation in her, like blood, would pump back in, traveling within her body and pushing the anger away.

"She's quite the catch, if I do say so myself." Skyler lifted Mia's shirt, cutting away the bandage as she spoke. She inspected the wound.

Regardless of how much Mia disliked her, Skyler knew her trade. The once sharp, stabbing throbs deep in her side had almost diminished completely. Skyler's other hand disappeared under Mia's shirt and, at once, cold fingers prodded her skin.

Skyler winked at Mia. "And you know what they say about Skadian women. They never say no."

"That's just a rumor." Mia frowned. "Doesn't mean what you think."

"Oh really?" Skyler smiled. "Have you tried?

Heat snaked its way up the back of Mia's neck.

Skyler glanced back at the wound. "We're almost to Helix, a few more hours and you'll be shipped off with the other criminals. Is that what you want?"

"Maybe," Mia said stubbornly. "It's what I deserve, isn't it?"

"Is that what Cassidy thinks?"

Mia answered the question with silence. Skyler nodded and leaned across Mia's body to grab a clean cloth from the equipment table. Her loose, white shirt fell off her shoulder, exposing pale skin and a pretty spiral tattoo. Mia focused on the design. As if an alarm blared deep within her, Mia realized there was something wrong with the tattoo. The black ink hid something all too familiar to Mia's trained eye. Her left hand twitched. Something evil.

Skyler pushed herself to a standing position, holding the cloth in one hand and pushing her shirt back up with the other. She stopped. Her eyes widened as she looked at Mia. She stumbled backward.

"You're one of them." Mia's voice shook.

"You...you don't have to be." Skyler left without another word.

Now. Mia jerked her arms up. The bonds snapped easily. Sitting, she yanked the ankle bonds free and swung her socks to the deck. Without looking back, she moved to the far bulkhead, unhooked the grate from the air duct, and shimmied into it.

So easy, it was so easy to slip back into her old ways, as if the past two weeks, the past six months even, had never occurred. It was an odd feeling, sneaking around on her own ship, using bombs she commandeered from a fellow crewmate, from a friend. No, there wasn't time to think like that. Now was the time to sever the links, break the ties. Cassidy. Now was the time to shatter relationships that could have been. She could not destroy her crew, not this one, not this time, but she could keep them safe another way.

Her plan was simple. She would plant the bombs, pull the alarm, allow her crew time to get off the ship, get off the ship herself, blow the *Eclipse*. In the escape shuttles, each crewmate would find an archivist detailing her plans, apologizing for her faults, and warning them of Skyler. One would find a message professing her love, the reason she had to leave, and the reason to never follow. Mia had already programmed one of the escape shuttles to jettison in the opposite direction from the others. She and Skyler would have a nice, long chat. She worked quickly, quietly, placing her explosives in areas that would do the most damage, by the engine coils, under the control panels, wedged next to the airlock, and the aft hatch. Secondary explosions would surely take place in those compartments, obliterating any stray remains of the *Eclipse* from sight.

So easy, too easy, to strip emotions once more. To find that void and cling to its serenity. It had clawed at her mind and, finally, she let it have full reign. So easy. She never worried about Harrison patrolling the corridors. Military officers were easy to apprehend, easy to find patterns in their patrolling to take advantage of. Harrison stuck to that code, and Mia easily slipped past.

Will and Jeff stayed in the kitchens when Mia snuck by, merely a shadow on the bulkhead. Snippets of conversation—"You have to calm down." and "I can't believe you're defending her."—drifted over to her. She tried to ignore them. Cassidy never left her cabin. Mia thought once, and only once, of going in to see why muffled sobs could be heard outside Cassidy's hatch. If Cassidy cried in front of Mia, she could never bring herself to leave. And she had to leave, to protect them. Mia stayed far away. Skyler concerned her. The woman in white had never failed to ruffle Mia, and now she was an Acedian, too? Mia couldn't predict where the nurse would linger. Thankfully, Mia had set her last explosive and was on her way back to the infirmary, with no sign of Skyler.

Love is a weakness. The thought pounded in her head, unbidden. *It makes you vulnerable, Mia.* Was it them? She put a hand on the bulkhead, pressing her palm, her scar, against the cool metal as it started to pulse. Was it him? Her vision blurred. The deck seemed to buckle underneath her. *Sympathy, empathy, you cannot have these emotions.* A memory of Cassidy, crying, surrounded by rubble. *You know what I'll do to her once I capture you. It will not be a quick death like Freya.* Cassidy blurred. The image spun. Will and Jeff obscured Mia's vision, from only moments ago. *I'll torture all of them to get to you.*

Mia blinked, trying to see clearly, stumbling as she pushed herself into the air duct that would lead to the infirmary, trying to ward away the claustrophobia that hit while in such a small place. Air pushed past, cooling her flushed skin. She pulled herself out, replaced the vent, and sank to the deck, overcome by images not her own. Even though she felt the smooth metal under her hands, she saw Cassidy being tortured, Will screaming, and Jeff struggling as metal burnt his flesh. *This is what I'll do.* Her head pounded. The panels swam back into a blurry reality.

Mia pulled herself onto the table, her chest heaving as she took in deep breaths of air, her limbs trembled. Not from exertion or stress. From fear. They had come. Somewhere from the dark recesses of space they had clawed their way to Mia once more.

There was no warning shot, no grazing off the starboard bow, nor voices over the intercom. The *Eclipse* jolted as shots shook Mia's ship. The blasts wouldn't damage much. Cut off their engines, disable their guns, just enough to make them helpless. Not enough to kill those aboard the ship, just to make it impossible for them to run. With each hit, Mia was thrown sideways, but she clung to the table. Her fingers dug deep groves in the metal beneath her, and Mia ignored the pinpricks of pain darting up her hands.

Her mind raced. If she blew the ship now, the Acedians would surely follow both escape routes. Her crew would be in danger. Cassidy. Mia's breath caught. She had to do something. Trying to keep her legs from buckling as another shot tore into the ship, Mia whispered the lights off. No sense in making their target easier.

Searching for a weapon, Mia stumbled around the infirmary, thrusting her hands into all the cabinets she could reach. Finally, she found a small, but lethal, laser surgical knife. She thumbed the laser on, and the tip of the hooked blade glowed blue. Feeling the smooth metal against her fingers, she breathed easier. At least the captain of this vessel had a weapon. Even a weapon as small as this. Darkness surrounded her. The shouting began.

She waved the hatch open to a struggle, down the corridor to Mia's left. Will, on his back on the deck, fighting with a white-haired Acedian. Will punched the woman square in the face. Her head snapped back, and the crack from her breaking nose could be heard, even over the shouts. Mia grabbed the woman's shoulder. The Acedian had already started her next attack. A bright blue light burst on Will's chest. He froze, eyes wide, then stilled.

A roar came from behind Mia. Something knocked her into the bulkhead. She pushed herself up again just in time to see Jeff throw himself at the Acedian woman. He grabbed her hair, yanked her up, and threw her into the bulkhead opposite Mia. The woman fell to the deck, her weapon clattering alongside her, and didn't get up again. Jeff turned, his eyes locking onto Mia. Fury painted his face an ugly mask of his former self, teeth bared, eyes wide, lines and shadows crossing his face like scars. Jeff lunged toward her now, and she sank back against the cold metal, not wanting to attack her crewmate. He wrapped a hand around her throat, but before he could do any more, a burst of aqua light snaked around him. Sparked her, too. Heat shot through her neck, her shoulders, her back. He sank to the deck.

Mia stumbled away. The Acedian hurtled after her. Male or female? It didn't matter. Mia was in no shape to fight, either way. The shot that sparked through Jeff had weakened her. She swerved to the infirmary. Heat grazed her shoulder, and she stumbled away from the pulse. The shot slammed into the edge of the hatch, dazzling Mia for a moment too long. The Acedian pushed her, and she fell to the deck, her hands taking most of the impact. Heart pounding frantically, she spun around. The Acedian, a male, leaned forward and pointed his weapon at her stomach. Knowing exactly what that shot would feel like, Mia yelled.

A grunt came from the Acedian instead. He fell. Mia rolled out of the way as another person grappled with the intruder. She struggled to decipher the two shapes wrestling in the dark. A flash of brunette hair caught a curtain of light. A hand jutted upward, decorated by an orange band. Cassidy. The fist thumped down, hard, on the other form.

Mia got to her feet. The woman Mia was trying to protect from these people had just saved her from one. Was there nothing Cassidy couldn't do? She moved toward the fight. Another grunt. The Acedian rolled off Cassidy. Didn't get up again. She had ended it. Mia extended her hand.

Cassidy breathed heavily. Her entire body trembled. Her lips parted, mumbling something Mia couldn't hear. One hand grasped the miniature knife, now dripping with blood, while the other grabbed onto Mia's hand. It took all Mia's strength to pull Cassidy to her feet. The dead body stayed in the curtain of light, but both women were cloaked in darkness.

"Thank you," Mia whispered.

"Anytime," Cassidy replied.

Mia took the blade from her shaking hand and wiped the blood off, sliding the weapon back in its holder. Cassidy breathed too heavily, too quick. Mia pushed her forehead against Cassidy's and breathed in and out, slowly, measured, until Cassidy followed suit.

"Good." The word passed Mia's lips like a secret, low, meant for no one else. She rested one hand on Cassidy's cheek, and with the other she rubbed Cassidy's shaking palm, willing it to stop. Trembling never helped in a fight. A second passed. The tremors ceased.

"Good," Cassidy repeated.

A shout from down the corridor caught their attention. Cassidy moved so she could see out of the infirmary, breaking their handhold. The next few moments passed by as if time itself stood still. Cassidy turned her head toward Mia. Their eyes met. A slight smile formed on Cassidy's lips. A ball of static formed on Cassidy's chest, glowing blue directly over her heart. Her eyes widened. Her hands flailed upward. Static burst out of the sphere. Aqua waves of light traversed her skin, traveling up and down the entire length of her body. Her cry pierced the cabin. She began to fall.

"No," Mia shouted.

Time snapped back into motion. Heartbeat thudding in her ears, she leapt forward and caught Cassidy before she hit the deck. She pressed an ear to her chest, finding Cassidy's heart still beating steadily. The shot was not meant to kill. The surgical knife in Mia's hand rested by Cassidy's shoulder, puncturing the orange stripe of her uniform. Mia breathed again and thumbed the laser off. She tore her gaze from

Cassidy's face. Skyler rushed down the corridor toward her. Other Acedians followed right behind. Harrison stood in the way. Skyler shoved him against the bulkhead as she led the charge. They readied their weapons.

Mia didn't know the one who fired first, seeing only blinding streaks of aqua light smashing against corridors. Her body tensed. She tightened her hold on Cassidy. And, even as shots traversed Mia's body, spreading sparks of pain, she did not let go.

Chapter Eighteen

MIA WOKE STRAPPED TO a table again. This time the *Eclipse* didn't surround her but a different hull, a different atmosphere pressed in on her. Her breathing quickened. The place looked familiar, eerily so, but Mia knew it could not be true. The rough bulkheads, white paneling plastered with paper, could not be covered by multicolored maps. There could not be bags littering the deck. Underneath her, a yellow blanket could not rest on the cushions. Her head sank deep into a pillow that could not possibly be there. Mia fidgeted, the surface beneath her contrasted too much with what she saw, what she knew to be true. This bunk, though it looked like her small cabin on the *Hekate*, couldn't be real.

The bulkheads shimmered, flickered green. Dark metal domed up around Mia, only to be replaced by another familiar sight. Branding devices dangled overhead. Blood dripped down the bulkheads. Mia's heart raced. While her bunk on the *Hekate* could not be true, this fresh Helix could. Her hands closed into shaking fists. Sweat beaded on her skin. She trembled. She squeezed her eyes shut. Breathed. She opened them again. The bulkheads shimmered, flickered green again and darkened.

Interesting where your mind will go when you wake in an unfamiliar place.

Mia shoved his presence away. An empty cabin loomed around her, now. Dark metal again, forming a large dome, and ending in a single glaring light above. The bulkheads seemed smooth, save for three square hatches. Brown and red smears stained the metal, as if painted on with a brush. The ball of fear forming within Mia told her otherwise.

Her nose wrinkled from the lingering stench of something she couldn't place. Or maybe she simply did not want to remember the coppery scent. She tested the metal bonds on her ankles and wrists, and realized with a groan they seemed much stronger than her ship's. Another strap pressed across her abdomen. Five bonds. They deemed her a threat, at least. Thankfully, she still wore clothes. And boots now covered her feet.

Mia's thoughts roamed, scattered, fled, only to come round again to her crew. What happened to Cassidy? And Will and Jeff? It surprised her that her concern reached out for Harrison as well, even for Skyler, until Mia remembered the scar on the nurse's shoulder. Where were the Acedians holding her crew? Her crew. Not theirs. A knot hardened in Mia's stomach. For a moment, she couldn't breathe. Slowly, air trickled back into her lungs.

"Mia Foley." A strange mechanical voice echoed into the cabin, shattering her panicked thoughts. The deep robotic voice rambled on, "Twenty-five years of age, female, Captain, unknown origin, born on the family-class shuttle *Hekate*, scarred for twelve years."

"That's me," Mia quipped, her panic transforming into anger. She was back on one of their ships. She struggled to push the memories down. The Mia strapped to the table was much older and stronger than before. She forced herself to breathe evenly. They were not going to touch her again.

"Activated one month, seven hours, thirty-six minutes, twenty-nine seconds."

Activated. Mia glared at the ceiling panels. "What do you mean by activated?"

The voice did not answer her question. Instead, it simply asked another. "How are you doing today?"

The absurdity of it all angered Mia. Balling up her hands, she yanked upward. Metal screeched, as her wrists snapped free of their bonds. Cold coursed through her arms and shoulders, fueling her. Ripping the metal off her stomach and ankles, Mia sat up. Her boots hit the walkway moments later. She gripped the table with one hand and pushed it over. The heavy bolts that held the table down twisted and screeched in protest, giving in to her strength. She didn't know how she could do that, but at least she was unchained.

"Free," Mia said in a low voice. "Now what do you mean by activated."

Silence. "I cannot answer the question. Please restate, or ask another."

"Fine," Mia huffed. "How are you?"

"Unimpressed."

A square machine skittered into the cabin, propelled forward by, at least, fifty tiny legs and armored with heavy, metal plating. The machine rushed toward Mia. She backed away, but readied for a fight, unsure of the bot's programming. It was Acedian, after all. The thing just sat there, unmoving and silent. Mia circled around, examining the machine. No distinguishing marks, no grooves, only the dark plates and the miniscule legs. And this was the robot chosen to test her strength?

The machine started to vibrate, and a quiet humming filled the air. Mia stopped pacing. At first, nothing happened, the machine merely trembled and hummed. She started sliding toward the robot, as if an invisible force tugged her to the machine. Her boots slipped over the panels. What? She couldn't stop. Only a foot away from the machine, the humming grew louder, deeper. Frightening. A crack whipped through the air and an aqua wave exploded from the bot, lifting Mia up and off her feet. She slammed into the bulkhead, the blow momentarily dizzying her. Her shoulder ached from the impact, her movements, sluggish. The shockwave must be created from the same energy source as their pulse weapons. Slow the victim down until she can't fight anymore or gets knocked unconscious from the waves. A crude but effective technique. However, if the device always pulled victims toward it, she could use that technology against it.

She pushed herself to her feet. The humming softened again, and the machine pulled at her, faster now. Mia smiled. Using the momentum already created by the device, she launched herself. The machine crackled, readying for the pulse. Too late. Mia had gotten close enough for her attack to work. She pulled back a fist and punched. The heavy panels crumpled under her fist. Impossible. That metal had to be at least six inches thick. She shouldn't be able to dent it. Yet she had made a crater deep enough that her knuckles stuck. The humming stopped. The robot stilled. She yanked her hand out of the metal and stood as others crawled out of the hatch to take their fallen comrade's place. Surrounded her.

"Strength assessed." The robotic voice droned. "Testing."

The four machines crept forward, inching closer to Mia. These robots were near replicas of the first. The only difference was the twin swords that jutted out of the front. As if a switch had been flicked, Mia calmed. She did not care. She did not care that she was outnumbered. She did not care that these machines had weapons. She did not care that her crew had been captured. Her task was simple—destroy the machines in front of her. That was all that mattered now.

One of the machines moved faster than its brothers, a glitch in the programming or perhaps it was meant to be their leader. Mia turned to a humming behind her. The machine on her flank started shaking. The swords shook and cracked, and the blast knocked Mia off her feet. She rose. Not fast enough.

Humming to her right. She had just turned when the aqua wave washed over her, propelling her painfully toward a third machine. That machine thrust forward and upward with its sword. Mia somehow managed to twist around the weapon. Still, the sword cut an arc so close, the air by her cheek sizzled. She slid into the bulkhead behind the machine. She lunged, slamming herself into the machine. The swords sliced toward her again. Mia ducked and grasped onto the base of the weapons. They twisted, snapped off the robot, and crashed to the walkway. She pulled her fist back. This time her attack dove through the metal, punching a hole in the thick exterior and finding wires underneath. The machine jerked. She hung on, grasping the wires and pulling. Green electricity hissed through the air. Dark liquid seeped onto her hand. The machine stopped twitching, as if its life drained out onto the walkway.

Deep humming came from behind her. Mia swung around, letting the wires fall from her hand. The three remaining robots condensed in front of her, creating a barrier of crackling swords. A familiar pull dragged her toward the others. The humming filled the space. Mia dove around the weapons, targeting the appendages first and ripping them off, before tearing through the metal until the feeble wires were exposed. She pulled their circulatory system out with her bare hands. So quick was Mia's attack, the machines didn't have a chance to explode a single wave. When the fight ended, scraps of metal littered the deck. When she had ripped open the last of the four, her hands had begun to shake, hard metal gradually winning against her hands. Finally, she walked to the center of the cabin, pushing scraps of metal to the side, and waited.

"Sufficient." The robot voice said, "Analyze speed. Testing."

The second hatch slid open. At first Mia could not follow the new aggressors' paths, hearing only the high-pitched whistle they created as they zoomed around her. She watched, concentrating on the movements. She began to notice blurs, outlines, and finally, the machines themselves. Oval and sleek. Tiny, compared to the others. They sped around her. She batted at one with the back of her hand, connected. The machine faltered and flew up toward the top of the dome. The other machine darted upward. They seemed to converse, circling around one another, until finally turning toward her.

The whistling increased in pitch, and the tiny machines began to fire. Rapid aqua pulses raced toward Mia. She dove behind the fallen table, landing hard on her shoulder. The pulses slammed into the space where she had just stood, onto the bulkhead, and finally the table. Mia moved before the next shot fired. She dodged again and again, each attack missing their intended target and denting the deck and bulkheads instead. Mia kept her vision trained on the devices. They moved lower with each pass, still too high for her to reach.

Suddenly, they plummeted toward her. She ducked. One of the machines countered her motion by flying lower. It smashed into her chest, sending Mia to her back, breath rushing from her lungs. The devices swung round to attack her once more, one aiming for her face, the other her stomach. She pulled her legs up and kicked. Her boot connected solidly with the one gunning for her abs. It spun out of control and smashed into the bulkhead. The force of Mia's kick was so great, the device's impact created a dimple in the metal wall. Mia used the momentum of her attack to jerk herself up and whacked the remaining machine with her hand. The device went spinning to the opposite end of the space, sticking into the bulkhead just like its partner. Mia breathed. She stood, waiting for the robot voice to return.

"Acceptable."

The simplicity of the answer shocked Mia. Fear returned and anger. Soreness radiated throughout her body. Slivers of red littered her skin as blood seeped from her numerous wounds. The back of her left hand sported a stinging purple welt. Her shoulder ached. Even her heart beat hurt.

She'd had enough. Enough! She stalked over to a depression in the bulkhead, curling her hand into a fist and throwing her weight into one solid punch. It widened. The metal didn't break, wrapping itself around her fist instead. She yelled, yanking her now throbbing hand out of the bulkhead.

"Surely, you would never think we would make it that easy for you, Mia?"

The deep, gruff voice startled her. She knew that voice. Mia gathered her courage, recalled the many nights she'd spent wishing him dead. She spun to look at the man who'd killed her parents. He stood across from her, hands behind his back, feet wide. The scar on his throat caught the light and shone, as if recently oiled. Her gaze landed squarely on Charles Donavin's gray eyes. His lips turned upward in a smile.

A dam broke and all of Mia's anger came flowing out in one piercing, unending yell. One moment she was standing still, looking at this man who had destroyed so many. The next she was rushing toward him, throwing her fist back as she crossed the space between them. She reached him in a heartbeat. Her fist flew forward, faster than even she could track.

She stopped. With only a hair left between them, Mia stopped moving entirely. Unintentionally. Mia could've screamed. Her fist should connect with his ugly face and finally enact revenge. Her muscles wouldn't listen. Her veins pulsed, searing her limbs as the cold permeated her body. She stopped so close, his sour breath filled her senses, but Mia could only move her eyes.

Donavin's smile broadened. He kissed her knuckles, his lips leaving a thin coat of saliva behind, and drew back. "Do you honestly think I would enter a cabin unarmed when you are this strong?"

Mia's gaze swept Donavin's attire as much as she could in her frozen state. Wearing only rough brown pants and a matching sleeveless shirt, there was little chance he could hide much in the way of weaponry. The needles the Acedians favored, however, could be hidden almost anywhere.

Donavin's voice lifted with the barest hint of humor. "Perhaps, instead of a weapon, you should be looking for this."

He drew his hands from behind his back and held out a small device. Rounded on one end and pointed on the other: a giant, opalescent teardrop. Donavin flipped the object over and rubbed his finger over the silver metal hidden underneath. A soft, white light painted the path of his finger on the smooth surface. As soon as his finger left the device, serenity washed over her. Anger, fear, and pain drifted away until only a calm emptiness remained. Her arms dropped to her sides, somehow relaxed, even in the presence of this monster. He stroked the device once more, sideways this time. Every muscle in her lower body relaxed further, and she crumpled to her knees. Move, she ordered herself through the void. Move! Her muscles would not listen. Captive inside her own body, she could only watch as he strolled around her, a hunter teasing its prey.

"A splendid device," Donavin said, "lovely little thing, really, once the bots have a chance to spread far enough."

Mia couldn't move her lips to ask about the blasted thing. Donavin answered her unspoken question. "The ones in your system have not spread entirely throughout your body, but, as you can tell, I can still control your basic motor functions and limited emotional responses." He put the device into his pocket and gestured to the dents in the wall. "You've proven your strength to me. You certainly aren't the strongest among my ranks." His footsteps paused behind Mia. "However, you may be the fastest."

He crouched down in front of her so suddenly that her breath caught. Her heart pounded against her chest, its quickening beat filled her ears. Defenseless. In this moment she was utterly defenseless. Anger boiled up inside of her, momentarily melting her frozen core. She grasped at that sensation, feeling it slip through her as easily as water over a smooth rock. The pinky finger on her left hand twitched, but the empty sensation returned too quickly for Mia to react.

The tip of a dagger resting against her chin called her back. Her vision focused on the weapon itself instead of the man who held it. Flames etched in the metal. Snowflakes inside the flames. Her own dagger.

"This is a dagger proclaiming allegiance to the Vespa government," he said. Mia rolled her eyes, the only area of her defiance allowed at the moment. Donavin laughed, his sour breath again wafting over Mia's face. He hefted the dagger, turning it over in his hands, staring at the blade. "There shouldn't be a government to pledge allegiance to, in my opinion. Do you want to know why?" Mia couldn't answer no, so Donavin blathered on. "Because, after leaving Earth to die, they came to attack the survivors who might have carried the radiation. Generations later, if you showed even the slightest signs of radiation poisoning, you got carted away. No background checks, not even a question asked or answered." He stopped for a moment, glancing into Mia's eyes. "They took my daughter, you know, my only daughter."

He twirled the dagger between his fingers and threw it, the clang from the impact echoing back. His fingers found her face, gently caressing Mia's cheek. Fury surged through Mia at even this slightest touch. Warmth seeped into her frozen limbs.

"You remind me of my daughter, Mia Foley, did you know that? Her eyes had the same shade of blue. A piercing, intelligent color." His fingers wove through her hair, playing with a lock. When he spoke again, his voice caught, "I knew you were a fighter the moment I saw you, just like my little Elanora. Where you acquired that kind of spirit, I'll never know. Your parents certainly weren't blessed with it."

Her mind raged. Her parents were strong.

They were old. Donavin smirked. *You were not. I need the power of youth for my plan to work.*

His telepathy trick didn't faze Mia, though the path his thoughts were heading certainly did. Instead, she focused on the anger boiling inside her. Only when she heard Cassidy's name did she listen once more.

He titled his head, scar catching the light again. "Remember Cassidy Gates? Of course you do, silly me, how could you forget? You love her."

Warmth spread throughout Mia's body, like a breeze caressing her skin. Mia's vision blurred, and images of Cassidy spread before her, making breakfast, sliding her extra pieces of meat, sitting on the couch curled around a hot drink, smiling as she accepted Mia's gift, the way her blush stained her cheeks and ears, the heat of her hand.

"I can take that away," Donavin murmured.

The images stayed, but the joy vanished, the warmth dissipated. Mia felt nothing, as if Cassidy were a stranger to her, as if the past six months had never happened, as if she watched a different life taking place, far from her own.

"Remember Freya? Will? Jeff?"

One by one they floated up into Mia's vision, vanishing as the next appeared. She felt nothing.

Donavin's voice lingered by her ear. He brought an old piece of parchment in front of her face. The list. Her list. "Remember this?"

He slowly ripped the list apart and let the pieces float the ground. Still nothing. Yet her fingers did move by her own accord, ever so slightly.

Donavin grinned. "I discovered if you remove the emotions from memories, the images become stale, worthless almost. The ties sever."

Mia's hand twitched.

"And if you remove those memories entirely, you become empty."

Mia's world disappeared. Who was this man? Who was she? All at once, memories flooded back with a sensation of snapping back into herself. Dizziness. Donavin came back into focus. He has the power to take memories?

"Yes. I usually do not remove memories, unless asked."

Who would ask?

"You'd be surprised how many do," Donavin replied. He sighed, a long heavy sigh laden with seemingly endless troubles. "Doing so makes control that much harder, so I've perfected my voiding technique instead. And I must say, your Cassidy Gates would be a fine specimen for my bots to inhabit. Her emotions run close to the surface. She does not hold back and, so, will be quite simple to control."

The pinky finger on Mia's left hand twitched again. Her hand broke the barrier of his control, grasping Donavin's neck. The quickened beat of his heart pulsed under her palm. He smiled, gray eyes crinkling. Mia's hand froze again. He tilted his head and broke free of her grip. Nodding, he stood.

One swift kick and Mia's chin was on fire. She lay flat on her back. Her vision blurred then sharpened. She put her hand to her aching chin. Move. This time she did. She pushed herself to her feet. For now Mia accepted there was little she could do to stop him, all too aware of how heavily she breathed, how tired she was, how much her hands shook and bled. He watched her for a moment, then walked toward one of the hatches and waved it closed behind him, taking her dagger and pride with him as the hatch slid shut.

"Good." The robotic voice echoed around the cabin once more.

Chapter Nineteen

AFTER DONAVIN LEFT, TWO more Acedians came to escort her from the cabin. She spared the barest of glances at the pieces of her ruined list. The inked paper torn, but the ships still in her memory. Mia hoped at least she would see the rest of her crew, if only to check that they were okay. How could anyone be handling this well? The corridors looked old, the bulkheads worn, held together by scraps of paneling and rusted bolts. A thin layer of dust covered every surface. Even with the dust, the air smelled clean, too clean. Her nose stung. What was the manufactured air laced with? White lights lined the sides of the deck and overhead, casting too bright a glow for the narrow area. Everything here on display.

Mia passed a viewport, chancing a quick look out into space. Infinite gems sparkled on a velvet backdrop of black. Not one of the star systems looked familiar. Although, a ship certainly did. The orb narrowed at the bow and an ATS was blazed on the metal. The *Eclipse*. Scorch marks blemished her sides, guns were torn off the starboard side, and a breach ripped the dark outer hull, exposing the lighter metal underneath. She still flew, floated, drifted more like, but flew nonetheless. A cuff to the back of her head pushed Mia's gaze forward. Idiot. Lingering on a ship. They would use that against her. Quiet dominated here. Gray-eyed people moved about the narrow walkways, squeezing past Mia and her two guards. No one spoke. No one had to.

Destroy the ship.

With the people still on it?

Yes.

Mia pushed the thoughts away. She stopped. Wait. People still on it? Was her crew still on the *Eclipse*? Was Cassidy? She shoved her two guards out of the way and pressed her hands harder against the glass. Her breath misted the surface. The lights from the panels above washed the viewport out. She struggled to see through the glow. The lights above her flickered to green, and the space outside became clearer. The *Eclipse* loomed closer than she expected, closer. Helpless. One voice eased itself easily into her mind, and it did not take long for her to realize whose.

Yes.

Wait," Mia muttered. Could Donavin hear her?

Isn't this what you wanted?

"Wait," she said again.

Isn't this what you planned for?

"No, not with them..."

The explosion began slowly—a flash of red there, a hull breach here—but it was enough to quell Mia's sputtering. With the secondary explosions basking them in such a vivid light, Mia knew it had to be the bombs she had planted that finally did the *Eclipse* in. She closed her eyes, only to force them open again. She had to watch. Even if there was nothing she could do to save them now. She could at least watch as her ship was torn to pieces, a horrifying display of fire spheres on a backdrop of the endless blackness of space. Only when the last remnants of the *Eclipse* floated out of sight did Mia turn away. She walked passed the guards, who then followed her, and trained her eyes on the walkway ahead, keeping her face a mask of outward serenity. She would not give them the satisfaction of her tears.

I gave you life, Mia Foley, life.

Life? She replied viciously, feeling the mental connection between herself and Donavin. Somehow they were tethered in this moment. She shoved her thoughts across the link. *You took my life. I would have been normal if not for you! These people would have been normal. My crew would still be living if not for you.*

If not for your plan to kill them perhaps. You planted the bombs. I merely lit the spark.

Mia couldn't think of a response. Donavin didn't give her much time anyway, pushing his own words into her instead. *I gave you health. Can't you feel it? You're better now. Better than your old form, at least. Even your wounds heal quicker.*

As much as Mia hated to admit it, his statement did carry truth. She shoved her thoughts again over the link. *I'd rather have my friends, my ship, and my life back.*

Your life will be with us, Captain, once your transformation is complete.

Donavin continued to force his way into Mia's mind. She willed herself not to listen. Words too terrible and foul crashed through her, whispering of death, of destruction, of chaos. To distract herself, Mia tried to keep a mental record of the turns, but the frequency of them, coupled with so many other voices in her head, caused her to lose track. She held tight her own musings the rest of the way.

They passed by a holding cell. This one had a resident already, a young boy whimpering in the corner. They passed by a large round hatch where screams could be heard even through the thick metal. They passed by another like Mia, whose golden eyes had not been changed. His demeanor had, walking slowly, slumped. Broken. Mia swallowed the lump in her throat and tried hard not to think of what was to come. For any of them.

Soon, they reached her cell. One guard, an ugly thing with too much neck and no hair, twice the size of a normal human, tapped a button. The other, a small woman whose arms were littered with scars, stood next to Mia, watching. The hatch hissed open before Mia, revealing a tiny empty cell. She shivered. This cabin was similar to the one she had occupied the first time around, a young girl whimpering in the corner just like the boy. Could it be possible that this was the place they kept her in so many years ago? Perhaps. The fear and pain slid in easily, nudging up to her like old friends, wrapping their arms around her shoulders and squeezing them tense. Her escorts shoved her into the cabin and the hatch sealed shut.

Silence. No voices filtered inside her. Only her own thoughts lingered now. Rubbing her eyes, she stalked around the cabin. Her breathing came heavy, gasping almost. She had destroyed another ship, another crew. And not just any crew, this time. Her lungs hurt as her gasps turned to heaves. Her vision blurred. Tears ran down her cheeks. What had she done? Cassidy's face welled up, her laughter, her smile, her warmth. Mia stalked the other direction. What would be left for her now? Her hands trembled. She clenched them into fists as the waves of guilt broke over her.

Finally it all came out in a yell, a shout, a blasted scream. There was nothing left for her. She eyed the bulkhead. Nothing left to do, but cause a Helix-level hell on this Acedian ship. She walked over to that bulkhead, pulled her fist back, and punched. A dent pillowed outward. The sharp sting radiating from that blow shocked her system. A good sting. She punched again, and again, and again. Each blow created a dent all its own. Tears coursed down Mia's cheeks, hot streams dripping off her face and down onto her neck. This bulkhead wouldn't give. Maybe another would.

She ran toward the other bulkhead, Jeff and Will's face submerging in her troubled mind as she roundhouse kicked that barrier. A depression creaked through the wall but didn't break. Each breath tore through her. Her entire body trembled now. Had she really destroyed her crew? Had she killed people she cared about? Again? She had to calm down. She tried reaching out to the others on the ship. Something blocked her thoughts. Silence, Mia welcomed it for only a moment before her insecurities crept back. Had she really destroyed her crew? No, she hadn't. They had. The Acedians.

Mia punched the bulkhead. It crushed under her strength. She yanked her hand back, and the metal bowls reformed to a smooth bulkhead. She turned away. Donavin had mentioned a transformation. She had changed in her dreams. Would she turn into one of them outside that dreamscape?

And, in that empty cabin, without knowledge of her crewmembers, without any soul to tell her otherwise, the blackness inside of her told Mia she already had. She walked to the corner of the cabin, leaned on bulkhead, and slid to the deck, head resting on the metal. She rubbed the welt on the back of her left hand, wincing. The metal sent shivers through her.

A few moments later not only her back shivered, the rest of her body did as well. The bulkhead Mia leaned on hummed, vibrated even. Pushing herself away from the strange wall, Mia turned to face the now shaking structure. The square bots. The pulses that sent her flying. Here too? She braced herself for the wave. It never came. The bulkhead still shook.

"What the quasar—"

The muttered curse barely passed her lips before the wall disintegrated completely. Metallic cubes crumbled to the deck only to shatter into smaller sections as they hit the surface. A wave of silver flowed toward her. She leapt back to avoid it but found she did not need to. The wave stopped just before touching her, froze solid, silver cubes sticking out of the wave at strange angles then melting into the deck beneath it. So shocked by the curious events, Mia did not see the person now standing directly in front of her. It took a strangled cry to remove her gaze from the smooth surface where the bulkhead once stood. Arms flew around her shoulders and a body crushed into Mia's. Brown hair obstructed her view and sinna wafted around her. A face burrowed into her neck. Lips brushed against her bare skin. Mia gently wrapped her arms around Cassidy's trembling body as they pressed together.

"Mia!" Cassidy's voice wavered. "I was scared when they took—"

"I'm fine," Mia interrupted.

Her heartbeat quickened as the warmth from Cassidy's body mingled with her own. Abruptly, Cassidy stepped back, out of Mia's reach. Were any noticeable wounds on Cassidy? No. Cassidy's clothes—idiotic military garb—looked fine save for a few minor rips. Her wristband was gone. Still. She was alive. Here. Whole. Relieved, Mia finally looked at Cassidy's face. Redness tinged her eyes.

"I thought the blast killed you," Mia muttered, moving closer to Cassidy.

Cassidy backed away from Mia, shaking her head. "No, I was just stunned."

Mia looked at her. Slowly, she pieced it together. Cassidy did not know about the *Eclipse*. She only remembered the gun pulse. Mia wavered in her choice to tell Cassidy. She decided not to. Cassidy was acting strange already.

"Are you okay?"

Cassidy bit her lip. "Yes, but..."

"They haven't done anything to you?" Mia stepped closer.

Cassidy stepped back again. "No, but..."

"Where's the rest of the crew?"

"That's what I've been trying to tell you." Cassidy frowned. "They've been taken."

Shock rippled through Mia. "How long ago?"

Cassidy shrugged. "I don't know, an hour, maybe two. It seems like I've been pacing this cabin for ages. I don't know what else to do. They haven't come back and I..."

"Have you found a way out?"

Cassidy's ramblings came to an abrupt stop. She trembled, lips pursed together, eyes shining with tears. "There is no way out!" Cassidy shook her head and backed up farther. She now stood an arm's length away from Mia. She looked ready to run, a trapped bird locked in too small a cage. Cassidy's words came out in a rush, tumbling over one another, drenched with fear. "Those stories you told, Mia, of what they did to you? I couldn't survive that. I'm not like you. We're locked in this breaching cell and there's no way out."

Mia cocked an eyebrow at Cassidy's use of Skyler's expletive. She ignored it for now. Cassidy looked to be on the verge of a complete meltdown. Mia took a step toward her. Cassidy stepped back again, shaking her head. Did she not want to be comforted? Cassidy had a rational side. The woman could calm a meteoroid shower if only Mia could get through to her. And Mia needed her.

She stretched her hands to the shaking woman and spoke in a low, even tone. "There is always a way out, Gates."

Neither woman moved. Cassidy still seemed frightened.

Mia tried again. "I got out of here once, remember?"

Cassidy nodded.

"So we can do it again."

A flicker of something, hope perhaps, skittered across Cassidy's brown eyes. She blinked, once, twice, then too rapidly to count. With a deep breath, she seemed to pull herself together, rubbing her hands over her arms. Her trembling ceased.

"That's logical," she finally said. "How? And what about the others?"

Images of Skyler rose unbidden in Mia's head, of Cassidy running toward her, of Will and Jeff cuffing her on the shoulder, only to have their throats slit by the woman who was not who she seemed. The raven-haired nurse. Mia blinked the images away. Her body tensed at even the imagined deaths.

"We'll find them." She turned away from Cassidy.

Mia took in her new surroundings. The cabin the two women now shared was merely a replica of the smaller version. Empty, save for them. Mia could only imagine Cassidy walking this way and that in the tiny cell, getting more worried every moment that passed.

She ran her hand over the walls. "Have you checked each bulkhead?"

"Yes, the blasted things are solid," Cassidy replied. Mia smiled at Cassidy's sudden influx of curses, preferring her anger over fear any day. Cassidy looked at the empty space where the bulkhead between them once stood. "Except for the one that crumbled. What was that?"

"I haven't the foggiest idea. I didn't know ships could do such a thing. Much less that the Acedians could." Mia stalked over to one of the bulkheads and tapped on the metal. "Do you think all the walls do that?"

Cassidy came over and put her ear to the bulkhead. "I don't know. Did you feel it vibrate before it fell apart?"

"Yeah."

"Maybe it's a certain frequency." Cassidy made a fist and knocked on the bulkhead, listening. "Like a high-pitched sound wave, higher than the ear can detect, but enough to shake the metal apart?"

"Wouldn't that shake us apart, too?" Mia leaned against the cold surface.

"I don't know," Cassidy muttered.

"Well, these bulkheads might be weaker than others." Mia looked at Cassidy and tilted her head to the side. "Move."

Cassidy backed away, arching an eyebrow. Mia pulled her arm close to her body, tightened her shaking hand into a fist, and threw her weight forward, punching the metal as hard as she could. The bulkhead creaked from the force of her attack, its metal folding over her hand, but still not shattering apart.

"Mia! What was that about?" Cassidy's exclamation and hands landed hard on Mia's shoulders. She pulled Mia to the side and gawked at the sight.

"Blast it." Mia yanked her hand out from the iron grasp. She shook her pained hand, rubbing it with the other. The welt throbbed under her fingers.

"Even you're not that strong," Cassidy inspected the dent. "You are freakishly strong, though." The bulkhead melted back into place, and Cassidy backed away. "Did the metal just do that?"

"Yeah, it happened in my cell, too. We have to get out of here." Mia looked anywhere but at Cassidy.

"We will." Cassidy looked at the welt on Mia's hand. Cassidy grabbed it, her eyes narrow. She flipped her hand over and looked at her scar. "Did Donavin do something to you? To your scar?"

Mia didn't want to divulge that she had met Donavin and could not fight him, that they had more control over her than she originally feared, that this organization seemed bigger than she originally imagined, and that she was beyond frightened of what that could mean. How could she tell Cassidy she was turning into a monster? That she had planted the bombs that destroyed the *Eclipse*? Mia's eyes searched the cabin again. There had to be a way out.

Mia tried to find the right words. "It was...it was some sort of test." Her gaze finally landing on Cassidy.

"A test?" Cassidy asked, hooking their fingers together. "What did they have you do?"

"I fought machines."

Cassidy glanced up, their eyes met. "That's it?" She sounded startled.

"Yes." The fib ripped through Mia. She welcomed the guilt. At least they could not control her emotions here.

A muscle in Cassidy's jaw twitched, her eyebrows furrowed slightly. "I doubt it." She dropped Mia's hand and stepped away. "Don't breaching lie to me."

That blasted curse again. Mia pushed off against the bulkhead and began pacing the cabin, analyzing every surface. There had to be a way out. She had to find one.

"Don't use that word," Mia said, glaring every so often at Cassidy.

"What?" Cassidy's eyes widened.

She eyed the spot where their shared wall liquefied. "Breach. Don't use it."

Cassidy scoffed. "Why?"

Mia glared at her. "Because she uses it."

Mia remembered the scar hidden beneath Skyler's tattoo and the evil that lurked within. Just like her. It felt too small in this cabin. Too cramped. She cursed herself, trying to replace the fear with anger. Failed. She stopped pacing and turned away, not wanting Cassidy to see her anguish.

"Skyler? So what?" Cassidy's voice carried laughter with it, brushing off Mia's anger. She touched Mia's arm. "I told you that you didn't have to lie to me. What else happened during the test?"

"Skyler uses that term, so don't make it your own. I don't want you imitating her." Mia ripped herself away from Cassidy's touch. Why were they fighting? Still, she couldn't let Cassidy trust Skyler. Not now. Not ever.

Cassidy took hold of Mia's shoulder and spun her around once more. "Stop avoiding my question! What's wrong?"

"She's one of them," Mia shouted.

Cassidy let go of Mia's shoulder and pounded her hand against the bulkhead. "Oh, breach it, you don't really believe that."

"You saw her running at us, leading the Acedians." Mia rubbed her neck, trying to quell her anger, her fear. Failed, again. Her chest tightened, making breathing painful. Of all people, Cassidy had to believe her. Even though she pushed her away before, even though she hurt Cassidy's feelings, there had to be a way to make her believe.

Cassidy expelled a puff of air and stared at the far side of the cabin. "Skyler was running away from them."

Mia shook her head. "I saw her scar! Besides, why else would I warn you about her?"

Cassidy folded her arms, tilting her head ever so slightly. She was silent for a moment before replying. "Because you're jealous of her, perhaps."

"Wha…what?" Mia stuttered. Jealous? Perhaps. Probably. That wasn't the only reason. Skyler was dangerous.

Cassidy pulled herself up to her full height. She glared at Mia. "Quasar, Mia! I've told you how I feel and what do I get in return? Silence. Anger. Pushed away! I've seen how you are around me, and you still don't tell me. You're just too breaching afraid to make a move, and she isn't. How do you think that makes me feel, huh?" Cassidy's voice wavered. "Or maybe you're just doing it to cover another lie, because, Foley, I never do really know with you."

A deep blush crept up Cassidy's neck during her last words, tinting her ears and cheeks. Mia gaped at her. Cassidy glared back, eyes narrowed, mouth set in a firm, trembling line. Making a move? How did they ever get onto this topic? And in the belly of an Acedeian ship, was there ever a worse time?

"I'm not afraid." Mia's quiet words carried deception Cassidy did not miss.

Cassidy scowled. "Liar," she whispered. A flash of something, pain probably, crossed her face.

A hissing noise interrupted the two women. Mia's gaze flitted around the cabin before landing on the source. A hatch slowly opened in the far corner of the cabin. Mia rushed to it. A heartbeat later, she froze. Cassidy crashed into her, hard. There was nothing Mia could do. He had control over her again. Her skin beaded with an icy sweat. Another heartbeat. Men stumbled into the cabin, and Cassidy started trembling again.

It took only a moment to recognize them. Harrison, the admiral's lackey survived the first torture session, as had Will. Where was Jeff? The men barely looked at Mia, seeming to want to get as far away from that hatch as possible.

A guard followed, a young man no older than any of them. Mia half-hoped he would take her. The guard latched onto Cassidy's trembling arm and began to drag her away. *No!* Mia forced her thought to the guard. Deadened gray eyes looked at her, but the only reply was a vision. Cassidy, arm broken, lay strapped to a table. Acedians loomed over her, pushing iron into her shoulder, branding her. A moment later the vision disappeared, breaking apart and drifting away as if it never occurred. Mia's heart quickened. She threw her thoughts over the link. *Take me instead. Take me!* Cassidy swung a fist at the man. He blocked it easily. She wasn't a fighter. Mia's arm twitched. Cassidy struggled, screamed. The guard kept dragging her away.

A blur of movement beside Mia startled her. One of the men—Harrison—punched the guard's face, but Harrison was too weak. The blow barely moved the guard's head and the one he gave back sent Harrison flying. Mia's leg twitched. Regardless of the emotions swarming within her, she could not break free. Cassidy's terrified eyes met hers once more, and the hatch hissed shut.

Chapter Twenty

MIA'S MUSCLES RELEASED, AND she lurched forward, stumbling toward the exit. Cassidy's shouts filtered through the hatch.

"Cassidy," Mia yelled, pounding on the metal.

She threw her fist forward, the impact of her punch ringing through the quiet cell. The metal screeched and dented. She hit again and again, fury charging her muscles, clouding her mind. Moments later despite being dimpled in many places, the hatch still stood. Mia sank to her knees, hands throbbing. A sob escaped her lips. Cassidy taken, already bruised by Mia's stupidity. Jeff, somewhere on the ship, undergoing who knows what. But, she could save them. The idea eased her worry. Regardless of what she may become in the future, right now Mia was herself, grounded, captain of the *Eclipse*, the woman who would escape this prison whole and with her crew. She breathed. Calmed. There would be time for fear later.

Harrison groaned behind her. He had landed spread eagle, strands of hair messy over his forehead, and a dribble of blood pooling by his nose. She scooted over to him. With his breathing regular and eyes closed, unconsciousness clearly took him away from this place. She frowned. Great. Just what she needed now. Mia left him where he was and looked to Will instead.

Will had sunk down in the far corner, hands on his knees. Mia went over, slowly, and crouched down beside him. The man flinched. Swallowing a lump in her throat, she assessed the damage done. Eyelids opening and closing, nostrils flaring, mouth set in a quivering line, he looked like he'd been through a black hole. He may have. Cuts lacerated his military jumpsuit, on the shoulder, the lapel, the chest. Blood seeped through. Not enough to worry Mia. Nothing seemed broken. He breathed, if not easily.

"Will?" Mia whispered.

He didn't respond, eyes were unfocused. Did he even know she was there? Probably not.

"Will, look at me." She touched his arm, expecting him to shrink away. Nothing. Not even a waver in his gaze or a sudden intake of breath. What had they done to him?

"He won't talk," a voice croaked.

Mia glanced back at Harrison. He had woken and pushed himself into a seated position, resting on his hands. Blood saturated his torn uniform, but he did not seem to notice or care about the cuts beneath. He coughed, dry scratching heaves that shook his entire body.

She winced at the sound. "Why not?"

"Why should I trust you?" He stared at her coldly.

The words held the accusation of her scar and past embedded within. Understandable. "I'm locked in the cell with you, you imbecile." She punched the deck, immediately regretting it as Will shied away from the sudden movement. "Why would they do that if I were on their side?"

"It would be an excellent ploy, placing a spy here." Harrison's face betrayed no emotion.

"And what would I learn from you that they don't already know?"

"Point taken," he muttered, an edge to his voice Mia had never heard before. "Although I doubted you were one since I saw you fight on the *Eclipse*. Why would anyone defend her crew against a threat they themselves were a part of?" Harrison's eyes never left hers as he spoke. Mia nodded and started to respond when he cut her off. "Either way, I don't trust murderers."

"Fine." She sat down on the deck, legs crossed, as close to Will as possible without actually touching him. Regardless of how far gone he was in this moment, he needed to know someone protected him.

"You don't need to trust me." Mia chose her words carefully. "My past will damn me when we leave this place, but for now, it's the only source of information we have. We need to work together if we are ever going to get out of here. Do you understand?" He nodded, and Mia continued, "Now, what happened? And talk quickly, we don't have much time."

"Torture. They tried it on him first." Harrison jerked his head toward Will. "They only did it to break me, though."

Mia must have looked confused because he explained, "It was an obvious way to make me talk. They interrogated him. After they brought out the knife, he didn't speak. Screamed, yes, but never an actual word. It worked, made me talk. I told them about my responsibilities as an officer, my transfer to the military, where the fleet was searching, how many ships they had, anything to get them to stop. I tried telling them Will had just joined. They were done with him anyway."

Harrison faltered. His gaze drifted down toward Will. After a moment's time, Harrison seemed to remember where he was, shook his head, and met Mia's eyes once more. "He never spoke ill of you, Captain Foley. They asked how he came into contact with you, how you acted and reacted to things, why you joined sides with the military. He simply said 'she's my captain' and never spoke again. I thought you should know."

Mia grimaced, the loyalty of her crew making her restless. Her idiotic loyal crew. She rubbed one hand with the other, her thumb pressing against the scar on her palm. Because of her, these people were going through this hell.

One look at Will, quivering, silent, and she rose to her feet, pacing the cabin. "Did you get any information about them?"

"Well, they deemed us unfit for their type of duty." Harrison's voice took on a sarcastic edge.

She glared at him. The man had no idea. "You don't want to be fit for their type of duty."

"After that, they no longer cared what we knew. I believe they mean to kill us, anyway, all of us." Harrison rolled his eyes. He pulled himself backward until his back rested on the bulkhead. "The man called himself Donavin. He spoke of battle plans, of his great and powerful army taking over the government and putting a rightful leader as head. He's a harried citizen that's all."

"A harried citizen who is attacking planets, killing, and capturing people isn't worrisome?" Mia stalked the other direction.

Harrison sighed. "He is, of course, but my death would simply be a causality of war. And the Vespa military is far too big to be taken down by one man."

She rounded on him. What about the people from Paradous? The children? "You've enlisted volunteers to help with the search."

He waved her concern away. "Only from Paradous, and that was merely to give the citizens something to go after. Our planet was decimated. The citizens needed an outlet for their rage."

Mia could hardly believe his arrogance. But she needed his help to get off this ship. She needed everyone's help. "Did you see anything when they brought you around the ship, something that might help us escape?"

"No, I was knocked out. The last thing I recall was a boot heading toward my face," Harrison muttered. He tilted his head toward Will. "He might have seen something."

Mia went over to the Dee brother.

"Will." She towered over his trembling form. He didn't move, didn't even look up at her. Enough! She leaned down and grabbed Will, hauling him to his feet. "William Dee, you are going to break out of this right now. We need you here!"

Her yells echoed in the cabin, bouncing off the walls. Will shook his head, and for a moment, Mia figured he would speak. His eyes widened. He knocked her hands off his jumpsuit and sprung backward, crashing into the bulkhead.

"That worked out brilliantly, Captain," Harrison said in the corner. "Don't you know anything about torture? People react in different ways."

Mia ignored him. Of course she knew about torture. With Jeff still gone and Cassidy taken, there was too much at stake. Harsh love didn't seem to work, so she tried a quieter voice. She reached to Will, palms down, in what she hoped was a calming manner.

"Will, it's terrifying, I know. We have to figure out a way to get out of here. I need your help."

He pushed himself against the bulkhead, his eyes wide. A knock came from outside the hatch. Mia turned to see the dents she'd created on the hatch melt away, metal vibrating and reconfiguring itself until a smooth surface appeared. The hatch hissed open, and Skyler walked in. No cuts on her person, no rips in her clothing at all.

Harrison let out a strangled cry. "Skyler, you're all right! Where did they take you?"

Leaving Harrison's question unanswered, Skyler's gray gaze lingered on all three of them, before finally landing on Mia. The hatch closed behind the woman in white. Mia moved between the traitor and Will, but Skyler raised her hand.

"Captain Foley, wait," Skyler said.

Mia tensed, ready to move, to fight, if needed. "Why should I?"

"Because I can help." Skyler eyed Mia's aggressive pose but didn't return one.

Mia scoffed. "You've helped enough."

"What's going on here?" Harrison said. There was a shuffling sound, a groan, and Harrison slid in between them.

"She's one of them!" Will blurted from behind Mia. "She was outside the cabin. I saw her. She's with them."

"Shut him up, will you?" Skyler snapped, her gaze sliding off Mia as Harrison went to calm Will down. With her gaze fixed only on Skyler, Mia couldn't tell what Harrison had done. Only muffled sounds came from behind her now. Mia shifted her position slightly, spreading her feet and balling her hands into fists. She wouldn't let Skyler close to the men. Not even Harrison, even though he infuriated her. Silence filled the cabin, pressing down on Mia with every moment that passed.

Finally, Skyler shifted her gaze off of the men and back onto Mia. "I know where your crew is being held."

"Of course you do. Like Will said, you're an Acedian." Mia spit out the last word as if it were poison in her mouth.

"What?" Harrison's yelp went ignored.

"And why do you say that?" Skyler didn't move, her hand still held in the air like a barrier between them. The hand—small, pale, undecorated—never wavered, never even shook.

Mia frowned. "Don't be stupid. We both know I saw your scar. You're one of them."

Skyler pointed to her own left palm. "You have a scar, too. Does that make you Acedian?"

Even the sound of it made Mia angry. Irrationally angry. "No—"

"Are you certain, Captain?"

A sudden heat crashed through Mia's system. Did she know for sure? Donavin did control her. Did take away her emotions for a little while. Did make her sink to the deck. But he didn't have all of her. Not yet.

"You kept going after Cassidy, kept bringing her up whenever we spoke. Right after she gets taken, you come in. Why? To get to me?"

"Breach it, Mia, don't be so self-centered." Skyler's hand dropped, her shoulders sagged, her eyes rolled. The action made Mia feel ignorant. "They took Cassidy, because she's strong and her emotions are raw. She'll be easy to control. But you're right, I did use her to assess how far gone you are."

"What?"

Skyler stepped closer. "Did he demonstrate his powers?"

Mia's chest tightened, remembering the demonstration. How defenseless she was. She forced her reply out. "Yes."

"You still have emotions, don't you?" Moving closer still, Skyler frowned. "You can still feel?"

The question startled Mia out of her memories. "Yes."

"Good, I'm not too late. We have to go." Skyler moved toward Harrison and Will. Mia blocked her. Skyler narrowed her eyes. "Breach it! We have to get out, grab Cassidy before they start on her, get Jeff, and leave. Now!"

"Why should we trust you?" Will's voice floated from behind Mia.

Skyler fished around in her pocket and pulled out a device, a small opalescent teardrop device. Mia recognized it instantly.

"This is a device that renders them IA," Skyler said.

"IA?" Harrison asked.

"Inactive." Even though she answered Harrison's question, Skyler's gaze still locked on Mia. "This controls them, not all of them, not at the same time, not for long, but it can stop them, like how Donavin was able to freeze you during your testing. Here." Skyler tossed the device across the span of empty space between them. Mia caught it. "Now, you can control them."

Mia hesitated. It made more sense if Skyler was an Acedian. They had not tortured Skyler like they had the others. The woman had even come at Mia and Cassidy with a weapon. She was a traitor, wasn't she? The IA device seemed too light in Mia's palm, insignificant, smooth and rounded. Tiny. Not strong enough to do the damage it promised.

Narrowing her eyes, Mia asked, "You know where Cassidy is being taken? Where Jeff is held?"

"Yes." Skyler's gaze never wavered. Although her answer rang true, those dark gray eyes warned Mia.

"This may be our only chance," Harrison said. Mia turned to look at the two men. Will stood, trembling. He shook his head, unmistakably a no. Harrison stepped forward. "We should take it."

Turning her back to Skyler as an indication of, at least, a tentative agreement, Mia walked slowly over to Will.

"I don't trust her," Will whispered, his eyes flitting from Mia to the woman behind her.

"I don't either," she said, calm and firm. "But trust me."

Will held her gaze for a moment before he nodded.

Mia turned back to Skyler. "We're in."

Skyler motioned to the hatch. "Let's go."

Chapter Twenty-One

MIA LED THE WAY out of the cell, Harrison followed, and Will shuffled behind them both. A quick glance back told her all she needed to know about the mindset of the men. Harrison walked straight-backed, eyes narrowed and forward, a man who believed they would survive this ordeal. Will portrayed no such confidence: eyes to the deck, arms close to his body, and shoulders hunched. A man who wanted to be anywhere but here. She heard a noise at the far end of the corridor.

As the noise became footsteps, Mia took out Skyler's small device that promised so much, intending on using it on whomever turned the corner ahead. A hand on her arm caused her to look at Skyler, who shook her head and tapped a finger to her forehead. Mia raised an eyebrow, not understanding. Skyler pushed Harrison and Will back the way they had come and into the cell, putting a finger over her lips as she did. They cooperated. Will looked more than happy to go back inside, tottering and trembling as he did. Harrison was not so willing, a clenched jaw his only tick.

"I thought we had to leave immediately," he whispered, blocking the door so the hatch couldn't close.

"Jones!" A bark came from behind Mia, startling her. She whipped around to see a short brunette woman staring at her. No, staring past her at Skyler. The nurse narrowed her eyes at the newcomer. Mia, caught in between the two women, heard everything.

What are you doing? The brunette's eyes flitted to the hatch door, where Harrison stood, gritting his teeth.

They were making a ruckus. I wanted to see if I could subdue them.

A ruckus? Who cares? I'm ordered to take Foley to Station Five. Charles would like to scan her.

I'll do it.

Fine.

With that the brunette left, no argument, no question, her gray eyes passing over Skyler, past Mia, past everything it seemed. Those lifeless, blank eyes frightened Mia. The brunette's footsteps echoed down the corridor as she left. Mia shivered. Skyler placed a hand on Harrison's arm and pushed him backward.

"I just got word I have to take Mia to a check-in station," she said. "Donavin is there. He'll be expecting us right away. It's just a routine scan to see how far the bots have progressed."

"We don't have time for a routine scan," Mia whispered, grasping Skyler's arm and squeezing it. "Cassidy was just taken. We don't know how long Jeff's been with them. We have to get them out!"

Skyler glanced at Mia's hand on her arm. "I know, and we will. If we try to leave now, they'll know something is up and my cover will be blown."

"I don't care about your blasted cover. They're my crew." Anger raised Mia's voice, quickened her pulse.

"One man and one woman are not enough to breaching blow this. The scan is quick, a few moments. We'll leave after." Skyler yanked her arm out of Mia's grasp and glanced at Harrison, who still stood by the door. "Be ready when we get back."

With those words, Skyler pushed a code into the control panel and the hatch slid shut, locking the men inside. Placing a hand on Mia's shoulder, the nurse pushed her down the corridor. The weight of it felt strange, awkward, foreign even to Mia. She tried to shake Skyler's hand off, but the woman tightened her hold. Mia gritted her teeth in reply. What if something happened to them? To Cassidy? The bulkheads loomed, lights glaring too bright, shadows stretching around her as if they too held her to this place. She did not like the feeling of being led to this man, quiet as a lamb to the slaughter, while the rest of her crew suffered.

"Look, I'm sorry. I know this is hard," Skyler muttered suddenly. "We really have to do this. It's safer this way."

Mia didn't reply. Didn't feel the need to. They walked in silence until Skyler nodded toward an open hatch. Mia fumbled for the IA device. Skyler shook her head. "We don't know how many are in there."

Skyler tightened her hold on Mia's arm as they passed the hatch. Mia glanced in. The cell, like so many others, was empty save for a man sitting on a stool. He seemed calm as the night sky, and just as silent. His hand moved with quick strokes, as he sliced a circular scar onto his arm. The cicatrix ritual. He raised his arm to her. A thought shoved itself into her mind. *My twelfth.* The Acedian smiled. Skyler pushed her faster down the walkway, away from the man.

"Ah, yes, I feel much safer now," Mia said. "Did you know this had to be done?"

"Yes. Though I didn't think he'd want you so soon," Skyler whispered back. "He usually lets the victims stew for a while. Sometimes, after the testing, he waits a week before anyone else comes in. It's a game."

Her words kindled a new worry in Mia's stomach. "Should we be talking about this? Can't they read minds?"

"Yes and no, the ones on this ship are weak. They can only enter into your mind if they keep eye contact."

"Donavin—"

"He's the exception. He's been Acedian the longest, and his powers are much more advanced. He surrounds himself with the weak so he can feel stronger. They just got a new shipment of people in, so he's too preoccupied to invade everyone's minds."

Mia frowned. A new shipment? The Paradousians or the Pargonians? Either way, guilt twisted her stomach.

Skyler held up her hand. A noise bounced across the corridor ahead of them, coming from one of the adjoining walkways. Skyler leaned into her and whispered, "There's someone coming. Try the IA device I gave you. Point it at them and rub a finger over the metallic plating."

A meaty, blue-haired man turned the corner. Mia had one quick glance into his dull eyes before she pointed and stroked the tiny teardrop. A soft glow emitted from the path of her finger. The man froze. His eyes stared straight ahead, mouth set in a line and arms stilled mid swing. Mia slowed her pace to inspect him, but Skyler pushed her along.

"Keep moving," she whispered in Mia's ear. "I recalibrated the IA device to include memory loss. If we hang around he'll be suspicious, and there's a greater chance he'll remember being stationary."

"Won't they notice him?" Mia asked, quickening her pace to match Skyler's so the woman didn't need to shove so hard.

"No." Skyler tilted her head and signaled Mia to glance as well.

Mia did. The blue-haired stranger had continued his journey, walking slowly, seemingly unaware of what had just transpired. She shivered and hoped the device would never steal her own memories. "Let's just get this over with." She clenched the IA device tightly in her hand.

Skyler nodded. Screams periodically punctured the silence of the walk. Mia tried hard not to linger on how young they sounded. She couldn't bare it. Wouldn't allow herself to. Soon, too soon, they arrived at the end of the corridor. A blue "Station Five" decorated the metal. Lights tilted toward it and washed some of the color out onto the silver surface.

"It won't hurt. I'll be standing right outside this hatch, waiting for you, and we'll leave. If he finds you with the IA, he'll know something is wrong." Skyler pried open Mia's fingers, slipping the device from her hand. She tightened her hold on Mia's shoulder in what seemed to be a reassuring squeeze. "And try not to think of your crew, he'll use that against you, okay?"

Mia nodded, her jaw too clenched for speech. Determined to think of nothing, she faced the hatch. Skyler pushed a code in, the hatch slid open, and Mia stepped through. The hatch shut behind her.

At first the only thing Mia could see was the light, white light so bright it was as if she'd landed in her dreamscape once more. Her eyes adjusted, and a cabin slowly came into view. Donavin stood behind a large control panel that sat in the corner. Images flashed over a transparent screen, flickering in front of him, although Mia could still see his gray eyes as he watched the display. His fingers raced over the top of the panel, madly typing as his lips moved. He reminded her of a scientist hunched over his work.

Donavin did not bother to look up. "Captain Foley, so good of you to come. Please, step into the center of the circle, and we'll begin."

Going a few paces forward, Mia stood in the center of a circle etched onto the deck. A blue, shimmering light materialized around her, a force field of some kind, Mia assumed. She tried to touch it, found her arms remained motionless at her sides. The blue light froze her within its beam, not painful nor accompanied by any sort of strange sensations. She could only breathe and blink.

"Try not to worry," Donavin said. "This will only take a moment of your time."

He fiddled with something on the control panel. A flash of green light blinded her for a moment and, when she blinked it away, a holoimage of herself materialized, just outside the circle. As she looked at it, the holoimage looked at her, as if a mirror reflected it back. She winked, the holoimage winked at exactly the same moment.

The holoimage shimmered, and a green light swiped down its body. The clothes it wore disappeared as the light moved, starting with its shirt all the way down to its boots. Mia gulped, thinking perhaps she was naked as well. No, her fingers still pressed against the fabric of her pants.

As disconcerting as it was seeing herself so bared, Mia was happy it was not her true self. The holoimage's pale skin gleamed in the white lights, the scar on its hand plainly visible, but the wounds on its thigh and midsection had completely healed, not even a trace left behind. Remarkable, really, that she healed so quickly. There were no dark circles beneath its eyes even though Mia had not slept well over the past few weeks.

Another swipe of green light, and Mia's skin disappeared, leaving behind the muscular system and veins. The sight made her slightly nauseous, as its heart still beat and blood still pumped through its veins. When she breathed, the holoimage's lungs expanded. Creepy.

"As you've no doubt figured out, this is a real time holoimage of you, Captain Foley." Mia tore her eyes from it as Donavin pushed something. Finally, he flicked the screens down to his control panel and glanced up to meet her gaze. "And this, this is what I've done for you."

Mia's gaze flitted back to the mirrored image of herself. The holoimage shimmered again, this time a gray substance flowed in place of blood. The gray had almost entirely engulfed its vascular system and was slowly seeping into its muscles. The gray had not reached the furthest part of its limbs, calves and feet, forearms and hands all still inked with red. Its head still glowed sanguine, but the gray had seeped next to the holoimage's eyes. Mia's breathing grew rapid. How was this possible?

"You are finally accepting my bots into your system. Do not worry. The bots have not replaced your blood. They merely swim in it, controlling you. You were quite resistant to it, actually, you're stronger than I originally anticipated." Donavin paused for a moment. He looked—lovingly?—at Mia's holoimage. He stayed that way, watching for a few breaths, then focused on his screens once more. Mia wished she could see the screens, but they were now hidden from her view. Donavin smiled. "Once they have overwhelmed your system, I will void you of these troubling emotions. You will be an empty shell of your former self, and mine to control."

Donavin was quiet, clinical, easy, like this was something he had done for years. With all the people on this ship, perhaps he had.

"Good, Captain Foley, very good indeed. I'd give you a few weeks, at best, before your transformation is complete." He touched the panel again, the holoimage shifted and disappeared, as did the light that held Mia captive. Her muscles released. Donavin nodded. "You may go."

Mia realized that only she and Donavin occupied this cell. Should she attack? Yes. A few quick movements and she could be behind that panel, hand ripping into his chest and yanking out that delicate muscle, squeezing the life out of this man's heart. Mia did a double take at the gruesome image as it drifted away. But he had one of those IA devices. One simple touch and Mia would be motionless once more. No, she had to wait. Another time. Another place, perhaps, she would give herself the satisfaction of killing him.

Donavin smiled. Mia took a step back and turned toward the exit. The hatch slid open, revealing Skyler, waiting outside. The nurse took one startled look at Donavin, grasped Mia's forearm, and led her away. Before the hatch slid shut, Donavin's voice entered Mia's mind.

I'll be waiting, Mia Foley.

Chapter Twenty-Two

MIA RUBBED HER ARMS, chancing a quick glance back at the closed hatch, half expecting Donavin to materialize in front of it. She couldn't get that holoimage out of her head. How the gray—bots, he'd called them—had seeped so far through her system. Dizziness weakened her. Her heart pounded against her chest. She looked at Skyler and whispered, "Let's get the blasted quasar out of here."

Skyler nodded, handed Mia the IA device, and led her away, a hand on her arm the entire time. They walked quickly down the corridor.

Halfway back to the cell, Skyler cleared her throat. "How far progressed are you?"

"How are we going to get out?" Mia replied, trying to change the subject. She couldn't answer that. Wouldn't. It scared her too much. "I want to have a plan before we get back to the men."

Skyler frowned and let the subject drop. "We'll get Cassidy first. She was taken away not half an hour ago. They couldn't have done much."

"They'd better not," Mia muttered. Her anger spiked, burning away the fear. If they did anything to her. Anything at all. The image of Cassidy's broken arm filled her mind, the one the guard had shot at her as he dragged her away. Mia glared at the deck panels.

"After that, I'll take you to Jeff. We'll escape by using pods. They have them scattered about the ship." Skyler pushed her harder, quickening their pace.

"Pods? Like an escape pod?" She glanced at Skyler and caught the woman's gray eyes. "That can't get us very far."

Skyler gave her a small smile. "Most of their escape pods have the same amount of drive and supplies as a small shuttle, so escapees can live for over a week inside."

They passed an adjoining corridor and fell silent as an Acedian crossed their path. The woman barely looked their direction, but she frightened Mia all the same. It seemed as if every muscle in her body tensed at the sight. She exhaled, attempting to quell the panic that rose like bile in her throat. They waited until the woman was far enough away before continuing their conversation.

"Won't they see a pod as it disengages from their ship?" Mia asked.

"Hopefully a drone will be watching and not Donavin himself. That's what I call these breaching people, walking around seeing nothing, feeling nothing, a drone, just another machine Donavin gets to control." A definite bitterness seeped from Skyler's words.

Mia had her fair share of bitterness. She eyed Skyler. A gnawing doubt had started in her stomach. "Why are you helping us?"

Staring down the corridor, Skyler said, "No one should undergo this type of torture."

Skyler's words, wise beyond her young years, caused Mia to fall silent. She would not wish this life on anyone, not even her worst of enemies. Not trusting her voice to remain steady, Mia nodded. She forced herself to calm down. Now was not the time to have a breakdown over things that had happened in the past.

Skyler pulled her to a stop in front of a hatch. "This is it."

Mia stared at it. The hatch looked just like all the rest in this corridor. Skyler pushed in a code and revealed Harrison and Will standing on the other side. Harrison, the closer of the two, barreled out first. Will followed, slower, head down. Mia took hold of Will's collar, the shiny fabric crinkling under her fingers, and jerked his head up to face her. "I need you here."

He nodded and muttered, "I'm here."

When he lifted his eyes, Mia knew he was telling the truth. At least partially. She turned to Skyler. "Lead the way."

"It has to look like I'm taking you to another cell," Skyler said. "I go first, Mia, you're second, the men last." She rustled around in her pocket and pulled out a metallic armband, slipping it onto her wrist. The band glowed white. A beam connected all four crewmates together, the light slipping through a wristband Mia hadn't even noticed. Apparently, no one else had noticed either.

"Where the quasar did that come from?" Will exclaimed, pulling his arm up and examining the wristband.

"Come on." Skyler began pulling them along. A jolt of hot prickles flew down Mia's arm as the light grew taut. She moved forward. The light slackened and the prickles stopped. The others stumbled along behind her. They walked for a few minutes in silence.

"Where are all the people?" Will's mutter floated up from behind.

Had Will not asked the question Mia surely would. The corridors were quiet, eerily quiet, as if the entire crew had disappeared. Empty. Just like the strangers that walked them.

"I don't know," Skyler replied. "Now be quiet, and count yourself blessed."

They fell silent as they strode down the corridor. Mia matched her pace with the others, but she wanted to go faster. To run. Drawing attention so obviously would be dumb. Idiotic. And even though she ached to get to Cassidy sooner, she would not allow it. Lights flickered around them, their shadows stretched up the bulkheads, and vents created a soft hum in the background. They neared a rather large hatch and screaming filtered through the heavy metal. Mia's stomach twisted into knots. It was there, in front of that hatch, that Skyler paused.

Mia's heart almost stopped. Her jaw slackened, eyes grew wide. "Cassidy?"

"Yes..."

Mia didn't hear the rest of Skyler's sentence. Will and Harrison's yells were muffled under Cassidy's screams. She yanked her arm upward, ignoring the pinch in her arm, and the shouts of the others. The light vanished. She pounded on the control panel beside the hatch, not knowing the code and still expecting it to open. And when it did not, she didn't see anything but the metal barrier keeping her from Cassidy. Ice spread from her core. She shivered. Mia threw her fist back and punched the hatch as hard as she could. The metal gave.

Mia welcomed the spreading shivers, for with the cold came strength and with that strength she would save Cassidy. She shook her hand out of the fist, willing the cold to rush there, the power to collect in that one limb. Hurry. Blast it all, hurry! A hand grabbed onto her shoulder. She brushed it off. The cold coursed through the back of her forearm, wrist, and hand and pooled in her fingertips now.

In one fluid motion, her fist connected with the metal again, dented it, and burst out the other side. One kick later, and the hatch peeled away enough to allow Mia through. The cold slowly retreated from her body.

Once her boots hit the deck on the other side, Will and Harrison's exclamations of disbelief, Skyler's harsh whispers, the angered yells of the Acedians, and Cassidy's shouts all filtered into Mia's consciousness. She tried to ignore them, taking in the scene before her as quickly as possible.

Tables were bolted down with hovering carts next to them. Metallic drawers lined the bulkheads and displayed a variety of torturous devices. Clothing lay in heaps. In the far corner of the cabin lay Cassidy, strapped down on a table, clothing ripped to shreds, blood pouring from a wound on her shoulder. She yelled something Mia could not discern, her attention now drawn to the five Acedians rushing toward her.

Balling her hands, she willed the cold back again. It came, crashing in waves, spreading through her entire body. She assessed her targets and readied herself, spreading her feet wide. Blood stained their clothing in arcs, bright red on the plain white fabric. She tried to ignore Cassidy struggling in her restraints.

From the far left, a young boy attacked first, blond hair flying as his face twisted into an ugly mask. His arm swung in a low arc. Mia blocked the blow easily, deflecting his momentum to the side. The boy stumbled, fell, crashed into the deck. She smirked. Easy.

Mia turned back as the next lug—a tall woman with black hair—had already launched herself. A guttural yell poured from the woman's mouth. Her wild gray eyes captured Mia. She froze, unthinking, fear taking control for a second. The cold withdrew from her muscles, warmth spreading instead. That moment of hesitation became a window of opportunity for her attacker. The woman engulfed her in a bear hug with one arm and landed a solid blow to Mia's stomach with the other. Breath rushed out of her lungs. White clothes dominated Mia's line of sight as she sank to her knees, her vision tracing a smear of scarlet on the woman's chest and abdomen. Before Mia could collapse completely, a white knee came up to greet her. The rough fabric scratched her chin. Her head rocked back, and she landed hard on the deck.

Mia snarled. Stupid, rookie mistake. She pushed herself sideways, spinning upward, knocking the woman's feet out from under her and standing, all in one fluid motion. The woman crashed to the deck, and before Mia could do any more, the other Acedians joined the fight.

Two grabbed hold of her arms. They pushed her backward into the ruined hatch. A shard of metal punctured her clothes and a sudden heat welled between her shoulder blades. Mia tried to ignore it. Hands pushed at her from behind. Her crew was trying to get in, their shouts and attempts muffled by Mia's own body. She could not see Cassidy, only two men, both slight and hairy, and a woman, face covered in scars. The two men held Mia and the scarred woman smashed her hand across Mia's face. Mia's cheek stung and tears formed in her eyes, blurring her vision. She blinked them away. The woman smiled, her thoughts entering Mia.

Weak.

Mia shook her head, vision catching the two men's gaze in the process. She reeled with their thoughts.

So weak. One echoed.

Pathetic. The third agreed.

Mia looked at the woman again, attention now on her instead of the two men.

Not pathetic, just young in the sphere of us.

The woman threw back her arm, and Mia gritted her teeth. The punch vibrated through her body. She willed the cold back, to her legs, her thighs, to strengthen them. It came, quicker than before. The heat in her back vanished as the bots spread throughout her system. She no longer tensed from the Acedian's punch. Pulling her legs up, Mia lashed out, catching the woman's midsection and hurling her back. The woman toppled over one of the trays. The metal cart crashed to the deck with her.

The men holding Mia seemed startled. One even slackened his grasp on Mia's arm for a moment. Perfect. She jerked her limb out of his hands and elbowed the man's face. His nose broke, but he grabbed for her arm again. Red blood spurted from his nose. After the scanning, Mia almost expected their blood to be silver. She was glad it wasn't. She smashed her fist into his face, felt the bone push against her hand, then give under her strength. The Acedian's eyes grew wide. He slid to the deck.

She twisted and punched the other man's neck, causing him to choke. He released his hold. Mia pulled her leg up and kneed him in the abdomen. He keeled over. Mia slammed an elbow into the small of his back, and he crashed onto the deck.

Not so weak. Mia pushed her thoughts outward, connecting with the Acedian minds, taunting them. A strangled yell pulled her back to herself.

"Cassidy," she muttered, glancing around.

Mia crossed the deck in moments, but Cassidy's eyes had flitted from Mia to something behind her, a sharp intake of breath her only warning. Too late. A heavy weight thumped Mia's back, limbs wrapping around her midsection. She was off her feet and slammed into the deck. She didn't feel the pain of the impact nor the welts on her flesh. The bots already flowed through her body, dulling it, freezing it. Mia looked up to see the blond-haired boy now looming over her. He moved to crush her skull. Grabbing onto his boot, Mia twisted, and the boy stumbled to the deck beside her.

Mia pushed herself to standing once more and took a few paces only to be wrestled to the deck again. The boy landed atop Mia, pushing down on her hands and using his entire weight to pin her to the deck. The stench of him, sweat from fighting, copper from blood, and some ugly thing she did not want to know assaulted her senses. Red from effort, his face hovered over her. His eyes glared into her. Crimson blood matted his blond hair and dripped onto Mia's cheek. He smiled. The boy was heavier than he should be. Stronger than he should be. Mia couldn't move.

Hands appeared on the boy's forehead, neck, and shoulders. Harrison and Will lifted the struggling attacker. His kick landed hard on Mia's shoulder, but Will yanked him out of reach. Harrison delivered a blow to the boy's neck. The boy sank to the deck. Skyler reached out a hand and Mia let the nurse pull her to her feet. As soon as Mia's boots hit the walkway, she rushed over to Cassidy.

Mia's breath left her as she saw what they had done to her. Only Cassidy's bra, the upper section of her pants and her boots remained. Blotches of red seeped through the limited cloth. Her exposed knees and shins had cuts on them, there was a slash on her left shoulder, and her abdomen had miniscule puncture wounds.

Cassidy's arm took Mia's breath away, but not for the reasons she expected. Normal. It was normal. Looked perfectly fine, healthy actually, except Cassidy kept shaking her head at Mia when she tried to touch it. This was nothing like the vision she saw when she looked into the Acedian guard's eyes. Cassidy's arm wasn't broken. Her arm didn't jut out at an odd angle, didn't bleed. Because her arm wasn't broken. And her shoulder wasn't branded, either.

"Mia," Cassidy whispered, eyes filled with tears. There was a hint of a smile on her lips as she said Mia's name.

Warmth rushed back into Mia's system, purging all shivers from her body. Agony knifed through her back. Her stomach writhed. Her entire body ached. It didn't matter. She looked into Cassidy's beautiful, brown eyes, and a deep fondness surged through her. For a moment, a brief, brief moment, Mia's universe narrowed its gaze down onto this one feeling. She gently touched Cassidy's hand and intertwined their fingers. Cassidy smiled broader in return.

"Can you get me loose?" Cassidy's eyes flitted to the cloth bonds that held her.

Mia followed her gaze and nodded. Cassidy had only three. Two bound her ankles, one on her left wrist. No need to waste more on her. She was no threat to them. Mia tried to be as gentle as she could, deftly slipping her hand underneath the heavy cloth to provide some barrier as she worked the knots. Tried to ignore the warmth of Cassidy's skin. The shivers rushing down her spine that had nothing to do with fear and everything to do with Mia's heart.

The ankle braces were easy to get free. Cassidy's wrist posed a problem. A sliver of blood ran down her arm under the cloth that held her wrist in place. Mia slowly tried to wipe the blood away, but a gasp from Cassidy caused Mia to jerk back. A cut opened beneath the blood. There was no way to remove the shackle without touching the injury. Sliding her hand under the cloth, the back of Mia's hand skimmed the wound and another gasp left Cassidy. This time Mia could only wince as she undid the final bond.

The moment Cassidy was loose, she sat up and gave Mia a one-armed hug. Mia gently hugged her in return, not knowing how far the damage extended within her body. Some types of torture didn't leave marks. Still, Mia hugged her. She drew back, keeping her hands on Cassidy's waist. Mia longed for that connection, and it seemed Cassidy did as well, for Cassidy's hand slid down Mia's shoulder and rested on her arm.

"I'm sor—" Mia began.

"You fought them for me," Cassidy interrupted.

"It was nothing." Mia tried and failed to keep her voice light.

"You tore down the hatch." Cassidy smirked, tilting her head.

The action caused her brunette and amethyst locks to cascade off her shoulder and even with the blood on her clothes and fear hidden deep within those eyes, Mia realized once more that Cassidy was stunning. No, not merely stunning—gorgeous. There was never enough time for this, but Mia, who was tired of waiting for the right moment, finally swallowed the fear boiling inside of her and locked eyes with Cassidy.

"Nothing could keep me from you," Mia murmured, her voice lower than usual. It was as close to expressing her feelings as Mia dared to venture, especially in this place, surrounded by these people.

Cassidy smiled. A blush seeped into her cheeks, and she grabbed Mia for a hug once again. "True," she whispered back.

Chapter Twenty-Three

AFTER A MOMENT TOO short, Mia and Cassidy broke apart, their time shattered by the sound of a throat being cleared. Heat crept up the back of Mia's neck, her ears tickling until they too filled with warmth. She straightened, her gaze flitting away from those brown eyes. Mia cursed herself. Some captain, forgetting everything on a whim. They were on an Acedian ship, for blasted sake, not a sanctuary.

"Does your arm hurt?" Mia asked, nodding toward it. The limb hung slack at Cassidy's side.

Cassidy's reply came in a whisper, "Yes. I don't know why. It doesn't look broken." She shrugged and winced. "This hurts more, actually." She looked at the gash on her shoulder.

Mia looked around, and her sights soon landed on Skyler. She stood only a few paces away, watching the pair. The woman lowered her hand that previously covered her mouth. Her lips turned upward in a smile.

"I didn't want to disturb your moment, Captain, but we don't have time for this now," she said.

Mia scowled at her. The nurse's pithy comments normally annoyed Mia. This time, they only heightened her awareness of her own stupidity. The truth they contained fell heavy on her shoulders. Time never was on their side, it seemed.

"Fix her," Mia ordered, her voice low, dangerous.

Skyler kept on smiling. The order hung in the air a bit too long for comfort.

"Yes, Captain," she finally replied. "Cassidy, lie back down."

Skyler moved to Cassidy's side and stared intently at her arm. Her gray eyes narrowed to almost closed. Her mouth relaxed into a soft frown. The nurse gently poked and prodded Cassidy's arm, touching her forearm here and there. Skyler pushed her thumb down once and Cassidy gasped. Even with her eyes closed, Cassidy still found and grasped Mia's hand. Skyler finished her examination.

"Harrison, Will, you'll have to find me a splint and some cloth, clean, preferably. See if they have helofoam for her shoulder and stomach wounds."

The men began sifting through the heaps of clothes on the deck. A few grunts and many discarded items later, Will handed strips to Skyler, and Harrison grabbed a few pipes from a broken cart. They hadn't found a helofoam dispenser. Skyler frowned.

"What do I do?" Mia asked.

"Hold her. This might hurt, and a person's natural reaction is to twist away. She could damage herself even more by doing so." Skyler motioned for Mia to stand by Cassidy's head. Mia did and placed her hands, gently, on Cassidy's uninjured shoulder. A grin flickered on Cassidy's lips before melting into a grimace. Skyler continued speaking, this time to Cassidy. "We need to do this fast. You have a fracture, not a bad one. I'm going to reset the bone and wrap it. This won't do much to help. The pods have medical kits. We'll fix you up better there."

Cassidy nodded. A strand of purple hair drifted across her cheek. A bead of sweat fell down her forehead. Her skin grew slick under Mia's hands. She tightened her hold. Cassidy's lip trembled as the men, too, gathered around her—William at her arm, Harrison at her feet. Skyler counted down, but Mia did not pay attention to the nurse, her eyes rested solely on Cassidy.

Cassidy's yells reverberated through the cabin. She jerked. Mia held her down. As the scream died away, a low guttural sound escaped from her lips. She rocked her head from side to side. Never looked down, never looked at the nurse or at her own arm being repaired. Her lips parted again, and Mia half expected another scream.

"Oh blast it all to a breaching black hole, are you done?"

"Not even close, Cassidy. Hold on," Skyler replied.

Cassidy moaned and shut her eyes.

Mia's gaze broke from Cassidy's face to the blood that trickled from her wounds to the deck, pooling at the base of the table. She smiled. The crimson liquid called to her. Cassidy's moan ended in a sob. Mia's grin widened. The pain from this woman excited her. They should inflict more, not heal. Wait, this woman? What was she thinking? This was Cassidy. Cassidy, her first mate, Cassidy, her friend. Cassidy. Not "this woman." Mia shook her head, clearing the frozen cobwebs that had suddenly spidered through her. A nudge on her shoulder helped, too, and she glanced at the person who pushed her.

Skyler had moved to Cassidy's shoulder wound and had just finished clipping the bandage down when their eyes met. Her gray eyes narrowed, and she opened her mouth to speak.

Before she could utter a word, Harrison interrupted. "Look alert, people. One of them woke up."

Harrison tilted his head ever so slightly toward the direction of the hatch. Will had gone tense, hands gripping Cassidy's arm even when she no longer struggled. Surprisingly, Cassidy looked calm, peaceful now. Her breathing came regular. Her head lulled to the side, away from her injured arm. Her eyes remained closed. Had she fainted? No, a crash echoed from the far corner of the cabin—one of the carts falling, no doubt—and muscles coiled underneath Mia's hands as Cassidy winced from the sound. The woman must be made of steel.

Mia shifted her gaze to Skyler last. The nurse kept touching Cassidy's arm, her head down seemingly focused on her work, but her gray eyes still narrowed at Mia. Rage boiled up inside of Mia. Those horrible gray eyes scrutinized her. Scared her. Condemned her to this life of empty-eyed people. This girl, this youth, this could not be her savior, this little pathetic excuse for a female. Mia blinked.

The crash came again. Skyler fidgeted. Mia put a hand on the nurse's arm and turned toward the awakening Acedian. She would take care of this threat, not Skyler. The wild woman kicked, and the heavy cart spun off, slamming into the bulkhead with a loud echoing clang. The woman got up and ran across the cabin, boots pounding on the deck. Mia moved in between her crew and this wild one. The woman stopped short, fists close to her body, crouching just a few paces from Mia. Their eyes met.

The woman's thoughts came through loud and clear in Mia. *I must finish the job.*

She pushed her own opinions out. *Not with me in the way.*

The woman crouched lower, her eyes wide. The woman was stronger, faster, and it was clear she knew it. Her lips pulled back into a sneer. Mia readied herself for the attack then relaxed. Wait. She didn't need to battle this woman. Mia stuffed her hand into her pocket, feeling the teardrop object, smooth against her palm. The woman lunged. Mia pulled out the IA and activated it, the white light trailing after her fingertip. Mia's attacker froze, as if all her muscles had suddenly turned to stone. One boot planted firmly on the deck. The other heel lifted. Arms wide, with hands grasping at nothing.

The woman's thoughts stumbled into Mia's head. *Where did you get—how did you—what's happening?*

Mia stalked over to her attacker's frozen form and, with one twist of the woman's neck, ended her life. It was only after the woman slumped to the walkway that the cold rushed through Mia's body, the ice flowing through her veins.

A rustling noise spun her around to face whatever horrors lay before her. It was only Cassidy, slowly getting up from her table, gingerly placing each foot onto the walkway. She stood, swayed. In a heartbeat, Mia stood beside her, holding her up.

The men's gasps meant nothing to Mia, nor did Skyler's arched eyebrow. Only that Cassidy remained standing, that was all that mattered now. Weak, she leaned heavily on Mia's form, eyes closed, head listing to one side. Hair fell in waves over her shoulders and down Mia's arms as she held Cassidy close. It was next to impossible not to touch Cassidy's wounds, but Mia stayed far away from the injured arm. It hung uselessly at Cassidy's side and scared Mia. Cassidy's arm was fractured. Not as bad as the guard's taunt, but broken all the same. Mia could not get over that simple fact. Broken by them. She dwelled on it.

Skyler shifted beside the two women, moved ever so slightly away from them. In a moment Mia realized that Skyler could have supported Cassidy. Mia also realized she wouldn't have allowed that to happen. The nurse could fix Cassidy's wounds, and Mia would be grateful, however grudgingly. But she would always see Skyler as the woman who made her late. Had they come straight here, perhaps they would have stopped the Acedians. Perhaps the Acedians would not have even had a chance to start.

"Come on, we still need to get Jeff." Mia slipped an arm under Cassidy's shoulder and helped her hobble to the exit.

Mia ignored the looks that the men gave her. Will started toward the hatch, but stayed far away from them. Harrison kept his distance. Even Skyler stayed a few paces behind. They were almost out of the cabin when a robotic voice filtered through the speakers.

"Improvisation, acceptable."

"Who the heck said that?" Will yelped.

"Where did the voice come from?" Harrison asked.

Skyler shushed them. "Shut up for a breaching minute. It might say more."

The robotic voice silenced the drone of questions. "Fight skills, lacking. Need improvement. Testing."

Mia shifted her stance and looked back at Skyler. The raven-haired nurse stood rigid, lips pressed together, arms tight by her sides. Something had gone wrong with her plan. If her back got any straighter it would probably break from sheer rigidness. Her dark, gray eyes swept the cabin. Mia followed suit. The Acedians on the deck didn't move. Would they regenerate? No. Her gaze searched the bulkheads. No hatches whooshed open. No machines outfitted with knives or guns rushed at them.

"Testing?" Mia whispered, her voice carrying through the quiet cabin.

The silence shattered around them as a fluctuating wail that could only mean one thing—an alarm—screeched out of the speakers. The siren blasted through the cabin. Will ducked at the noise, and even Harrison flinched. Cassidy sank closer to Mia. Skyler merely came up next to Mia and caught her gaze. While Mia couldn't hear the words that left the nurse's mouth, it was easy to guess what the woman would say.

"Breach it."

Chapter Twenty-Four

CASSIDY TREMBLED AGAINST MIA as they traversed the corridors, her movements so pronounced they shook Mia as well. She had one arm wrapped securely around Mia's neck, while cradling the other close to her chest. While Cassidy's eyes were fixed on the deck, Mia kept her vision securely on the nurse stalking down the corridor ahead of them. Skyler had led them out of the cabin the moment the wailing began. After a few turns, Mia was lost. The wail reached its highest pitch. Cassidy flinched, her face burrowing into Mia's neck. The sudden hot breath sparked an untimely response in her. Ignore it. She had to.

Will flinched, too. He helped Mia, keeping an arm looped around Cassidy's waist and holding her upright. Just like a good soldier and friend would. The alarm peaked again. Mia glanced around Cassidy, and Will's face jerked down as if hit by an unseen force. Even in such close proximity, connected by the weight of their friend, his hazel eyes would not meet Mia's. Why wouldn't he look at her?

Harrison trailed behind, rear guard as he called it. How he could guard them, with no weapons and such a slight body, Mia would never know. She certainly didn't feel safe with the lackey protecting her back. It would be better if a worm crawled behind them rather than the useless officer. A useless, pitiful, weak man.

Mia blinked. Her head ached. Cold slowly traveled up her neck. The bright lights washed over them, sharpening the fear on Skyler's face each time she glanced back. Her eyes seemed lighter in the gleam, dark gray brightening to silver. The woman kept her shoulders hunched. No one confronted them. No lost souls wandered the corridors. A ghost ship.

Unsettled by the odd circumstances, Mia focused on her breathing. Tightness knifed through her lungs. She breathed as if they had been frozen solid, encased completely by ice. What little air could seep in, she expelled quickly. The ice traveled up her throat, her mouth, even traversing her tongue before stopping at her lips. She couldn't breathe.

Couldn't speak. Mia stopped short. Will and Cassidy stumbled at the sudden break of momentum.

"What's wrong?" Cassidy glanced at her.

As quickly as the sensation came, it vanished. She felt whole again.

"Nothing." Mia blinked rapidly, rubbing the back of her neck. The cold would not go away. Instead, it traveled slowly down her spine, tingling as it went. She grimaced.

"Liar," Cassidy whispered.

Mia glanced at her and Cassidy narrowed her eyes in reply. Mia slowly shook her head. Cassidy exhaled, and her gaze drifted forward again. Her mouth still tightened in a firm line, a sure sign of her annoyance.

At Mia's nod, her crew continued down the corridor. They had only gone a few paces when it happened again. This time her entire left leg could have been splashed in icy water and sliced with knives. She stumbled to the side and crashed into the bulkhead. Will let go and Cassidy fell with her, pinning her to the wall. Mia's gaze dropped. The cold spiked now in her right knee, traveling fast throughout her body. More painfully, too. What had Donavin said—that she had finally accepted the bots into her system? Could that be true? No, she wouldn't allow it. As she straightened, it became clear. Saving Cassidy had taken more strength than Mia ever had by herself.

"It's getting worse isn't it? The cold." The nurse stood in front of Mia, arms crossed over her chest.

"I can handle it," Mia replied. She rested on the smooth bulkhead, enjoying the way it curved to the deck. The sensations in her legs passed and her muscles relaxed. Instead of grimacing, she sighed. Satisfaction filled her. And drowsiness. Her eyelids closed. She would be content to stay here, forever, leaning against the metal.

Skyler shook her and turned to the men. "No, you can't handle it. We have to get out of here before it gets worse."

"Worse?" Will stepped closer to Mia. Harrison moved back.

Mia pushed herself off of the bulkhead. She could feel her crew's eyes on her, their silent scrutiny of her condition. She had to be strong. Forced herself to be. Mia nodded, tilting her head down the corridor ahead of her.

"Let's go." The words lumbered off her numb tongue.

"We're almost there," Skyler said.

They passed by hatches with symbols painted on their surfaces, but Mia did not pay attention to them. Her free hand balled into a fist at her side. Her other hand tightened its hold on Cassidy's waist. Mia's jaw clenched, her muscles coiled. Her right arm now seared. Her thoughts drew inward. Anger filled her, fueled her, overwhelmed her. Everything infuriated her, from the weight of Cassidy, to Will's heavy breathing, to Harrison's boots pounding on the deck, even Skyler's dark hair swinging against her back. Not the fact that she was on an enemy ship. Not that she was surrounded by Acedians. Not that her friends were hurt. Anger, for all the wrong reasons and coming from nowhere. Her lips numbed, pulled themselves into a sneer.

"Mia, are you okay?" Cassidy's whisper filtered through Mia's thoughts. She didn't want to be angry right now. What was happening to her? They stopped moving. The others huddled around her and Cassidy. Conversation droned around Mia but only snippets got through.

"Jeff is in there."

"How could you know?"

"Have to take it by force."

"My brother."

"Mia?"

The anger disappeared. Mia blinked. Her eyes watered. The white lights flooded her vision. The deck paneling blurred. Skyler's form became hazy. She focused her vision on something close by, something recognizable. Cassidy's hand hung over Mia's shoulder and her ring glistened in the light, the one Cassidy twisted when nervous. Silver, simple, tiny swirls etched into the metal. Beautiful.

Voices filtered in. She could not distinguish one from the other, only emotions seeped through the fog. Worry, anxiety, fear.

A stabbing sensation shot through her back and stomach. She leaned against the bulkhead and groaned, letting go of Cassidy and reaching her hand out to catch herself from crumpling to the deck. Her hand met the cold metal underneath. Unable to move as a sudden onslaught of sadness crashed over her. Riding a wave of emotions she could not control. Tears slipped from her eyes. Her thoughts raged. But he stole emotions not amplified them. Her body quivered as the cold pressed in on her. The wail of the alarm became nothing more than a hum.

A voice whispered inside her. *Time to see what you can do.*

Her hand slipped from the metallic plating, arm falling to her side. A woman with an arm brace mouthed words. They did not reach Mia's ears. She assessed her targets. She focused on the closest one, the woman in front of her attempting to speak, brunette, weak, broken. No threat. She shifted to the next female—black hair, gray eyes, Acedian, no threat—then again to the males of this enemy regiment. The black-haired male came closer, attempting to connect with her.

William Dee, brother to Jeffery Dee, born on the planet Paradous. Other data could be called up. Unneeded. The target seemed vulnerable, scared. Perfect.

The broken one shook her slightly. "Ready?"

She nodded. Others tilted their heads. The broken woman beside Mia breathed, slowly, painfully. Mia smiled. The Acedian woman punched in a security code controlling the hatch. So many security codes throughout this ship. So many safeguards. The metal barrier slid open revealing two more of her allies. One heartbeat later, Mia attacked.

She coiled her muscles and lunged, pushing the broken woman out of her way, slamming William into the cabin and onto the deck. Pain registered in every wrinkle of his face, his lips parting in surprise. William attempted to push her away. She sank a fist deep into the man's gut.

"Mia!"

The cry came from behind her. She ignored it. Only one thing mattered. Annihilate the enemies on her turf. Starting with the one struggling beneath her. She punched his face. Blood spurted from his nose and poured onto the deck. Cold coursed through her shoulders, her arms, her hands, even her fingers as she wrapped them around William's neck. He tried to pry them away.

He drew a leg up and kicked, boot landing squarely on Mia's stomach. The sudden blow shocked her enough to slacken her hold and send her sprawling. Pushing herself up, she moved once more toward her target. He struggled to his feet. Grunted when her boot connected with his ribs. Falling once more to the deck he heaved, his breathing ragged, heavy.

Mia smiled. She dropped down to the deck beside him, pushing a knee into his chest and wrapping her hands around his neck again. A simple snap and his life would be over, her mission partly complete. His eyes widened, fearful perhaps. Mia felt nothing. But when his hazel eyes met hers, a spark of recognition passed through her. The cold in her hands ebbed slightly. She released her hold. William—no, Will—breathed, pushed her off him, and scuttled backward. A voice shouted. *No, finish it!*

Mia's mind emptied of recognition, of emotion, of anything. Her entire body pulsed now. She launched herself forward once more. This time William was ready. He blocked her charge by grasping onto her hands and pushing her over him, using her momentum to throw her across the corridor. She twisted midair, landed on the toes of her boots and her hands.

Straightening, she drew herself up to her full height, preparing for another attack. Someone shouted, "Harrison, hold her."

A strong arm snaked around and grabbed her neck. The man's face appeared beside hers, whispering, "Mia, calm down."

She accessed data on this new target: Jer Mi Harrison, newly minted officer of the Vespa military, born on the planet Paradous, trained fighter. Her new target could prove more valuable alive than dead. Yet it was easier to destroy them than to ask them questions. Harrison pushed her into the bulkhead, her cheek pressed against the cold metal. She tried to push off, but his scrawny figure held much more strength than she could have imagined.

In her limited range of sight, she saw the Acedian woman attacking one of their own, winning the confusing duel between allies. The Acedian male smashed to the ground and remained still. The other ally had also been eliminated. The bandaged woman had escaped her line of vision. William rushed over to a table holding Jeffery Dee, the brother. Mia recognized him as another enemy. Five against one. The odds were not in her favor.

The Acedian woman rose from her attack, leaving the body. She narrowed her eyes as Mia searched her face for some recognition within her data stream. Information came to her moments later. Skyler Jones, eldest sibling among three, activated three years, the lost one. Mia attempted to connect with her, pushing her thoughts outward. Skyler's mind would not allow the intrusion. Something blocked Mia's way.

"You can't burrow into me, Charles. I won't let you." Skyler stopped a few paces away from Mia glanced at Harrison, at the brothers, and finally at the broken woman. "We have to get her out. Donavin should be weak from controlling so many newcomers so fast, remind her of something."

The broken woman stumbled over to her, placing her free hand on Mia's cheek. Their eyes met. "This isn't you, Mia. You don't attack your crew, and you'd certainly never attack me."

The broken woman stood—no, Cassidy stood—who was this woman? Data streamed into Mia's thoughts then left it. Cassidy stood before her. Memories dragged themselves into the forefront, the *Eclipse*, her crew, the attacks, the gifts exchanged. Cassidy.

Attack them. Keep fighting!

The real enemy crystallized. She pushed the intrusive voice away, shouting over the link. *You'll have to try harder than that.*

Mia was herself again. Furious at being taken control of so easily and by being pinned to the bulkhead by Harrison, she concentrated on the twinge shooting through her arm as he tightened his hold. The pain lingered even though the cold pulsed through her system. But Mia was herself once more.

She struggled against Harrison's hold. "Harrison, you blasted lackey, get off me."

He smiled. "Does that mean she's okay?"

Skyler leaned in close to Mia. Their breath mingled. Mia's ragged, scared, Skyler's calm, easy. The nurse searched Mia's face, her gray eyes flitting over every inch.

"Yes...Donavin is gone. Let her go."

Harrison released his grip. Mia's aching shoulder flared as she let her limbs go slack. She turned from the bulkhead, rubbing her shoulder and taking in the entire cabin for the first time. Harrison and Skyler moved away from her. Cassidy sat, shaking, next to the closed hatch, cradling her arm. The two Acedians lay dead or dying on the deck.

Where was Jeff? There. Will stood in the far corner by his brother, ripping off pieces of cloth from his own uniform and slapping them on the small wound puncturing Jeff's upper body. Blood seeped from the cut on his chest. It wasn't deep, though. Not dangerous. Aside from being unbuttoned, his jumpsuit looked amazingly whole. No rips at all. The wound on his chest and a dark bruise on his cheek were the only signs of trauma. Perhaps they had interrogated him a different way? Mia made a note to ask about it later.

"What happened?" Jeff's voice took a higher pitch than normal. He did not even limp as he stalked toward her.

Mia's mouth opened and closed. How could she explain this to him when she didn't understand it herself?

Skyler, thankfully, answered for her. "Donavin is controlling her."

"What?" Jeff asked.

"These people have the technology to embed picobots into the bloodstream, into the muscles. Donavin activates the bots and two months later, sometimes less, you become a drone, Donavin's plaything. Your emotions get voided and, in their place, you get his. Your thoughts are not your own and your actions are not your own. You are not your own." She glanced toward Mia and asked, "You were activated a month ago?"

Mia nodded. A gasp from Cassidy brought Mia to her senses. As much as her crew needed, and deserved, this information, this was not the time. Off the ship, far from these people, they could figure it out. Not now.

"He's not controlling me now, so you need to go." Pushing Harrison toward the hatch, Mia gestured for Skyler to follow.

"Yes, it's time we leave," Skyler agreed.

"We?" Jeff's voice dripped with mistrust as he glared at Mia.

She couldn't blame him. Were their positions shifted, she'd be suspicious as well. Hence her saying "you need to go." It seemed Skyler had ignored that part of Mia's statement. Will lingered at his older brother's side, he, too, glancing warily at Mia. His gaze flitted back to the bodies on the deck.

"Of course, we." Cassidy pushed herself into an upward position, still leaning heavily against the bulkhead. "In case you idiots have forgotten, that alarm hasn't ceased. We're likely going to have to fight our way out, and we'll need every hand we can get."

Will let out a strangled noise halfway between a whimper and a shout, and Mia hoped he did so to agree with Cassidy. Yet, when she looked in his direction, it seemed he had not heard Cassidy at all. His eyes were trained on one particular body sprawled on the deck.

"That's Bob Narison," Will exclaimed. Mia glanced down at the dead body drooling blood and spit onto the panel. His face had flashed on the screens of Paradous. Not so missing anymore. Mia smiled. She blinked, forced the smile off her face.

"That's Bob Narison," Will repeated.

"I know," Jeff muttered.

"Like I said," Cassidy interjected. "We should really leave."

As if in reply, the alarm changed, growing louder, higher, unwavering in its persistence. Will clamped his hands over his ears, hunching against the sound. Cassidy suddenly blanched, color entirely draining from her face. Her knees buckled. A moment later Mia caught her.

This time Mia paid attention to the gasps around her. Understandable. She had crossed the entire span of the cabin in a mere moment, a feat no human could do. Yet there was no time for the others to ask questions, no time to wonder how she could do such a thing, no time to judge her loyalty. The hatch beside the two women slid open. On the other side awaited the real enemy, a whole hoard of them. Mia counted twenty at least. Gray eyes stared blankly into the cabin, as Mia held Cassidy in her arms.

The robotic voice filtered through the speaker beside Mia's shoulder. "Testing."

Chapter Twenty-Five

FOR A FEW MOMENTS they stood, watching each other, as if even the Acedians didn't know what to do next. The static from the speakers faded away. Cassidy wilted further into Mia's arms. The atmosphere in the cabin shifted. Tensed. Still no one moved.

Mia did a quick assessment of her crew. It was painfully clear this wasn't going to be a fair fight. Half her crew was either too broken or too scared. The other half didn't trust her enough to follow her lead. Skyler perhaps. Harrison? Jeff? Even with the truth hanging in the air, why should they believe it? She had no proof.

It wasn't going to be a fair fight, but she could make it one. She shivered. Goosebumps emerged on her skin as the cold crept through her body. She hated relying on the strength Donavin had forced upon her, yet, it gave her the power to protect her crew. For now, that was all that mattered.

"Stay here." Mia met Cassidy's eyes. When Cassidy nodded, Mia slowly leaned her against the bulkhead. While the action didn't draw attention to them, the slight movement colored Cassidy's face a shade of green.

Mia turned toward the Acedians. The cold had finished spreading through her system, drenching every inch of her with a clammy sweat until even the air around her chilled. Closing her fingers into fists, she breathed, steadying herself. A flash of bending metal on Paradous, of throwing sheets too heavy for her, of climbing too high, came to her mind. Time to see what these powers could really do. The eyes of her first mark met hers. She noticed no other detail, only those gray eyes.

One moment Mia stood next to Cassidy, the next she stood amidst her attackers, hand squeezing the life out of a man's throat. Her hand grasped his neck so tightly he died within moments. The indecision of the Acedians broke.

Two of the brutes grabbed Mia's arms. Mia smacked her head into one, and he released his hold. The other got a kick to the groin. The man kept coming. Mia threw a punch at his face. He ducked under it and launched at her. The sudden bulk toppled her backward. A fist sank deep into her stomach, doubling her over. Yet, even though she wheezed for air, the pain of the blow never came. She coiled her muscles, noticed a surge of ice flow through her hand, and her uppercut connected solidly with the enemy's chin. He tumbled over the Acedians gathering behind him.

It was impossible to tell who punched her next. The avalanche of assaults heading toward Mia kept her focus entirely on defense. Scarred faces loomed around her, regardless of where she turned. Grunts and yells, sweat and musk, skin and fabric. Fists swung toward her, forcing her to either block the attacks or suffer the blows. Still, only a few strikes connected.

Mia grabbed a fist heading toward her chin and pulled the assailant forward. Their eyes met and his thoughts drifted into her. *From the side.*

One of their party lunged at her right side. She stopped the lunge with a kick that sent the boy flying. Of course. The easiest way to defeat these people was to use their own minds against them. From then on Mia looked each attacker in the eyes. Their thoughts filtered into her. Now the Acedians were on the defense.

One by one, Mia fought them all. A punch here, a kick there, and the Acedian number dwindled. Her attacks were flawless, precise. Deadly. Not her usual style of fighting, her techniques seemed more brutal. Animalistic. A crack on the skull didn't seem like enough, a bone snapped in two did. With each hit Mia's shivering increased. The biting cold washed over her, flooded, and engulfed her. Her fingertips, toes, even her face tingled.

Mia stood in the center of a jumble of bodies. None of the drones had attempted to invade her, to probe her thoughts. Strange. Breathing came easily to her, no sweat dripped on her brow, no aching pierced her body. Even the cold had dissipated. A slight tingling traveled through her now, as if her skin was alive.

Her eyes swept the corridors. When no more Acedians rushed out, Mia finally turned back toward the cabin. The others stood, gaping at her. As far as Mia could tell, not one of them had even moved from their spots. Cassidy slowly raised a hand to cover her parted lips. Disbelief and anger boiled inside Mia at the sight.

Mia marched into the cabin. "Why didn't you help me? It was twenty against one out there."

Not one of her crewmates moved or spoke. Not even Skyler.

"Why didn't you help me?" Mia shoved her hands onto her hips, glaring at the rest of the crew. They exchanged tense glances. The action grated on her nerves.

Slowly moving toward Mia, Will spoke in a quiet voice. "We didn't have enough time to help you."

Mia glared at him. "Blast it, what are you talking about?"

Will pointed to the fallen Acedians. "The fight only lasted a minute, less even."

Harrison spoke up. "You were a blur, Captain Foley."

"That doesn't make sense." Mia's heart pounded in her ears. "I don't understand."

Another round of glances. Another pang of annoyance.

"She's still ours, for now." Skyler's rough voice cut through the dull pounding in Mia's skull. "I'll go first with Mia. Harrison you take Cassidy. Will, Jeff, you two are the flank, make sure no one sneaks up from behind."

It pained Mia to see how quickly the others reacted to Skyler's orders. Harrison marched over to Cassidy, taking her good arm around his neck. Will and Jeff fell behind them. Yet, when Skyler moved past Mia, it shocked her how easy it was to follow the nurse's command. For now, anyway.

Static burst from the speakers. "Testing."

One quick swing, and the speaker crumbled under Mia's fist. Skyler put a hand on Mia's shoulder before stepping over the fallen bodies and heading down the corridor. Mia matched her pace. When she looked back, only Jeff followed. Will still stood next to a fallen Acedian, a woman. Will shook his head when he noticed Mia watching and rushed over to Jeff, averting his gaze. They twisted and turned through the pathways, each one similar to the next, passing an endless number of hatches. A noise caught their attention, and everyone stopped.

Skyler motioned for Mia to come up beside her. "Use the IA. Hold it ready. If there's only one Acedian, use it. If there's more, we'll have to fight."

Pulling the device out of her pocket, Mia held it before her, wishing she had a gun instead of an oval in her hand. The IA had proven itself before. She grasped it tight. They moved on. Every sound seemed amplified. Cassidy's ragged breaths, the quiet whispers of the brothers, even their boots seemed too loud on the deck. The wailing of the alarm grew dim compared to the ruckus of her crew.

Jeff's annoyed voice drifted up toward them. "Shouldn't we be running now?"

A fair question. With the alarm blaring, Acedians obviously on the guard, and Mia's issue growing ever worse, Donavin had to know something was wrong.

Skyler shook her head. "If we run, we'll be easier to track."

Jeff pointed at Mia. "Aren't we already easy enough to track?"

Skyler put up her hand. They stopped. Hurried footsteps bounced off the corridor ahead. Mia crouched down, and the Acedian rushed toward her. Mia stroked the IA device, and the Acedian froze mid stride. She signaled the others to move, quickly. They snuck into an adjacent corridor, moments before the Acedian unfroze. The woman continued running in the opposite direction.

"This might be easier than I suspected!" Will flashed a thumbs up.

The alarm stopped blaring. Will's smile faded into a look of horror as the lights changed color. Instead of washing the corridors with white light, the orbs now shone crimson. The lights in the adjacent corridor remained white, as did the lights a few paces away from the group. Only the orbs directly under and over them had changed. Mia advanced a few paces down the corridor, and the crimson light followed. Footsteps, multiple footsteps, echoed from down the pathway.

"Now, we should run." Mia sprinted back to her crew, fear creeping into her limbs. She pointed down the adjacent corridor. "That way."

Skyler nodded and started at a fast clip. Will paled and seemed to freeze, so Jeff dragged him along. Harrison, however, stayed put. Cassidy wavered in his arms. The crimson light followed the larger group, leaving a single red orb behind. The footsteps pounded closer.

"What about Cassidy," Harrison began. "I can't—"

Without a word, Mia gathered Cassidy into her arms and dashed after her crew. Harrison trailed behind her, and the red light, behind him. They caught up to the others in a matter of moments.

Skyler led them through the labyrinth of corridors, changing direction often. The pounding behind them grew louder still. Soon, the pounding came from ahead of them as well. Skyler stopped and thumbed a code into a nearby hatch. The hatch slid open, and she beckoned them inside. Darkness surrounded them for only a moment until the crimson light burned the blackness away. Mia expected to find a tiny cabin. Instead a cavern loomed around her. A gaping pit opened under them, just a pace away, and a narrow walkway traversed the empty space between their hatch and the next. Skyler turned to the men.

"Don't look down," she whispered. Her gaze flitted to Mia and Cassidy. Skyler's thoughts pressed into Mia. *I took a wrong turn. This won't be easy.*

Mia couldn't ask any questions for Skyler had already pushed a barrier back and started down the walkway. She stepped cautiously, lightly even, and Mia followed close behind, still holding Cassidy in her arms. The men followed. The red light shone over them, washing the walkway in an eerie glow. Cassidy felt light in her grasp, too light for the curves of her form, but Mia tried hard not to dwell on her strength. Cassidy's pale face was set in sheer determination. She never fidgeted or winced, even when Mia accidentally touched her shoulder wound. It seemed her gaze never wavered, always looking forward, not even a flit down toward the pit beneath them. Though in spite of the warnings, Mia looked. Immediately wished she hadn't.

A sea of eyes looked back. Men and women, a hundred of them at least, all young, not yet in their thirties it seemed, and all looking upward. Their eyes gleamed in the bright crimson light, catching and reflecting it back, tinting their silver eyes red. They never moved, never spoke, never even blinked. Frozen, it seemed. Mia turned her gaze back to the walkway and tried to ignore them. They were, after all, strangers to her. As long as they posed no threat, there was no reason to wonder why they did not attack. Or who they were. Or where they came from.

A gasp echoed behind her, and Mia looked back. Will was on his hands and knees, pointing, while Jeff leaned over the edge to look at the people. It seemed they weren't strangers to the brothers.

"That's Rika and Cade Wes, and those are the Qi twins!" Will said.

"It seems we've found the missing families," Jeff whispered.

"We should try to help them." Will leaned over the walkway.

Skyler rushed over and jerked him back. "There's nothing we can do for them right now."

"Bilg!" Jeff shouted, cupping his hands around his mouth. His voice echoed a thousand times louder.

"Stop it," Skyler said, pulling Jeff back as well. "Do you want to get us all killed?

"Brooken!" Jeff shouted again, yanking himself from Skyler's hold and stalking back to the edge.

"Harrison, grab him," Skyler ordered.

Harrison didn't move. His eyes transfixed on a woman wearing a red coat, standing amidst the motionless crowd. "Ellen," he murmured.

He, too, moved toward the edge of the walkway. Mia glanced at Cassidy, who shifted her weight off Mia in reply. Mia strode over to Harrison's side and grabbed his arm. The crimson light flowed with her. The strangers blinked, rustled, and as one synchronized unit, pointed guns at Mia and her crew. They began to fire.

"Move!" Mia shouted, pulling Harrison away from the edge as a shot whizzed past. Skyler yanked Will to his feet and grabbed Jeff, hauling them toward the other hatch. Cassidy moved toward it, stumbling as shots burst past. Mia dragged Harrison toward the hatch, too, ducking as a wave of shots blew by their head. Bursts of blue light skimmed their path, yet none connected with her crew, slicing air and exploding on the ceiling instead. It seemed, thankfully, that these Acedians were not yet trained in the art of guns. Mia wrenched Harrison down as a shot flew past his neck. Together the two women were able to force the men over to the hatch. Skyler punched a few codes in, and the barrier slid open.

They stumbled into the next corridor. Skyler already ran ahead of them, not even bothering to close the hatch again. Mia shoved the men in Skyler's direction, pulled Cassidy into her arms, and raced after them. Cassidy winced as Mia held her tight. Mia knew her fingers pressed into Cassidy's wounds, but she could not relax her grip. She didn't want to, either.

Skyler skidded to a halt before a round hatch. Mia's head ached. The corridor tilted. She listed to the side, caught herself by leaning back on the bulkhead. Will leaned down and gasped for breath, hands on his knees for support.

"This is it?" Jeff looked over his brother's head.

"Yes, this is the entrance to the escape pods." Skyler slid the control panel up and revealed a myriad of multicolored screens. "I just have to get the hatch open, and we'll be out of here."

"We don't have much time," Harrison said.

A hoard of Acedians pounded their way into view. They hurtled down the narrow corridor, some old, some young. All ready to capture or kill.

"I only need a second." Skyler tapped on the colored screens, and the hatch swirled open, revealing a tiny, square cabin with four hatches on the far side. "Get in!"

The crew struggled through the opening. Will and Jeff first. Skyler. Mia pulled Cassidy through. The pounding almost reached them before Harrison fell into the cabin.

He pulled his legs inside. "Shut it!"

Skyler tapped the screens. The hatch wouldn't shut. She tried again. Nothing. She stared helplessly at Mia. There was little, if anything, in the cabin to stave off the attack.

"We could bottleneck the hatch," Harrison suggested. "Hope that a lot of them try to come through at once—"

Skyler kicked the control panel, smashing it. Sparks flew out of it. Without warning, without codes, the hatch spiraled shut. The pounding on the other side of the bulkhead stopped, only to be replaced by the batter of fists on metal.

Mia wanted to smile. Wanted to say good job. Wanted to help. She couldn't. Her head suddenly swam. Her vision blurred. She felt the probe into her mind and battled against Donavin. He was trying to take control of her again. Her crew did not need an enemy on this side of the hatch. The agony in her head spiked. She shouted in spite of herself, sinking to the deck. It rocked beneath her. The cold that had never quite left her body was consuming her.

Shouts washed over her, like water over stone. "We have to go now!"

Holding her head tightly between her hands, Mia tried to force him away. Donavin came back, sifting through her memories. Mia clamped her eyes shut. The visions still came, one after the other, of her mother dying, her father bleeding on the deck, their ship exploding. Underneath those memories Mia could sense Donavin trying to lay some foundation, to push her down beneath it. A void began to spread through her.

"Jeff, Will, take that one."

I can make you forget.

"Harrison, ready the one to your left."

Memory after memory passed through Mia's head. Of Freya dying, of the Dee family sobbing over their lost daughter, of families being ripped apart by her mistakes.

"What about Mia?"

I can make you forget everything. Join me!

Her own scarring flashed before her, the sudden torture jolting through her system as if it was occurring this very moment. That memory enabled Mia to drive Donavin out. She latched onto that agony and flooded her soul with it, recalling every moment as it crashed through the void that Donavin tried to set. She pushed a single idea over the strand.

Never.

The strand snapped. The world righted again, and the cold left her. She trembled. Sweat dampened her clothes, but his presence no longer snaked into her, the empty place, gone. She pushed herself to her knees.

"Grab her. Drag her if you have to!"

Mia opened her eyes to see Skyler's face looming before her, gray eyes peering intently into her own.

"I'm me," Mia muttered, waving a hand at Skyler's anxious expression.

"Not for long," Skyer replied.

Skyler hauled her over to one of the escape pods. The pods were cylindrical, tilted slightly downward, and, like everything on this blasted ship, empty. Harrison slid into it. The pod looked to accommodate only two. Mia's vision blurred then sharpened. The hammering on the closed hatch grew louder. She glanced down the line of pods, determined to make sure her crew got off this blasted ship. Jeff and Will had squeezed in the one furthest away. Cassidy waited in a third.

Skyler attempted to shove Mia into the pod Harrison was in. Mia tore away from her grasp, crawling over to the one that held Cassidy.

"I don't care which one, just get in the breaching pod," Skyler yelled, sliding into Harrison's pod instead.

Mia slid into Cassidy's, feet first, trying not to land on her.

Cassidy clutched her arm against her chest. Even then, she smiled. "Couldn't wait to be near me again, huh?"

"I just didn't want to be in the same pod as that blasted lackey."

"Liar." Cassidy breathed heavy, tightening her hold on her arm.

The hatch above them spiraled shut and plunged them into darkness. A green light flickered, then orange, then red. Soon the entire bottom of the pod danced with multicolored lights. The pod jerked.

Two thick rods burst from behind Mia and Cassidy, making both women yelp. The rods spiraled down their bodies, holding them in place. Cassidy grabbed onto the metal. Her hand shook, and her knuckles whitened from her grip. She squeezed her eyes shut. Mia held onto her brace, wishing she could hold onto the trembling woman in front of her instead.

Skyler's voice filtered through a comm system behind Mia's head. "All systems go. Eject EP Units Two, Three, and Four."

The pod jerked again. Hard. Colors flickered—once, twice—and lit up the pod with a solid yellow glow. A holoimage popped up between them, displaying three blue dots jettisoned from a larger green. A blue icon winked, their icon Mia assumed, and showed the engines flaring to life. The pod jerked again. Harder. The force of the engines pushed Mia into the bulkhead. Cassidy's eyes flew open. Mia smiled in what she hoped was a reassuring manner. Cassidy only gripped her rod tighter.

The holoimage between them shimmered out. The metal beside them swirled open, revealing a viewport facing a bulky transport ship. The Acedian ship.

Skyler's voice filtered through the comm. "See the aft engine?"

Mia nodded before realizing Skyler couldn't see her reaction.

"Yes," Cassidy replied, a smile tugging at her lips. Now, in the escape pod, she looked somewhat revitalized, her pale skin reddening with health.

"Watch this," Skyler said.

An explosion rocked the ship askew. Blue and yellow flames orbed from the hull. Secondary breaches burst through the starboard side, balls of fire bursting forth. The Acedian vessel listed sideways, and shouts erupted over the comm as the Dee brothers celebrated. Mia could hear Harrison's whoop amidst the cheers. Even Cassidy released her hold and reached out to Mia with her good arm. They grasped each other's forearms. Covered in cuts on her shoulder and abdomen, skin bruised, hair a tangled mess, Cassidy's smile could still light up even the darkest corner of space.

Mia gently squeezed Cassidy's forearm, a gesture that caused Cassidy's gaze to break from the viewport. Heat traveled across Mia's neck, reaching her ears in record pace as Cassidy focused on her.

"A gift from me to them," Skyler muttered through the comm.

The nurse continued speaking, uttering words that might've been important. At that moment Mia didn't care. The Acedians had been stopped. Her crew had escaped. If only for a moment, they were safe.

An impossible joy spread through Mia. Safe. She grinned. Cassidy's smile widened. When the harnesses finally let the two women go, when the engines stopped jerking the pod and slipped into a faster clip, Mia and Cassidy embraced. Mia made sure not to crush Cassidy's arm, but Cassidy pulled her closer, not seeming to care about the wound.

"We're okay," Cassidy murmured.

"Yes, we're okay." Mia pushed a stray hair off Cassidy's cheek.

They were so close. Close and safe. Mia's breath hitched. Her heart skipped a beat. The timing, finally, seemed right. Mia leaned down and kissed Cassidy. She tasted of blood and sweat, but Mia didn't care. Cassidy tightened her hold, fingers digging into the small of Mia's back. Warmth seared through her body. A sudden ache spiked up Mia's neck, and she jerked, breaking their embrace. She grabbed her neck with one hand and held Cassidy tight with the other until the agony passed.

"What's wrong?"

"I must have torn a muscle or something," Mia muttered, even now unwilling to confess how far Donavin's bots had gotten into her system. The holoimage of that gray traveling through her blood still burned in her memory. Of how close it seemed to completion. Yet the Acedian ship had been damaged, stopped for now. They could've killed Donavin. Mia held onto that hope as she lifted her gaze to Cassidy.

In the confines of their tiny compartment, after a kiss that should have lasted an eternity, Cassidy shrank back in fear.

Mia tilted her head. "Cassidy, what's wrong?"

"Mia?" Cassidy's shrill voice echoed in the pod as she leaned away.

"Please, what's wrong?" Mia said.

Mia ran a hand through her hair, distracted by a sudden chill in her eyes. She stilled. Cassidy didn't need to answer. Mia shifted her gaze to the viewport beside her, focusing hard at the reflection staring back. The glass showed Mia's face, a face she had known for twenty-five years. Red choppy hair fell over her forehead and freckles covered her nose. Yet something had changed, and for a moment, Mia didn't realize what. Shock ran down her spine. Instead of her blue eyes, bright silver ones glinted back.

A single thought, not her own, invaded her. *I'll be waiting.*

The pod jerked again. Lights flickered once and blinked off.

[The End of Finding Hekate: Book One of the Cicatrix duology.]

Losing Hold

Cicatrix Duology Book 2

After Mia Foley and her crew escape Donavin's grasp, they crash land on a the prison planet Fissure. Mia begins to hear Donavin in her mind once again and knows the transformation into one of his drones isn't far off. But will her crew stick with her after she turns into an Acedian? Will Cassidy?

Coming in Fall 2016

About Kellie Doherty

Kellie Doherty is a bisexual writer living in Portland, Oregon. She is currently a student and hopes to graduate with a Master's in Book Publishing from Portland State University in June 2016. She is also a freelance editor, taking jobs whenever they come her way.

Kellie has been writing since she was young and living in Alaska. Her work (fiction and non-fiction) has been published in *Pathos, Alaska Women Speak, F Magazine, The Chugiak-Eagle River Star*, as well as the blogs of 49 Writers and Ooligan Press. She also writes fanfiction under the name SerenityQuill. She is currently working on the sequel to Finding Hekate, Cicatrix Duology Book 2 - *Losing Hold.*

When not writing or editing, she enjoys reading, taking walks, playing video and board games, and hanging out with her friends.

Contact Information

Website - http://kelliedoherty.com/

Editing - http://editreviseperfect.weebly.com/

Twitter - https://twitter.com/kellie_doherty

Facebook - https://www.facebook.com/KellieDoherty89

Email - kellie.f.doherty@gmail.com

Other Fantasy and Science Fiction from Desert Palm Press

Amendyr Series by Rae D. Madgon

The Second Sister
ISBN: 9781311262042

ELEANOR OF SANDLEFORD'S entire world is shaken when her father marries the mysterious, reclusive Lady Kingsclere to gain her noble title. Ripped away from the only home she has ever known, Ellie is forced to live at Baxstresse Manor with her two new stepsisters, Luciana and Belladonna. Luciana is sadistic, but Belladonna is the woman who truly haunts her. When her father dies and her new stepmother goes suddenly mad, Ellie is cheated out of her inheritance and forced to become a servant. With the help of a shy maid, a friendly cook, a talking cat, and her mysterious second stepsister, Ellie must stop Luciana from using an ancient sorcerer's chain to bewitch the handsome Prince Brendan and take over the entire kingdom of Seria.

Wolf's Eyes
ISBN: 9781311755872

CATHELIN RAYBROOK has always been different. She Knows things without being told and Sees things before they happen. When her visions urge her to leave her friends in Seria and return to Amendyr, the magical kingdom of her birth, she travels across the border in search of her grandmother to learn more about her visions. But before she can find her family, she is captured by a witch, rescued by a handsome stranger, and forced to join a strange group of forest-dwellers with even stranger magical abilities. With the help of her new lover, her new family, and her eccentric new teacher, she must learn to gain control of her powers and do some rescuing of her own before they take control of her instead.

The Witch's Daughter
ISBN: 978131672643

Ailynn Gothel has always been the perfect daughter. Thanks to her mother's teachings, she knows how to heal the sick, conjure the elements, and take care of Raisa, her closest and dearest friend. But when Ailynn's feelings for Raisa grow deeper, her simple life falls apart. Her mother hides Raisa deep in a cave to shield her from the world, and Ailynn must leave home in search of a spell to free her. While the kingdom beyond the forest is full of dangers, Ailynn's greatest fear is that Raisa will no longer want her when she returns. She is a witch's daughter, after all—and witches never get their happily ever after.

Desert Palm Press

Dark Horizons Series by Rae D. Magdon & Michelle Magly

Dark Horizons
ISBN: 9781310892646

Lieutenant Taylor Morgan has never met an ikthian that wasn't trying to kill her, but when she accidentally takes one of the aliens hostage, she finds herself with an entirely new set of responsibilities. Her captive, Maia Kalanis, is no normal ikthian, and the encroaching Dominion is willing to do just about anything to get her back. Her superiors want to use Maia as a bargaining chip, but the more time Taylor spends alone with her, the more conflicted she becomes. Torn between Maia and her duty to her home-world, Taylor must decide where her loyalties lie.

Starless Nights (Dark Horizons Book 2)
ISBN: 9781310317736

In this sequel to Dark Horizons Taylor and Maia did not know where they would go when they fled Earth. They trusted Akton to take them somewhere safe. Leaving behind a wake of chaos and disorder, Coalition soldier Rachel is left to deal with the backlash of Taylor's actions, and soon finds herself chasing after the runaways. Rachel quickly learns the final frontier is not a forgiving place for humans, but her chances for survival are better out there than back on Earth. Meanwhile, Taylor and Maia find themselves living off the generosity of rebel leader Sorra, an ikthian living a double life for the sake of the rebellion. With Maia's research in hand, Sorra believes they can deliver a fatal blow against the Dominion.

Desert Palm Press

Chronicles of Osota – Warrior by Michelle Magly

ISBN: 9781311834324

Alina knew that one day she would return to the heartland of Osota, even after eleven years of isolation. But how could she know her return to the capital would coincide with the arrival of young Warrior-in-training Senri? Beautiful and strong, Senri makes for a pleasant distraction from Alina's troubles. But as the prospective ruler of a nation, Alina can hardly devote time to pursuing a romance. As a new threat looms over the kingdom of Osota, she is left with little choice but to turn to Senri for help.

.

Desert Palm Press

Journey To You by AJ Adaire

ISBN9781311571854

What do you do if you are one of the few who remain alive after a mysterious, flu-like virus claims most of the global population? This is a question Kim Robins and Peri Henderson have to answer when the world changes and society falls apart.
Violent gangs of looters make it unsafe to remain in the city. Hoping to improve their chances for survival, Kim and Peri decide to hike into the remote forest area of Maine.
Dangerous circumstances along the trail cause the women to join forces with another hiker and her dog. The longtime friends and their new companions set off on a daunting trek filled with both menacing and

kindhearted survivors.

With evidence of the illness everywhere they go, will this journey bring each of the women the happiness and safety she seeks?

The Broken Coil by Sy Itha

ISBN: 9781972976042

Secluded in the Dainlock Woods, Jacquelyn Fletcher makes her living trading furs and occasionally escorting travelers through the dangerous forest. Disguised as a man, she hides from the mistakes of her past. As a favor to an old friend, she finds herself agreeing to guide Avalon, a Paladin of Sel, through the woods to safety. All Avalon has known is the temple life. When her fellow Paladin is murdered, Avalon is framed for the crime and must flee her home to find the source of the attack. Her only clue is an ancient tome that she is unable to decipher. Traveling with the ranger Fletcher, Avalon thinks she is safe. Neither of them realize the danger that follows them.

Cover Design By : Rachel George
www.rachelgeorgeillustration.com

Note to Readers:

We have made every effort to edit this book. However, typos do slip in. If you find an error in the text, please email: lee@desertpalmpress.com so the issue can be corrected. We appreciate you as a reader and want to ensure you enjoy the reading process.

Bright blessing.

Desert Palm Press

www.ingramcontent.com/pod-product-compliance
Lightning Source LLC
Chambersburg PA
CBHW070914180626
46817CB00003B/1048
9781942976066